DAW Books proudly presents
Sara Hanover's novels of
the Wayward Mages

THE LATE GREAT WIZARD *(Book One)*
THE NEW IMPROVED SORCERESS *(Book Two)*
THE WAYWARD MAGE *(Book Three)*

SARA HANOVER

THE
WAYWARD
MAGE

BOOK THREE OF WAYWARD MAGES

DAW BOOKS, INC.

DONALD A. WOLLHEIM, FOUNDER

1745 Broadway, New York, NY 10019

ELIZABETH R. WOLLHEIM
SHEILA E. GILBERT
PUBLISHERS
www.dawbooks.com

Magic believes in each and every one of you!

CHAPTER ONE

STARTING OVER

HAVING MAGIC WOULD be awesome, if only there weren't people willing to kill me for it.

There are, as far as I know—and my knowledge is like Swiss cheese with a number of holes in it—only three ways to naturally have magic. It can be studied and practiced for years on end to gain skill, or one can simply be born magical like an Iron Dwarf, harpy, or an elf. Don't ask me about vampires, I've been told they're extremely rare, and no one likes discussing them.

My friend the professor, wherever he is, has learned several lifetimes' worth of skill, being a phoenix wizard who can rejuvenate himself when time weighs too heavily. He has unlimited lifetimes to spend learning his spells. I can't pontificate about those born with it. I'm just learning about the different folk who exist in a world I never thought possible.

And then there's the third, reviled way—theft. Out-and-out stealing magic from those unsuspecting or unable to defend themselves. The professor wouldn't tell me how it's done, but I gather it's really something terrible, like stealing a soul.

There are articles which can store power in their core, but they are few and far between. Someone has to have charged them in the first place, so the magic in those items is simply transferred.

As for me, I've been possessed. A relic known as the mael-strom stone has decided to embed itself in the palm of my left hand and there it stays until I give it away or die, which is why I've been hunted. Now the stone itself has power which it lends to me when needed, and it also absorbs other relics, increasing its ability almost at will. I could easily be convinced that it is alive, somehow, and . . . well, hungry. One of those relics made a sorceress of me, but don't ask me what happens if I lose the stone. I don't know. I don't even have a good guess, unless I lose it in the most drastic way possible, over my dead body.

What I do have is a healthy respect for self-defense. I'm an enforcer for my college field hockey team, meaning I can run— and I can hit, jar, bump, trip, tackle (discreetly), and scramble at will. Off the field, the stone can help me throw up a defensive shield and so can the awesome bracers the Broadstone dwarven tribe gave me for my twentieth birthday. As a sorceress, my power lies in recognizing the magic sunk into other objects and calling that power into my usage. This is a little dicier than it sounds because I didn't used to have the Sight necessary to recognize and name the power so I can own it. I do now, thanks to shards of the Eye of Nimora which my stone absorbed. That's another magical object possessed by the Iron Dwarves and which they use in their judicial system. There was a slight accident when I retrieved the Eye for them (it had been stolen) and it broke when dropped. Not much damage, thank goodness, but two distinct splinters snapped off, and my maelstrom stone didn't hesitate to gobble them up. They reside in the stone and are a little temperamental about opening and viewing, but we've reached an agreement. I think. I would have given them back so the Eye could be whole again, but their loss doesn't seem to have weakened the original relic and my stone has never regurgitated anything it's swallowed. And my power grows.

No, I don't rest easy, even at night.

Especially then.

I wasn't surprised when something woke me. Nights are the worst, because things can creep in and out through the veil of dreams, the sort of things that nobody wants to deal with.

So when I rolled over in the dead of night, in that still, silent, and frozen week after Christmas and New Year's, an unwelcome presence took me right out of my sleep. It ran across the edge of my conscious thought like a tiny beast with razor-sharp and ice-cold toes.

I blinked up at the ceiling, and listened. Had something entered the house? It shouldn't have been possible, but the professor no longer lived here and his wards might be weakening. My overgrown pup, Scout, snored from the corner of the mattress. Whatever I'd heard, he hadn't. My bedroom felt cold outside the covers, and I didn't want to leave them. I pulled them up under my chin until I realized that I'd already passed the point of falling asleep again. I hate it when that happens. I slid out of bed quietly and found the bedroom floor as chilled as the air. It could have been the weather, with snow that comes and goes and icy rain following it in, and everything seems interrupted and left for dead.

My robe didn't hang on its usual hook by the closet. My mom must have taken it to wash, so I grabbed my favorite oversized T-shirt and pulled it on over my boy shorts and athletic bra. I don't sleep in cozy nightgowns or pj's in case I have to react. In the faint light from the hallway, my shirt proudly read: We Ar the Champi ns. I tend to wear my favorite shirts to smithereens.

In the hallway, I still heard nothing, but something hung in the air. It smelled moldy and musty and left a slimy feeling down the back of my throat. I'd never encountered anything like it before and wasn't happy about meeting up with it now.

Just past my doorway, there's a niche in the hallway wall. A vase and a bouquet of what looked to be budding red roses about to open, resided there. They're not flowers. They're tell-tales, a mostly reliable alarm system. As I approached them, I could see that every flower had opened wide, looking like daisies scared straight. I put a finger out and stroked a velvety petal. It shivered under my touch and then leaned into it. Something had definitely alarmed them.

They looked toward the street side of the house.

Turning, I made my way slowly down the hall, trying to avoid squeaky boards. Scout joined me, a little sheepishly, his golden tail hanging low in an apologetic wag for letting me explore the unknown alone. I put a hand on his head. "Quiet."

He gave a little snuff of understanding.

I opened the next bedroom door, which had been the professor's room, although it had been empty now for months. The bed stayed made and no dust lingered on the wardrobe or nightstand, but the area had that smell of being unoccupied. Or maybe the musty smell from the hall followed me in. I looked at the bed where his walking cane with the large quartz decorating its handle caught a bit of starlight through the curtained window. It glowed like the diamond it resembled. I smiled to see it so bright and clean. It had been through a lot, that crystal, turning dark and opaque, and we'd thought it would never recover. I guessed that's why the professor left it behind. It's one of those relics I mentioned.

I stepped around the single bed and headed to the window. The curtains were askew the tiniest bit, and if I were careful, I could look outside on the street without being caught spying. I positioned myself, Scout promptly sitting down on my left foot to anchor me.

Down below, a mist danced along the street and sidewalks, up and down the block, and I could see frosted patterns on the ground. Lampposts up and down the block seemed a little dimmed; the shadows they cast were barely decipherable in the overall gloom. I could see two porch lights on down the block but no lit windows in the houses. Everyone in the neighborhood but me seemed to be safely asleep, but it was the streetlight directly below that drew my attention. It cast shadows where none should be, shaped like nothing I'd ever seen before, and which didn't belong there. How can something cast backward silhouettes?

The curtains at the window wiggled a little as I pulled one aside, just a slit, to better look down at our street. It's odd, but our streetlights change intensity. They burn brighter once warmed up. On a winter night like tonight, with a heavy mist that might turn into a light snow by morning, the streetlights barely seemed to cut into the evening. Midsummer was like that, too, as though the day had been long and bright enough that we deserved a milder, gentler illumination. Tonight, every light seemed to be pitching a losing battle against the cloak of evening. I could see little more than outlines although many were longer and deeper than expected. That hair-tickling feeling didn't go away. Something was leaning against a lamppost out there. I saw it.

I leaned close enough that my breath fogged the window a little. I watched it for the briefest of moments, trying to separate true shadow from illusion, and then—it seemed as if I had caught its attention as it looked up at me.

If it hadn't moved, I wouldn't have seen it. Stretching and turning, it seemed, as if suddenly becoming aware of my study.

Instinct jumped me backward. I dropped the curtain, breath thudding out of my lungs for a brief moment as my heart did a skip and a thump, and I fought to inhale. But the thing I found watching . . . just the hasty glimpse before I retreated . . . had looked up with blazing red eyes.

I'd seen Steptoe like that once when he'd lost control over his demonic powers, and I'd hoped never to see such a sight again.

I stepped back two, three steps from the window, just in case my silhouette could somehow be visible. I didn't want to draw attention. I took a ragged breath or two. My hand remained in the air, and I stared at my palm, my left palm, where the Eye of Nimora often looked back at me, and it awoke.

Two, small red slits opened to observe my world. But these eyes, though supernatural, held absolutely no resemblance to what I'd just seen below. There was no malevolence, no sinister aspect, but on the street—I'd felt a wave of malignance turned upward, toward my window, toward me, as the thing below searched.

My foot took a step all by itself. The rest of my body wanted to follow. To go see what the hell was going on, to find out what sat on my street by my front door and driveway and glowered at the world. I knew that would not be smart. I could feel the icy presence of malice drifting outward from it, whatever it was. I stared at the curtains, transfixed, while my heart thumped heavily.

What had I just seen? Like watching a train wreck, I couldn't stay away from the vision.

What was it doing here?

Eyes narrowing, I looked for it, and then I spotted it among the spiked silhouettes. Something nearly impossible to see.

Not a wisp of the curtain moved. I hadn't given myself away, but it had caught me . . . or had it? If it was surveilling the house, it could be gazing all over, not just where I stood. I waited until my heartbeats steadied and Scout went from sitting on my foot to lying down on it, paw across his nose as if he could also smell the evil odor creeping through the upstairs. When I leaned close to look again, the shadows had scattered— splintered across the road and sidewalk as if they had never been out of the ordinary and grotesque. It had disappeared or melded into the evening. I couldn't detect it even though I *felt* it. Slimy. Rotten. Evil.

So I did that thing that one should never do—I went downstairs, determined to go outside in search of what might have been happening. Nearly every Gothic horror written or filmed tells you Do Not Go Out Wandering. It's deadly. It's exactly what the enemy wants. It is usually fatal. But this was my house. We'd been driven out of our other home by poverty and addiction and found refuge here, and I wasn't about to let it happen again.

So I went anyway, my dog tucked against the back of my leg as if knowing what I planned to do and hoping I'd change my mind. Scout is smarter than the average dog, being of exceptional bloodlines . . . half elven, half Labrador retriever . . . with a predicted longevity of thirty years or so. His devotion to me is endless, except now he took a corner of my droopy T-shirt in his jaw and didn't want to let go when I got to the door. He had no intention of going out the front door and worked to keep me from accomplishing it.

I pushed him aside with a stern "off," and he retreated with a whine, his eyes sad and his ears drooping. The moment my bare feet touched the porch, I nearly turned around and bolted back inside. Cold radiated upward as if attacking; my whole body went icy, setting my teeth to chattering. I'd explore, but I'd do it in a damned hurry, I decided. Something inside me, probably my common sense, tugged at me to go back.

I didn't.

The shadows had all shrunk to normal size and dimensions, with no sign of what had been there. Something wicked had been here . . . I could feel it in every tingling nerve . . . but it had passed, and I was no closer to knowing what it was.

I walked about the lamppost and watched the shadows dance as I did: all normal, no grotesque rendering. I peered at the iron structure itself, to see if anything had been left behind but hoarfrost and saw nothing. Even that smell had dissipated, or I had gotten used to it because it no longer hung on the evening air. Yet . . . when I looked at the ground, I saw one distinctive shoeprint outlined there. It seemed to be fading even as I studied it. I hadn't brought my phone with me, so I had no chance to take a shot. It looked like a boot print, long and narrow with a distinctive heel but definitely man-sized, and then . . . it disappeared into the mist.

I retreated back to the safety of the house and had trouble closing the front door because of Scout's relieved and exuberant welcome. My feet tingled in the warmer air. I tugged on his neck.

"Enough already. Back to bed. Let's not disturb anyone else. I don't want a lecture."

And I could hardly wait to shove my toes back under warm covers again.

As I passed the tell-tales upstairs, I saw they had lost their exaggerated pose and slumped back into sleepy buds as though nothing had ever been wrong. I wondered if Steptoe, my friend who'd given them to me with the express purpose of having an alarm in the house, had even noted their panic. If not, then something dangerous had been watching the house—and almost nobody knew it. What measures we had in place hadn't been enough to protect us. That would have to change.

As I pulled the covers back up, and Scout arranged himself alongside, I thought of how we'd been driven out of the home that had been my safety and haven for most of my life. If not for Aunt April and her generosity, we wouldn't have the place we did: rickety structure, old-fashioned plumbing, and all.

Once upon a time, I had had a father. I thought him awesome

until he caught the gambling bug, so I killed him. And no, I
didn't shoot him or take an ax to him although half my high
school at the time thought I did when he disappeared suddenly.
We'd had a shouting match when I found out he'd cleaned out
my college fund, and I shoved him away. Magic's greedy jaws
swallowed him whole. He hasn't been seen by the general pub-
lic since. I didn't believe in him or magic then. In the ensuing
years, my mother and I lost our house, our savings, and our
credit cards, but at least we had each other.

If I'd known then what I know now, I might have done things
differently. Yes, he had an illness, and magic had a grip on him
as well, for he'd used it to increase his luck which fed his addiction. Can't do that. The House always wins.

Magic has a price; when it comes to take its due, it can be
fairly messy. It's not pretty. Don't ever believe it is. It is the stuff
of blood, sweat, and tears. Add a little cursing—but that will
lead you into the dark side. Avoid that, if possible. Because the
price is high enough as it is. I lost a father . . . and gained a
family I never expected.

Power imbues all of us, like sunlight and shadow, and those
who can see it, sense it, or bend it hold a definite advantage over
those of us who cannot. I want to use it to right those wrongs
in my life that changed everything—but magic doesn't work
backward, only forward. There's a balance to the powers of life,
and then there's chaos which thrives on the messy bits. The
forgotten pieces. The ragged overlaps.

I wouldn't have magic at all, but it chose me for reasons I
have yet to understand. Chaos decided to burrow into me and
stick. It seems permanently attached, and don't think others
haven't tried to take it any way they can, including over my
dead body. As for devouring . . . well, my stone has inhaled a
cursed ring and a book on Dark Arts, as well as those bits of the
Eye I mentioned. As for why the breakage of the Eye of Nimora
didn't really seem to hurt it, well, the darn thing is a gem big
enough to choke a horse.

Sorcery struck me, not that differently from a bolt of lightning, but forgot to leave me with a set of directions, and I've

been struggling ever since. Lightning not only struck twice, but it darn near incinerated me.

There's a steep learning curve to dealing with my new reality and, if not for my sake but others, I'm running out of time. The power I have to manipulate is stubborn, sometimes angry, possessive, and impatient. Chaos stones are adept that way, I've been warned, although there are excellent moments. I've also been told by those who know that magic mirrors the person who wields it, but I don't think so. Maybe. Maybe not.

Magic can't mend things, well, magically. Not in reality. It's like pulling a piece of elastic to change its shape. The form will change, but conditions alter and oftentimes—abruptly— everything snaps back. The snap can be killer. Like super glue, power is best used in small, very careful doses, trying not to get your fingers stuck together. I can't trust magic to do the ordinary stuff I need done, but I have this situation.

Two floors below me, in the basement of this creaky old house, I found my missing father, fallen into a crack between dimensions. He's out of place. I drove him into that jeopardy, and I need to get him free. I'm fairly certain a conjuring put him there, and it's going to take the same to pull him out—and it needs to be soon. He's a poltergeist in our cellar, and he's fading. I can't get him out without knowing how he got in, and I haven't been able to determine what happened. It's time for me to go visit my father and see how he's faring. It's one of those not pretty, very messy moments I hate.

I fell asleep in a tangle of thoughts and emotions and didn't wake until Scout put his damp nose to my cheek, signaling he needed to go outside and be fed. I got up and prepared for my day, deciding I could wait no longer to check on my father.

I sat down on the cellar steps, pulled my glove off my left hand, and put my palm out, hoping the little red slits highlighting the marbled stone set in my hand would open, which they often will not do. They glow red. They also bring heat into the marble of the stone. One sees, the other consumes, and all of it is a pain in my existence. I hadn't known about any of this until I met Professor Brennus Morcant Brandard, a crusty old guy on a charity senior meal route. When he set his house (and himself) on fire, the phoenix wizard called me for help, and I answered. I've never been certain why it was me he called. Maybe no one else answered his first or second attempt, but then I showed up. Life has not been the same since. I've met a host of magical beings, good and bad, and been infested myself. It's rather like having a virus that can cure one fatal disease but gives you another, highly troublesome one, in exchange.

While I sat, hand open in the air, thoughts stampeding through my brain, I took stock of my current situation, including the apparition which had awakened me.

Other life projects loom in front of me, besides rescuing my father, which include falling in love with Carter Phillips, finding our now missing phoenix wizard professor, establishing world peace, and curing childhood hunger. Oh, and declaring my major at Sky Hawk CC. I really don't count on any other burdens because these seem tough enough as it is. Well, Carter isn't tough. I mean, he is tough, but loving him isn't, and I've had strong hints that he might feel the same way back.

I sat in a moment of quiet and searched the cellar for my father. I felt it the moment the Eyes opened in my palm, and a subtle warmth traveled from my hand to my face and eyes. What was dim was now illuminated. Storage boxes piled hither and yon glowed with magical possibilities—they belonged to the professor and were all we could salvage of his former life and burned-out house. Although the boxes are battered and look like ordinary cardboard, I can see the auras that dance about them. Tiny motes of starlight have drifted in from upstairs, whirling about like fireflies. And there, in the corner, stood my transparent father. He lifted a hand in greeting. A green haze surrounded him; if he were a tree, I might think that was good. But he's not, and it looked sickly to me.

"Dad."

A small gust of cold air surrounded me. "Don't try to talk," I tell him. "I'm just checking in. Goldie and I are visiting Broadstone Manor tomorrow, so I'm hoping to finally get some of the information on how this happened, so we can undo it."

The ghost reacted not at all. Did he understand what I said?

I waved my palm. "Goldie is the harpy who was married to Mortimer. She knows he kept journals, and he told me once he thought he knew how all of this might have happened, so I am thinking he noted it down before he died." My dwarven friends were detail oriented, and the Broadstone clan was a pillar of their community. I counted the late Mortimer as a friend and his son, Hiram, as a close friend.

My see-through dad cut a hand through the air, a negation, a warning, a signal to stop, as emphatically as he could.

"No? Why not? This is good news."

He drifted closer but stopped halfway across the cellar as if the maelstrom stone put up a barrier he could not cross. And it might. It's a very defensive item and has saved my life more than once. Now I needed it to save his. I might add that any saving it had done was probably self-preservation of its own interests and not necessarily mine.

But he halted and shook his head.

"The Broadstones are friends. So is Goldie. I'll be fine. You can't wait much longer, and this is the only break we've had."

The air about me grew so chill I expected snow or hail to start falling.

"I did this to you," I told the apparition. "We fought and I sent you away, and you got into some kind of trouble and shoved between dimensions and this is all my fault. I'm the only one who can fix it. I thought . . . I thought you'd taken everything away from me that I'd planned, but what I have now instead is . . . well, it's better. I have friends I could never have believed even existed, and Mom is doing well, finally, and we not only survived, we thrived. But you belong here, as part of us, and I have to find a way to bring you back. I won't lose you again. So you better get used to the idea that I intend to undo what I did."

My father held both hands palm up and stood watching me.

"You're not going to talk me out of this. If I do nothing else with the magic I've got, I will free you. I will."

He sliced a finger across the air again, an unmistakable gesture, killing my plans.

I stood up abruptly. "Look. I know what I'm doing. I'll be fine. You're the one I'm worried about, all right? I have the stone and my bracers for protection, and a harpy warrior on my side, and the Iron Dwarves, not to mention Carter and Steptoe, and you've no one but me. I'd say I'm in good shape. I'll check in with you tomorrow when I get back."

Upstairs, I heard Scout's toenails clicking on the floor as he scrambled to go bark at someone at the front door. I closed my fist, shutting down the Eyes, and although I could feel the ghost-touched cold, I couldn't see him anymore.

"I'm doing this," I finished. "And you'll be happy I did."

As I shut the cellar door in the kitchen behind me, I half-expected to see the lesser demon Steptoe looking like the dapper chimney sweep he emulates, or my mom, or just about anyone else appear but my best friend Evelyn Statler.

But there she is, with Scout doing half-grown Labrador puppy circles around her feet, in hopes of 1) tripping her or 2) getting a treat. She is as slender as a willow sapling, dressed in expensive casual, and her blonde hair is tousled down below her shoulders. She puts me to shame. I'm taller than she is, but lanky, with a dusting of freckles accenting my blue eyes, and my brunette hair cascades down also but somehow never looks so casually wonderful and windblown as hers.

Before she could be knocked over by Scout, she plopped down in a kitchen chair. "You're going to the Broadstones tomorrow and I need you to take me with you and you have to introduce me to Hiram's folks, and then you have to come home with me and introduce Hiram to my parents."

I'd obviously had other plans after my visit and had no idea how she'd found out about any of them. Needless to say, I was not expecting to get my ears assaulted with what I'd just heard. Nor had I any idea their dating had gotten this serious sounding.

"Please," Evie coaxed. "You've got to help me on this."

Scary as it is, I'd rather wrestle magic to a standstill again than get in between Evelyn Statler, her new boyfriend the dwarf Hiram Broadstone, and her parents. Even if she did plead for help.

I'd also rather stand on my head and poop bricks, but she is my best friend on the human side and Hiram on the magic side. There shouldn't really be "sides," but that appears to be a major facet of my current life. And there she sat, eyes open wide and slightly weepy, begging me to be a bridge. I'm pretty sure she doesn't know Hiram is an Iron Dwarf which means he hasn't decided to share his antecedents with her yet, and that tells me I shouldn't get concerned. Why get involved in a fight sooner than necessary, right?

I shifted slightly. Evelyn's eyes narrowed suspiciously. She stood up and held her hands out.

"You're not going to do it, are you?"

"What does Hiram think about this?"

"Oh, he . . . ah . . . well . . . he's fine with it."

"You didn't tell him."

She swung her chin away from me, and her light blonde hair bounced about her shoulders. "Not exactly."

Hiram is what I would call a grown-ass man. More grown than Evelyn has any idea because Iron Dwarves live about two hundred years near as I can figure and, although he's a young man in his clan, he's probably close to Evelyn's father's age. All of which means, if he wanted my help and thought he needed it, he'd be here asking for it.

"I think you're jumping the gun on this," I told Evelyn.

She still wouldn't look at me. "Meeting my family?"

"Not that, but making a big enough deal out of it that you feel you need muscle on your side. You don't need muscle to say 'Hi, Mom and Dad, this is my date Hiram. We'll be back before midnight and bye!'" I told her.

"I don't have a midnight curfew."

"Maybe you should. I can advocate that when I handle everything else if you wish."

"Oh, shut up." Evie sat down again and twisted her hands in front of her. "It isn't a casual date. I'd like him to escort me to the swearing-in, and that's a big deal." Her father had won the mayoral electoral contest in November, and she was right. It was a big deal. Hiram's presence there probably would need parental approval.

I thought I still might be able to dodge the bullet she aimed at me. "The party celebration? Or the actual inaugural?"

"Either. Both."

I sat down next to her and bumped shoulders. "You guys have been going out for two months now and he's not met your parents?"

"No."

"Why?"

Her fingers knotted. "We agreed we weren't going to date. I had classes and he's in business. But we just couldn't stay away from each other."

"Awwww."

She punched me in the arm. I pretended to rock away from the blow. Actually, it wasn't bad. She'd taken up some self-defense classes since getting caught in a political riot and having someone bash her in the shin. Seriously, though, I couldn't believe the honor bound and solemn Hiram hadn't taken steps to meet the parents early on. Time for me to narrow my eyes at her.

"Wait a minute. You haven't told them you're dating at all. You've been . . . oh, I dunno . . . at study groups or cheer practice or over at my place."

Evelyn blushed, a lot deeper than I ever have, starting at the hollow in her throat and working its way up her neck and turning her face a cherry color.

"No wonder it's awkward." I ticked facts off on my fingers. "One, Hiram doesn't know you've been fibbing about him and two, your parents don't know you've been lying to them, and three . . ." I raised an eyebrow. "These things come in threes. What have I missed?"

"Nothing."

"Hiram doesn't know you have been sneaking around to see him."

"No."

"And your parents truly have no idea?"

"They've been busy getting Dad ready to take office. It's a lot of work. I didn't want to bother them."

"A relationship with Hiram is a bother?"

"No, no . . . he's wonderful. Fun. Intelligent. A gentleman."

"Then what's the problem?" I waggled my raised eyebrow.

She sighed. "I might have asked him to marry me."

"What?!"

"We agreed that's too serious too soon, but . . . it feels so right, Tessa."

I felt as though a brick wall had fallen on me and it was difficult to get words out. "What are you thinking? You hardly know each other. Nothing about this is going to feel right to Hiram when he finds out they don't even know about him. And your parents—" I stopped, not finding any words to describe her parents' probable reaction.

She drew close and leaned her head down onto my shoulder. "I know," she said miserably. My shirt grew wet under her cheek as she wept quietly. If I were in the same spot, I'd need friends who wanted to help. I couldn't not help her.

Plus, I wanted to stay on Hiram's good side. The invite to his home was not easy to come by; the harpies and the clans have been at odds for decades, and Mortimer's and Goldie's marriage had gone against all those bad feelings. But I needed her to find his journals. Those diaries could hold invaluable information on what had happened to my father and how to help him. This, for me, was literally a matter of life and death. Putting Evelyn in the middle of it would complicate things horribly. But it would be worse to try and put her off. She could be relentlessly determined.

"All right," I said, not altogether selflessly.

She pulled back, her face lighting up. "Great!" Evelyn had another thought and gathered up her purse onto her lap. The purse in question is the size of a briefcase that could hold a small elephant or maybe even Scout, and her entire arm disappeared inside it as she reached for something. "I almost forgot! This was on your front porch."

The envelope she withdrew was sized 9 x 12, a beautiful parchment structure with a wax seal on the back flap, and my name in calligraphy on the front. No address, though, which made one wonder how it had gotten delivered, and that gave me a Harry Potter flashback.

I slid an invitation out.

YOU ARE SUMMONED, TWO EVENINGS HENCE, TO

THE SOCIETAS OBSCURA. AN ESCORT WILL PROVIDE
TRANSPORTATION.

The black borders edging the paper seemed both appropriate and threatening.

Aaaaaand here came more trouble, right behind the shock
and awe.

WITH THE PROFESSOR no longer in my daily life—well, that wasn't quite true, we spent a lot of time searching for signs of him—I couldn't ask his advice on the Society. I knew only that he had disdained it and did not trust it, but I didn't know if I should hold the same opinions. I was as curious about the governing group of magicians as they were about me. And I needed a teacher. Every time Nimora opened her eyes in my stone, I could feel a surge of power and a sharp hunger to do things that I might possibly regret. I needed to know how to tame those impulses. I needed to have the discipline to change the things I should and bear the things I should not, like that popular saying. Plus, once I had Morty's journals in my hand, I might need their assistance with setting my father back in his true dimension. Carter, I knew, would help me, but I also knew he worried about backlash from the Society.

"Who died?" Evelyn leaned close and ran a polished fingernail along the edge of the invitation.

"Nobody. Why?"

"It looks all solemn, like something a funeral home might send out." She gave a little shiver. "Glad nobody died." Then she added, in a different tone: "Yet."

Evelyn dipped a shoulder as if she thought to either take the invitation from me or read it, either one of which I couldn't allow. But she didn't notice my defensive maneuver to keep it away. Instead, one of her dark blonde eyebrows arched and she added, "More good than ill will come from that, and yet it's up to you to make the choice which gives you the best destiny. Death and doom fall before you. Beware."

Like that wasn't creepy. I shoved the paper back in its envelope before saying to her, "Why are you spouting all witchy woman and Shakespearean?"

She blinked a few times. "I'm not. Am I?"

"Then what was that you just said?"

"What was what?"

"That bit about good and ill and destiny."

"I didn't. Did I?"

"You most certainly did." I fingered the envelope. Without the professor, I needed a mentor on how to handle the new me, but he'd always despised the Society and I tended to think he had valid reasons. My experience so far had been mixed. I didn't know whether I should show up or not, and Evelyn's little speech didn't help my indecision. "You don't remember?"

Evelyn shook her head. I considered her a moment, before adding, "You've done that a couple of times."

"Said something I don't remember?"

"More like intoned. Predicted." I considered what she'd intoned lately. It couldn't be, and yet it was. "And, come to think of it, you've mostly been right."

"Well, thank sugar for that. I'd hate to go around saying something stupid."

I grinned at her. "Oh, I didn't say they didn't sound stupid. Just . . . correct." And she had been, and because of what I'd been exposed to over the last year, I crossed my arms and asked, just in case, "Any witches in your family?"

"Witches? No, for heavens' sakes. Maybe a horse thief or two and a prohibition runner." She punched me lightly in the shoulder again. "Now who's being stupid?" The movement flashed her watch in front of her eyes, and she straightened. "I've got to fly. Don't forget, you promised me."

"Be here by nine."

"All righty!" she fled, the kitchen side door banging in her wake, Scout chasing after her until the door shut in his face. He sat down, a disappointed look on his doggy muzzle.

"I'll take you for a walk in a bit."

His tail thumped. Sidestepping him, I went to the front door, then out the kitchen door, and then through the mudroom to the backyard but found no sign of its delivery. I should have asked Evelyn where exactly she found the invitation, but it probably wouldn't have mattered. It would have poofed into existence wherever it was most likely to be picked up quickly. It felt substantial enough, but I was a little surprised that it stayed intact under Evelyn's touch. I tapped the envelope. "You forgot to include the time."

If the Society thought I was going to get all fancied up and then sit for hours hoping to be collected before I wilted, they had another think coming. The envelope grew warm between my fingers and I eyed it suspiciously before opening it enough to peer inside.

8:00 PM appeared below the original missive. Magic, ain't it wonderful. I let the envelope snap shut. I'd be ready by eight, but not a minute sooner, and I still didn't intend to sit around all night waiting to be picked up. I didn't even have to sleep on that idea.

Mom had chores lined up for me, filling my day, so when bedtime rolled around, I collapsed. We're a team, the two of us, and although University was on break for her, and community college for me, her dissertation had her pretty well tied in knots, so I worked at keeping the house Aunt April rented us in as good a shape as I could. It's really old (for that matter, so is she) but it's not a Victorian, just a framework almost Craftsman style two-story. It needs a daily cleanup, cooking, laundry, dog care, the usual. Also the unusual, but I tried to keep most of that as unobtrusive as possible. Sure, Mom's paper touched on reality and magic, but I had no intention of letting her know how steeped in it I'd become. It was enough she knew about Dad and my friends and the stone in my hand, but most of the rest of it I'd kept quiet. Or I hoped I had. I didn't want her to worry. Even when the wicked elf Devian had taken her, he'd kept her under a glamour so she really didn't know what was happening. Getting her released from his hold had been an ordeal. Luckily, the professor and Carter had blasted Devian back through his elven portal and didn't think he'd be able to reappear again for a decade or so. Equally hopefully, he'd learned a lesson not to mess with us.

Sometime after midnight, a tap-tap-tapping came at my bedroom window. I struggled out from under my comforter and my Labrador, whose body was thrown over my legs as though he expected a high wind to come blasting through and I needed an anchor. His watchdog instincts had gone to sleep with him, his pink tongue hanging out with a bit of dog drool as I staggered to the window and wrestled it up.

A lady harpy sat on the sill, the detached window screen in her arms as if she held a harp. I say lady because, although all harpies are female, this one usually dressed in battle armor and tonight she sat wrapped in a stylish silk dress, matching heels dangling from her feet. Harpies are shapeshifters, and in their battle mode they are winged and wicked. She could also manifest entirely as an owl, a hunter of the night. But it was a good-looking woman who faced me now. Goldie handed me the screen as she swung inside my room. I pried one eye open enough to peer at my clock.

"A little early, aren't you?"

"Early morning rain expected, and I didn't want to ruin my dress. You've got room on your couch." With that, she marched past and through my door, headed for the downstairs sofa. I propped the screen against the wall, wrestled the window shut again—old houses, what can I say, with enough paint on the frame that I was lucky the window could be moved at all—and I went back to bed.

The sounds of voices drifted up the stairs to greet me as I came down for breakfast, and I could hear Goldie and Mom laughing over something or other. A pang hit me that the two-men-in-one our professor manifested as wasn't there to partake. I'd spent months trying to help him reconcile his soul with the rejuvenated body of his younger self, but we hadn't been able to succeed for quite a while. Brian had been all left-coast surfer dude, laid back and very naïve because he'd been born at the age of twenty and had a lot to learn about the world. The professor now—crusty and knowledgeable and altogether magical—well, he was supposed to have morphed soul AND body into Brian but hadn't, his phoenix ritual going wrong. Not entirely wrong because his personality resided inside Brian, so the poor guy had two people wrestling for control of his body. The professor usually won. We'd managed to get it right, finally, or I hoped we had. He'd disappeared when we'd attacked Devian to get Aunt April and my mother freed as hostages and knocked that evil elf deep into his own realm. With any luck, Devian wouldn't get his shit together for a decade or two. If he were smart, he wouldn't bother us then either, but no one could accuse Devian of being able to let bygones be bygones. Had Evie somehow been warning me against Devian?

All of which went in a full circle to my missing Brian/the professor at the breakfast table with the rest of us. I sat down with a sigh, putting the envelope next to my place, and both women swung around to face me.

My mother said brightly, "Goldie here has been telling me more about that stone in your hand."

Wonderful. The rules of magic seem to be on a need-to-know basis, and nobody seemed to think I needed to know much in case that made me dangerous. "Anything interesting?" I responded as I took two pieces of bacon, some lukewarm toast already spread with melted butter, and poured myself a glass of orange juice.

"Many think it thrives on chaos, but there are other opinions on it." Goldie passed me the spare teacup and saucer as she answered, and my mother filled it with coffee as it was passed along to me.

Mom kept her gaze on my face as I ate my bacon and swallowed before saying, "Oh?" I feared to say anything less or more in case I might be in trouble later, so I dropped my sight away from her blazing blue eyes to concentrate on cream and sugar in my coffee.

"Indeed," Goldie continued. "You know, of course, that the stone tends to absorb magical relics—that cursed ring of Professor Brandard's and the book on the Dark Arts, as well as the benevolent shards of the Eye of Nimora—" She smoothly ignored the gulp and near splutter from my mother's direction, and added, "Which seems to support the theories I've heard that the stone is not one of chaos but balance."

"Balance?"

"It purportedly acts like a fulcrum in the powers of magic." Goldie smiled at me as if totally unaware of the chaos she was currently bringing to my life. "You took physics in high school? You know what a fulcrum does?"

I put my teacup down. " 'Give me a lever long enough and a fulcrum on which to place it, and I shall move the world. Archimedes.' I got an A in the class."

"Good quote."

"So . . . this thing . . ." and I rubbed the thumb of my right hand over my left palm. "Seeks balance?"

"That's a theory I'm inclined to believe. It's not sent you down any paths of evil, has it?"

"Maybe a little reckless now and then, but no."

My mother coughed.

Goldie smiled. "Still so much to discover in this world!" She pushed back from the kitchen table. "I'll leave you two to finish your breakfast in peace while I go talk with the neighborhood guardians and see if there is anything afoot."

That gave me a hope that something else besides myself had seen that apparition watching the house the night before last. I wanted to go with her, but chances were the spies she hoped to contact might not show if I were there, so I stayed in my chair and studied my breakfast plate.

The kitchen door had banged solidly back into place before my mother said, "Neighborhood guardians?"

I shrugged. "No idea. Maybe crows? An owl or two?"

"Seriously, Tessa?"

"I really don't know."

"I'm finding out new things every day."

"Welcome to my world."

She stared at me wordlessly while I stared back.

Finally, Mom said, "There's a chance that thing could go evil?"

"I don't think so. I mean, the professor and Steptoe were a

little astonished when it embedded in me, but they didn't wave a cross in my face or anything."

"Don't make fun of me."

"I'm not! I think, but I'm not sure, that they don't want to suggest anything to me in case that brings on the problem they're worried about. Anyway, I've had this for what—six months?—and I'm still on an even keel." I shoved the envelope back and forth a bit. "Or I thought I was. The Society wants to see me in two days."

"Mandatory? I know the professor held nothing but scorn for them."

"The feeling is mutual, near as I can tell, but I don't think I have an option here. I really need training."

"Should I worry?"

I looked at my mother, examining her face which is not at all like mine except that I have blue eyes, too. Her dark blonde hair looks to have strands of silver here and there, and her eyes had laugh (and maybe some crying, too) wrinkles at the corners, and she had one crease across her throat that may develop into some serious stuff as she gets older. So, yeah, she looks a little worn but still pretty, if stern and worried, and I can see why my father fell in love with her. I love her, too, but then she's my mom. I wasn't about to tell her that my trip today was vital and for information that might bring back my father. I didn't want to offer hope I couldn't deliver.

"If I told you no, you would anyway."

"True." She finished her cup of coffee. "I wish the professor was here for advice."

"No, you don't. Not about this anyway. He had nothing but spite for them and he'd be spitting nails now and telling me not to go. Threatening them for requesting my presence. Trouble we don't need."

"Right again. Okay. I've got a meeting at the university, a short planning committee to prepare for the new semester. Can you start the dishes before you go wherever with Goldie?"

"Got it." I finished my breakfast and listened to her gather up her tote bag and laptop before leaving, and wondered if anything Evelyn said might come true this time.

Scout snuffled around the backyard, chasing off a few birds and marking his territory to warn off the raccoons and possums near the trash cans. It wouldn't work, and he would be unhappy if they stopped coming around because chasing them off seemed to be one of his great joys. He bounded through the grass, golden Lab-half something else. Our yard was no longer green and lush, and I didn't miss the need to have to mow and hack back shrubbery. Winter does have some advantages. I saw no sign whatsoever of Goldie. That early morning rain she'd predicted began to fall, first as an ice-cold mist and then a steady drizzle. The pup and I ducked our heads and hurried back into the house, more from the cold than the wet.

I found Goldie sitting at our breakfast table, sipping a mug of hot tea; she pointed helpfully at the nearby kettle on the stove. "Should still be piping hot."

Scout plopped his butt down near his food bowl, put a paw into its empty interior, and looked up at me hopefully. He watched with soulful eyes while I fixed my own mug and left it to steep on the counter before heading to the small bucket we used as a kibble bin. Goldie watched as I poured his scoops in and the pup did his celebratory dance, which consisted of hopping around in a joyful circle three times before diving in.

"Are you taking him with us this morning?"

I sat down with my mug and dosed it with sugar. "I don't think so. Should I?"

She shrugged, powerful shoulders moving under her silk dress. "Perhaps not today. You and I will be very busy and not able to tend to him. But someday. He needs a forest run. He was bred for it. And the retriever part, too—he would love splashing through the rivers." She paused and tapped a nail on her mug. "I wouldn't let the Society get a close look at him, though."

"You think?" I had been buttering a day-old biscuit to go with my tea before considering Scout as he ate as if he'd never, ever, in his months of lifetime, been fed before. Carter had certainly evaluated him closely; the dog was a gift from him, a reject from the police department when a basket of orphaned pups had been left for the canine unit. Scout hadn't fit well into the training program. After months, my birthday had come up, and so he'd brought Scout over to see if the dog would take to me. And the two of us had bonded. I'd never been quite certain why the dog hadn't fit in, but I had an idea that he had been very selective over whether or not he'd obey commands. He and I had a few similar talks lately. Mostly though, he respected my discipline, and I tried to respect those times when he had a different agenda in mind. Unless it was eating. Heavens knew Scout would eat himself into a food coma if I let him.

She gave an indifferent wave of her drink. "It might be wise. The Society might try to take him from you."

"I'll keep that in mind." I finished my second breakfast, funneling biscuit crumbs to Scout's eager red tongue and waiting for our guests to show up. I bolted upstairs to brush my teeth and run a comb through my hair to be ready.

They showed up within minutes of each other, Evelyn first as she came in the kitchen door and footsteps after that, as Hiram approached. The house always moaned and groaned under the hefty weight of the Iron Dwarf—but it was relatively quiet this morning and I realized that Hiram had done that thing, lightening his body, to prevent undue strain on the building's structure. I was certainly used to the wood and iron and stone of the house awakening to him but not so much to Evelyn, I realized. That told me at least two important things: one, he hadn't explained his background to her yet; and two, he knew she'd come in the house just ahead of him even though from the expression on his face he hadn't expected her at all.

I eyed Evelyn up and down, and she caught on to what I was doing, looking to see if she'd changed clothes from yesterday or was doing the infamous walk of shame. She slapped my elbow lightly as she passed me, saying "I do declare."

I arched an eyebrow at her. "Just checking."

Ever the gentleman in spite of his surprise, Hiram held a chair for her to sit, even though we were all at home in our kitchen.

"I hope you don't mind," Evie told him. "Tessa said I could come along, and I thought it would be nice to meet your family."

"Why wait?" Hiram forced a smile. "This is my stepmother, Goldie Germanigold."

Evelyn's jaw dropped, and she swiveled about. "Goldie! I didn't know you were part of Hiram's family."

The two of them had only met briefly during a heavy rainstorm on a country highway, but the meeting had been rather unforgettable since we were all fleeing Silverbranch Academy for one reason or another.

Goldie reached out and squeezed her wrist. "Six degrees of Kevin Bacon, right?"

"No kidding!" Evie leaned back in her chair, hoping perhaps to also lean back against Hiram, but he'd moved quietly away and stared at me.

The look was stern enough that the thought went through my mind that Iron Dwarves didn't need mining tools; they could just stare at a rock hard enough and it would chip away. I tried to fend it off with a weak smile but wished I had my bracers on or my shield up instead.

Goldie sensed the tension. Even Scout sat in the corner, his ears in a downward droop. In fact, the only person in the room who didn't seemed to be keyed in was Evelyn.

Evie smiled. "I thought," she said brightly, "that today would be a terrific day to meet everyone."

Hiram's hands flexed. "Actually, a better time would be when we can host you properly, with a grand luncheon or dinner, and I could gather the clan in, because my aunts and uncles and brothers and cousins are a hard-working group, most of them out on crews and such. It would be a near empty house today. There will be no one for you to meet, and I would hate to disappoint you and my family."

Goldie slid her hand out and patted Evie's wrist. "I'm just going up today to pick up some odds and ends from the estate. A melancholy trip, at best."

"Oh." Evelyn dropped her gaze to the table where she was drawing tiny circles with one index finger.

He leaned forward. "How about this weekend or the next? Even the Broadstone family has Saturdays off, and we can meet everyone properly. Tessa could bring her mother and we'd have a grand time. Might even be a bit of snow in the forests awaiting us. It would be beautiful to host you then." His slight Dwarven accent showed. I could never decide whether it was Scots or Gaelic, though definitely a brogue of some sort, and a little old-fashioned.

"Oh!" Evelyn's expression glowed. "That would be wonderful. I guess I'll phone my driver and have him circle back. I should be home helping plan Dad's event if I'm not off with you."

Disaster was averted, at least for now, and we all sat and talked amiably until her driver knocked politely at the front door and swept her away. I expected Hiram to turn on me and bellow, his color still high, but he just brushed past me with a low grumble.

"Not my idea," I offered by way of apology.

"That I know," he answered slowly. "Lass has a mind of her own. She can be a bit hasty."

Goldie simply lifted her mug to her lips, obviously realizing it might be wiser to say nothing at all. I decided that, due to his culture, any of us might be considered hasty and didn't attempt to defend Evelyn.

He let me make coffee for him and accepted the last of the biscuits, without saying much one way or another until he wiped his hands on a napkin and stood up. "We should be leaving."

Goldie smiled at him. "I'll be right out as soon as I use the facilities. Tessa, care to show me where they are?" and she stood in the hallway, waiting for me as he went outdoors.

I started to show her the downstairs bathroom, which was little more than a closet, but she stopped me. "I needed a moment."

I waited.

"Remember that I told you there was a traitor among the dwarves? That someone betrayed me as the keeper of the Eye of Nimora so that it could be taken?"

"And we determined it wasn't Hiram."

"True, but despite his words to Evelyn, I imagine we will have quite a welcoming committee today. Those four remaining suspects should be among them. I'm not expecting a welcoming. The marriage between me and Morty was extremely unpopular."

That I had learned over the last few months. I didn't want to say it, but Goldie deserved my cooperation. "Should we not go?"

"Oh, no. This was a victory too hard won. But you should be wary and careful."

I certainly hadn't expected this but nodded. "And you, too."

Goldie gave me a wry look. "I always am when surrounded by enemies." She added, "And friends. These are chancy days. You'd do well to remember that."

I could hardly forget it. Way back when I was early into magic, a sorceress named Remy had warned of the exact same thing. She hadn't been wrong, either.

We caught up our coats and rain slickers and then I walked out with her to Hiram's SUV, misgivings unsettling me. Scout watched me dolefully from a corner of the living room window, unhappy at being left behind. I leaned forward in my seat. "Maybe I should bring Scout."

"Not this trip," Hiram responded as he started the vehicle, put it in gear and pulled away. That was when he pulled the blindfolds out of the center console. "And you'll be needing to wear these when I advise you to."

CHAPTER THREE

FAMILY KNOTS

I KNOW. FAMILIES should have ties, but in Hiram and Goldie's case, they tangled almost beyond repair. The blindfolds seemed a bit extreme, however. I opened my mouth to protest, but Goldie stopped me. "He's right. We're going into old forest, beyond a kind of veil, and the trip can be very disorienting."

I shut my mouth. Thought about it. Iron Dwarves and other clans stayed as hidden as any of the other magical races and it stood to reason they had their own sanctuaries. I wasn't certain about what kind of veil Goldie might mean, but I'd seen through an elven gateway not long ago, and the landscape on the other side certainly had been different in strange and awkward ways. I stretched the blindfold across my lap. "Ready when you are."

"Oh, it'll be a bit," Hiram told me. "It's a drive."

I understood a little more why he hadn't wanted Evelyn along. Explaining the blindfold might have been a little difficult. Although, for all I knew, she might think it delightfully kinky.

That light rain increased to a wintry, dark storm that grew heavier as we motored outside the city. A chill hung over the car until the heater kicked in while I pondered what Goldie had meant by old forest. North America is, compared to many of the other continents, a relatively new world. There are the redwoods and sequoias that negate that thought, but the rest of the area . . . well, I haven't met a tree over five hundred years old that I know of. Admittedly, I hadn't even thought of introducing myself to a tree until lately. But where magic users are concerned, I had the feeling even five hundred years wasn't considered ancient. I tried to watch through the windshield to see which direction we were headed, but Hiram had turned almost immediately onto a thoroughfare I didn't recognize, and there weren't that many in and out of Richmond. After listening to the windshield wipers slap back and forth for about fifteen minutes, Hiram said, "Blindfolds, please."

I caught Goldie giving him a look, but the Iron Dwarf said firmly, "Even you," so she reached up with her hands and began to fasten it over her eyes. I slipped mine on then, too.

I could feel it the moment the SUV slipped away from modern-day Virginia and into . . . what, I didn't know. The pelting rain stopped and might have turned into a light snowfall, I couldn't see to tell, but it wasn't the heavy kind of snow that muffles the immediate world. The windshield wipers slowed to a more deliberate rhythm, and the tires and bumps told me that the road of asphalt had turned into something else. Hard-packed dirt, possibly. I didn't hear the occasional slippage or ping of gravel coming loose, so we didn't drive over that. I really, really wanted to see what we headed into, but then the Veil hit.

A feeling shivered through me, and for a moment I felt as if I were doing a somersault. It wasn't awful, but I really hated having my eyes covered so I could deal with gravity and the lack of it. It got worse. My stomach turned inside out, and the breakfast I'd pushed into my throat demanded an automatic eject. I swallowed convulsively, determined not to embarrass myself by spewing all over Hiram's backseat, but my stomach fought back. I pushed my hands to my mouth and must have let out a moan as my ears went wild and my brain reeled. I could barely hear Goldie say, "Steady."

But there was nothing steady about what happened to my body. Had Hiram driven onto a roller coaster track and were we now hurtling along at seventy miles an hour *upside down*??? Because that's what my brain told me. And then it said sharply, reverse! And we did the whole course backward. My stomach ran for another exit, and I held onto the seat belt then, with both hands, certain my knuckles had gone white.

My ears popped and then—it all stopped. Well, the SUV kept moving but in a normal, orderly fashion; my stomach promptly gave a last spasm before settling down. My brain stopped whirling in circles and the whole, terrible, sensation faded away. I sat back weakly in the car, muscles limp. I hadn't embarrassed myself—barely. I could feel a drop of sweat trickle down my face from my temple and blotted it away once I unclenched my hands. If passing the Veil were this difficult every single time, I seriously doubted that they would have any trespassers to worry about.

After a few long moments, during which my senses convinced themselves that everything had turned out all right, Hiram said, "You can take off the blindfolds now."

With slightly shaky hands, I reached up, unsure if I even wanted to take it off. What if we'd just driven into, I don't know, *Jurassic Park*? Was I prepared to see a stegosaurus stumbling through the foliage? On the other hand, that might be rather neat until it charged the vehicle.

I pushed the silk scarf off as Hiram turned down the heat setting on the dashboard and saw that I'd been right about a light snowfall. Huge flakes twirled down from the clouds, melting almost before they landed on the grass or road, their fall slow and deliberate against a vast, green forest the likes of which I had never seen before and likely would not see again, unless invited and escorted in. I began to realize what old forest meant.

Either I had shrunk, or these trees belonged to a species of giant evergreen unknown to me, every one of them rivaling the legendary sequoias. Clouds threaded through the tops of them, shredding where the pointed crowns struck through, almost as if the clouds themselves were merely white puffs decorating the dark green branches. Saplings pushed through here and there, stretching nearly as tall, though thin and supple, and the older trees that canopied them allowed just enough view of the sky that sunlight could nurture them. I thought of owls winging through, like a slalom course on a ski slope, moving in and out for the sheer joy of it. Below, grasses still held a slight green despite the snowfall, and I wondered what animals might pad through to crop at them. Would there be a wide and commanding river or fast-moving brooks somewhere beyond? And what about mountains? The Broadstones were miners of legend. Where did their veins of gold and gemstones hide? I had my nose to the window glass as tightly as Scout would have, if he'd come along, and I felt no shame in it.

"What do you think?" Goldie asked.

I breathed out slowly. "Awesome." I worried, then, about Evelyn. She's got a sharp mind, and I knew that she would see this forest as being somewhere outside of the world we'd both grown up in. There would be no explaining this. Not even an outright lie such as "Protected Forest" would justify what I viewed now.

Hiram looked over his shoulder briefly as if alerted by my thoughts. "Tessa?"

"What will you tell Evelyn?"

He paused. "I have a nice home in town. I won't need to tell her anything, for a while."

That made sense. When he came by or answered a distress call from me, he was never more than fifteen minutes away or so, and we'd been on the road this morning for at least an hour. I pondered a moment. "That might be a good idea," I answered. "Although she should see this someday. It's amazing."

"We think so."

"So . . . how far out of time are we? And could this survive a nuclear blast?"

"Out of time?"

"Like Wakanda."

He laughed. "It is a wedge," he told me. "In time but not quite out of it, either. And we think it might survive a disaster, but we're not willing to test that theory—and we certainly wouldn't want to risk the outside world. As for the Wakanda reference, you're probably right. We do have it shielded although not in the marvelous way the movies would have it. This ward took a heavy toll when it was put in place."

"Blood, sweat, and tears."

"Precisely." He guided the car about a big sweeping curve, and the rooftops of homes could be seen. Immense and sprawling roofs, but not close together in the valley opening up.

I undid my seat belt so I could scoot closer to the front seat. "I take it back. That's not Wakanda, that's Rivendell."

Goldie admonished me. "I wouldn't repeat that here. Rivendell is the legendary home of elves."

"You mean Tolkien got it right?"

"I mean that one never associates one ethnicity with another ignorantly, even using literary license."

Hiram grunted. "We prefer to call it simply Old Home."

"So are you American dwarves or European dwarves or what?"

I sat back quickly as Goldie twisted in her seat as though she might slap my hands. But she merely glared at me over her shoulder. "Mind your manners."

I'd seen battle harpies angry and decided to retreat, even though I wasn't quite sure what I'd done to offend. "Yes, ma'am."

The road twisted about again and again, avoiding huge monoliths of rock that interrupted its pathway here and there, and I stared at each as we passed it. I noted the resemblance to Stonehenge and other similar monuments, wondering if the dwarves had had a hand in placing them. As for these . . . Had the road been carved around them, or had they been placed there to mark the passage? If they had been placed, what did they signify? Did the ward surrounding them expand over the years as the population flourished? I stared at them as we passed and saw tiny mosses and lichen covering the surface, weathering, and erosion marks, and—could I be wrong?—runes etched here and there. I wondered what they said. My breath fogged the passenger window, and I sat back with a slight laugh.

Again, I caught a look from Goldie, and saw the tension in her body. She'd lost the Eye of Nimora and most of her nest to traitors; I realized she must be wondering what she might lose this time. She had vowed to Hiram that she would not start a battle, but that did not mean she would head into trouble with her hands tied. Not that battle harpy.

The road dipped downward and headed into a final stretch, passing the lanes of manor and estate houses, aimed at the grandest one of all at the far end of the valley. The sun broke through, the snowflakes melting into glittering diamonds of dew before slowly disappearing altogether.

And, as Goldie had predicted, it looked like most of the clans had turned out to wait for us. I saw Hiram's construction crew buddies who had come to work on repairing/replacing our old cellar and breathed a faint sigh of relief because none of their names had been on Goldie's very short list of possible traitors. Of the others, I hadn't been at all sure who I would meet. I knew the Iron Dwarves but had never met one of the Sylvans or Timber men or even one of the Watermen as I knew. I could see by the colors of their shirts that they wore them just as a Scot might wear his tartan: there were blues and greens and red-wood fabrics, and they tended to stand in bunches rather than stirred about to blend and almost every one of them had arms crossed over their broad chests or fists resting on their hips. Talk about defensive posture!

Very few of them were female, but they dressed in pants and shirts alike, only their luxurious hair and flashing eyes to tell them apart. Unlike female dwarves in old tales, these ladies did not have beards and looked very feminine as well as determined.

Goldie made a slight sound at the back of her throat, though whether it was fear or dismay I couldn't guess. She had warned me about the reception, but—even so—I got the feeling she hadn't expected this. The excitement filling me at meeting so many of the dwarven clans receded as I realized she watched for trouble. I gritted my teeth shut. I was so close to getting some idea of what happened to my father, and it looked as if we were going to come away empty-handed.

Then I spotted a gleaming crimson ray as the sun struck something brilliant and altogether marvelous. One of the Broad-stone clan wore the Eye of Nimora upon his brow.

I touched Goldie's shoulder. "Wow. Looks like they brought out the big guns."

She nodded. "They want retribution against me however

they can get it. Well, I've nothing to hide." Almost before the SUV stopped, she unclipped her seatbelt and swiveled in her seat to step out.

I waited for Hiram to extend his hand, a little cowardly I knew, but I wanted the crowd to know I was on his side. Or maybe that he was on mine. I could hear the rumble and grumble of voices as we all appeared.

A bent old man, wrapped in green, lifted his bewhiskered chin and shouted out, "By what right are you even here, Goldie Germanigold! You brought death to Mortimer Broadstone."

"Perhaps that is true, but before that, I brought him many years of love and regard. I'm here because I asked to retrieve what few things are mine from Morty's holdings and to give my respect at his headstone."

Headstone? They had a grave for Morty? The last I had seen of him had been a ghostly whirlwind of metallic elements and gems spinning away from the sidewalk where he'd died in New York City. No body, just a cloud of debris that represented his life. I'd have to visit that grave myself. I owed him for a few things.

No one standing there answered her.

Goldie inclined her head. "If you won't allow me that last, I have already asked for and received permission for the former from his heir."

It didn't look as if the crowd would let us through. "Hiram," I whispered in desperation. "I have to get that journal. Please."

The merest wave of his hand indicated he heard me. I didn't know what he could do, and I couldn't see us having a brawl on the steps of his ancestral home. I stood very still, with the stone warming itself in my hand as if preparing for action.

"And I," Hiram spoke up, "have permission from the elders. She did help retrieve the Eye of Nimora."

"Her fault it was stolen!" came a shout from the back of the crowd. Goldie swung her sharp gaze over everyone, identifying faces she knew, no doubt, as Hiram held up his palm.

"Let it go," he said. "She is a guest."

He shouldered his way through those blocking the entrance to the estate, an impressive building built of river stone and redwood from the looks of it, and split logs I didn't recognize, but Hiram touched them in passing and said, "Chestnut. The old trees are gone, killed by a fungus. New resistant trees have been created, but those who fear science will not let them be planted." He stopped and rubbed the beautiful wood stud again. "At one time they covered this coast. I would like to see that growth again."

I realized then that it might be great to live a long life and yet be filled with regret for the things lost in doing so as he cleared his throat and moved to the double door to open it for us. I waited tensely for the crowd to pull us back, forbidding entrance but no one moved though I heard a few low and unhappy mutters.

Goldie swept in ahead of me, moving very quickly and yet without seeming haste as if she could not wait to leave the crowd behind her but did not want to be seen as fleeing it. I hurried a bit to catch up.

Broadstone Manor did not creak or groan as my Iron Dwarf friend stepped into its lobby. Wood and stone polished within an inch of their lives gleamed at us, and from the side, an immense sweep of gem-studded stained-glass windows reminiscent of pictures I'd seen of Notre Dame let sunlight dapple the floors and walls. Every piece of furniture sat as a massive, carved structure strewn with pillows and cushions and lowered to fit the frames of those who would sit upon them.

Hiram started to give me a tour, but Goldie swung on him. "We haven't much time," she told him. "It's possible that when I begin to search for the journals, the Jewel of Nimora will reveal my lie which is unspoken though action will tell."

"It has that power?"

She looked back over her shoulder, one foot on the curving staircase, and gave a wry smile. "It has many such powers, Hiram, that you will learn if given the time." She hurried up the stairway, the case broad enough that an eight-foot sofa could have been carried crosswise up it without trouble, continuing up to the third floor. "You are the designated wearer, are you not?"

"Sometimes."

Hiram kept his hand on my elbow, not for fear of my tripping or getting lost, but I think more to hold me back and give Goldie a bit of privacy as she faced a home she hadn't been in for decades, yet which held distinctive echoes of Morty's influence everywhere. My friendship with Morty had been brief but deep, and I could feel his influence pulsing about me. He had given everything to help the professor and me in the hunt for the items needed for that last phoenix ritual. Yes, he'd betrayed us along the way but only to unsuccessfully ransom Goldie. How torn he must have been, and what a great friend he still had been. Hiram's hand rested on me warmly as I gave a little hiccup of emotion, my eyes brimming.

"Now, then," he said to my ear. "No mourning. This home stands because Mortimer lived. And it will continue to do so in his honor."

"A legacy."

"Indeed. In our blood and in our bones."

A door opened somewhere ahead of us on the third floor, the hinges giving off a faint noise of usage and Hiram made a little "Hrrmmm" in the back of his throat. I realized he had held a notion that the rooms might not have opened for Goldie, but they had.

She hadn't moved from the threshold when we caught up with her.

I could understand why when I stood at her flank. It spoke of Morty, every handspan of it, with a plaid shirt hanging from a nearby peg and a pair of colorful suspenders that had seen eye-blinding times next to it. Framed shards of gems arranged like tiny suns and stars hung everywhere. A stand in the corner held two cudgels that might have been used as canes rather than weapons, a sledgehammer, an ax, and a crossbow. The crossbow Goldie gathered up and put on the edge of the double king-sized bed. Then she went to the armoire/closet in the corner of the room and flung it open.

She drew out a set of leather armor that obviously belonged to her, although this one was a stunning white leather, fitted with bronze parts here and there. She smiled at me over the handmade hanger that held it. "My wedding armor. It is a family heirloom. Centuries and centuries old."

I gawked at it a little before asking, "How do you keep the leather from going to pieces?"

"Oh, my dear, dragon leather is practically invincible, and unicorn oil keeps it supple." She winked at me as she said it, and Hiram covered a snort by coughing briefly instead.

"Fine. Don't tell me." I leaned into the closet as she withdrew all the silken dresses hanging there, five in all, and all fit for a queen. She tossed them onto her pile. "Shoes?" I prompted.

"Boots," she corrected, and withdrew three handsome pairs, one of which was white to match her wedding outfit. Then she pulled open a drawer built into the cabinetry which rattled with jewelry as she did. Hiram produced a drawstring bag and she emptied the glittering collection into it quickly. I only caught the barest glimpse of 24 karat gold and many, many gems before she fastened the bag shut.

Then, with a lift and a twist, she pulled the drawer out, and the one under it. Goldie knocked once or twice, experimentally, and motioned for me to join her. Having been in the professor's study, I had an idea what she was looking for, concealed book shelves, and I tapped around until I found a likely square.

"Here. I think I've found it."

Hiram held the armoire/closet doors open while we broke a few fingernails trying to get the hidden bookshelf unlatched, but nothing worked until she fisted her hand and punched the corner. It popped open with a squeak.

Now, I had been through enough of Broadstone Manor to know that the noise had to be intentional, a kind of alarm of its own, that the shelf had been opened. It wouldn't have been heard beyond this room (at least, I didn't think so, but I had no idea how keen dwarf hearing could be) but it would definitely have alerted anyone sleeping in the double king-sized bed or sitting at the desk and suite in the corner.

Goldie gave a little nod and reached inward through the opening. She took out no less than ten massive, leather-bound books. I closed my mouth as I spotted her armful, reminding myself that Morty had seen a lot of history. My mother would have given her eyeteeth to have a look at them, but that would be out of the question. Goldie shook out the one on top. "This is the most recent."

I took it from her. I could tell the ones that had been filled out by that rippled, written upon in old-fashioned ink quality to them, but even if he'd only written half a page a day, I held maybe a hundred years' worth of journal. The diary was close to full. I felt as though I held one of the professor's massive lore books, containing nearly as many possible and obscure an-swers to the world, in my arms. Hope for my father rose in me. I should find something in those pages that would tell me what happened. And then I could work on undoing it.

"That will do it," she said to Hiram. She paused. "Shall I put them back, or are you wanting to read any of them?"

"Thanks to you, I know where they are when I need them."

She nodded to him and redeposited the journals; this time the hidden bookshelf door closed with a nearly imperceptible click. She hung her bag of jewelry from her arm and gathered up her armful of wardrobe. I tucked in the sweeping skirts to keep her from tripping over anything and then hugged the journal to my chest.

"You'd better hide that."

I looked at the leather book. The only place I could fit it in was the backpack I customarily used for a purse, so I slid it in there. "Will I be searched?"

Hiram scratched his chin. "I doubt it."

But he hadn't guaranteed it. I stood hesitantly. "Maybe I should try to read it before we leave?"

Goldie shook her head. "They'll want me out of here as soon as possible."

Hiram seconded her assessment of the situation.

I shrugged. "All right. Good thing you talked Evelyn out of coming with us."

He frowned. "I'd like to know how she got the idea in the first place."

"Not from either of us. But she seems to be jumping the gun

on a couple of ideas." I stared at him pointedly till a faint blush pinked his dwarven cheeks. He decided not to say anything further.

Emerging into the sunlight on the front steps, Goldie stated, "I have retrieved what was mine and thank all of you for the hospitality." I followed her out into the sunlight, and everything looked fine, when the elder who had been wearing the Eye pounced on us. The jewel on his brow gave off a ray of glistening crimson.

"Liar!" he shouted and pointed at Goldie.

CHAPTER FOUR

STICKS AND STONES

FOR THE BAREST part of a second, I had the inane thought of "So that's how it works" run through my mind and then I plunged to a halt. The Eye of Nimora had been alerted to something about us. On Goldie? What the . . . and then I had it.

I turned on my heel, but before I could say anything, the elder in question, in a rippling blue-and-green–plaid shirt and dark blue cotton pants with a sharply defined crease, pointed again and repeated, "Lies!" Just in case we hadn't all heard him the first time, I suppose.

A niggling suspicion went up my spine, and I swung around to look at my friend.

I raised my voice a little. "No kidding. Goldie, I thought you were serious when you told me your armor came from dragon hide and unicorn oil!"

A groan rolled through the assembled crowd. Goldie gave a light laugh as I looked over my shoulder at them. "How was I to know? I'm new at this. No dragons? No unicorns?"

"Not in this century, lass," a tenor voice answered me. I looked into the crowd and saw one of Hiram's construction crew grinning back at me.

I waved both hands in the air in frustration. Goldie stepped down to join me, Hiram's hand on her elbow as if he might buffer her from any further challenges from the crowd, and everything seemed fine until a woman pushed her way through.

Not only was she not bearded, she wasn't short and stout

either. This one was as tall as any of the men around her, and slim as well as curvaceous. No longer young but no telling how old she might be, as dwarves wore their years like trees grew rings, quietly if steadily. I could, however, tell she held some power within the group because they gave way to let her through.

"Not so fast," she said. "Goldie Germanigold has not been an honored guest here for a number of years. Have we all forgotten why that came about? And one lie may hide another."

But the shining ray from the Eye of Nimora had gone out, and it looked as though the falsehood matter had been settled. Goldie nodded toward it before she turned to face the other.

"And shall we have a duel of words, Ludcrita, to see which one of us alerts the gem? I daresay you might be cautious in that regard because there is a traitor amongst you."

Hiram made a tiny noise at the back of his throat as if he wished Goldie had not brought up that little accusation, but she continued speaking, as headstrong as the harpy warrior I knew her to be. "Perhaps it might be said that falsehoods amongst the tribes are not as important as lies outside them."

"You are a guest here," Ludcrita answered, her eyes holding a gleam deep within them. I had a moment to wonder if the two had, at one time, been rivals for the widower Mortimer's favor. Likely there was another reason for the dwarf's animosity, but I stood in fascination, mouth half-open, to watch and listen.

Goldie threw her head back a little. "While it is true," she declared, "that my own nest sisters betrayed the place where I kept the Eye safe, it is equally true that they had no inkling whatsoever of the bridal gift Mortimer had given me, not until told of it by a dwarf. Their treason began here. Without that knowledge, they could not have planned a theft. So which one of you—or your sons and daughters—betrayed me? I left no stone unturned until I was given names and one of them, Ludcrita, belongs to your son Milardi."

A gasp ran through the crowd, and the comely Ludcrita's face paled into a color close to ashes. Her head swiveled to the Eye of Nimora, but it did not reveal a lie. She put a hand to her face and stepped back, disappearing into the crowd, words choked to silence.

"I pray you find out differently," Goldie called after the woman as she ran from the gathering, her skirts knotted in her hands.

"It is well you leave, Germanigold, before you harm us further." The elder wearing the gem beetled his brows at her in a hard stare.

"I concur." She swept past Hiram to the SUV and stopped one last time. "I have given the names of three others to Hiram, and if you're brave enough to investigate, ask him what he knows."

I think I heard him mutter "shit" as he opened the car door and hustled her inside, dresses, armor, jewel pouch and all, before shutting her away from further provocation. I hopped in alertly, thinking he might well leave me behind if I didn't hurry.

We bounced onto the gravel road when well away from the manor houses and Hiram paused only long enough to throw our hoods at us.

Goldie batted hers away serenely. "Not needed."

I grabbed for mine and pulled it on. I had looked forward to seeing Hiram's home, with Morty's touch everywhere within it, but the afternoon felt soured now. I really hadn't expected Goldie to lob verbal grenades as she left. I'd no idea of the grudge she'd carried.

Hiram said little to me and nothing to Goldie as he dropped us off. The screech of tire rubber on the road as he drove off, however, spoke volumes. Goldie looked after his vehicle and gave a little shake of her head. "So young he is. And, as Mortimer might say, opinionated." She smoothed the heavy bundle she carried over her forearm. "If you have any questions about the journal, you know how to reach me. I hope it holds some of the answers you need."

Indeed, I did know how to reach her, although talking to an owl and asking for her seemed on the odd side, but nothing like what I've been through the last year or so. The corner of her mouth quirked as though she could read my thoughts. "He didn't write in code, I believe, but he might refer to names and events as though you should know what they are, with little explanation. The past influences the present more than you might guess."

"How old was Morty, anyway?"

"Nearly four hundred years when he died in battle."

"Four—wow." I revised my opinion of Hiram's probable age. "Seriously?"

"Very." Goldie tilted her head. "I was a child bride, barely more than two hundred years myself."

I tried to smother down my reaction and ended up hiccoughing. She pounded my back with her free hand. She laughed when I finally lifted my head to meet her expression. "Tessa, all of us . . . all the ones of us you might call magical . . . we live in a niche outside of your time. If we didn't, we wouldn't exist today."

"Truth?"

"What do you think?"

Before I could answer, she wrestled her car phone out of a heretofore unseen pocket in her dress skirt.

"Can I drive you anywhere?"

"No, I'm going to call for a car. It should be here soon." She shifted her booty in her arms. If I'd thought she was out of ammo, I found myself greatly mistaken when she began to speak again.

"Your house is being watched," she told me. "I wish I could say it was Brandard, looking the situation over before he comes home, but it doesn't appear to be. You and your mother need to be very careful."

"Watched? How would you know?"

"My little friends about the neighborhood have sharp eyes and ears and noses. They know."

"I've got Carter. And Scout. And Simon."

She tilted her head dubiously. "I'm not certain any one of those could help you in time. So promise me. You will take care?"

"I will, if you'll promise me that you'll let me know anything else you find out."

"Done."

Before she finished, a car swept up to the curb, a limo, and its trunk bounced open. It must have been waiting around the corner. Goldie leaned over, brushing her lips across my forehead.

"Be safe, Tessa." She said it like a benediction, sending shivers down my back as she walked to the car, stowed her things, and got in. She did not look back as the car drove away.

For a brief moment, I wondered if I'd see her again.

CHAPTER FIVE

HOME AND HEARTH

SCOUT DID HIS usual riotous welcome home dance when I unlocked the door and entered, his youngish body with gangly long legs in jeopardy of tripping both of us up before I convinced him to go out the back door and run around the yard. I watched him, a little in disbelief so much time had passed, but it had. My hands itched to pull the journal out, but I knew I wouldn't be able to read it easily in the dusk. Outside, as night fell, smudging the corners of our yard in shadows, my pup ran about in big loops, with an occasional return to nudge my hand with his cold nose and then to race off again. If we were being watched, he gave no sign of it, and despite his half-grown puppyhood status, Scout was a great watchdog. So whatever it was escaped his senses. What could a dog not smell or hear?

I fed him his dinner kibble and went upstairs as he ate noisily, the hard chunks rattling around in his stainless-steel bowl with great commotion. Upstairs, in their vase standing in a hallway niche, the tell-tales brightened at seeing me, little magical rose faces turning up to me without alarm as well. I shook a finger at them. "I hear someone's been watching the house. How could you not tell me?" I'd only been alerted that one, awful time.

The roses reacted very little. If there was a danger, the tell-tales seemed unaware as well, which made me wonder how they had reacted so strongly that once.

I knew the professor and Carter both had wards on the house. I didn't know if they faded with time or distance (no one knew where the professor could possibly be, not even Simon whose demon tail had an intimate binding with the wizard after having been used as a relic in a bonding ritual). I decided to ask many questions of several people because Goldie's warning had seemed solemn and important.

I checked my phone to see when Mom would be home. Not long from now . . . her office work and staff meetings finished, she had only her dissertation group to get through and she'd be home. Dinner was on me tonight, then, and I headed down to the kitchen to rummage through the fridge to see what I could fix without too much trouble that would please both of us. I wrinkled my nose as I came across a container half-filled with blueberries that needed to go out in the trash, their little round buttons dotted with white. I shoved them over on the counter and found the fixings for chili, a mix we didn't often eat, and which would be welcome to stave off the winter chill. Also, about as easy to make as I could hope. Mind occupied by worries, I chopped onions and a not too hot pepper, and mixed them into browned hamburger along with chili pepper. Then I threw everything together in a deep pot with a can of diced tomatoes and set it on a back burner to simmer for an hour or so as rich smells filled the kitchen. Scout occupied a corner, his belly to the floor and his front paws crossed in sincere yellow Lab interest in our dinner as well. I paced around him.

"What could possibly have been out there that slipped past you?"

Scout's ears went back as though I'd insulted him. I stared at him. "Don't give me that look. Goldie informed me. What we need to do now is find out who or what and run it off."

He shook his head energetically, ears flapping.

"No?"

I raised my palm at him, and he snuffled in response. "Point that somewhere else?" I considered Scout's silent advice. "I suppose I could sit in the window all evening with my hand hanging out and see what the stone sees. That doesn't sound the least bit practical." I dropped my arm. "Maybe the Society will have an idea if I can figure out an oblique way to ask them without revealing much on my side. This being a sorceress has got to have some advantages, right?"

Scout sneezed. It meant nothing particular to me except that perhaps the aroma of freshly chopped onions on the air got to his sinuses. I laughed at him and set to making corn bread to accompany the chili.

I was deep into my laptop, going over the course catalog—not for this upcoming semester but for summer and fall—when my mother straggled in, her hair wind-tangled and her briefcase bag hanging precariously off one arm and carrying her laptop case in the other. I jumped up to rescue the bag before it spilled her paperwork all over.

"Thanks, hon," she got out as I followed her to her down-stairs office.

"Tough day?"

"Not really, but they want me to teach one class this semester."

"I thought your sabbatical was approved?"

She shrugged a shoulder. "The committee giveth and the committee taketh away."

"How did the read-through go?"

She dumped her laptop on her desk and reached for the bag I held. "It didn't."

"You didn't get to present what you have so far?"

My mom took a moment both to collect herself and finger-comb her blonde hair away from her face. "I did present . . . the first chapter. But we only had half the review group show, and they stopped me. Tessa, their faces were like stone. I have no idea if they liked or even understood what I'd written. I let them know I'd finished all four chapters and wanted to make what-ever changes they deemed necessary, rewrite, and publish in the next three months. Four chapters don't sound like much, but I'm talking 130 pages of work and citations. Not to mention that I suspect each of them has an agenda and wants to see me express it."

"No reaction to that, either?"

"None. I'd have gotten more reaction out of a statue."

"Then that's their problem."

She leaned on the desk and looked across at me. "Do you think it's the magic?"

I paused to consider that thoroughly. Having read her paper at least once, I knew that she didn't draw heavily on magic's actuality, at least not in the first three parts of her examination and argument. Instead, she traced the history of magic realism in storytelling, oral and written, through the past to the present. Rather like saying: If there's smoke, will there be fire? I finally answered, "I don't know. It could be, but shouldn't be. Are you facing a stubbornly conservative review group?"

"All academia tends to be conservative, even if they're liberals. They have the school's reputation to consider, as well as their own, when it comes to degrees and publication." My mother sat down heavily with a sigh. Her eyebrow, however, ticked up. "What did you cook that smells so good?"

"Chili. With cornbread."

"Oh, I'm in! Start some tea for me, too, please. I'll be in soon as I put my laptop in to charge."

"Tea's already made, but I'll get it piping hot."

"Thank goodness."

I left to the sounds of her fiddling with her computer.

Because she worried, I did. After semesters of nagging for her to finish her dissertation, now they (or someone) balked at giving her the time to do so and had gone back on the sabbatical agreement. That sounded political to me, and although my mother kept her job worries fairly quiet, I still had a good idea of some of the situations. If the professor were here, I'd rope him in to actively help her, for he'd retired from the university in extremely good standing and influence. I'd have to find him first to manage that, though.

I set the kettle back onto high after fishing out the tea leaf infuser. The chili went back on simmer and the corn bread had kept nice and warm in the quilted basket for baked goods, so all I had to do was set her place at the kitchen table. I thought about it for half a minute and set a third place, just in case.

When she joined me, I'd already scooped out a second bowl and wedge for myself and she'd scrubbed her face clean of makeup for the day and put on a moisturizer that gave her a glow despite the fatigue in her eyes. She'd barely begun to eat when a knock came at the kitchen back door, and our visitor didn't wait for us to let him in.

Simon approached the table, tugging on his suit coat to make himself absolutely presentable. He looked like a chimney sweep, regardless, dark old-fashioned clothing and often a bowler hat. "That smells fabulous, ducks. Which one made it?" His tail twitched from side to side, rather like a cat approving of the sensory information about him.

"I did. Place all ready for you."

He helped himself and when he sat, he took a deep draught of the tea before anything else and leaned back in his chair. "Ah, that's a good one for a cold night. Might add a bit of brandy to it . . ."

"No brandy." My mother gave the dapper lesser demon in his suit, tail and all, a look that stopped any protests. "If it's too cold out there in the garage, Simon, you might want to consider sleeping in here. Or perhaps in the basement."

"Basement? No." He shuddered. "Too warded for the likes of me. Although I might consider bunking around here somewhere—" He looked about. "Might be some room in the mudroom?"

"But that's where the dog crate is . . ." And we all turned at once to look at Scout who perked one ear up innocently.

"Aye, but that begs the question, doesn't it? Does the pup ever sleep in it?" And Steptoe twisted about and stared at me as if he knew perfectly well the answer to that question. He probably did because the tell-tales undoubtedly told him all that happened that they could sense in the upper hallway, including visitors in and out of my bedroom. That would be me and my dog and occasionally my mother.

"You know he doesn't," Mom said patiently. "Why don't we store that in the garage and . . . well, what would make you happy?"

"A little cot of my own. I've got a nice down comforter, I have, to put on it."

"No pillow?"

He winked at me. "Wouldn't mind a little pillow. Nothing fancy."

"I'm sure I have extras in the upstairs closet. Move yourself in soon as you're finished with supper." Mother picked up her spoon again. "Now eat before it goes cold."

So he did. Where his tail went, I never quite saw. Unlike a cat, he didn't sit with it curled about him. I had the feeling it came and went as it pleased. He hadn't had it for centuries, and now that he'd recovered it, it seemed to have gained a certain independence from its owner. We ate until the chili pot was scraped clean, much to Scout's disappointment, and all but the last half of cornbread wedges which Steptoe crumbled into his bowl, on top of the last spoonful of chili. Then he put it down on the floor for Scout.

"What?" he said defensively as Mother frowned. "I'm dispossessing him of his crate and mudroom. I think he deserves a sop for that, doesn't he?"

"No more than that. I don't want to deal with a dog and chili gas all night."

Steptoe roared a laugh at that and cleared the table for us, rolling up his suit coat sleeves so he could wash the pot.

"Who would think a demon would have such good manners?"

He tossed us a look over his elbow. "Maybe it's because I grew up in Britain where they are generally a polite group, except for that lot in Parliament. Come t' think of it, Canadians are polite, too."

He got a smile from my mother as she left the room, and I tossed a silent thank you at him for that. "No worries."

"Sure you'll be warm enough in the mudroom?"

"More than. Might even send a bit of heat throughout the entire house. That's how I got 'ere, you know."

"Oh?"

"Bit of a cold, cold winter even for Scotland that year." He scratched his eyebrow, cockney accent fading a bit as he talked.

"A handful of hedge witches got together and decided to conjure up a fire imp, to keep the home fires burning a bit easier. They managed to open a tiny hole—and who popped through but me. I'll admit my mistress on the other side at the time gave me a boot in the arse to push me through, but they were taken aback and didn't keep ahold of me like they intended. Thus I was free to work my mischief in the world. I wandered down to old London soon enough and, as the years went by, shipped to the new world. Eventually," and he stopped to rub the side of his nose. "Eventually, Brandard and I ran afoul of each other and he bested me. Took my tail and bound me to this great city and that blessed church. Enough years of that and I decided, takin' a look about me, that I needed to be changing sides. So I have, and 'ere I am."

I blinked. Decades of history all swiped right, as it were, and my fingers itched a little. To have some idea of what he'd seen, what he might have meddled in, settled about me . . . but it was not something to be done now. When, and if, Steptoe wanted to talk, he would, and hopefully I would be able to listen. Yet he'd never given any sign at all that he knew anything about my father. Ran in different circles, I suppose. I wanted to get upstairs alone to look through Morty's precious journal.

He dried the pot and set it in the cabinet under the stove top. "Your mom is a bit down in the mouth."

"College politics."

"Politics is everywhere. If Brandard were 'ere, would it help?"

"Might. He's about somewhere."

I hadn't mentioned the professor, but Simon thought the same as I did, evidently. It would be nice to have the old guy as an ally.

Since our missing phoenix wizard had bound Simon to the earthly plane by taking his tail from him and performing some ritual or other, more or less nailing Simon in place, that observance from the lesser demon was about as reliable as we were going to get, unless the professor decided to phone home.

"You're sure."

"Positive. My bond would be gone if he were lost to th' world."

"But you can't tell me where," I sighed.

Simon shrugged a shoulder and rolled down his sleeves. "I try what I can, ducks."

"I know." I pushed away from the table, made a hand sign to Scout to head back outside, and as we went out the door, I found a lone figure sitting on the steps. My heart beat a little faster as I recognized his silhouette in the evening light.

CHAPTER SIX

OATHS, BIG AND SMALL

I THINK I would have recognized Carter anywhere, even in absolute darkness. Scout bounded ahead of me after snuffling him a welcome. I sat down on the stoop next to him, and he turned to look thoughtfully at me.

"I smell old forest on you."

I lifted my arm and sniffed my sleeve. "I would have thought onion and garlic and chili powder, but okay."

Carter raised an eyebrow. His looks wouldn't knock the socks off a girl, being on the plain and trustworthy side, except for the scar/dimple in his chin. I could see beyond the surface, though. He was the whole package: strong, funny, heroic, thoughtful. And tall. "Hiram take you in to the family estate?"

"He did. Goldie retrieved her things and a journal for me."

His mouth tightened a little. "I would have gone with you."

"No need. Wasn't a real friendly welcome but not awful either, and Goldie got what she wanted, and then she dropped the traitor bomb in their midst." I paused before adding, "Although I would have loved it if you'd come."

He made a sound of disbelief. "She made accusations?"

I crossed my chest. "Believe me. And Hiram isn't happy about it, either."

"Don't blame him. Harpies like to stir up trouble."

"Well, she did."

After a long moment, as if he wanted to weigh his words, he said, "I could skim the journal for you."

"Nope," I told him. "I can hardly wait."

"You might get a little dismayed by what you read." He put his hand on my arm, warmth bleeding through the shirt and into my skin, comforting and strong. He took my hand in his and traced my outline, fingers and all, with a gentle touch. Each slight caress sent a thrill through me.

"I know. Gotta do it anyway." I leaned into him. "I missed you."

"Work." He cleared his throat. "I've been assigned to something dangerous. For you, not me."

Those words chased away the comfort and his stroking ceased. "Are they moving you?"

"No, but I might have to transit up and down the coast a bit."

"Ordinary or magical research?"

He gave a short laugh. "I can't tell you that. But I need you to be a little circumspect. Cautious."

I felt as protective toward Carter as I could feel he did toward me. I answered, "The more I know, the less I'll have to go find out."

Tension instantly coursed through his body. "You can't do that. I need to know you're safe, and the way you'll be safest is not to know anything about what I'm doing. This is deadly business, Tessa, and I can't share what I know with you. I don't want to, but it's what is best. It's the only way I can keep you secure."

"Sounds like Mafia or a drug cartel."

"Not much different, and that's all you need to know. I'll be around except when I can't."

I turned to look at him closely, lines deep about his mouth, that offset little cleft that was really a small scar of some kind, his plain yet handsome to me features, the sheer determination that sculpted his face, and the inner heat that always managed to shine through. Goldie called him a sun lion. The professor had called upon his ability to project the massive heat of a solar flare to bust open an elven gate and send our enemy through it. Yet he was human. I knew that through every nerve and bone in my body and felt it keenly as he leaned in and kissed me. Tender and yet demanding that I return it, so I did, closing my eyes and falling into the sensation. He moved his hands up to cup my face, and I encircled my arms about his waist although I couldn't reach all the way around him. We finished one kiss and began another, a yearning one, open and deep that made my body pulse and my blood rise until finally we both pulled away reluctantly. He brushed my hair from my eyes.

Then he gently put his fingertips on my chest, on the breast-bone, and I could feel a warmth flood me, a heat that went somewhere secret and stayed.

"What—"

"A bit of love. So you will always know it, and that it comes from me."

I put my hand over his for a brief moment, and then he pulled away.

"I don't like not being able to talk freely with you," he told me.

"But I'll see you. And you'll send word if you need me?"

"I don't know yet if that will be possible."

I couldn't believe what I was hearing. "No?"

"I have to be careful."

It hurt him to say that, I could see it in his eyes, barely view-able where we sat on the back stoop, with the moon half-hidden by clouds and the porch light off, but I could still see it. I had had plans, a lot of them, and it ached that I wouldn't be able to carry through with them, at least for now. "It won't—it won't be long, will it?"

"Might be."

"How long? Six months? A year?"

"Not a year. Beyond that, I can't tell. It's a job that needs to be done, and I am uniquely qualified to do it."

So it was magic, my question answered sideways, at least a magical edge needed that only he could provide. That brought all sorts of possibilities bubbling up. "Is it the Society—" but he stopped my question with his index finger across my lips. "No, and no more questions."

I managed to say "But" and that was about all before he took me in an enormous hug and just held me close, until our heartbeats matched and my breathing became slow and easy, and even then he didn't let me go. The heat he'd given me glowed as well, and I savored it. Not until Scout finally came trotting up and shook cold evening dew all over us, effectively a cold shower, and reminded me that there was supposed to be frost in the morning.

That passage of time he'd given me meant I might be soaking in summer heat and humidity before he could hold me like this again. I burrowed my head against his shoulder; he tightened his grip on me, and we both knew he didn't really want to let go. I knew then, deep down, what I needed to know: I hadn't driven him away as I had my father. He didn't want to go. Duty demanded he be blocked from me and had dragged him off.

I didn't tell him what Goldie had said to me because I couldn't bear to see him torn between duty and me. It wasn't something I could ask of him, not now, and I didn't want to add to his worry.

To break my silence, I muttered into his body that the Society had ordered me in for an appearance. His answer, when it came, tickled my ear as his breath grazed me.

"You'll do fine. Just don't go in spoiling for a fight."

"I wouldn't!"

"Of course you would. I know you. But don't. Try and stay open to what they might have to say and ask of you. They're going to be curious about the stone, but you know that already. Don't tell them you're a sorceress. Let them figure that out. You might have other abilities we haven't thought of, and they're a good way to find out the depth of your power."

"So I can't set their asses on fire if I get angry?"

"Wouldn't advise it." He muffled a chortle against the side of my head. "Look, the professor has spent months trying to turn you away from the Society but he wasn't always right on everything. You know that."

"He did have his faults."

"Keep an open mind. But not so open they can crack you like an egg."

I pulled back with a "Hey!"

Carter started laughing. "Just checking to see if you're listening."

I thumped him lightly. "I will always listen to you!"

"I know." His eyes glistened a little. "I'll be around before you know it."

I told him, "I take that as a solemn promise. And if you're not, I'm coming to get you."

He put his hand up. "Pinky swear?"

And so we did.

I admit it took some nerve for me to open Morty's journal when I retired to bed. I wanted to chase away my worry for Carter, but as I sank into the first few pages, I realized that reading the inside and detailed workings of a culture I'd no idea existed most of my life wasn't the way to do it. I paged ahead, my mind filled with secrets and pacts and cautions . . . what a precipitous life the Iron Dwarves and their other clans lived. One slip off a tightrope of existence and their whole world would fall, crashing. The modern world would rush to crush them, no matter what good intentions existed, and common sense told me the intentions would more likely be those of greed. I counted myself lucky any of them would bend enough to call me friend. Me, a disaster without any help at all. They trusted me. I'd never promised any of them I'd keep silent although the necessity to do so seemed obvious. Now.

So how was it he had faith in me? Did I keep it? Morty had failed himself and all of us in our intrepid little troop, but he had redeemed himself. Who would tell me to find redemption if I slipped? Would the others even be able to let me know what I'd done?

I closed his journal on my finger, keeping a placeholder. "Morty, wherever you are, and I refuse to believe such a strong and true soul went nowhere, had just simply ceased, and so— wherever you are, I promise to do my best to keep your secrets." My words fell on air that reacted in no way whatsoever, as if nothing listened to me. What had I expected? That his profoundly bass voice would rumble in my ear, verifying my vow? Yeah, seriously, a little. I had hoped for some response.

And getting none, I fervently hoped that I hadn't already broken that vow.

Reopening the journal, I read a little more, than I came across a name I knew: Potion Polly.

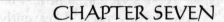

CHAPTER SEVEN

NAMES AND OTHER PORTENTS

I SAT UP straight in my bed, for I had been slouching lower and lower, about to drift off.

That had been . . . what had Aunt April told me a few months ago? . . . her grandmother? Great grandmother? Someone in the Andrews family line, with magic in her. She'd made homeo-pathic medicines, folk medicines, back in the day when every-one took them, and her cures had been true and helpful. She'd had a reputation for being a nurse one could rely upon, in that century of chancy medicine of the late 1800s. I dove into the page a little more intensely and found that Aunt April's recol-lections were absolutely correct. Even the Iron Dwarves came to buy Polly's elixirs. Morty's clan had marked her as someone to value . . . and to keep an eye upon.

Humans with magic, it seemed, could occasionally pierce the veil the others had drawn about themselves for safety. They had to be watched with caution.

I stopped reading again, wondering when the Dark Arts book came into the Andrews family line, and from where? That book had taken its toll from the family, taken far more than it had ever given, although Aunt April and my father both had treated it like a lucky talisman. I'd seen the family tree, though. Early deaths, some of them horrible. A life for luck. If they'd known, would they have thought it worth it? Although Morty had penned this diary, he hadn't lived through all of it. He'd taken it upon himself to relate his clan's history, from memory that could be verified. I'd read one tall tale so far, but he'd marked it as such, and I hadn't put much stock into it, something about unicorns and Europe, and although I wouldn't mind meeting one, I doubted they'd ever truly existed. I hadn't forgotten being laughed at by the dwarves when I'd mentioned one.

Vampires, now—Morty had warned they did exist. Those words sent a chill down my spine. Rare but powerful and intensely dark, he said. I closed the journal on that, not wanting any more nightmares than I usually had, although mine were normally filled with a three-tailed Kitsune who carried a katana and aimed for my neck. Restless, I got up.

I stood at my bedroom window, looking down at the moonlight-dappled backyard. Something tickled at the hairs at the back of my neck. I wanted to look out on the street. Well, I didn't want to, but a nagging feeling came over me that I had to. So I padded barefoot into the hall, checked on my vase of telltales and discovered that they all faced the back of the niche, as though something on the other side of the wall drew their attention streetside. Their little rose petal faces didn't seem terribly alarmed but definitely alert.

I went into the professor's room again, never changed or altered, with only the bed made, just in case he made his way back from wherever the blast of power and phoenix fire had carried him. We knew he lived. That was about all, except that Steptoe felt certain he'd find out more to the story. I ran my hand down the cane, wondering if he'd feel the touch wherever he was. "Come home," I whispered. "We miss you."

At the window, I couldn't discern anything except that the shadows once again jumped and stabbed in riotous discord. Something watched us. Probably not all night, but I'd caught it twice now. I backed away carefully.

I'd tell Simon in the morning. And Goldie.

I decided not to worry Carter.

I wanted the professor then, more than anything. He'd lived a number of lives, accumulating knowledge as well as ability, and he'd know what to do and what not to do. He would hand out sketchy information here and there, in his grumpy old way as usual, but I'd always known I could count on him.

I couldn't now, wherever he was.

I thought of the Society then, and if they'd have answers. Maybe, but I'd have to be extremely careful with my questions. It might be one of them who watched because I knew firsthand that not all of the Societas Obscura were as good or even neutral as they professed to be. I'd faced a judge from the Society who had been neither honest nor honorable. Part of magic's terrible price, I presumed.

I wanted to look at the street again, just to confirm I'd really seen a shadow move, or perhaps it had gone on, done with its surveillance, but I couldn't get up the nerve to do it.

The tell-tales ruffled at me as I crossed the hallway again while they settled back into their neutral bouquet. I sincerely hoped that meant that whatever stood sentry had left. To quote both Shakespeare and Ray Bradbury, "something wicked this way comes." Gone or not, I wouldn't forget it.

When I got back to bed, Scout was curled up in the middle of it and didn't want to shove over to let me in. We tussled a bit and my hands lost a chill I hadn't realized I'd picked up, and when we finally went to sleep, all I could hear was big puppy snoring.

When I woke, I realized I'd had a good, sound sleep without even one magical battle in my dreams. In fact, I couldn't remember any dreams at all, rare for me. I always had dreams, scattered and nonsensical as such things could be, but I dreamed in color, flew sometimes, and could even read a book in them. Scout tugged the cuff of my jeans, urging me to take him downstairs and out, and I realized we'd slept in late.

As I stood on the back stoop and watched him take his patrol, I rubbed a small crust of sleep from the corner of my eye. Warily, I looked at it before flicking it away. Had I slept too solidly last night? And if I had, what had I missed?

Scout galloped up and snorted at me.

"Yeah, I know, this whole thing is making me a little paranoid."

He wound around me and whined a little.

"Hungry?"

He darted to the kitchen side door and danced eagerly,

waiting for me to open it. I did, looking down at his wriggling golden body. The mudroom door was at the back, off the yard, and I entertained the idea, for a moment, of letting the dog in there, to dance all over Steptoe's sleeping form. From the slant of the sun, however, I doubted Simon would still be there.

Scout bounded in ahead of me and pushed his stainless-steel bowl across the floor so I could reach it easier and fill it. He liked being helpful like that.

I did my part and leaned against the counter as he dug in. He'd grown, his Labrador retriever form staying slimmer than most, confirming what Carter had first told me when bringing him to my door. He had other blood in him. I didn't think it was elven hound, but it might be. I'd found stranger things in the world than that recently. If it was, it only contributed to his personality, not detracted. I waited until the crunch level had dropped in decibels before saying, "So . . . hear or sniff anything unusual last night?"

He licked his bowl three times to ensure no crumb remained before sitting down and eying me.

"Nothing?"

He seemed secure in his assessment.

"Not in the backyard, anyway, huh?"

Scout sneezed. I took that as a "no way."

"I saw something out front again. Want to go inspect?"

He shook his head, rattling his collar, which I decided meant an affirmative. What dog doesn't want to explore his neighborhood? Every pup likes to check his pee mail.

I picked up his harness and lead, just in case, but Scout raced out the door before me, so I just carried them to make it look like I could be in control.

Down the driveway past the two cars, my little red Corolla and my mom's older, sedate sedan, we went. Scout raced, I jogged after. The sky looked leaden and the ground covered in hoarfrost which the sun had only begun to melt. Grasses had already gone brown, trees leafless except for the evergreens, and the wind bit at me. The earthy scents of autumn were long gone, and the whole area held the signs of being shut down and hunched over for winter. I should have grabbed my hoodie, too, even for a few minutes out. It looked like it might snow in earnest later in the afternoon. My ears chilled.

We passed a telephone pole with a note rippling in the air, and I slowed to look at it. Someone a few blocks away seemed to be missing a long-haired cat, a family pet greatly loved. As I stood reading all the particulars, a man walked up, his shoulders hunched against the weather, reached up, and tore the poster down.

"Oh! You found her?"

He looked at me then, eyes red-rimmed, wrinkles in a face showing years of outdoor, hard labor, and he managed to answer, "What was left of her." He shambled off, shoulders still bowed, his grief like a cloud around him.

I yelled after, "So sorry!" but knew that wouldn't help much.

We took our exercise and when we got back home, I decided to try him out on the scent trail of whatever had been watching the house. Scout gave me a wary, brown-eyed look but ambled in the general direction.

He coursed back and forth across the front yard, but when I directed him toward the lamppost, Scout's gait faltered. He slowed to a reluctant walk and looked up at me, several times, brown eyes under a furrowed dog brow. Finally, he just sat, a good ten feet away. I snapped on his harness and leash and pulled on it. He didn't budge.

"That's it?"

Scout put a paw up.

"I don't want to shake hands. I want to know if you smell something weird around here."

He tilted his head at me and, before putting the paw down, rubbed his nose with it.

"Here," I told him and went to the lamppost myself, looking up at the light bulb and then winding around the pole. Scout came to me, head down and tail between his legs, either ashamed or afraid.

He shivered when I put my hand down to rub him. I could feel the vibes coming off him. Something had spooked my bouncy, happy-go-lucky dog.

"Nothing good or just too wintry for you?"

He cast his gaze up at me and rolled his lips back off his teeth in a half-hearted snarl. Not meant for me, I felt sure, but for whatever he smelled lingering in the daylight.

And I was certain because I felt it, too, smelled it a little but couldn't quite identify it. Something dank and dark and maybe with death in its aroma. Something unsavory and unnatural. Something wicked.

I chirped at him, and he sprang away from the dreaded lamppost, galloping toward the house, towing me along behind him as if determined to rescue me. He didn't stop until we hit the porch and he leaned against the closed door, waiting for me to open it. Thresholds, I remembered, held a magical portent, a ward even the unmagical could, and did, unknowingly utilize.

The Society might want to see me that night, but I had a feeling I needed to see them as well, for a little well-orchestrated snooping if nothing else. If I scratched their back, they sure as hell better scratch mine.

CHAPTER EIGHT

CELEBRATIONS AND OTHER FUN OCCURRENCES

I DIDN'T EVEN realize that my mother left later and returned. My nose was stuck off and on in the journal between loads while I caught up with the laundry. I became aware as she entered with paper bags full of great smelling containers from the best Chinese takeout in our end of town and began to decorate the kitchen table. I came out of the laundry room; my jaw dropped, and Scout began hopping around in celebration. He sneezed once or twice as the garlic and ginger and savory goodness overwhelmed his senses.

"Wow. What's the occasion?"

"My dissertation is finished, whether they like it or not." And my mother dropped a binder on the table next to the aromatic bags. She'd written her title in permanent marker on it: Magic Through a Broken Mirror: How Magic Avoids Discovery in Literature and Fact by Mary Andrews.

"I thought you'd said three months."

"I did. But over half of them have submitted suggestions for reworking and I've done that, and I'm tired of the rest of the committee sitting on their hands. They can agree with the revisions that have been done or give me input of their own, but they need to do *something*."

I knew it, had seen it many times before, but seeing it in bold and capital letters made it seem more real as my mother rustled around getting plates and utensils. Looking at it hit me in the gut. What would Morty have thought of this? All those decades—no, make that centuries—in his journal of avoiding such a close look at his clan's existence. An uneasy knot settled in my stomach. Had we betrayed him somehow? Would this break my vow to keep their secrets?

Yet I knew what she'd written, mostly, having helped her proof it for months. If she'd betrayed him and the others at all, I hadn't seen it. No, her observation had been more geared to classical writings and poetry, music and the like, and the link they might have had to what might actually have happened. Her paper had been precise and thought-provoking, but she hadn't given away any secrets. At least, not in what I'd read. That last chapter could be a real doozy. Conclusions have a reputation for that.

"What happens now?"

"I've given them five days to respond. It's up to the secretaries now, I think, to schedule a pub date. Then I have to sign up for graduation, the official doctorate ceremony."

"Wow."

Mom dodged me to set down serving spoons and forks and pull a chair out for me to sit. "I know it's a surprise, but I didn't expect you to freeze in shock."

"What? Oh, no, I just stopped to think and forgot to get started again. It's been forever."

"I know. At this point, I think we're all tired of it. I know I am, but it's finished. I've had it proofread and waved that last chapter under their noses. They have to accept it for print, I think. I've done everything they've asked of me."

I took my seat and pulled a box toward me. "Dumplings! You got dumplings!"

"I certainly did, and steamed buns, too. The whole megillah." She paused before sitting down herself. "I decided that, considering my own objectives, that I was done, and I would submit it as such."

"But there might be more rewrites."

"Sometimes a bit here and there. I expect an edit or two in the appendices, but those will be easy to do. The committee has to look like they're doing some real work. But this stalling they've been doing, dragging their heels on one end while my department head on the other is saying, publish or quit or be fired—I won't tolerate it anymore."

I filled my plate with a respectable number of dumplings, their sauce running in a thin brown and savory puddle as I did. "Congratulations! We should have champagne. Or Chablis. Or something."

"Thank you!" She waved off the suggestion for wine though as she shook out a napkin and passed me one of those little packets of soy sauce. She paused. "Where's Simon?"

"No idea. Not like him to miss a feast, though. I think the tell-tales upstairs alert him to freshly cooked food as well as problems."

"That would explain a lot."

We didn't say much for the next few minutes, turning out house special fried rice, chow mein, chow fun with shrimp, and Mongolian beef onto our plates. Heavenly smells filled our kitchen to the rafters. We dug in, paying little attention to the third place setting which remained empty. Scout put his paw on my leg and got a few noodles for the polite effort. I don't think he'd ever had Chinese takeout food before which explained his restraint in begging.

I sat back, getting full and pondering whether I wanted seconds on shrimp or beef or both, then decided to ask: "Going to take that binder down and show it to Dad?"

She paused, fork in midair, noodles dangling and dripping sauce into her rice. "I hadn't thought of it."

"He may not react, but he's always been aware. I mean, you were starting your thesis before he left, right?"

"Not this one but yes." My mother chewed thoughtfully for a moment. "Maybe I will." She tilted her head. "Visit him often?"

"A couple times a week. I don't know if he has any real sense of the passage of time, though. He can't indicate that to me." I hesitated a moment wondering if I should tell her my worry. "I think he's fading more and more."

"He's running out of time?"

"Maybe. Maybe energy, maybe more." I stopped short and just shrugged. "I don't know."

"Going to ask the Society?"

"They don't know we have a ghost, and the professor and I never discussed if we should tell them about Dad. Brandard was mostly concerned about the stone."

"Mmmm." She considered the dumpling carton and then speared another for herself, commenting, "Steptoe better hurry, or he's going to miss out entirely." Halfway through nibbling it, she said, "Where does Simon get his energy?"

"I've no idea. He's not a ghost, though. He's a lesser demon."

"Still, he's, what, centuries old? He's got to have a life force of some kind."

"You're thinking he might have an idea how to recharge Dad?"

"It might be possible. And since you're going tonight, they're going to see or sense that stone anyway. Maybe it can charge your father up."

I looked at the handsome piece of marble. It took power from me, although usually not a lot. It might be worth pondering her suggestion, but it would have to be done cautiously because I had no idea how to send him energy without draining myself dangerously. I might be able to find out from the Society if I asked questions carefully, without revealing too much. The last thing I wanted was for a team of ghostbusters galloping into the house and going after my father.

Anything I might have said was interrupted by Steptoe as he burst into the room carrying the chill of the late afternoon weather with him. His nose matched his apple-red cheeks as he chafed his hands. "Oy, it's a brisk one out there."

"That it is. Sit down and have supper."

"Don't mind if I do!" He grinned cheerfully and reached for cartons before he even properly finished settling. "I had some chores to undertake, but it looks like we're going to get a good snowfall tonight. Late tonight, but sometime." He doled out his share of food. "What a feast. Good news, I take it?"

"I finished my paper and have submitted it for final review."

"Despite their puttering around? Good show, Mary." He ate with relish. "And a good idea, this."

"Steptoe," I began. "Do you ever run out of energy?"

"I sleep like you lot. And eat. That what you mean?"

"Not exactly."

He waved a near empty carton in one hand and his fork in the other. "Ah. You're wondering if I have to return to the demonic essence sometimes. Indulge in blood sacrifices and brimstone and fire and such." He winked at me, as if enjoying his teasing remark. "Well, the answer is no."

"Seriously?"

"Very seriously. Do you think old Brandard would have left me standin' if I'd been about any of that? 'Course not. The professor would 'ave blasted me away. Almost did anyway." He brandished his fork.

"I wasn't thinking brimstone."

My mother raised an eyebrow at me.

"Well, I wasn't. Sort of like a demon's version of solar energy."

"Ha." Steptoe snorted. "It's like this. The earth is gridded with ley lines, elemental energy, and I tap into those. If I went back to my origins, I'd be swallowed up and this whole bit of redemption and goodwill and friendship would be for nothing. And I don't want that, ducks, not at all. Put too much time and effort into it, and I'd miss all of you far too much." He dug the last of the fried rice out of the bottom corner of its container. "That answer your question?"

"For you, but—"

Mom cautioned me. "Don't ask questions we really don't want answers to, Tessa."

"Superstitious?" I shot back at her.

"Sometimes a little caution brings big dividends."

"Not on the hockey field."

My mother shot me a glance. "Life is not a hockey field."

"And curiosity and the cat is a good lesson," Simon added before devouring the last dumpling.

My mother took my plate away. "Done?"

Done but not defeated. "Definitely," I answered and pushed away from the table. "And I've got studying to do before tonight."

He looked puzzled a second before brightening. "Ah, I'd forgotten. Goldie got some information for you."

"Yup." I waved and tromped upstairs, but I'd lost my faithful shadow who figured another noodle or two might come his way from those still sitting at the table. Seems he decided he liked Chinese food.

Upstairs, I sprawled across my bed and opened the journal again. Next thing I knew, Scout had curled up with me and I was fast asleep.

I don't even remember dreaming. It didn't feel like it. It had that clarity of real life except I didn't know where I was. I walked through a thinning crowd of people I did not know or recognize or even care about, which made me feel awful. It seemed like a number of them were in distress, but I hadn't time for them. I had another destination.

A shadow fell over me, and I turned to see who it might be.

And there he stood: Malender, with his intense expression and smoking hot attitude. His dark hair curled back from framing his face as his brilliant green eyes trained his attention on me, his tall form dressed as always like a troubadour. Of all the centuries he'd lived through, he must have loved that one best. He held a whip handle. The lash draped down to his ankles where shadows hugged him, coiled about his legs as if alive. I peered closer. Razor-sharp thorns studded the lash, and as I looked, flames erupted up and down the length. But they didn't entrap him. He raised his hand and snapped the whip into the air, thorns flashing and fire erupting. Holy moly.

"Maybe," he said to me, "it would have been better if you hadn't freed me from my prison." The whip relaxed back to coil about him, almost seductively.

Maybe he was right.

Sometime around then came the realization that those people I had passed by, those throngs of strangers, had all had their backs flayed open in ragged, crimson stripes. I could hear their moans faintly, even though they had staggered out of my reach, out of his reach. Had he done that to them? I couldn't believe so because of the aura of wrongness that hung in the Butchery where I'd once seen similar torture. I'd never sensed that about this being, this man that I knew. Danger . . . yes, but not wanton evil. I wanted to trust him but couldn't quite. I didn't know what he really was, even. Perhaps one of the old gods who'd survived the turns of the world.

I stared at Malender. The most beautiful being I'd ever seen. And possibly the most wicked.

I jerked awake. My heart beat wildly and my throat had gone dry. It took me a few breaths to become truly aware of myself in my bed and bedroom. What meaning had that dream had? Or was it even a dream? Malender had power, a terrible power. Most of my magical friends feared him; I'd always wondered why. That whip was new. I'd never seen him carrying it before, but I had no doubt that he knew how to use it.

I grabbed my laptop to try and identify what I had just seen. It took a bit of poking about, but not long. Everything, it seems, is on the Internet . . . even medieval scourges because that is what it was. A whip to end all whips in pain and punishment, for the purpose of justice and cleansing. Biblical even.

I wouldn't have believed I could dream up such a thing, so it helped a little to just sit and stare at it. Well, minus the flames. My imagination must have added that little detail.

Go me.

I couldn't have imagined seeing Malender with one, though, tormented magical being that he was. I had never thought of him as the rising evil that everyone had feared returning to life, to kick ass and take names. Powerful: yes, evil: no.

The dream gave me second thoughts.

He knew how to handle that whip.

For the briefest of moments, I wondered if it could have been Malender standing at the lamppost, watching us from the dead of night. It left me chilled.

I got up and headed to the shower as if that might somehow wash the dream and thoughts out of my head. Then I had to find out how to fritter away the rest of the day.

CHAPTER NINE

INVITED AND UNINVITED

I DECIDED TO dress down for the Societas Obscura: jeans, black-and-silver shirt, black jean jacket, running shoes. I considered wearing my leg guards from field hockey but decided that might be a little distrustful and left my favorite hockey stick behind as well. The maelstrom stone goes everywhere with me, so that was a nonissue.

I stood at my windowsill where my dwarven bracers had been gathering daylight and storing it in the golden gems studding them. I finally put them on, but under my blousy shirt sleeves. They gave a little hint I wore something about my wrists but weren't entirely revealing what as I grabbed my jacket and trekked downstairs. Scout trotted down beside me, missing the last step, and should have sprawled at the bottom but twisted in midair and managed to land on all fours. He shook his head vigorously as I snorted at him.

"Grace."

He gave me a look before leaving my side and heading into the kitchen without me.

My mother and Steptoe sat at the table, having an evening snack, sipping hot tea and enjoying fresh muffins. I hadn't smelled them baking which told me how preoccupied I'd been with armoring myself for the meeting. No wonder Scout had missed a step in his hurry to get to the smells. It's a wonder he hadn't busted through my bedroom door to get downstairs.

"Smells good."

"Cherry wonders," Steptoe managed before reaching for another muffin. My mother shot him a look, a warning I recognized but didn't think he would. It was the "you better slow down and leave some food for the others" stare.

I sat down and helped myself. Still warm. I watched as melted butter trickled through his fingers as he picked it apart delicately and gobbled each fourth down. I ate slowly, savoring the tart/sweet cherry chunks. "Aunt April's cherries?"

"Of course. No one puts up fruit the way she does."

My great-aunt had the devil's own luck gambling, addicted to it but fighting her obsession successfully, yet I think her better talent was in preserving. Maybe that was because Potion Polly hailed not too far back in her line. Whatever it was, Aunt April had the talent to can and bake with the best, and Southern belles had a reputation for those abilities. I quickly snatched up a second muffin before Simon could clear the plate, and my mother shadowed the movement. That left a solitary pastry on the plate which he eyed sadly before looking up at my mom.

"Go ahead."

His hand moved so quickly I barely saw it, reminding me that despite his veneer, he was not and never would be human. I found myself shrinking back just a little. My mother's foot jabbed my ankle lightly, jolting me, and I managed a grin before slipping a corner down to Scout who'd decided he owed allegiance to me after all.

Steptoe arched an eyebrow at me. "Date night?"

"Society."

He winced. "I can 'ear the professor now."

"Me, too, but it wasn't one of those invites you can refuse. Besides, I need more teaching than you can give me."

"Ow. You wound me." He placed a hand on his suit jacket over where his heart should be, leaving a tiny buttery fingerprint. It disappeared even as I noted it in fascination. "Be that as it may, do you need an escort?"

"You weren't invited."

"Nonetheless." And he shrugged in his magical jacket which could render him invisible once removed and used as a cloak.

He ignored the expression on my mother's face as her lips tightened.

I traded a look with her. Did she want me to take along help or feel it might be courting more trouble? Not that I knew I was in trouble; it just seemed a foregone conclusion. She said nothing. "Mom?"

After a long pause, she shook her head. "That's not a decision I can make for you."

I shrugged. "Thanks for the offer, Simon, but no."

"Sure, ducks?"

"Pretty sure. Scout is staying home. It'll just be me, the stone, and my bracers." I smiled at him as I finished the last of my treat.

He twisted slightly in his chair, and I'm fairly certain Mom couldn't see the wink he gave me. "As you wish."

I stood up quickly, gathering teacups and saucers to load in the dishwasher before the expression on my face gave me away. I had three of his signature flash-bangs in my pocket so I probably wouldn't need his backup, but it might be kind of nice to have. All said, it was a heck of a thing to need assistance if I was going to be visiting friends. Still the idea appealed to me. If the professor were here, he'd probably insist on going with me. I missed the idea of Carter being available, no matter what. The thought made me sigh.

My mom turned around at the sink. "What is it?"

"Just thinking about Brian and the professor."

She put her hand on my shoulder. "I know."

I made a little face. "He'd probably just make trouble, anyway."

"Too right," Steptoe said. "He hated the Society."

"I never really understood why."

He dusted himself off after standing and pushing his chair back under the table. "That history is not one I'll be telling. He'd have my ears as well as my tail again if I did." He gave a half-bow. "I've got some things to take care of, and it'll be a late evening for me, Mary. Don't be alarmed when I come in."

"Oh, I won't. I have the intrepid Scout here protecting me."

The dog in question let out a woof. Steptoe disappeared out the back door. I checked my phone for the time.

"I'd better head out to the front porch. They said eight o'clock but might be early."

"I have a feeling everyone in that bunch is precise to the second."

"I know." I slipped my phone back in my pocket. "It figures."

Mom started the dishwasher cycle. "Anything on Dad yet?"

"Not yet, but there's a lot of history in that journal. I should probably skip ahead, but I'm afraid of missing a detail or two." I leaned a shoulder against the archway to the living room and foyer. "You know there's scattered magic all through Dad's line?"

"There's a weird kind of logic to that, knowing what we know now."

"Do you think he magicked you?"

"Into loving him?" My mother gave a slight laugh. "Oh, you should have seen him in college. He was a star on the golf team, with his talent and his slight southern drawl. Girls couldn't keep away from him. We Yankees find southern gentlemen irresistible. I saw something in him the others didn't, though, and it took him a while to realize that I wasn't interested in dazzle but substance."

"But he chose you."

"Eventually." She dried her hands on a dish towel and corrected me. "We chose each other."

"What happened to the pro golfing?"

"He tore a rotator cuff. Never was quite right after that even with surgery, and he gave it up, long before we were married. It shook him more than he wanted to admit. Most of the Andrews families were hard workers, calluses on their hands, uniform shirts on their backs, and dust in their eyes. He didn't want to work that hard, tired to the bone all the time, and thought he had a different life planned. That's why he jumped at the golf scholarship, even though it was so far from here, from home. It was the best offer he had—and mind you, he had several golfing offers, but he took the most profitable one. Then he lost it all. He settled for an office job after college, in insurance, but you and I know, now, that he'd become addicted to dazzle. He wasn't sure if I'd follow him back to Virginia. He liked to joke that it was the coast and pine trees that made up my mind."

That was the most she'd ever said about the private things between her and my father. Things parents don't usually discuss with their children—the uncertainty, the bumps in the road. Then, as she'd noted, we'd weathered a lot of those bumps together in these last few years. I put my hand out, took her in, and hugged her.

"Things are better now."

"They are, aren't they?" Her face brightened a little.

"I've got to leave." Letting go, I gave her a little hand wave and set off for the outdoors.

A slight but very frigid wind slapped me in the face as I closed the front door behind me. A voice said, "I'm here and ready to go."

"And cold, too, I bet." I hesitated and then said to invisible Steptoe, "I appreciate the backup and you're wonderful to offer, but I need you to stay home with Mom." I knew from the wink he'd given me that he would use his suit jacket as the invisibility cloak it could become, and follow me when I left. But I didn't want him to; I wanted him at home protecting my mother.

"Why?"

"There's something that's been watching us on the street. Goldie let me know. Scout didn't catch scent of it until I hauled him all the way out to where it had been standing, and the telltales don't seem very aware of it."

"That's not good."

"It might be a guardian Carter put on sentry because he's on assignment and worried about collateral damage. Or it might be something nasty," I added, remembering Scout's fearful reaction and my dream.

"Don't you worry, then. I'll be right here. But not outside, I think."

"That's fine." I heard very faint footsteps as he took his leave.

Scanning the neighborhood, I could smell smoke from two or three nearby chimneys, and lights on the block seemed steeped in that golden glow that deep night brought on. The wind touched its icy fingers to my cheeks and nose as I shrugged into my jacket's collar, thinking I should have brought my nice wool scarf with me. The sky had begun to cloud up, skirling in on that breeze as if it wanted to be an actual storm front as Simon had predicted, and I debated darting back inside long enough to fetch that scarf and some thicker gloves.

A white-blue beam cut across the end of the street as a car turned the corner and headed right to our address. My ride had shown up, and I was out of time for last-minute decisions.

The car stopped, and a back door swung open silently.

No one got out, but I knew the vehicle waited for me to step in.

It seemed a cold welcome but nothing to the one I anticipated receiving when I got delivered.

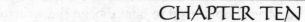

CHAPTER TEN

WHOOPS

SNOW STARTED AND stopped, more in icicle drizzles than drifting flakes, and it never held together long enough to hit ground. It just splattered the car windows in streaks before sliding away to oblivion. Each hit in long, spiky splats and then melting started. To my current train of thoughts, the weather looked more like spite than a natural phenomenon. The inside of the car felt terribly chilly as well, and I found myself huddled on the rear seat, trying to catch a glimpse of the driver's face in the rearview mirror, to no avail. To the Society's credit, this driver was neutral, quiet, and forbidding all wrapped up into one.

The leather seat warmed, but the air stayed cool enough that my breath showed its haze when I exhaled. The fact I had on my jacket seemed little help. I leaned forward. "Could you turn up the heat a little back here?"

All I could catch was a flicker of a look, nothing clear, as if the driver checked to see if he even had a passenger. But he/it didn't move to turn on the heat, so I guess arriving semi-frozen was on the agenda. Maybe they expected to warm me with their hospitality later, at least in contrast. I folded my arms across my chest and crossed my legs, imitating a snowball. The drive seemed to take forever. Hunched over as I was, I almost missed what direction the car moved in. But I didn't.

The hair stood up on the back of my neck as we approached the trendy area with the brick roads and the old buildings which had changed little in a few hundred years. Especially the bar/restaurant called the Butchery in honor of the killing and carving shop it used to be. I'd been there once, in a dream, and it had looked as deserted then as it looked now, when it should have been bustling with business. In my dream, it had been silent and deadly.

Only I thought I was awake this time.

I should be. I hadn't closed my eyes. Too cold to sleep unless I had just passed out or— I peeled my leather glove off my left hand as my stone warmed, and I clutched both hands together tightly.

Inside the Butchery on my previous visit, I had found bodies and souls hanging from meat hooks. Swinging desperately. Tortured. Most of them still alive and hurting. I hadn't found neon lights and high-backed stools, and a long serving bar wiped glossy by two or three busy bartenders. Clients drifting in and out. Clusters of loud laughter and soft, sincere talk. No. I'd discovered a nightmare of vast proportions with misery and more hanging there. I hadn't been able to free them, being lucky to escape with my own mortality.

I'd found a nightmare before. It seemed equally possible that I'd find one again. I had no intentions of letting the driver deliver me to this destination.

My left hand slid to the inside door handle. Locked. Naturally. But I have talents now, and it wouldn't stay that way if I could help it.

The car slowed to a bare glide, cutting through the night like a shadow, lamp lights dimming as we passed them. I could walk faster. I cupped my left hand and then twisted it, ever so slightly, and heard a faint click.

Before the driver could react, I flung the door open and tucked and rolled to the street, hitting the bricks hard but not hard enough to cause damage and got back on my feet.

Then I sprinted in the opposite direction, through alleyways and across darkened doorways, and heard the car racing after me, searching. Tires squealed. Sometimes near, sometimes a little farther off as I zigzagged past buildings that were all closed, shut tight, abandoned to the night as they never should have been. Winter or not, this was a booming district.

I ran until my side hurt and finally skidded to a stop inside a deep arched doorway, moving back until my spine went to the wall. Then I brought my hand up and began, despite my shaking, to weave a shield with Steptoe's wonderful invisible suit coat in mind. I didn't know if I could mimic it, but I had to try. Nothing to see. Nothing to detect here. Not a thread, not a breath, not even a footfall. I was underneath, behind, below, obscured to any vision no matter how sharp or magically acute or diabolically focused. Not even my inhalations could be seen or heard.

I felt something fall over me. Something tangible curtained me, hid me. Something I had made and held. I brought the palm of my hand close to my chest so that even the beat of my heart would be hidden. My body heat. My trembling soul. All undetectable.

It would work. I had infinite faith in Steptoe's coat. This, woven in copy, should work as well. He'd protected me amply on several occasions. Now I had to protect myself. From what, I had no idea. None. If this was the Society, I could now fully understand the professor's scorn for it.

Until the car screeched to a halt, a door opened and then crashed shut, and something stepped into the alleyway as if it could sift me out of the night, smell me, hear me. Incredibly loud, or perhaps I just stood, incredibly muffled.

My lips thinned as I concentrated on taking away whatever odor I might carry. Not myself. Not my mother's touch, or Steptoe, or Scout, not the fabric softener in my clean clothes or the faint sweat in my shoes. And especially not the smell of fear.

It scanned the alleyway. I saw, once, as its gaze spanned over me and moved away, blazing red eyes. My hand jerked against my chest in recognition. I still had no idea what the hunter was, but knew it had kept watch on my house.

A feeling rose in me, cresting over my icy fear. It warmed me as if I'd just swallowed a hot mocha coffee, spreading its tingling from my throat and stomach outward. I recognized it for the spark Carter had given me. It kept me from spiraling into an icy death and let me feel. Anger rose. I wanted to launch myself at the abductor, kick it down, and turn my shield into an edged weapon that would slice whatever it was to smithereens. I shoved that instinct down. Took the barest of quivery breaths to tame it. For all I knew, the thing that hunted me counted on drawing me out, either in a panic or in a raw, fighting mode, whatever it took to bring me out of hiding. I dared not even use my flash-bangs.

I retreated to patience, a deep well of it, thinking of the professor's teachings, once so enigmatic to me who preferred action to thought, but he'd pounded it into me anyway. I stilled. Stayed that way, deep as a bottomless lake, serene, reflecting nothing back at the hunter. Carter kept me floating without drowning in this beingless state. I would not be the prey who lost this night.

Footfalls. Sharp as if its shoes might have taps. Or did it even have shoes? Perhaps I heard the click-clicking of talons. It walked the alleyway. Up and back. Once, twice, thrice while I breathed so little that I thought I might pass out but told myself I wouldn't.

Then it growled.

No. Not a growl. A . . . hiss.

Well, not a hiss either. A noise I couldn't possibly imitate but knew I would identify immediately if I ever heard it again.

Then it turned on heel in its immaculate black suit and left the alleyway. I heard the car pull away in a squeal of rubber.

I did not move. I wanted to. My arm ached from holding my hand up motionless. I dared not relax.

I waited. Long, long moments. Until I decided that I might be wrong, I *must* be wrong. And I needed to breathe deeply.

I almost let go.

Then I heard the faint crunch of a step, grit between the brick pavers and a shoe sole getting ground down, and I caught the slight swish of fabric as it stepped back into the alleyway.

Whoever, whatever it was, had sent the car away and waited for me to emerge from whatever cubbyhole hid me. It walked the course one more time, head moving back and forth from building and doorway to doorway and building, its gaze searching. It put its hands out, long, thin, white fingers, and combed the air delicately as if it could pull clues out of nothingness and weave them together to find me.

I found nothing human about its stance, its hands, or its painstaking efforts. I didn't know what it was. It stood and walked as if human. Drove a car. Wore a nice suit. Had an overcoat on as if the winter cold might affect it slightly.

If it had hair, I couldn't tell. It wore a newsboy cap, and the forward brim hooded its face extremely well, except for the crimson glow of its eyes. All I knew about it, as I stood and prayed that it wouldn't detect me, was that it was nothing I wanted to meet.

Ever.

I wasn't sure if I could survive such a meeting.

It clucked to itself, tongue against teeth, and then made that grating hiss again, before pivoting and striding off.

Again, I stood stock still until I thought I'd fall over, and realized the stone was taking its energy from me. I wasn't sure if I could walk away. But nothing came to ferret me out again, and I finally dropped my hand and let myself exist once more.

Noise came in, surrounding me, whirling about, laughter and teasing and a masculine voice saying, "Hey, hey, hey!" and a feminine voice answering, "Hey yourself, and be on time next time!"

The streetlights overhead and about blared with their full illumination, and music drifted out and over and bounced off the walls, and I could hear cars passing back and forth, with an occasional horn blare of indignation. The world as it should be caught up with me. I managed a breathy "Carter, Carter, Carter," and waited. Nothing came to meet me. Disappointment arched through me, but I had outrun trouble for the moment. I told myself I could handle the rest of the evening. I let out a quivery breath and exited the alley, saw a convenience store, went in, and bought a small bottle of OJ and downed that as quickly as I could, without taking a breath. Then I bought a second. I tapped that hidden well of warmth and goodness inside me, thankful for Carter's gift.

Outside, I scared something at the corner. A striped tabby bolted behind a trash bin and then peered out, green eyes glowing. It looked thin.

I turned around and went back into the store which had "food" on its grill, little rollers turning it over and over and over. I pointed. "Chicken wings. Are they buffalo or teriyaki or what?"

"Plain old grilled," the bored teen said to me. "Last of the evening. I can give you a deal." He named a price for six and I bought them.

Outside I put five in a row next to the trash bin. I could hear a sound. I backed up and ate the final one. Opened my second container of orange juice and sipped it slowly, feeling a lot more human than I had moments before.

A paw reached out and snatched a wing. It disappeared.

The sight made me smile. As I walked away, a claw hooked two more wings and then a tiny gray kitten pounced on the remainders.

I walked under the lights, wishing that I'd bought a hot chocolate instead of an OJ, anything to warm me up from the inside out. I came across a bus stop, read the route sign and realized I could take it to head back home. Or at least close enough that I could be located and picked up without too much worry.

The bus chugged up a few minutes later and I got on. The moment I did, my phone lit up. Texts came in and at least two missed calls, as though the thing had died and suddenly come back to life. Perhaps it had. I thumbed through and then it rang.

"Miss Andrews. I am disappointed you have missed your summons." A stern yet educated voice I did not recognize.

"Actually," I said, "someone got to my house before you and I got in the wrong car. A very wrong car."

"Oh? Are you all right? Do you require assistance?"

"Yes, on both counts. I'm on the bus, but I can disembark at the City Hall."

"We will pick you up there."

So, legs shaking a bit, I got off in two stops and stood in the bright evening lights of the City Hall, which held night court two nights a week and this appeared to be one of them, the steps spilling over with people going in and out. I stood at the curb and eventually a sleek silver car pulled up. This time I knew better. Leaning over, I tapped on the window.

"ID."

"Societas Obscura," came a whispery response.

"You say the sexiest things." I slid in as the back door opened silently. I settled myself and clipped the seat belt in place, leaning forward to see if I might recognize who drove. I didn't, but then I only knew two or three of the Society although I figured I'd probably run across more without an introduction.

The car transited the town more smoothly than had the bus, and I spent the time examining my hands, the stone in particular. It seemed not to have changed at all despite the intense shielding it had just held for me. And it made me wonder . . . that thinning of the world . . . that veil across what I knew to be real, a curtain drawn across all my senses that so that I might be truly hidden from the menace that sought me. I felt as though I had fallen into a pocket between dimensions and that if I had not fought to get myself out, I would have stayed there.

Was that what possibly could have happened to my father? And if it had, it meant that—at one time or another—he'd possessed the maelstrom stone and had used it, or it had misused him. But if that were true, why hadn't it slipped into the in-between with him and stayed there? How had I found it lodged in a locked drawer in the old basement's armoire? If it had come forth, he should have as well. I had no answer and a ton more questions tumbling in my thoughts as the car pulled into a curved drive and came to a halt.

I opened the door and emerged into a chilled evening to face what could only have been at one time a tobacco drying shed. A huge one. If I inhaled deeply, I could still catch a faint scent of the leaves that had been hung here to cure. This barn looked big enough to house a manor and although there were ample vents at the eaves of the roof, the sides had been enclosed, something that would likely never have been done when it was still in use.

I looked away. "Nice clubhouse."

Double doors swung open silently. Feeling uneasy, I flexed my shoulders and walked in. Only to walk right back out abruptly.

"Oh, no," I declared as a couple of people followed me. "I am not going anywhere if he's going to be there."

And I pointed at Judge Maxwell Parker, a nemesis who would undoubtedly love to see me hung by my heels since I'd bested him in a magical battle. I was on a recon mission trying to locate Goldie, and I found her. He was the one without honor I'd been thinking of earlier. "I was told he was on probation. He abducted Goldie Germanigold."

"Hearsay," the man in question said, staring me down, jaw clenched and eyes intense. He wore an impeccable suit, Italian name brand of some sort or other, with a mauve shirt and matching handkerchief sticking artfully out of the pocket. Someone had styled his hair to look casually perfect, but it was his eyebrows that fascinated me. Trimmed into pointed wings, they angled sharply down to frown at me. "You haven't a word of proof or defense for your attack on me!"

"I found her bound at the Silverbranch campus, locked into a statue, and she told me you had done it. In my book, that's proof enough."

"Nevertheless, did you see me abduct her? No. There is only her word. And harpies are not the most dependable of truth tellers. Nor, it seems, are those who associate with them."

I was not about to back down, to the Society for having him here to oppose me or just to push back on his existence in general. "You attacked me when I attempted to free her. That is firsthand testimony."

"Perhaps I was just defending Germanigold in her vulnerable captivity from you. You were then—and still are—unknown in the magical community. Who is to say that you were not the menace?"

I swung about, addressing the watchers, perhaps a paltry group that reminded me more of a jury than a meeting, all more adult than I, and with expressions that told me little about their inner feelings. After the night I'd already had, I wasn't eager to face any judgmental types. My inner self reminded me about the professor's determination that he and I should never cross paths with the Society for reasons he never quite delineated to me. He'd held little but scorn for them in the time I'd known him. I began to realize why. I threw my words at them anyway. "Are you all just going to stand here and let the lies fly?"

A carefully calm and modulated adult spokeswoman answered me, "Goldie has been asked to appear and give her statement at her convenience. So far, it has not been convenient for her to do so." She stepped back as if she'd been at a recital and given her part, her white hair in waves about her face, back ramrod straight, and navy pantsuit absolutely without a wrinkle.

I began to walk back to the car that had delivered me. "I think she has the right idea about avoiding you-all . . ."

From all the someones I didn't know, a middle-aged man with a full head of curling hair under a caramel-brown fedora and shrewd eyes stepped forward to put his hand on my shoulder. I suddenly became so sensitive that I felt it through every fragment of my body and I halted. Magic jolted through me from my shoulder to my toes as if I'd been hit by lightning. The strength of it scared me and reminded me that I was playing with the big dogs tonight.

"Pay no mind. He is just leaving."

I half-turned to see if that was so. And, apparently, someone else had told him it would be prudent to go.

Parker pushed past me in the doorway. "The situation is temporary, Miss Andrews. It will behoove you to remember that. Whatever disfavor I might have earned, the truth will out."

"Back at you."

He made his way into the night to a car park I hadn't noticed earlier, it not being lit until he produced a fireball in the palm of his hand to see where he walked. As he found his car, he turned and tossed the fireball my way.

I ducked out of reflex even as the sorcery fizzled into nothingness far short of where I stood. Parker grinned before getting into his car.

I flung up a hand and let a bolt of my own energy go, a little surprised to find it responsive when I had had virtually nothing at my beck and call after the Butchery. It lanced into the ground in front of his car, making it buck a little before he could pull away in a squeal of tires. I think we understood our farewells. When next we met, it wouldn't be words we exchanged.

I knew I could pop tires on a car. I'd done it before—not intentionally but figured I could duplicate it. I raised my left hand, but before I could form a coherent thought of action, a hand closed about mine and brought it down.

"Don't do it," the owner said lightly from under the shadow of his fedora. "Even if he deserves it."

"No?"

"No."

"You don't even know what I had in mind—"

"I have," he said, smiling at me, "some idea." Tucking my arm under his, he wheeled me about and headed me back to the building. "It wouldn't make for a good introduction."

"I had earning some respect in mind."

"That," he assured me, "will come about naturally."

"I'm going to hold you to your word on that," I told him as he delivered me into the hall and dissolved back into the waiting crowd. I didn't like not being able to see his expression. I couldn't read the truth or honesty in anything he'd claimed.

He disappeared so quickly that it left me wondering who he was. Because of nighttime shadows and dim lighting about the car park, he'd been obscured. The thought bounced about my mind briefly that it could be Carter in disguise, but I dismissed that quickly. He didn't have the age and magical gravitas of the helpful stranger. Not that Carter didn't have powerful magic— he did, extremely powerful, but he let few people sense it. I doubt if even the Society knew how much force he carried. Also, I'd never seen Carter wearing a hat, other than the one or two military pictures I'd seen of him, and then it had been a scuffed and well-used helmet. And, mostly because I knew his touch. His walk. His hands.

The members dressed in business casual parted as I entered. I looked about, seeing few faces I recognized but almost being surprised by the ones that I did. There was a professor as well as a custodian from my community college. Another elegant woman I knew from my mother's University, a secretary. Department secretaries may seem to be low on the totem pole in administration, but my mother would swear that they had more power than many of the professors and even deans. As our eyes met, she raised pewter-colored eyebrows as if surprised herself. Faith Hawkins, I remembered her name. Her gaze narrowed as I came to a halt, and I could feel other stares at my back uneasily. I'd have to let my mother know, once I determined her stance on things. She could be friend, or she could be foe.

A tall, older man with streaks of silver accenting his dark hair came forward and bowed slightly. "I am glad you found your way here." He wore a formal suit with a morning coat and even gloves, but it didn't look out of place on him. For the most fleeting of seconds I wondered if he was a funeral director.

"I was waylaid, but I managed."

"Waylaid? I heard a rumor of that. Do explain." A few indistinct murmurs from around the watchers in the room underscored his words.

"Yes."

"How so?"

"I was expecting a car and driver, so when one showed up, I got in. I shouldn't have. And, word to the wise, don't ever go to the Butchery on a dark and dreary night."

"The Butchery? That bar in Old Town?"

"That would be the one. It has bad vibes."

That brought up a startled buzz which my welcomer squelched with an upraised palm. "How so?"

I considered giving him a full explanation, decided against it, and merely said, "It's haunted."

A wry smile crossed his expression. "We will keep that in mind." He drew me farther into the hall. "We have a few questions and a trial or two—"

"I just bet you do." Because of Parker and other extenuating circumstances, I decided not to confide much of anything in the Society. It would have to prove itself first.

"Yes. Well, this inner sanctum has been built to withstand just about anything that can be thrown at it."

The tobacco shed morphed into stone. We stopped inside a

massive cavern with masonry walls that might have been five feet thick, to look at the stonework, and probably would have taken a direct hit from an atomic bomb from the looks of it. Its walls had scorch marks and maybe even blood soaked into it, leaving behind a rusty cloud here and there although I didn't go searching for the stains. I let a "wow" escape, suitably impressed.

"Let me introduce myself."

"That would be nice." I dragged my attention away from the cavern and smiled up at the gentleman.

"Hmmm. Yes. You may call me Archer. And you are Tessa Andrews."

"In the flesh." I smiled a little. "Got a title?"

"Title?"

"Mage, sorcerer, grand wizard or whatever."

"All in good time, young lady."

"Oh. This is one of those interviews."

"Those interviews?"

I nodded. "If I don't pass, I get my memory wiped or some such. The less I know, the less you have to clean up."

His nostrils flared slightly with what I hoped was a suppressed laugh. "Something like that." Archer took a slight step away from me. The group that had followed us throughout the hall gathered, more or less, at the entrance. Out of range.

"We've been informed you're in possession of a maelstrom stone."

"That would be correct."

"We'd like to see it."

I stripped my gloves off and held up my hand accordingly even as I said, "I'm not removing it and passing it around."

"I should imagine not." He removed his own gloves and took my hand in his, his fingers strong yet gentle and quite warm. He did not touch the stone itself, although I could see from the gleam in his eyes, he wanted to. I marked him down on my list in my mental notes of People Who Coveted the Stone. "Impressive, and quite handsome, actually." Then he held my hand out so others could admire it. Rather like a reception line at a wedding or some other function, people passed by the two of us to get a look at it (and me). When they were finished, they retreated again. Archer asked, "Any thoughts?"

"Well, I—" and he held a finger up, shushing me. "Not you, Tessa. I was addressing the panel."

"Oh."

Archer turned to one side. "Newhart?"

"As rare as they are, a number have been cataloged, but I don't recall any mention of ones of this coloring and size." A squarish looking man with glasses hanging on a cord around his neck spoke up. He wore corduroy, top and bottom, olive green and rather boring. He looked as if he would occupy a massive desk, the two of them vying for size. "I don't suppose you would care to illuminate its properties?"

I wouldn't. It sounded too much like telling the enemy all my secrets and then hoping it would come out all right in the end. I did say, "It devours other magical relics."

I have never seen a squad in a room back up two or three steps in one movement. You would have thought it was a dance step and they were all participating. I thought that line dancing was now a bit passé. But they did it as if they'd been drilling the movement all week just for my entertainment.

Archer, to his credit, stuck to my side. Or maybe he just didn't have anything magical floating about his person that my stone could eat.

"Please elaborate."

I put my hand in the air again and hoped what I would tell them would manifest. "Two red slits . . . ah, there they are. Shards from the Eye of Nimora. They're like eyelids. When they open, I can see a great deal, beyond my normal sight."

My stone blinked at them sleepily a few times and then the red slits faded entirely. I couldn't blame the stone; I felt a little bored myself. But before the eyes closed, I had felt the energy of the talented watchers, along with curiosity and malice.

"However did you obtain a splinter off the Eye of Nimora?"

"It's a long story, but they became available. The Eye itself isn't harmed at all, mind you, but there were these tiny flecks and, well . . . my stone ate them."

"Did you command it to do so?"

"No."

Archer stirred slightly. "Did you know it was going to do so?"

"Not really. It had eaten a gold ring belonging to the professor, but . . ."

Another movement of the crowd, in a giant step backward. I looked toward them. "You guys are creeping me out."

"An excess of caution. Under the circumstances, I can hardly blame them." Archer stayed rock solid where he stood.

"You must be the only one with stones, then. The other kind."

Archer laughed. A full and hearty laugh that brought along with it a small tide of other laughs that were pale imitators. "When dealing with the unknown, it's wise to be a little cowardly."

"Right." I curled my hand up, hiding the stone away.

"By the professor, may I assume you meant Brandard?"

I nodded.

"Did you gain your powers when the stone embedded itself?"

I didn't feel like telling him about the Dark Arts book the stone had absorbed, so I didn't. "No, they came about later. I discover different facets every once in a while, mostly defensive at first and then offensive later."

"Care to elaborate or demonstrate?"

I really didn't, but it seemed that was why I had been brought here. I braced myself and said, "Come at me."

Archer inclined his head slightly, stepped back five paces, and proceeded to raise his hands. I had no idea what kind of attack he planned, but basic shielding seemed advisable, so I spun mine out and enlarged them so that I, for all intents, stood behind a wall.

Almost before I set myself, flame hissed out, bounced off my shields, and slewed up to the ceiling before burning out.

"Well done. Were you taught that?"

"Yes. The professor taught me some basic shielding, and I learned to enlarge it."

"Have you been attacked before this evening?"

"A few times."

"And, again, this professor you name would be Brandard?"

"Yes." I wondered why he'd had me repeat that and then realized when I'd said it before. We'd been standing nearly toe-to-toe, and it was likely that our audience hadn't heard. They did this time.

That brought a loud muttering through our listeners. Archer lifted his chin and looked about, the stern expression on his face quelling more remarks, even though he'd definitely solicited them.

I couldn't let it go, saying, "He didn't approve of you all."

"No, he didn't, and we might have saved him a good deal of trouble if he'd been a bit more . . . flexible. We understand that he is no longer a guest in your home."

"No."

"Do you know where he is?"

"No idea at all. He completed his phoenix ritual and left." I heard a murmur of surprise run through our little audience. They hadn't known? Interesting. As to where he could be . . . I thought of mentioning Steptoe and his demonic tail as evidence that the professor still existed, somewhere, but that seemed unwise. I merely shook my head.

"Phoenix wizards are notoriously tough. He will turn up, no doubt. He prides himself on being a thorn in our side and isn't likely to give that up."

"He is stubborn," I admitted.

"What else has he instructed you in?"

"Reading. A lot of reading."

"No drills?"

I knew drills quite well, being on a varsity field hockey team with a coach who lived by fitness training. But no training that he'd given me, per se. We'd done plenty of magic together, in defensive situations, from marauding harpies to sorcerer samurais, to devious elves but nothing repetitive day-to-day. At least it hadn't been boring. I shook my head.

"Any particular books he had you read?"

Again, I felt as though I might be giving out information that I ought to keep close. "Herbs," I finally said. "And some sympathetic magic stuff that I just didn't get." I kept scanning those watching and listening for sight of Carter. This was his Society.

Wouldn't he show up to give me some guidance? Surely, he wouldn't abandon me.

An intense stare drew my attention for the briefest of moments, the behatted gentleman who'd steered me away from Judge Parker. He was taller than some and shorter than others but had a certain presence that made him stand out. A frown settled on his face as our stares caught, then he turned away abruptly. I felt as if I should know him but didn't . . .

"Miss Andrews, would you mind participating in a few exhibitions and tests?"

They weren't about to share any of their educated magic with me but didn't mind prying to see what my secrets were. I shrugged. "Sure. If I can't run with the big dogs, I might as well stay under the porch."

Archer hid his laugh with a slight cough. "Come with me then," he requested and proceeded to lead me farther into the stone works, the crowd trailing us seeming to thin out a mite. Worried about fallout perhaps? From the scorch marks crawling about the granite, it seemed a real possibility.

If I had been wondering about where the junior members of the Society were, I had to wonder no longer. Eight of them faced me, in two rows, their expressions avid and expectant. They ranged from my age in their early twenties down to one young lady who couldn't have been more than twelve. Without seeming to, I focused on her. She wouldn't be in this bunch if she didn't have a bucketful of talent, and because of her age, many might overlook her as just a kid. I couldn't afford to. She didn't look like the kind of person who would be easily forgettable, either, with her golden-bronze skin and snapping dark eyes and hair. She looked wholesome and at the same time, a bit decadent, like graham crackers hiding luscious chocolate and toasted marshmallow.

I didn't have time to wonder as Archer ordered, "Flame."

I don't think Archer said "Present arms!" but he might as well have, because all eight held out their hands, and their palms filled with a globe of fire. It seemed to be more of an illumination spell that I'd watched the professor ignite a number of times than an offensive one. I raised an eyebrow and looked at Archer.

"It's a basic skill," he said. "Do you possess it?"

Of course, I did . . . now. I mostly called on it for a fight, though, but I didn't think I'd make anyone happy by lobbing fireballs around. What worried me was the drain it might make on my reserves. I didn't know what Archer and the Society might demand from me this night and I'd already gotten pretty low earlier. I didn't know how much OJ and a few chicken bites had refueled me. I tamped down my effort and produced a globe the size of a shooter marble. My fellow magicians snickered, except for the youngest one I watched out of the corner of my eye. She frowned a bit, as if calculating something.

"Float them."

That seemed to be cheating a bit, as they were all floating just off their wielder's skin, but I inhaled and brought mine up nearly chin high. That brought out a gasp or two from the gallery of watchers and I knew immediately what I'd done. Me and the maelstrom stone had just exhibited a vast overachievement. No one else had hefted their fireball higher than four or five inches above their wrists. The young one inhaled and got hers boosted up to chest high where it bounced unsteadily in position.

Were they heavy? Mine wasn't, just combined of gas and air, so how could it be? But from the actions next to me, they seemed to be floating bowling balls from the strained expressions on their faces. Or maybe it was just the effort needed to keep the fire compact and contained.

"Release," snapped Archer quickly, before his protégés had a meltdown.

My presentation didn't snap out as it should, but rather melted down like liquid rain into my hand and then into the stone. I'd never had that effect before and when I looked up, I could see a lot of pale expressions. I wished I knew what I'd done wrong/differently, but I don't think anyone here was going to tell me. Yet. Again, I seemed to have achieved something far more difficult than Archer suggested.

I still battled the drained effects from earlier. I felt thinned out and unsubstantial. I scanned the room and saw a few tables in the back, pushed up against the wall, filled with finger foods and juice drinks and urns for coffee and tea. I broke away from the lineup, trotted over, and tossed a bruschetta or two down, my mouth filling with the taste of fresh tomato, olive oil, and a touch of garlic. They had to have been hothouse tomatoes, because we were in the dead of winter, but this group could afford to pay for what they wanted.

Archer cleared his throat. "Miss Andrews. We are far from done."

"Oh. Sorry." I returned to the lineup.

My wary student target gave me a crooked grin, reinforcing my s'mores label. Layered, different flavors, complicated textures, and the need to be careful while handling in case she was still flambé. I'd like to know her name, but Archer wasn't into introducing his students. Protective? Perhaps. It reminded me that I stood in a hall where true names could be used in power rituals. Unfortunately, they'd made it clear they knew mine.

We did two more tests which I failed utterly, in the line of sympathetic magic where you took a sliver of an item and replicated it in its entirety. The professor hadn't drilled me in its aspect, although I'd read his book, but we'd never gotten around to discussing it or applying its principles. I didn't push myself to accomplish something I wasn't skilled in and ignored the low laughs amid muttered sneers. I could produce a rose from rose petal if I had to, but why strain?

Then we did some aura reading. Opening the vision to see outside the box of our own world is not common or easy and, quite frankly, until my stone gobbled up bits of the Eye of Nimora, I hadn't been able to do it. Not unless Carter or one of the others touched me and used their own power to open my inner eye; since that is taxing to my partner, I'd only experienced it once or twice. But as a sorceress, my skill comes from knowing the real name, the intrinsic existence of another thing, so that I could manipulate it or draw power from it, or even give it an exact reality by naming it. To do that, I have to be able to *see* it.

My ability in that area had been nonexistent before acquiring the pieces of Nimora. It expanded slowly, as if I were learning to do it on my own with coaching from the shards. I could almost do it consistently without the eyes. That night, however, I felt too weary to even try. I watched the others scan their compatriots, and I'd no clue if they were right or wrong or scamming me. I would only know when it was my turn, and eventually it came down to me.

"I don't read auras," I told Archer.

"To be an effective magic user, one must have the Sight."

One also shouldn't reveal all the cards in one's hand. I allowed myself a smile and answered, "I do all right."

"I'm not certain you understand why we invited you here this evening. We're trying to ascertain not only your power but also your control of it. There is a minimum amount of magic required to keep one's powers in check as well as in tune. We have to certify you can do that, or we will . . ." Archer's crisp voice trailed off.

I read him then, quickly so that he would have no hope of detecting it, and saw condemnation behind his words. He wasn't nearly as friendly as he projected. I reacted. "Or you'll what?"

A ripple went through the Society. A number of them shuffled back a step again, their attention fixed on my inquisitor. That put their backs to the wall. Would they turn and run next?

I had a good guess for his silence. "Strip me of my power?"

Archer produced a piece of pewter-gray metal, very shiny, rather like a gold ingot bar, from an inner pocket of his nicely cut coat. "We will do whatever is necessary."

I eyed it closely. "What is that?"

"A relic," he said. "One that has proved quite useful and can be very effective. A nullifier, if you would."

"I would rather not. I came here tonight because you invited me—and because I had hoped for some basic schooling."

"Your aura indicates you have a great deal of power, untapped and undisciplined. We can't let you be a menace to others. As for schooling, you seem to be resistant to the idea."

"Ah." No wonder the professor had been adamant about my not getting mixed up with the Society. When they were good, they were very good . . . and when they were bad, they were *awful*. Also, he had had some idea about the first impressions I tend to make i.e., I often come on a little brash. I held up my hand, palm outward, and waited for a tense moment for my eyes to open. They did, instantly, as if eager to jump into the situation. I waved my hand in front of Archer and then the double row of students. As suspected, the youngest one was the real power-dealer in the bunch, after the adult. I could see more than the auras of their talents; I could read their emotional standing as well. Most of them were wells of animosity. S'Mores hit me as intrigued and a little sympathetic.

But Archer—well, Archer reminded me a bit of my nemesis Judge Parker—full of power and not about to be crossed if he could help it. I don't like dictators, good or bad, if there is such a thing as a benevolent dictator.

The maelstrom stone vibrated a little in my hand, warming up, leaving me wondering as to its intentions. It can be very independent.

Archer stepped close to me, his nullifier in hand, and as I swung about to meet him, to fend him off—my stone jerked my fingers to his relic, sticking to it like a powerful magnet. Before Archer could gasp or I could warn him—the stone swallowed it.

Like that. One minute he held the shiny ingot and the next it had disappeared into the palm of my hand. I could almost swear I heard the stone burp in satisfaction.

"My god." Archer stared at me. "Can you get it to release my relic?"

"Mmmm . . . I'd say no. At least, it's never spit anything back out yet." Not the whole truth, but I didn't feel like giving him false hope. Or anything else, under the circumstances.

"But it—it contains the powers of those it's erased until it's emptied."

"Then I'd say definitely that it's gone. I told you it absorbed items."

"Did you come here with that intention?"

I tilted my head. "Should I have? Because it's beginning to look to me like I should have, to protect myself if nothing else. But I don't see as how I could have. I didn't know what to expect here. I've never heard of a null stone. And I don't think the swell of animosity," and I swung about indicating everyone else in the cavern, "is going to make my defensive shield feel any more secure."

S'Mores edged close to me. Her whispery voice reached me. "Make a trade."

I took it as a sound idea. I opened my eyes a little wider at Archer. "How about a proposition?"

"A proposition! Tell me why we shouldn't drop you in your tracks?"

"Well, one, the stone will protect me, but I can't control any backlash. And two, with a bit of schooling, I might be able to figure out how to get the stone to relinquish what it's gobbled up. I know it's absorbed one or two things, but frankly, I can feel the nullifier. I'm thinking it might react like that grain of dirt that irritates an oyster into manufacturing a pearl. I ought to be able to force it out when the stone is ready." I couldn't sense it, but it certainly sounded plausible when I said it.

A slight tic at the corner of his forehead developed. I didn't know if this meant he was thinking hard or annoyed or, hell, he might even have been receiving telepathic opinions from members of the Society around us. I stood very still and gathered my power as quietly and inconspicuously as I could to defend myself. It would have to be a one-punch strike, hard and decisive, because I didn't have the stamina right now to do anything sustained. Someone said, very close to my ear, close enough that I did not think anyone else could possibly hear it, "Don't antagonize."

It sounded like advice.

Late advice.

When I looked about to see who it might have been, absolutely no one stood next to me but Archer.

I wanted to walk through their ranks and set off the little items they all wore to augment their magical skills, because if it has magic stored in it, and I can sense it, I can access it.

That's one of the things a sorceress is good at. It wouldn't take more than a slight nudge of the resources I had left, too. It might be enough of a power play to make the Society back off, it or might be a very bad idea. Did they really consider me one or just a half-assed magician with a far more powerful stone embedded in her hand?

Truth to tell, I had no idea how much magic I might hold if it was taken/moved upon, but I had some. I had felt it before and one day I would feel it again.

But now . . . right now . . . I could own them. All of them. At least until one of them decided to drop me in my tracks. The actions I wanted to take, though, would give them fair warning how dangerous and brash I could be. So not a good idea. It's always better to have the enemy underestimate you. If they were the enemy. I hadn't decided yet.

I took a step back, out of the range of both Archer and little Miss S'mores.

CHAPTER ELEVEN

NEGOTIATED POSITIONS

HIS IRE SEEMED as restrained and formal as the morning coat he wore. Archer flicked off an invisible bit of lint from one cuff, frowning, but when he looked up, he nodded. "Your proposition is accepted. The main intention of the Society is education, after all, and you've offered to participate in that. We will, of course, insist on the remittance of our nullifier—and it isn't the only such relic we have in our possession, merely the one at hand—for your information."

I didn't appreciate the threat even as he agreed to a deal. I'd remember that. "Done. I shall work diligently on getting that relic returned. But you'll have to schedule any classes you want me to take around my college and athletic obligations."

"Field hockey, I was informed?"

"Yes."

"Your season is finished, then."

And, it was, but that didn't mean the coach would let us go fallow. No, indeed. Most of us were added to the track and field team, to take advantage of the "legs" we'd already developed. "I still have classes."

"You shall have to forward me a calendar of the best available days, then." He produced a business card with a fluid movement of his hand. Archer must have been, at one time, a very adept magician with astonishing sleight of hand. Trickery, I knew, but still impressive. The professor wouldn't have thought so. I could almost hear his cantankerous bluster. I missed him, almost as much as I missed my own father. The business card held a private postal box as well as his email address.

"I'll get my hours to you as soon as the school has confirmed them for the spring semester. That should be any day now." He nodded briskly and then turned to the double line of students. "Dismissed."

I watched them scatter, rather hoping that they might take flight like refugees from Hogwarts, but none of them did. S'Mores dared a half-smile as she disappeared into the crowd, veered to grab some food goodies from the table, and then whisked out a side door.

Archer waited until the students had all dispersed before leaning in and saying, "If this trade of ours doesn't work out, we shall have to take steps."

I didn't think he meant baby steps either.

A corridor opened, leading back to the double doors and beyond that, the car park steeped in night shadows. I took it as a sign that I should leave posthaste, and so I did. The driver opened a door for me, I stepped in—and found Miss S'mores waiting for me.

She tilted her head and smiled at me. "Hi! Archer sent me to start your lessons."

"Isn't it past your bedtime?"

She giggled. "My day starts at sundown." She put up a window between the front and back and did a little finger wave. I hoped she was soundproofing the car.

"You've got my name. Fair is fair . . . yours?"

"Sophie," she told me as she leaned over to offer her hand.

"Sophie," I finished. She looked like one.

With a laugh, she tapped her hand on her jeans as if I had static-shocked her. Maybe I had.

Sophie glanced at me. Now her eyebrow went up. "That's a bit of a burden."

"What?"

"The power snapping at me. See, that's telling people what you are. You've lost any advantage you might have."

"But you can handle it, right? I didn't hurt you."

She stared at me solemnly. For an eerie moment, I saw what

she would look like as an adult—chiseled face, serious eyes, intelligent consideration, and—perhaps—even a tinge of sadness. Sophie gave an abrupt nod. "Of course not. The issue is control. And there won't be anybody but Master Thigpen about tonight who can report on you, and he won't know."

"He won't?"

"First lesson. I'll show you how to distract being assessed." Her mouth thinned in thought, before she knocked on the glass to tell the driver to leave. "All ready."

"That's a deal, then." I reached behind me to lock the door and off we went.

My experience with unknown cars and drivers made me look back, over my shoulder, as we pulled away. I turned back, settled in the car seat, and gathered a bit of power to my stone.

In the car, she tapped the back of the driver's seat, and the window obligingly rolled down between us and him. Sophie waved her hand again. "Catch that?"

The barrier stayed down, but I detected a muffled sound to her words.

"Sound waves?"

"Yup. I've cut off one of his major senses, so he will disregard us." She made the motion again as I looked at her warily.

"It's not so much the sigil you're sketching but the intention behind it."

She beamed. "Fast learner!"

I tapped the back of the driver's seat, and the window whined upward. She leaned toward me and sniffed. "Do I smell dog on you?"

That unnerved me a bit. "He just had a bath a few days ago, too. But yeah, that would be my pup. Do I reek of it?" I lifted one arm and then the other.

"Just to me. Labrador retriever and . . ." Sophie waited for me to fill in her sentence, but I didn't.

"And?" she repeated.

I shrugged. "No one is quite sure."

"Oh, wow. Something magical, then, maybe." She sniffed again. "Not hellhound. They always have this smell like an old fire pit."

"Sulfurous?"

"Maybe." She rubbed the side of her nose with one finger as if the very memory made her itchy.

"So . . . is this a sanctioned lesson, or did you just decide to drop by?"

She gave me a side eye. "You won't tell?"

"Never."

"I volunteered. Archer wanted someone to follow you, to put a tracer on his nullifier. I just wanted to see you on your own. I mean, who you really are, you know?"

And she wanted to evaluate me on her own. I wasn't sure if I found that encouraging or not. Suppose she was a pint-sized Joanna? As nice as she seemed to be, even though her offer might be genuine, I couldn't discount that she was fully immersed in an organization the professor mistrusted completely. I sat quietly and gave her the merest of nods and tried to think of my curmudgeonly wizard in his grand old tradition.

That made me even more cautious. Though I didn't think she'd detected my weakened reserves which told me that Miss Sophie S'mores wasn't as all that as she thought she was.

I was more than certain Master Thigpen would be.

"We'll be at a neutral practice area in a few." Sophie lapsed into silence, or perhaps she was working to keep her ward going. The smile on her face stretched thin, and she didn't really focus on anything but the back of the driver's head.

Because we'd turned into the quarter of town where I'd gone to high school, I caught a pretty good idea of where we were going this time and paid attention. Next time I'd drive on my own, thoroughly disliking the idea of being at the mercy of a driver/car I didn't know. The car, however, cruised past and toward the city limits.

Try as I might, I couldn't catch a glimpse of the driver in the rearview mirror. That disturbed me a little, wondering how it was possible to avoid being seen. I couldn't even tell if it were male or female although I had a feeling of female. Something about the shoulders and arms in the uniform coat, and the gloves covering the hands. Not delicate but nearly. It crept over me, like an ice-cold feather tickling against me that I didn't like riding in strange cars with unknown drivers. Nor was I headed toward the Butchery area, which gave me a little comfort . . . but not enough.

I turned around on the car seat to face Sophie. "How much farther?"

"Oh. You know." She gave a little waggle of her fingers.

"I don't know, or I wouldn't ask."

She didn't answer right away. I watched her for a moment, noted that her color had paled, tiny drops of sweat trickled from her hairline down her forehead, and one of her hands had begun to tremble. Not, I thought, from the soundproofing spell which didn't need to hold much power since the window stayed up. What unnerved this young lady so much? She wouldn't look back at me, her gaze fixed to the front, as landscape blurred a bit around us. The realization I was being taken somewhere I probably didn't want to go became much more than a suspicion. And Sophie was no more a willing participant than I was—someone had leveraged her. She hadn't volunteered, whether for Archer or someone else. She'd been forced to participate. That angered me more than my own situation.

I dropped my voice to a barely audible whisper.

"Unauthorized visit. Unknown location. You've been manipulated into getting me out to . . . wherever . . . so someone can take a closer look at the maelstrom stone. This isn't going to be pretty."

She twitched a look at me. Her lips had paled to nearly the unnatural washed-out color of her skin. She gave a bare shake of her head to steer me away from trouble. It didn't work.

I put a hand on her arm. "I got this."

I have no sympathy for bullies. Never have had, and even more so after what I went through in high school when my father disappeared, thought to have been killed. Now that I was adult, I knew how to fight back even better. I slipped my gloves off my hands and put my palms together, to feel the stone warm up. My bracers warmed as well.

I murmured, "Ready."

I knocked on the driver's partition. It lowered slightly. "Pull over. I'm going to be sick. Spent too much energy." My voice wobbled convincingly.

Sophie rolled an eye at me. I shrugged.

The window came down all the way. "Sick?"

"Seriously, pull over unless you want puke all over this back seat!"

The car slowed quickly and headed toward the berm. I muttered to Sophie, "Run as soon as you get out."

I don't know if she trembled or shook her head in acknowledgment because I was throwing open my door and getting myself onto the street.

The driver moved also, quickly, and I found the two of us nearly toe-to-toe. I'd thought the driver female but that mostly definitely was not the case. Maybe half elven, but he glared at me over the collar of his long coat, and I caught a gleam in his eyes. I knew dark elves when I met them. I reacted with a low growl that would have made both the professor and my dog proud. The driver retreated two or three steps quickly, one hand up in the air as if to forestall anything I had planned.

Or get off a blistering magical attack.

I put up my own hand, letting the stone deploy my shielding. It spun out in a golden disk, covering not only myself but also Sophie who'd run all right . . . directly behind me. Bite me, but I still didn't know if I could trust her.

I spun my defensive shield out a bit more as I faced the driver. "Thigpen, I presume?"

"What's in a name?" His lips twisted, and his long face pulled a bit to match the sneer, lanky brown hair hanging down from what passed for a chauffeur's cap. The suit, however, was both too fine and too outdated to be a uniform. And he had, heaven help us both, a Confederate flag pin stuck on his lapel.

Now, because my mom is from the North (and west), we've always been considered Yankees here in Virginia. It's a thing. Unfortunately, it's become more and more of a thing in the last few years and I have worries for the future. But that's in the big scheme, and—frankly—I have enough to worry about with me and my mom and our close friends . . . and Aunt April. The rest of the states need to get together to take care of themselves. All the same, I can feel the prejudice and so can she. It might even be one of the reasons the university is holding back on her finalizing her dissertation for her doctorate. We don't know. It's not always obvious. But she will always be a Yankee.

I raised an eyebrow at him as he curled the fingers of his left hand about that self-same pin. I caught, for a brief second, the bitter copper tang of blood and thought he'd cut himself on the stupid thing before realizing it had been intentional. That was no ordinary pin. Dude was about to send some dark, dark blood magic at me through his charged relic.

Anger surged through me. "Stealing power? Not got the spine to learn it on your own? You think you have to rip it out of someone? You're not getting anything from me or Sophie. I'll take you down first." And I would. I was a fighter and had earned my scars the past few years, mostly on the field hockey grounds, but I didn't intend to roll over and let this ugly string bean of a being take the stone from me. Over my dead body.

Which might be exactly what he intended.

I narrowed my eyes. "You're not powerful enough to do this on your own. Who's pushing you?"

"Shut up," Thigpen said. "Give it over. You will save yourself a great deal of pain if you do." His gaze shifted to somewhere behind me. "Or save her. You can't control the power you think you have to stop me."

"You haven't got what it takes. You'll have to scamper back to . . . could it be Judge Parker . . . and admit you failed."

"I won't fail! You're as good as dead! I will have it one way or the other."

The stone coughed. Or hiccoughed. Neither of which it had ever really done before, and I prayed it wasn't staggering to a powerless halt. I didn't feel fatigue, but maybe the magic Thigpen had begun to drum up had closed off my connection with the maelstrom. I felt an icy coldness wrap about me, gripping tight. My arms and legs went half-numb, tingling with pins and needles. I stomped both feet to restore sensation as I advanced. Another two feet and I would be within kicking or punching distance.

If I could make it that far. Despite my vows, the power he summoned fastened around my chest and then my throat. I had my arms up in hope the bracers could block it, but they didn't. Whatever he cast pulled the breath from my lungs and blocked me from getting a new gulp.

The spell he coiled against me wrapped around my throat, getting tighter and tighter, and I suddenly, desperately, needed air. I fought it, afraid to drop my shield and expose Sophie to the attack, and I doubted she had the power available right now either. I wrenched myself a step forward even as my lungs began to scream to breathe. What air I did have was sucked away from me, and I could see from the glitter in his eyes he didn't intend to stop. If I could get closer for a good kick, I'd drop him to his knees.

But my own knees threatened to give way, my limbs shaking from lack of oxygen. Black spots danced in front of my eyes. I wanted to claw at my throat, but I needed to keep the shield up. If I did drop it, I didn't know if it would protect me or if we'd all be at Thigpen's dark magic mercy. He laughed, but I barely heard it. My blood pounded in my ears. My left leg buckled, and I went down on that knee.

"Not so brave now, are you? I am moments away from taking everything you have. Your stone, your life . . . even that mongrel family of yours. As for Sophie, she won't remember a thing."

I couldn't find what I needed to answer, but I knew the anger flashed in my eyes. Then, slowly, I saw the Eye of Nimora awaken in my palm. I wasn't about to give up or give in. White spots joined the black ones dancing in my vision, and I swiped at my eyes with my right hand. Still wordless, still gasping in hope for air.

The stone coughed again, then I saw it burp out that pewter-gray ingot it had swallowed, courtesy of Archer. It hovered in front of my nose and practically danced into my free hand. I grabbed it out of midair and wrapped my numbed fingers around it, wondering if Thigpen had seen it. Hopefully not. I levered myself back onto two feet, two legs. It hurt yet, at the same time, felt incredibly numb and unfeeling. Did I have asphalt, the edge of the berm, under my feet or what? I stepped forward. Well, truthfully, it was more of a collapse against Thigpen as my vision threatened to black out entirely. I felt his hands grab my elbows as he gave a triumphant crow. Then I jammed the nullifier against Thigpen's lapel and bloody pin. It sucked at him greedily.

Air rushed back into my body like the surf at high tide, carrying feeling and strength with it. Not all my faculties yet—but enough. I twisted slightly out of his hold and put my knee where ladies were told never to hit a man. Crude, but effective. Thigpen yelped and toppled, hands cupping himself. His eyes rolled up, and he passed out from the magical and physical attacks.

My shield collapsed. I slipped the nullifier into a pocket while I stepped back and shook Sophie loose from my protection.

"I'm s-sorry. I didn't want to."

Anger still burned throughout me, and I think Sophie saw it because she scuttled to the far side of the car, watching me from behind the fender.

"You know who he is?"

She gave a slight nod, before adding in a burst of words, "Not well. He's just an elder, and I don't get lessons from him, and I would have avoided him if I'd known what he was going to do."

"I take it his actions aren't exactly sanctioned by the Society."

She shook her head abruptly. "Never. Archer will be furious."

"He a friend of Judge Parker?"

"I don't know."

I scanned her face a moment before accepting what she said. I didn't like myself for being skeptical, but I could almost hear the professor inside my head, repeating what he'd always said: the Society was not to be trusted.

I motioned to the car. "Get in. I'll get you home."

She hesitated. I shrugged. "Unless you want to stay out on the road with him." I scanned the roadway. We were slightly west and north of Richmond, in the country, with little traffic.

She might have to wait a long time for a ride, and I could almost guarantee Thigpen would awaken before that.

She hopped into the front seat. I slid in and checked the dashboard. Yup, he'd left the keys in the car. No imagination.

When we were all buckled in and headed back, I told Sophie what I wanted her to tell Archer and made her repeat it back to me until she got it perfect.

CHAPTER TWELVE

SHELL GAME

I DROPPED HER off where she said her home was. I don't know if I quite believed her or not, but we'd debate that some other day. Then I drove my borrowed transportation to the downtown rideshare lot and left it, calling Steptoe to come and pick me up. I strode up and down the lot to keep warm. The fleeting memory that I thought I'd recognized Sophie before actually meeting her tickled my thoughts. Where? How? At the far end of the lot, I could see the beginning of the cobblestone street that led to the trendy yet old part of Richmond, where the Butchery awaited its nightly collegiate crowds. At the thought of it, I fought for breath again, Sophie's mystery fleeing out of my grasp entirely. This was the last place I wanted to be. What if my stalker still lurked, searching for me? Where was my car?!

Simon didn't drive that often, but I knew he could find me. I waited around, a trifle uneasily, until he pulled up in my little red car, his elbow hanging out the window as if the coming storm on an ever-frostier midnight didn't bother him one whit. Scout hung out the other window.

Getting in, I realized why the windows had been down.

"You were smoking one of your stinky cigars in here!"

"Never." But his apple-red cheeks got redder.

"You know I hate those things."

"I smoke maybe one a year, ducks, on account of you lot. Nobody else was home, I thought I could indulge. I was outside the whole time. Well, until I was in here."

Scout sneezed heartily as he flopped across the backseat.

Simon put his other hand in the air. "I will divest the vehicle of its aroma when we get home."

"Promise?"

"Indubitably."

I settled back in my passenger seat, enlarged to hold a much heftier rider—the car had belonged to the professor once; the person accompanying him most often would have been Morty. A bucket seat had to be substantial to hold an Iron Dwarf.

I filled Steptoe in on the Society happenings, and we tossed some ideas around before pulling up in the driveway. Scout snored lustily in the back.

All those ideas fled as I got out of the car and saw the side door to the house swinging wide open in the breeze.

"It's a broken latch, is all," Steptoe announced after inspecting the door jamb as I bounded inside to see what might be disturbed and what might not. He produced a screwdriver out of midnight and a shiny new latch. "I've got things put to right."

The house rested, cool and quiet, my mother already tucked away in bed upstairs, and a note on the kitchen counter: chicken and dumpling casserole in fridge. Nothing seemed amiss, but it had been a dreadful night so far, and I didn't trust it to get any better.

He patted me on the shoulder. "I'll run a patrol, me and the pup. You eat something. I don't read auras much, but yours is waving a flag. You're about all used up." With that, demon and pup disappeared.

I couldn't deny I felt ravenous.

Eating sounded heavenly. I microwaved myself a hearty portion and sat down. I'd polished my plate halfway before I got up to get myself a drink, bypassed the ever-present decanter of sweet tea, and opted for a non-caffeine soda.

Steptoe called out, "All good. I'm for bed," as the mudroom door clicked shut.

I sat down and dragged my fork across my plate, thinking. I juggled around the problem of getting the stone to regurgitate the nullifier permanently and realized I would be on borrowed time if I couldn't. Maybe I could approach it from a self-defense angle. Return the Society relic, or I get terminated. Would the stone recognize the peril in that scenario? Would it care?

It wasn't until I sat back that I realized Scout hadn't shown up to help partake of the festivities of dinner. My ever-growing pup believed in bottomless food dishes and showed extreme disappointment in us that we hadn't provided such a thing. Here I sat having eaten a late-night dinner—demolished, was more like it—and he hadn't made a reappearance. He and Steptoe had finished searching, finding everything had been in its proper place. Except the dog himself. Highly irregular.

Pushing my chair back quietly, I got up and rinsed my dish in the sink, leaving it there to load in the morning. Then I set about finding my dog.

Scout looked like a typical Lab mix, with a golden hide, big paws he'd yet to grow into, intelligent brown eyes and a mega ton of energy. Because of the "mix" in his heritage Carter strongly suspected, he'd probably live to be thirty or forty. Accordingly, his body matured in time with that longevity. How and why the species mingling had occurred, neither of us had any idea, but he hadn't bonded with his former owners (the police department) and had with me, so that was that.

Except he was gone.

I went through the lower level of our aged home. Compared to the house we'd lost, the current habitation was far older, creakier, and more difficult to deal with. Plumbing could be cantankerous . . . even fickle. I think we've just about persuaded Aunt April, the owner of the place, to invest in a new hot water heater. As for the rest of it, well, it was just the way it was. At least, it was ours for the moment. I searched through all the rooms on the first floor, looking for my dog. The floor creaked a little on certain steps over the wood or rug-covered surface, the doors opened and shut smoothly on well-oiled hinges, the windows stayed locked, and even the mudroom door seemed to be bolted as it should be.

I looked through the upstairs as quietly as I could, not wanting to disturb my mother. I expected to find Scout sprawled across my bed but no.

That left the cellar.

I went down the steps cautiously because a cellar is . . . well . . . below ground and historically creepy, but also because a good many of the professor's remaining possessions were stored there, in a somewhat ordered heap of boxes. And I had no wish to interrupt my father again in whatever metaphysical state he might be in.

The cellar carried a vibe; it always had, but most of that had calmed since Hiram brought a crew in and remodeled it extensively. It didn't smell old and musty or have leaning bookshelves filled with creepy glass jars of who knew what-all floating in them. That had been the old cellar, before remodeling. I don't think my father's ghostly self added to the atmosphere as he had little enough essence to spare, but it might have. Maybe a touch of his despair or loneliness. Personally, I blame the cardboard boxes for the leakage of disturbing effects.

I paused halfway down the stairs. I couldn't be certain, but it looked as though the stacks of boxes had been reordered, somehow. The one box that always had a trail of blackish powder from one of its loose-seamed corners remained on the bottom as it always had, but the box above it and the third one on top of that . . . I stared at them. Yes. They had been shuffled about. The top one had been in the middle and two stacks over. The middle one had been on the top in the back.

Someone had been rifling through the professor's goods.

Only Carter and Steptoe had free access to our home. And Aunt April because she owned it and probably had an extra set of keys. Hiram could have gotten in, if he wanted, but I knew he wouldn't without asking solemnly for permission first. We knew the professor wasn't to be found in Richmond or even the state of Virginia. So, then, who had?

And why?

The idea that it might have been a Society member tickled through my thoughts. Tonight could all have been a nasty diversion, even the kidnapping before and after. It seemed a little contrived to be believable, but it sat in my mind uneasily anyway. I peered at the tape shutting each and every carton, but nothing seemed to be opened. Someone had just decided to arrange them? Of what use would that be? No use unless someone had been interrupted.

Then again, Simon had been home alone until I called. Mom had come home sometime after, defrosted a dinner, and gone to bed before we got in.

Steptoe seemed the likeliest suspect from that perspective. There were those who did not think his lesser demon personality had truly switched from the dark side, but I wasn't among them. I didn't want evidence I could be wrong. I sighed . . . and heard an unlikely echo.

I tiptoed around the end of the stacks to find Scout sitting, his ears on alert, watching the backside of the stored goods. His head swiveled about when he saw me, and his mouth stretched in a goofy grin which left little doubt in his delight on seeing me. He'd been concentrating so hard that he'd failed to scent or hear my presence. His tail thumped on the floor in sudden recognition.

"Get locked in? Why didn't you go to the door and bark to get out?" And, why hadn't Steptoe noticed?

He flicked a look at me and went right back to staring at the boxes.

"I get it. Someone got in and moved them around. Your nose tell you who?"

He tilted his head slightly, sneezed, and rubbed his muzzle with a forepaw.

"No dice, huh. Odd." I went to his flank and rubbed one of his soft ears. For the intruder to have left no scent trail seemed ominous, but other than the shuffling, I couldn't see that anything had actually been taken. Not a whole box at least. I'd have to ask Steptoe what, if anything, he might know. I think he'd tell me straight out. If not, I was fairly certain I could tell if he lied. That tail of his, now reattached, had a life of its own and was a definite tell. I pulled on Scout's collar. "Let's go. It's late, and whatever happened, the deed is done."

He resisted my tug at first, then gave in and bounded ahead of me to the stairs, leading the way. I gained the top step myself and looked back with a wave of my hand, wondering if the Eyes would open and give me an insightful look. My father wavered in a corner, bowed over and sitting on the floor. He looked as if he might be asleep, if ghosts could do such a thing.

Nimora's lids opened, but I saw nothing new about the boxes and their various auras, only that they'd been shuffled a bit and their presence seemed strong.

Great. Another one of life's mysteries to ponder while trying to fall asleep.

As I gave Scout a bit of kibble for a midnight snack, I told him about the Societas Obscura meeting and my reaction to it: that we definitely would have an uneasy marriage. He had little opinion about it, one way or the other, and I allowed as how the professor hadn't really expressed an opinion to Scout the way he had to me, and that might sway the pup's ideas about the evening.

When I told Scout about the happenings around the Butchery, however, he skinned his lips back, showing his teeth. I agreed with him as I closed and locked the cellar door before leaving the kitchen entirely. I also said, "No chasing down anything like that without me. That thing has bad juju, no doubt about it. In fact, we should have a whole hunting party with us if we ever run into it again."

Scout bumped my knee with his big Lab head, and I took it for agreement. I felt a little relieved as the more I thought about it, the more I equated it with whatever had been watching the house underneath the lamppost. I didn't want to be facing it down whatsoever in the future but knew I probably would. It stalked us for a purpose, and I would stop it however I could . . . but it would be nice to find out the purpose first, in case, you know, this sort of thing became a habit.

Morning came eventually. We all slept in while my mother left early on business. At the breakfast table, I brought up the worries at hand.

"I resent the inference in that, ducks." Simon gave me a sad look, and his tail drooped to emphasize it, down the back of the kitchen chair to the floor.

"I didn't say you did it. I asked if you knew anything about it." I leaned over to refresh his cup of tea.

"Means the same, doesn't it?"

"Only to the extremely suspicious. It doesn't to me. I thought since you were taking up nights in the mudroom, you might have heard something before I called you. That door latch didn't break on its own." I paused. "I thought you might have had a unique vantage point. If you say you didn't see or hear anything, I quite believe you."

His dark eyes blinked. "You do?"

"Of course, I do."

His eyes brimmed. "Benefit of the doubt?"

"No doubt involved. I consider you trustworthy."

His tail twitched. "I wish I could say I had knowledge or evidence, but I don't."

"Since I have no idea when the incursion occurred, I am pretty much in the dark, too." I sat down and added a bit of lemon to my sugary tea. "Wait. I'll be right back."

I jumped up and thundered upstairs to the tell-tales in their vase. They all swiveled about in sudden alarm at my abrupt and noisy appearance, and almost as quickly settled back into their preferred appearance of a lovely bouquet of roses. "Hi, guys. I'm not upset with any of you, but we might have had a stranger break into the house in the last day. Notice anything?"

They all wheeled about and looked downstairs and gave the equivalent of a blossom shrug. All except one. It waggled its leaves in a frenzy of excitement that I couldn't interpret.

I heard Steptoe on the stairs, entering the hall behind me.

"Understand what it's saying?"

"Not alarm but excited, I do believe. Not much help there. And," he leaned over, nose to vase. "You're supposed to report to me immediately."

The flowers sagged.

He jabbed a finger at them. "You've got an important job here, right important, and I expect you to do it to high standards. Buck up, my beauties."

The tell-tales straightened on their stems, except for the

exuberant one who kept bouncing and finally came to a tired and wilted halt.

"I think she had something to say."

Steptoe nodded at me. "I think so, too, but she isn't communicating well. Maybe if she mulls it over a bit, I can understand her later." He said to the flowers, "Too right, loveys. You stay on duty like I know you can."

I wouldn't have been surprised to see them twist their leaves about and salute though none of them did. We made our way back downstairs and microwaved our tea back into steaming hotness. The two of us sat there, silent, faces down as if inhaling the vapors for our health and concentration.

One thing and one thing only came to mind, along with the fact that I had probably put too much lemon in my tea (a little goes a long way for me). The tell-tales and likely Scout, too, had been spelled by the infiltrator and thus weren't too alarmed.

Hell, that one tell-tale was absolutely ecstatic over who it was. I attributed its attitude toward the charm put on it. The intrusion felt harmless, almost benevolent. Which brought me back to the impossible: the professor. But Steptoe hadn't sensed him. It became worrisome that someone or something might have mimicked his identity.

That did not leave me with any conclusions except that we were probably not at risk since nothing had been taken and no one menaced. We would, however, have to take precautions that it didn't happen again. I couldn't afford to be complacent. If there's one thing I've learned over the last year, it's that the magic side of the world can be tricky.

I cleaned house. Mom came in late and somewhat defeated, so I left her alone. When late evening came, the three of us— Simon, my pup, and I—went around the house testing and reinforcing wards. The maelstrom stone showed me a new facet of its defensive capabilities, and I managed to weave a few extra layers of protection. Steptoe's eyebrow arched in surprise until I tapped my palm in explanation.

"Ah. Too right—that bit of marble ought to be useful."

I didn't tell him that Sophie had gifted me with a bit of spellcasting that helped. "All done?"

"And a right good job, if I say so myself." Steptoe nodded at me. "Any cookies about?"

"No, but I could make some biscuits."

He rubbed his hands together. "Delightful!"

We settled down to relax a bit downstairs. Steptoe and I played some cribbage. It was about the only game where I could keep pace with him because he . . . well, he cheated at other games. I guess he wasn't as reformed as he liked to think.

CHAPTER THIRTEEN

DUE AND OVERDUE

THE ANCIENT PENDULUM clock in the living room chimed out midnight, something it rarely did although it did keep time, and I realized how dead late it was. We bid each other good night, Steptoe retiring to his cot and me upstairs to my room, Scout on my heels. He preferred sleeping with me, although there were still nights when he sought out the back of the house with its big window overlooking the backyard shadows and the movement of the moon. When he did that, I wondered if memories of another life prodded at him, but then—what did dogs know about other lives?

In his case, probably more than I did.

I propped myself up on my bed and opened Morty's journal. I'd thumbed through several decades to get anywhere near our own time period, although it would have been fascinating to just sift through page by page and learn about a world that I had no idea had ever existed.

But a name popped out every now and then, one denoted as the Master. Carter had mentioned it once and once only, and he wouldn't discuss it except to say that if I heard a title like that or anyone referring to it, to walk away and stay away. I hadn't, not until I opened the journal and now what I read did not elaborate except that the Master had to be treated carefully and with the utmost respect and caution. Who in the hell was this? A dark elf like Devian? Worse? It settled at the back of my mind and itched, something I knew I shouldn't scratch. I decided I'd ask Evelyn if her father knew anyone by that nickname, since he was now a player in local politics, having been elected mayor and all. He hadn't settled into the office yet, but he had to know some of the behind-the-scenes personalities.

That satisfied the annoying itch a bit and I kept reading through. It was interesting—Morty had kept a kind of eye— what we all call the side-eye—on local magic pushers. Most of course, were con artists or ordinary magicians who got by with sleight of hand and tricks, but he'd made mention of a few who weren't. I'd already gone through a few of the notes on Potion Polly, but she seemed to have garnered his respect as well as attention.

And, accordingly, he'd taken note of the family's history, including some of the heartbreaking deaths in the various branches. I couldn't decipher the symbols he used in his margins to draw attention or delineate a discovery, but even I could tell that death by accident or illness seemed to happen frequently, even with the mortality being what it was a hundred years ago. His writings confirmed what I'd already known. Two of the young ones had died of polio and one of tetanus. I lingered over that page a moment, appreciating the change in medicine. Another one of Morty's cramped symbols decorated the margin. I screwed my eyes up and peered at it as closely as I could. It looked like . . . but it couldn't be . . . a monetary symbol. Another cramped few words stated that a debt had been paid. To him? Or if not him, who? Or . . . I let the journal settle to the bed comforter. Magic's price? A shiver ran down the back of my neck. Morty had been a debt collector once. Had he been privy to the harsh dues magic users paid? Had he been a *collector*?

Scout stirred and came to the side of my bed, tail slowly wagging. He put his head on my knee.

"You get the floor tonight."

He pleaded with soft brown eyes, but I shook my head. "No. You're a cover hog, and you've got the old comforter right there, all lumped up the way you like it, just for you." His muzzle followed my point. The tail thumped, once.

But he'd made his point. We both needed sleep.

We yawned at each other and crept into bed. He took up the

diagonal lower half while I curled into the upper half despite our earlier discussion. Sleep came quickly, and only once did I wake up, having dreamed that I'd thinned myself out so much that no one could hear me when I tried to call for help.

But the dreams returned. A quicksilver elf entered my arena, and I knew those silvery eyes and that figure of grace and steel. Devian, the local elf lord who'd pitted himself against us and lost.

He smiled in my thinned direction.

"Caught yourself, have you, and made it all that much easier for me. I may be gone, but you are not beyond my reach. Not yet." And, as he spoke, he did stretch out a hand toward me, icy and deliberate. It started to break the fragile threads that kept me tied to this world; I could feel myself begin to drift away. Helpless. Hopeless.

That brought me awake, with the blankets tangled about my arms and hands, and sweat dappling my forehead. When my pulse quieted, I sagged back into bed and fell back to sleep again, with dreams I thankfully didn't remember.

Scout's low growls woke me again. I unwound the covers from my legs and one arm, and sat up very carefully, uncertain as to what alarmed him.

He stared, not at my bedroom window which faced the backyard but into the hallway.

Even for winter, the house seemed terribly chilled. Had Mom not set the thermostat before going to bed? We weren't flush with money, but we did have enough to carry us through for six months while she finished her dissertation and picked up a new load of teaching assignments. We could even think about moving if she got some full-time job offers along with that doctorate, the only good thing about losing our mortgage and now living rent to rent.

I looked past Scout to the bedroom window and saw the crystal patterns of frost on the outside. No, it was definitely cold, inside and out. I swept my bracers off the sill where they were stored, to absorb the sunlight in the morning, and put them on.

Not again. I got up. Scout stayed fixed on the hallway. Had our intruder come back? Or was it our watcher?

I hadn't heard a thing, but I'd been wrapped up in ugly dreams. I listened intently and heard only the occasional breathing that a wooden house does now and then. Even the furnace stayed silent. No wonder it felt chilled.

Fear sent bumps coursing over my arms, even under my bracers which gave off a soft, golden glow. Nothing like advertising my presence. I hesitated, then slipped them off and stowed them at the edge of my dresser. If I needed defense, running would be my better option over standing my ground. Slipping my tennis shoes on, I stopped long enough to throw on a flannel shirt and grab my second favorite hockey stick. I may be foolish, but I am not stupid. Really.

I went in search of whatever was spooking Scout and haunting our house. Not including my father, of course.

Nothing met my cautious glance out between the curtains at our front window. Same at the side kitchen door which looked out on our driveway to the garage in the back. I decided not to check the mudroom because of waking Steptoe. I'd never awakened him rashly and had no idea how he'd react, and even though the professor had blunted his powers long ago, he still crafted flash-bangs with a fair amount of punch. I didn't want any lobbed at me because he had no idea who'd come at him in the middle of the night.

In spite of my original intentions, I stood at the front door, unable to open it or cross the threshold. My inner voice rattled away that it was astoundingly stupid to go out and investigate—well, I have two inner voices, and one was for it and the other vehemently against it. I'd done it before without harm, so why poke the bear again?

They made such a racket in my head that I opened and skittered through the door just to turn it off.

The cold outside stabbed all the way to the bone and even made my teeth ache. But the sky stood crystal clear, brilliant and free of smoke trailing from nearby chimneys. It wasn't snowing yet, but it might have been too cold for it to snow. That is a thing that can happen, although usually not in this part of Virginia. The shadows that fell across the road, sidewalk, and lawns looked sharp enough to cut.

And yet I did not see what I feared and hoped to see. Whatever had lurked out front appeared to have moved on. I walked to the lamppost and found a patch that seemed even icier than the rest of the street. I knelt down on one knee and put my palm to it, checking my impression. So cold it burned. I snatched my hand away. Had something crouched there, watching? That thing with red eyes? If I'd even seen such a thing . . . but I thought I had, and Scout had backed that up.

Which reminded me. Where was my dog now? Certainly not at my side, ready to leap into action if warranted. I turned on my heel. Scout sat on the front step, flank plastered to the now closed door as if he could will himself to the other side. I put my tongue to the roof of my mouth and let out a high chirping whistle to gather him. I know he heard me. His ears perked forward and then back again. He lifted one paw tentatively before setting it back down. Now, if he were still an eight-week–old pup, I could see the hesitation and fear, but Scout had a good six months under his growth belt before being gifted to me. He'd never shown an ounce of cowardice before these visitations. That he did now brought my inner voices back online, telling me how reckless it was to stand out here relatively unprotected.

I heard a whisper of sound behind me, catching the barest hint of movement as I turned. And there he stood, Malender, just as I had dreamed him. He held that whip handle and the leather thong draped down to his ankles where shadows hugged him.

Words escaped me without much thought. "It wasn't you."

He arched an eyebrow, a feat accomplished without a single wrinkle on his ageless, surely immortal face. A tiny lock of hair had escaped to trail down to the other brow, and his jade eyes stayed fixed on me. "It wasn't?" His hand twitched, and movement undulated the length of that astonishing whip.

"Out here. Before. I mean," and I paused a moment, searching for the proper words. "The threat I felt couldn't have come from you."

Not to mention the prevailing cold. The flames licking the length of the whip smoked against the pavement, sizzling little puddles of what had once been ice. He tilted his head slightly.

More perfectly handsome than any man I'd ever met, he smiled
slowly, the corner of his mouth quirking slightly. I loved Carter,
but he couldn't hold a match to Malender in looks.

"Not that you aren't awe-inspiring," I added hastily.

"Tessa of the Salt, you freed me. If for no other reason, I am
indebted to you. You should fear me but only as it would be
natural to—and not be afraid of me otherwise."

Confused, I merely said, "Right." He had, for months, worn
a black cloudlike, shroud so menacing that every one of the
supernatural beings I'd met had held him in fear. His very presence brought up vague memories of ruin and disaster and corrupted power so that not one of my new friends trusted him.
We'd crossed purposes more than once before. I'd fought him
off several times and defeated him more with the simple com-
pound of ordinary table salt. Then I'd noticed that not only had
it stopped him in his tracks, the shroud that imprisoned Malender shrank visibly upon each contact. I couldn't prove him evil
one way or the other, but I could definitely tell he'd been imprisoned. Following a gut instinct, I dumped a thirty-pound
bag of salt on him one night and nearly killed him. But the
shroud had dissolved away and, along with it, his menacing
persona. He'd been something else, and began recovering it,
whatever it was. I hadn't thrown salt on him for weeks, and
wished I had a pocketful now, just . . . just in case. I still couldn't
be certain on which side of the line he stood.

"I'm here," he said softly, "to warn you."

That couldn't be good. "All right."

"You and yours have been marked for both Death and Justice. You must take very close care of those you love."

Not that I wouldn't, but I frowned, and felt my nose wrinkle
slightly. "Or . . ."

"You will lose, Tessa. All that you value."

"And you can't help me?"

"I'm here tonight, am I not? Take care."

With that, he flicked his wrist. The whip lashed out with a
sharp crack, flames leaping out and the smell of the burn cir-
cling us both. Then Malender disappeared.

Scout bounded away from the door as if released and thumped into me hard enough we both almost fell over. I dropped a hand to his dense head.

"I think," I said to him, "I've had enough for tonight."

I don't remember what I dreamed when I finally fell asleep again.

"Tessa! Ever getting up?"

Sometime during the night, the pup and I had changed positions for as I pried my eyelids open, we were nose to nose. He had one pillow and I the other. And no matter what anyone says, past a certain age, puppy breath is *not* adorable.

I rolled around him and made it to my bedroom door. "Down as soon as I shower!"

"I'll wait breakfast on you, then."

I yelled out my thanks and headed to the bathroom that serves as mine. Scout slept in, nearly oblivious until I dressed and laced on my shoes at which point he sensed that his own breakfast loomed. He lumbered past me, leaving me in his dust.

This time I put my bracers on and left them on, under the long cotton sleeves of my shirt. Malender had warned me, and it wouldn't be much use if I just shrugged that off. Against what, I'd no idea but any advance notice was appreciated.

Mom, true to her word, sat up straight at the table and smiled softly as the two of us walked in and plunked down. Scout went to his feed bowl, but I sat at my mother's right, as I had done for most of my life.

She'd made an egg and potato scramble that smelled heavenly, with bits of Vidalia onions caramelized and stirred in, and I grabbed for my fork.

She didn't follow suit, so after gulping down my first big bite, I stopped.

"Something wrong?"

"Nothing I can put my finger on."

"Did you sleep well?" I wondered if my nighttime adventures had disturbed her.

"Like a log. No, it's the paper and the committee and . . . stuff."

I stabbed another forkful of eggs and good things but didn't lift it. I wondered if I should tell her about the university personnel I'd seen at the Society or any of the other things that had gone bump in the last few nights. I decided on partial transparency. I waved the fork at her. "Want to know how the meeting went?"

"If it distracts me, yes." She watched me with tired eyes. Normally her eyes blazed blue, but today . . . today they seemed a bit clouded. I hadn't noticed that expression on her face since we'd found out that Dad had sold off the mortgage on our home without telling us.

"They didn't know the professor had completed his ritual."

"Really?" She unfolded her paper napkin with the delicacy others used on linen. "I thought they were supposed to know everything."

"They didn't. And they were all terribly interested in the maelstrom stone."

"Naturally. Did they give you any trouble?"

"No. Inferred but nothing overt. I kept a lot of my ability under my hat, so to speak. It seemed best."

"You're not going back," Mom stated.

"Actually, I might. I've arranged a few lessons that I need. The professor neglected some of my education. However, I think I'll approach the Society cautiously."

"Hmm." She picked up her own fork then.

"There were people there, Mom, that I didn't expect. I recognized some from the university. Like Faith Hawkins."

"Really?"

"Yes, and Nyanga from my campus, even though he runs the custodial department."

She thought about it. "Camouflage?"

"Maybe. Maybe he just enjoys having a relatively stress-free job. The one that worried me is from your area, though."

My mother sighed. "That rather jibes with what's been bothering me. I have this overwhelming sense of disapproval regarding my work. Faith may or may not be on my side. She holds a bit of power, and I've acknowledged that, which pleases her, but . . ."

"Trying to discourage you? It's a little late for that, isn't it?"

"Over a year late. Although I must admit my writing didn't really take off until I changed my main focus last fall. Knowing what I know, I don't think I could write any differently, at least, not on this subject."

"Then plow through. Insist that they finish their review so you can get your diploma."

"And if I get dismissed altogether? No paper, no job?"

I took my bite although it had grown cold. "I graduate in May. We'll move or whatever we need to do. Find work. We've friends now, and connections."

She laughed at that. "We could disappear off the grid altogether."

"We could."

We both started eating then, a little buoyed by our options, and determined to buck tradition as we had done before. The only thing I had to worry about would be leaving my father behind in the cellar.

CHAPTER FOURTEEN

TROUBLE TO THE RIGHT OF ME

THAT'S NOT QUITE how it goes, that earworm stuck in my head from some classic vinyl station my mother listens to, but the lyrics, clowns to the right of me, jokers to the left didn't quite fit what I was feeling. It had to be trouble, and I definitely felt stuck in the middle.

I stood in front of my closet, sorting through clothes that might or might not be appropriate to wear to the Statler Inauguration and wondering how warm/freezing cold the venue would be, and how damaging the shoes would feel to my toes after, oh, say, five minutes, and other crucial fact considerations. What I really searched for was a truly excellent reason not to go, but Evie was counting on me, so I couldn't really devise an alternate plan. Not unless, say, my house blew up or something. Which, after the warning Malender gave me, was not as improbable as it sounded. My bracers were becoming a steady part of my everyday outfit.

Whether I wanted to or not, the Society lessons had become a necessity, if only because I had a need to keep an eye on certain members. I wasn't sure where the threat could be centered, outside of Judge Parker, but he was enough, and if he'd had the likes of Thigpen in his pocket, there would be more. If he had friends in low places, I needed eyes in the back of my head. Although, with Evelyn, I might not need them. Her predictions came true much more often than not, and I had to face the fact that my best friend had become a seer of sorts. Time to give her credit and see if she could help me head off potential disasters.

As if divining that I thought about her, the phone rang. I fished it out of my back pocket and said, "Hi, girlygirl. What's up?"

"Do you think Hiram really wants to host us at a luncheon?"

"Why wouldn't he?"

"I've been a little . . . pushy." And I could hear Evelyn sigh.

Maybe she was coming to her senses. I could hope. "Just a little."

"It's just that everything feels so right!"

"If it is, it will not only last but get stronger."

"You're trying to tell me time won't ruin it."

"Not if it's real," I told her. "And I think it is, you think it is, and I can't speak for Hiram, but he's acting as if it is. Hiram strikes me as the sort who stands by his word whenever he gives it."

Evelyn's voice got very small. "He hasn't told me he loves me."

"Yet. He will. He's taking into account all sorts of things that you don't know about him. He's not a hasty sort."

That brought a little laugh. "You're making him sound like a character out of *Lord of the Rings*."

She wasn't far wrong, but I couldn't tell her that. I left it to Hiram to tell his story. I laughed back at her. "You need to chill, Evie. This is a good thing happening. Stop trying to talk yourself or Hiram out of it, okay?"

"Like you and Carter?"

"We're different but the same. Everything will work out for the best."

"I wish I could believe that, but I have this . . . I don't know. This bad feeling."

I didn't like the sound of that at all. I dug the toe of my shoe into the floor and answered, "Now you're just trying to spook yourself. Cut that out!"

"Yeah, yeah. You're right. I've been jumping at shadows. Talk to you later?"

"Absolutely."

She hung up. About then, a dress fell off its hanger in my closet, and I caught it on the way to the floor. Its light green chiffon draped nicely over my arm. I hadn't ever worn this, a leftover from last spring's big event. About time to give it its day in the sun, I thought, and hung it back up where I could easily find it.

I tried to have no qualms whatsoever about what pulled it off its hanger. Its history, though it shouldn't have had one, because I'd never worn it . . . well, its history bothered me. Joanna Hashimoto had brought it over with a couple of others, including my favorite which I had worn near to death. I hadn't known then that she was anything but a super smart tech kid with a father who owned a country club and several other high-toned businesses . . . nothing about them had suggested that he was a samurai mage and she a three-tailed and very wicked Kitsune. Either one of them would have killed me for the stone, and they were twice as deadly as a team. Just goes to show that one never knows what goes on behind closed doors.

I'd learned that samurai held a vigorous code of honor, but this one hadn't—he was all about power. I'd also been told that Kitsune, Japanese fox goddesses, were wise and good . . . but Joanna had been as corrupt and power-hungry as her father. On any scale, they had a lot: wealth, prestige, intelligence . . . so what made them so hungry? The need to be immortal, I suppose, immortal and unstoppable. I tried not to think about it because there would be no clear-cut answers.

But they were gone now, although I battled Joanna once in a while in my dreams. The pale green dress really did look pretty enough and sedate enough to wear to the mayoral inauguration ceremony. I would show a little neckline and shoulder, and maybe a sweep of my ankles, but the rest seemed pretty conservative. Not that I needed to be conservative, but it was Mrs. Statler's and Evelyn's night, not mine. I patted the dress as I shut the closet door. I'd had Carter as my plus one, but got the feeling he wouldn't make it, not to a high publicity event like this unless he was working it. My mom and I had had each other's backs for years, and she could use a ritzy night out.

Scout let out a sharp bark from the backyard, to let me know he wanted a walk/run and attention, so I went to retrieve him.

Steptoe was waiting for us both when we got inside, me

chafing my hands for warmth and Scout dancing around because he liked to dance.

He'd started a fire in the living room, and I sat cautiously.
The demon looked dreadfully serious, unlike him, and I knew
we were in for more trouble.

CHAPTER FIFTEEN

TWITCHES

"I'VE BEEN THINKING," Steptoe ventured, his hands wrapped around each other as though chilled beyond measure.

Normally, one of us would have teased him, but I was the only one still in the house, and neither of us felt quite like laughing just yet. "Of what?"

"Time to test the old twitches out again."

It had been weeks since we'd tried. At a certain point, there seemed to be no reason to. I poked in a small piece of kindling while I considered it before asking, "What's changed?"

"Outside of a broken latch and a few switched boxes? Nothing. But we won't know for sure unless we go looking."

I couldn't argue with that. "Got an itch?"

Steptoe frowned. "My tail is not to be a subject of your skepticism."

Attitude much? But he seemed to be genuinely upset, and I decided not to rile him up further. "How do you want to go about it, then?"

"Drive around a bit. Circle the city, I'm thinking."

"In case he's here somewhere."

Steptoe nodded. "I can't rightly think he wouldn't come back. He had his roots here for quite a while. And you've got trouble, Tessa. You need him."

I checked my watch. "Well, Mom's at meetings till after six. I've got the time."

We bundled up, or rather I bundled up, Steptoe was always

mostly in his suit although he did add a natty red muffler about his neck before he got in my car. It had begun snowing and then stopped although wind still rippled through all the trees. Clouds had boiled in, turning late afternoon almost as dark as night. I would have to drive cautiously and slowly, which helped the search actually, as long as we had room on the road and didn't stop traffic.

As we pulled out of the neighborhood, I suggested, "Let's start at the church."

"St. John's?"

"That's where it all started, right?"

"A lot of things started there, including bits of the Revolution, but you make a point."

I watched him, side-eye a bit, to see how uneasy it made him. The historic Episcopalian church, famous for Patrick Henry's "Give Me Liberty or Give Me Death" speech was also where the professor had cornered Steptoe and bound him. For decades he'd thought that was where Brandard had also hidden his stolen tail, but that proved not to be true. After the fire that hit the professor's house, while sifting through the ruins, it became clear that the tail had been stored there in his massive desk, in a hidden compartment, until someone else stole it from the ruins. We finally identified it in the hands of dark elves and liberated it after a number of misadventures. But we hadn't been able to break the bond, not even with the professor disappearing.

Our partially redeemed lesser demon was also only partially free. Not an easy state to try and exist in, I knew. He seemed a bit uneasy on the drive to Broad Street, but that could have been alertness for ice on the streets and cars that couldn't maneuver on it. The statues we passed held a gleam of frost on their metallic structures, looking even colder than usual.

Steptoe considered a couple of them as well. "Not nice people," he finally stated. "Don't deserve a memorial."

"Did you know any of them?"

"A few. None of them knew what I was, but they thought me a villain and tried to hire me, now and then, to create a spot of trouble."

That was news to me. "Trouble?"

"Theft, robbery, disruption behind the lines. General mischief. I wouldn't do it, but enough humans answered the call anyway." He gave a sniff. "War is not a noble profession."

I nodded as the stark shadows arrowing across the road worked on my mind as if it tried to remember and couldn't.

We got to the parking lot of the plain white-painted church. It didn't soar like Notre Dame had or rear itself in stone majesty like Westminster Abbey or St. Patrick's Cathedral in New York. Wooden and relatively simply structured, it looked practical and sustaining. Whatever magnificence it carried was on the inside.

I'd been there a few times, school field trips to instill history in us, successfully in the church's case. I'd always been able to feel the weight and importance of a relatively small building in comparison with its place in the scheme of things. I'd also been here once, very quickly, with Steptoe. I didn't expect that today would be any different.

Except that it was. My companion tensed in his seat, both feet pressed downward as if they rode a secondary brake and attempted to push it through the floorboards.

"Steptoe?"

I waited for him to relax or melt or at least acknowledge me before reaching over and putting my hand on his arm. Muscles felt like steel under my touch, but he did turn to me.

"Leave, Tessa. Turn the car around and get out while you can."

"What is it?"

"I'm . . . not sure. But it has nothing to do with our mission. It is far bigger and more dangerous." He moved then, all of him, rocking forward a bit as if he might leap out of the car.

"Drive!"

It seemed best not to argue with him. I put the car in gear, backed up, and sped out of the parking lot. "Where to?"

"Somewhere far from here." He looked over his shoulder, as if transfixed in horror, and unable to look away from whatever caught his attention.

I drove to the Dairy Queen not far from my old high school,

almost diagonally away from the Broad Street church. It was closed for the season and maybe due for some fresh paint before it reopened, but it seemed relatively harmless. More than harmless, it seemed a little forlorn on a wintry day. I shrugged that off as I turned to Steptoe.

"Better now?"

"Too right." He shrugged a bit, as if getting his composure back together. An uneasy ripple followed along his coat, as if it might be echoing his movement or maybe heaving a silent sigh of its own. I often wondered if the coat was like his tail, an extension of whatever his actual form might be.

"What happened?"

"Can't rightly tell you. Creeped out of my gourd, I was." His face closed up a bit in concentration. After a long moment, he faced me. "There's something rotten in Denmark."

"But do you think that's what's been watching the house? Broke our door latch?"

"No way of telling until we run into it." He sniffed. "But it's bad, Tessa, something dark and ugly, hiding, and getting ready to emerge. It's been there since I've been here in the States, but now it's creeping into the open. To pounce, as it were."

"Well, let's hope you're wrong on that score. Still up for cruising the city?"

He reached behind him and curled his tail across one thigh, regarding it sadly. "No use. It's gone dead. Not a twitch in it."

I eyed him dubiously. "You can still move it, right? I mean, it's not really dead."

His tail lashed across his legs. "Affirmative. And yet, it seems to be entirely numb when I think of our crusty old wizard."

"What does that mean?"

"I'll tell you what it doesn't mean. It doesn't mean that he's dead and gone, not by any reasoning. I'm bound. I won't lose that feeling until he is deceased or he destroys the bond."

"I guess that reassures me."

"It's about the only good news either of us is going to get," Steptoe added glumly. He put a hand on the dashboard. "Home is probably best."

He'd lost the ruddy color in his cheeks, so whatever it was

that struck at him from St. John's hadn't left him untouched. I could maybe pry some explanation out of him, but it didn't seem fair. He'd tell me when he was ready about whatever bothered him in addition to what we already had going on. Home did, indeed, seem best.

Or it did until I pulled into the driveway and saw that the kitchen door was once more flapping in the wind.

CHAPTER SIXTEEN

SNITCHES

STEPTOE BEAT ME to the door. "Blimey, I swear I fixed it!"

The door frame hadn't been kicked in or had a tire iron taken to it, but someone had definitely forced an entry. I stood there for a moment, glaring at it. Then I got the great idea to raise my hand and see if the Eyes could help me spot anything. Scout stayed behind me, his muzzle at my knees, and Steptoe behind him. I could hear Steptoe rattling something out of his pockets.

"Got my flash-bangs, dearie, if we need them."

"Good." The stone stayed quiet in my palm, and the eyes shut, so I didn't discern anything unusual. "I want to call Carter."

"Official police?"

"I haven't got a reason until we get inside." Scout pushed his head forward a bit, and I dropped my hand upon his skull.

"Pup doesn't seem too alarmed." I could feel Steptoe shiver next to me. He added, "I think we'd best get inside. It's going to be nasty out here in a few."

"Fine, fine." I crossed the small landing steps and went into the kitchen where I could hear the furnace winding up to blow hot air accommodatingly through the old two-story house. The outside door to the kitchen closed behind us as if it had never been forced. "Traitor," I scolded it.

No sooner had we all entered than the rack on the wall where we kept keys, hats, and a few pots rattled at me.

I blinked. The poltergeist I knew was my dad—and he hadn't

had the energy to rattle at us for weeks. I pushed Scout aside and ran for the cellar door and stairs. I could hear the scrabble of dog toenails after me, as well as Steptoe's leather soles, but I didn't stop until I hit the basement flooring, with the lights going on brightly about me.

The professor's boxes lay scattered about, one had split its cardboard sides, guts spilling out, and not a one remained stacked in place. Whereas the last intrusion had been minor, this was definitely major. Whatever wards had protected it seemed well and truly destroyed. My only questions were who and why.

"Cor," murmured Steptoe. "What's missing?"

"A few books, near as I can tell, although the boxes have all been—I dunno—plundered? Not thoroughly, but not all of them are still taped closed like the other night. And they're all out of order as if someone rummaged about."

"Something particular wanted."

"Yeah." I scanned the basement, wondering if my Sight could catch anything. It did, but only briefly. My dad looked wispier than ever as he gave me a worried frown before winking out. "Thanks, Dad," I told him. "Go get some rest."

I backed up and sat on the bottom step a moment.

"He doesn't look good."

"I know. Believe me, I know. And he's not there enough to tell me what happened, only that it did."

Steptoe put his hand on my shoulder. "We'll make it right, luv."

"Right. Search the rest of the house first, and then I'm calling Carter."

"I'll be directly behind you."

On some other day, that might have struck me a bit funny. Today seemed determined to be altogether different. We left the cellar without putting the boxes in order.

The living room, foyer, and even Mom's downstairs office seemed okay. The small fire Simon had started earlier had burned out. When he made his way toward the backyard, he put his head in the mudroom and muttered, "My cot's in place. Bugger could have made the bed, though."

I gave a little snort. "Like they broke in to do our housekeeping." I took the stairs up two at a time. In the hallway, we could see immediate trouble. The tell-tales lay scattered on the hallway runner, their little bodies wilted and drying. I grabbed them up as quickly as I could while Simon found their vase thrown somewhere down the hall and went to fill it with water. The two of us tucked the flower creatures in, while he gave them a soothing pep talk on how well they'd done and how quickly they'd feel better. I doubted him at first until I saw the browning petals begin to uncurl and gain color back again. I sprinted to the linen closet and pulled out an old towel to mop up the spilled water, wondering why our invader had swept the vase out of its niche. Steptoe had told me once that they could stun when alarmed, but if they had, it hadn't stopped anyone this time.

Steptoe gave the vase a solid pat. "Carry on, then."

Their little rose faces looked almost back to normal, and I felt anxious to examine the rest of the upstairs.

From there, we went room to room. I had a habit of hiding Morty's journal whenever I put it down for any length of time, and found it just where I'd put it, buried in the old athletic shoes and sox compartment of my field hockey gear bag. It smelled like a musty old sock when I pulled it out, but it seemed undisturbed otherwise. Good. I left it near the window which I opened a sliver to air it out.

My companion stopped short at the threshold of the room the professor/Brian had occupied for months. The door stood firmly closed in front of him. I raised an eyebrow at him.

"Warded," he told me. "I can't even touch the doorknob."

"Seriously? It's never bothered me."

"You," he said emphatically, "did not spend centuries sparring with him."

"Or lose."

"Too true, that." He retreated a few steps so I could open the room up.

Fear touched me for a moment. I'd been in and out of that room several times this past week and never felt a thing. But what if I'd been cursed anyway? I shook it off. The professor wouldn't have done that to me. Never. Not in a million years.

I hoped.

I reached for the doorknob, twisted it, and pushed the door open.

The thing I least expected flew up and hit me squarely in the chest. The room looked untouched, absolutely pristine . . . but his cane, his crystal-knobbed blasting rod, was gone.

I got a sound out before Steptoe could move in behind me, but he saw it, too. Or rather, didn't see it.

"Damnitall. The cane's gone. Could it have been the professor?"

"You tell me." I looked pointedly at his tail.

Steptoe twisted about a bit and did the same. "Noooo. No, it probably wasn't."

"And if it had been, why would he break in? Why not just come home and claim it? It's his. Same thing with the boxes in the cellar. It's not like we wouldn't have welcomed him."

Steptoe ran a thumbnail over a bit of shadow on his chin. "If he remembers us."

"Why wouldn't he?"

"The phoenix ritual can be a rough one. Last time he did it, I had three decades without him in m' face. Nice break, that was. Then his recollections came back."

My stomach felt as though it had plummeted toward my feet. "Thirty years? Before he was himself again?"

"Indeed. Of course, times were rough back then. A bit harder to get on your feet and stay out of trouble. He might have just been laying low. We haven't discussed it. I think he was a tad embarrassed about letting me have free rein."

"Well, it could be worse this time. Him or not."

"Why?"

"Because the crystal's gone absolutely clear again, so it's powered up for . . . whatever. Whoever has it can use it for just about any kind of trouble." Worse than that, someone had definitely been in my house again. Where no one should have been but me and my mom and one or two other people we trusted.

We were under siege. I looked at Steptoe over my shoulder. "Would the tell-tales have seen anyone? If they had, would they remember? Could they tell you?"

Wordless for once, he merely shook his head.

"And whoever it was really went after the tell-tales. I don't remember the professor feeling one way or another about them." I let out a sigh. I went into the room and patted the bed-spread down, in case the cane had . . . I don't know . . . rolled under the pillows or off the bed, as if it could move on its own volition. Nothing. The floor stayed empty and silent as well. It was gone, well and truly gone.

"Someone had to know it was here."

"The house is being watched," I told Steptoe.

"It is? Blimey. Those little gits haven't said a word to me." He shook a fist in the general direction of the hallway and the tell-tales.

"Outside their range, maybe? It wasn't close, whatever it was. And whatever it was could have been watching since the professor and then you moved in."

"Gives me the creeps it does."

I gave him a long look. "Simon, you're a demon. What could frighten you?"

"Oh, ducks. I'm a reformed demon, and as things go, I'm way, way down the ladder. I've my tricks and a few of my powers, but I couldn't stand up to an attack of any kind. You want high-powered help, get that Malender of yours to move into the backyard."

"He's not mine." And, after my last run-in with him, I wasn't any more certain of his good/evil alignment than I'd ever been.

Scout gave a woof from downstairs, reminding me. "Could you go feed him? I've got a call to make."

"Will do." He tugged on his suit jacket as if straightening out his whole perspective on the world and left.

I went to my bedroom and sat down on the corner of the bed, pulling out my phone. Rather than call, I typed out a text.

Can you talk? I need to.

And waited.

It rang about five minutes later, but it felt like an eternity.

"Are you all right?" Carter asked.

"Somewhat," I told him. "I have some things to talk over with you."

"You picked a good time to have a crisis. I'm alone and available."

His warm voice and tone enveloped me. I started off with the break-in first, then backed up to the abduction after the Society meeting, and the meet with Malender, and the thing that I'd found watching the house. I left out the stalker and the Butchery, though, uneasy that I might conjure it up by just thinking about it. When I'd finished, I found myself breathless.

He waited a measured moment before saying, "Looks like trouble caught up with you."

"You think? I don't know what to do."

"You've been minding your own business?"

"As much as I ever do. You know me."

A soft laugh that gave me a shiver, even over the telephone. I added, "I miss you."

"I miss you, too. Any idea about who would have taken the professor's cane?"

"Not a one." Then one did come to me, absolutely unbidden. "Unless it was a harpy. They fought us for it in New York last year." It didn't seem all that long ago, but Morty had been alive then and things had happened.

"That's right." He'd forgotten, it seemed. "But the nests around locally have been pretty upset and disorganized. Goldie's been taking them apart. I doubt one of them would have dared a heist."

"All the more reason they felt they might need a blasting rod." She had never forgiven her sisters for turning on her, and if there were any traitors left, she seemed determined to root them out.

He made a noncommittal sound, not all that convinced, I realized. I added, "If not the harpies, who?"

"Dark elves possibly. Devian is gone for now, but he had ambitious elves watching him, I'm certain."

"Oh." I didn't like the sound of that. "Would Scout have alerted us to them?"

"Hard to tell. Not unless you'd had unpleasant dealings with someone specific before and he had a scent to remember. Listen, I might come by later, but it'll be very late, middle of the night. There's a spell I can put on the room if you close the door and leave it alone."

"Both Simon and I have been in there."

"That shouldn't throw it off too much."

"Can you really come by?"

"For you, I can."

"All right, then." We murmured a few other things to each other and hung up.

We didn't bother pretending to each other that things were all right. I was worried about him, and Carter was now worried about me.

My mother still hadn't come home from the university, so we returned to the cellar to put the boxes back in their correct array. First, I strapped them back together. Then, I started stacking on my own and pointed out to Steptoe what went where. After one or two switch-arounds, he straightened and peered at me.

"They're just boxes. What's the point?"

"I dunno. It's just that . . . well, this belongs here and that one belongs there, and the leaky one is at the bottom corner, there."

"You remember this—why?"

I couldn't tell him exactly how, only that I felt extremely uneasy if they were stacked any other way.

He jutted his chin at my left hand. "It's the stone, luv, and those eye shards of Nimora. Their memory is set in marble, as it were, and don't like to be changed out."

I looked at my palm, where the Eye of Nimora remained stubbornly shut, but the maelstrom had warmed slightly. "Maybe," I admitted. I pointed. "Put that one there."

A little bit of sweat ran down his right temple. He made a slight face. "You do it."

I gave him a look, but I did it. I had forgotten that the many wards down here probably made him prickly, uncomfortable, and a bit jumpy. I waved at Simon. "You go on up, I'll finish."

He lunged for the stairs. At the very top, he leaned down

and said, "Colder than a monkey's brass ass up here. What's for dinner?"

"Get out a jar of the tomato puree Aunt April gave us, and a small jar of the roasted red pepper, too. I'll make soup and grilled cheese sandwiches."

He disappeared, and I could hear the upstairs door click shut.

I muscled the boxes into order and stepped back. Without the eye shards opening, I couldn't see my father, but I could feel a faint chill lingering in the air, colder than the wintry outside, creeping in.

"Thanks, Dad, for warning us. I'm sorry you were here to see all this happening." I sat down on the bottom stair step. Without warning, I could feel my eyes sting as tears began to slowly roll down my face. "I have Morty's journals. They're packed with information and detail, and it's like wading through red clay mud. I haven't found anything about you yet, just Potion Polly and that's too far back. But I'll find it, I promise. I did this to you, and I won't stop till I can undo it. I won't!"

I brushed my arm over my eyes, wiping away the wetness with my sleeve before turning and fleeing upstairs myself.

DINNER WENT WELL, and I put the lid on the pot of soup and tucked the whole thing into the fridge so Mom could warm it herself when she got home. Bagged the grilled cheese sandwich left over—I'd had to wrestle it from Steptoe—refrigerated it as well, and left a note under one of the many magnets on the freezer's door. It was too early to go to bed, but I did anyway, with the idea of doing more reading.

I fell into an uneasy sleep instead. I kept trying to catch Steptoe's wildly thrashing tail and missing, even as something dark and dreary chased us. No idea where those dreams came from, right?

A tap-tap kept interrupting my dreams. Finally, it was irritating enough that I jolted awake, shutting my mouth and wiping away a bit of drool from the corner. The entire house seemed enveloped by the deepest of night. Even Scout, sprawled across the lower corner of my bed, seemed dead to the world. I watched his rib cage rise and fall in slumbering breaths to make sure he was okay, before sliding my feet from under the covers and sitting up.

My phone stayed dim on the nightstand. I didn't dare set it to silenced hours, in case one of my odd friends needed help whenever. But it hadn't sounded either.

Tap TAP.

I struggled to the window, rubbing one stubborn eye awake and then the other, where I saw, like something out of a Stephen King novel, a figure floating outside.

Carter waved at me as soon as he saw the curtains part. I opened the window to remove the screen to swing out on the sill. His hands went to my waist, lifting me up, and I discovered he hadn't levitated at all, but climbed a ladder up. He carried me down carefully while I held my breath lest I topple us both to the ground.

When my bare feet hit the frosty grass, I shivered. He held his hand up, and I saw a key in his hold. "Don't want to wake Mary. Let's go talk here," and he led the way to my little car, opening it.

"Where'd you get the spare key?"

"You have one of those magnetic key boxes fixed under the passenger fender."

"I do?"

"Well, the professor did. I don't think anybody's used it in years. I'll put it back when we're ready."

I yawned in spite of myself and could feel my cheeks warm in mild embarrassment.

"I'm sorry I woke you."

"I knew you were coming. I just thought I could read until you got here. Who knew that reading Morty would put me to sleep!" I yawned again and wrinkled my nose in irritation.

"It's stress," he said. "Normal reaction."

"To abnormal events." I rubbed an eyebrow that seemed to have developed a tic. "Look, I don't know what you're investigating, but does it overlap any of my trouble?"

He shook his head. "Doubtful. I mean, it might. Richmond has a rich and varied history, as much of it underground as above, but I'm not seeing any warning signs."

"I haven't been turning any rocks over. At least, not on purpose."

"We don't know what your dad was about when he disappeared. It could have been pressure from his gambling, or it could have been supernatural."

"I'm voting for supernatural because of what happened."

"He might have triggered that himself, trying to get out from under. There's a strain of witchery that runs through his family."

I rolled that word around in my thoughts, uncertain if I liked it or not. "Maybe that's what attracted the stone."

"Very likely. You had potential, buried, and it sought that out. What I don't understand is how you found the object hidden here, and why John hadn't used it to leverage himself out of trouble when he could."

"Maybe he tried using the Dark Arts book instead."

Carter tilted his head slightly. For a very brief moment, I could see the other side of him, the side Goldie referred to as a sun lion, shining through. "No," he said shortly. "He should have known that way would lead to substantial trouble."

"It seduced me into finding and hiding it."

He waved a hand. "You hardly knew what you were dealing with. Your father knew; he'd been handling it for years, although they didn't know what they had, exactly."

"Not to cast spells."

"No, he and your Aunt April used it more like a lucky rabbit's foot. Totally unwise for what it is. It has to have plagued the family for a few generations."

My eyebrow tic worsened. "There are early deaths in the family tree."

Carter nodded. "It does take a toll. Luckily, Steptoe and the professor shielded it from you. Near as we can tell, you got the sheer energy but not the evil intent."

"It made a sorceress out of me," I reminded him.

He rubbed his hand over my shoulder. "I think you'd have become one, anyway. You're remarkable."

I muttered a wow, which I don't think he heard, as he stared out the windshield which had begun to fog slightly on the inside. Louder, I said, "Where do we go from here?"

"We find out what's been watching you, and why . . . and who broke in, and why."

"The cane isn't reason enough?"

"Whatever it was, the intruder might have found it, entirely

THE WAYWARD MAGE
149

by accident, canvasing the house. Didn't Goldie warn you that the dwarves had a traitorous streak?"

I sat back. I'd forgotten that. "She sure did. Do you think it could have been one of them?"

"The wards in your cellar were placed by the Broadstone crew and they're not likely to have affected anyone from one of the other clans. They're not used to thinking of themselves as one of the enemy." He shifted. "I don't think they'd have been watching the house, though."

"No." The spindly silhouette I'd seen had been anything but a square and blocky Iron Dwarf. Traitor or not, I'd never felt evil incarnate from any of them. "But they could have ransacked the cellar and bedroom, though?"

"Highly likely. I think the cane was taken to negotiate with. Tessa, it's highly likely that Goldie inherited something additional from Mortimer that she shouldn't have been given—"

"And they want it back."

"Precisely. You need to find out what. And I need to find out who and why something is shadowing you. What was it Malender told you again?"

My mouth went dry. I recalled the exact words, words which I had tried to forget, and couldn't. "You and yours have been marked for both Death and Justice. You must take very close care of those you love."

The words hung in the air.

Finally, Carter cleared his throat. "Exactly?"

"Word for word."

"His saying Justice is interesting."

"Telling me someone wants us dead is interesting?" My voice went up and, I think, even squeaked a little on the last of that. He reached for my hands and grabbed them tightly. He felt warm even as I shook with a sudden chill. I could take care of myself, but my mother was a vulnerable target.

"We don't know who or what Malender is, but I think that pronouncement of his is finally revealing."

"That someone put a death judgment on us, yeah."

"He didn't come to carry it out. If he had, you wouldn't be sitting here with me."

"Thanks."

Carter pulled me close. "Listen to me. Did he carry a weapon of any sort?"

His shoulder muffled my answer. "Like a flaming sword? No, but he has a wicked looking whip now. Something from medieval times. I googled it . . . a scourge. Barbed thorns and actual flames." I felt like I could bury my face against his chest and shoulder forever and be safe, but he pushed me back a little, peering into my eyes.

"You saw it?"

"Of course, I freaking saw it. Do you think I could make anything like that up?"

He studied me for a few seconds longer. "No," he answered. "I can't see you making that up. That makes him, if I'm right, an ancient deity. A demigod."

"Of what? Whips and lace?"

"This is serious. He metes out what he perceives as Justice and Punishment. He's warning you that you are someone's target and may become his."

I tucked my chin in. "I set him free." My tone made it clear that I thought he owed me.

"Of the shroud?"

"I salted him until it disintegrated."

Carter winced. "Then he may consider his warning to you nothing more than a discharge of his debt to you."

"A warning for his freedom?"

"Old gods have very strict viewpoints."

That tic in my eyebrow gave a mighty twitch; I rubbed it, hard. "So what you're saying is that the next time I see Malender, I should duck and run?"

"A good idea if you'll remember it." He let go of me entirely then, and I immediately missed the wash of warmth and strength. I folded my arms in front of me in a vain attempt to keep it. I had more on my mind but couldn't decide how to say it. He seemed to sense my tentative silence.

"What else?"

"I never told my mother about the fight I had with my dad."

"I know it wasn't part of the police report."

And he would know that because he'd been part of the follow-up team when my dad was finally reported missing. I hadn't told him then, either, because I didn't want to be a Person of Interest, and guilt already festered around me.

Carter added, "None of the neighbors said anything about an argument, and I only have hints from you."

"We had an early spring thunderstorm that night. Loud and flashy. I doubt they would have heard me screaming at him." I fought for a breath as my chest went tight. "I threw him out. I was writing checks to go with my college applications, from my own account, and he stopped me. Told me I had no money left. He'd taken it all. Stole it. Not only could I not pay for my applications, but at least two full years of part-time work had disappeared, too. I didn't know then that he'd also raided the mortgage equity . . . everything. I just know that I felt he'd attacked me. So I attacked back. He was my dad and I loved him, but he'd done this awful thing. He'd ruined what I'd planned for my future. I couldn't hear one thing he'd said, the excuses, the promises. I just screamed him down and threw him out. He went. And that is the last we saw of him."

"Mary never knew?"

"No. I couldn't tell her." I curled up both hands at my chest, as if to protect myself. "I don't want her to know what I did. And I couldn't tell you then, either. I'm a horrible, terrible person." I turned my face away from him, afraid I'd see agreement in his expression.

"No, you're not."

"I have to be! Look what happened."

"It was his job to be the parent, not yours. He should have protected you with all that he could manage—that's part of the job title. You can't carry that burden, Tessa. You were never meant to, and you shouldn't. You didn't plan to react the way you did, but we both know he'd already been through a few years of lying and denial. You just ran into it face-first, and hard." He shifted his hands to rub my shoulders.

He continued. "I'm a cop. I understand perfectly why you couldn't tell me then. People don't always lie. More often, they omit. I knew you wanted him back when we were investigating.

I also knew that teenagers can say the angriest things. Any parent knows that." He paused before adding, "I won't say you didn't do anything, but I know you're not responsible for his disappearance. He turned to someone or something he never should have, because he'd put himself in a desperate situation. I think he tried to make it right, and it failed. That's not on you." Drawing close, he kissed the top of my head to try and soothe me. "But you should tell your mother. One way or the other. If you bring your dad back, or if you fail and we lose him, she should still know the truth. This is a weight you shouldn't keep carrying."

"I'm not despicable?"

"Never."

I took a quavering breath then. "I should tell her."

It hadn't been a question, but Carter answered. "Yes, you should. You may very well find that your mother had some idea. She's a wise woman. Anything else on your mind?"

I had not yet told him everything, particularly about the Butchery. I couldn't prove it had happened, and I didn't want him suspecting my soundness of mind any more than he already did. Which he didn't, I felt sure, but who wanted to take a chance? I needed him to trust me and felt that I'd already pushed that boundary a bit with Malender and my father. I sat up straight. "What else do you think I should do?"

"You've two problems: your dad's predicament and your break-in."

"No, three."

"Three?"

"Evelyn and Hiram."

Carter did a double take. "What about Evelyn and Hiram?"

"Their love at first sight, Romeo and Juliet worthy, is sticking and she wants me to run interference with her family."

"Good gods. And you agreed to this?"

I shrugged a little, saying, "She's awfully hard to refuse."

"Does she know anything at all about Hiram? Really know?"

"He hasn't told her, and I haven't."

Carter gave a faint growl. "Well, somebody needs to. The Statlers are going to be very powerful politically, and the Iron

Dwarves already are. We don't want heads butting. Can't you talk her out of it?"

"I don't think so." I thought it over more. "And Hiram is just as crazy about her, so it's not entirely her fault."

"Fault is not what's important here. Reality is. You're talking about two worlds colliding and disastrously so. Hiram is an outstanding young man, but there are those in his clans who may well kill to keep their secrets. You have to talk her into being sensible."

"But you and I—"

"Are entirely two different beings, Tessa. Promise me you'll talk to her?"

I didn't want to. I couldn't see myself breaking Evelyn's heart—or Hiram doing that to her, either. My eyebrow gave one last final twitch as I mumbled a half-hearted vow to do something.

I just didn't promise what.

HE RETURNED ME to my window as quietly as we'd exited. Leaning in, he gave me a long and simmering kiss, and I didn't want to let go of him. The warmth inside of me flared a bit. He pulled back reluctantly with a soft smile. "Someday—but today is not that day—I won't have to say goodbye to you."

"Promise?"

"Always."

And then he was gone, and the ladder quietly disappeared from the side of the house as well. I sat on the corner of my bed, feeling a bit unbalanced. Scout still hadn't turned a paw in my absence, so I padded down to the kitchen to get some juice and noticed in relief that my mother had come home. The soup pot stood in part of the sink, soaking for cleaning in the morning, and she'd made a few extra grilled cheese sandwiches beside the leftover I'd fixed for her because bread had disappeared and the skillet was dirtied, too. Oddly enough, there were two soup bowls also soaking. I'd loaded mine and Steptoe's, and stood looking at her dirty dishes in slight surprise before deciding that Simon had probably had a second dinner. He didn't have a digestive system like we did, and I think he burned every last molecule for energy every time he ate. Like my Scout, his appetite qualified as voracious. Hiram's wasn't skimpy either. Luckily, they wouldn't eat us out of house and home; they brought groceries as often as they shared meals with us, and right now our bank account had a comfortable pad. May it stay that way.

I found the glass juice pitcher, poured myself three fingers, drank it, and headed back upstairs. Somewhere close to my bedroom door I found myself wondering if my mom had entertained a different guest.

That kept me wide awake for about three minutes, but I gave up thinking to dive back into my bed, nicely warmed by one sprawled golden dog body.

The morning breakfast came accompanied with a nice thick stack of paper, bound in a card stock wrapper. I stared at it. "Wow. Is that it?"

Mom bustled around the kitchen as if she had energy to spare. "It is, indeed."

"Where does it go now?"

"To the university printers if Faith delivers the disk as she should. It will be ready when I walk in early May." She stopped at my elbow. "It's been a long time coming."

"But worth it, right?" I hefted the manuscript. "Copies?"

"They made about twelve. Six to the committee members, two to me, and four for . . . well, I don't know who those are meant for, but they're only photocopies. It's the bound ones that will take my breath away." She looked down at me. I could see some silvery hairs among her natural blonde, and a few fine lines at the corners of her brilliant blue eyes, and something else. Satisfaction? A job finished and done well? We didn't have a lot of successes in our lives that we could enthusiastically point to; like most people, we just kept surviving with our heads above water. But this was a real achievement.

"Congratulations doesn't say enough."

"We should celebrate, right?"

"We should!" I dug my phone out of my pants pocket. She reached over my shoulder and pushed my wrist to the tabletop.

"Phone later, breakfast now. And I've already put kibble down for Scout. Simon's nowhere to be seen, so it's just the two of us."

The animal in question wiggled his butt as he sat next to the now very empty bowl and looked at me as if he'd been neglected. I pointed at him. "You get my toast corners. That's it."

He licked his lips in anticipation.

I dug into my breakfast as Mom sat down opposite and, every once in a while, one of us would look at the binder and let out this crazy, crooked grin. Mine faded as I considered what Carter and I had discussed. I put my fork down.

She noticed the change in my mood immediately. "What is it?"

"How can you tell it's anything?"

"You get a shadow in your eyes. And a few bags underneath. I can always tell when you haven't slept well. I usually chalk it up to our varied group of friends, many of whom seem to be primarily nocturnal. But mainly, now, you look worried."

"Ain't that the truth." I traced my finger over a pattern in my paper napkin. "Dad's not doing well."

She stopped with her hand in midair. "Are we losing him?"

Words jammed together in my throat. I nodded instead.

She put her cup down. "What can we do?"

"I don't know."

"Who would know? Carter? Hiram and his clan? The professor if we could find him?"

I managed a shrug, still fighting with the lump of words, and ended up just shaking my head.

"I thought that you thought that Mortimer might have observed something, noted something in his journal."

I grabbed for my juice and gulped down a big swig of slightly sweet and acidic orange juice. Winter season oranges were never as good as spring and summer. My tongue stung a bit. "Nothing yet," I managed. "And there's something else I need to tell you."

Her gaze narrowed ever so slightly.

I didn't want to say it, but I had to. "I chased him out of the house when I found out he'd emptied my college fund."

"And where was I at the time?"

THE WAYWARD MAGE

157

"Evening office hours. I think you were trying to talk a student out of dropping too late and getting a horrible grade on his record."

She slid her hand over the table to mine and gripped me. "Honey, I'm sorry. So, so sorry he did that to you."

"No. No, no—you don't get it. *I* did that to *him*."

"Don't think that. Ever. I knew something was going on and should have called him on it before it got that far. You reacted."

"I overreacted."

"Maybe. But it wasn't your fault then, and it isn't now. Your dad caused most of his own problems, and I got tired of running interference for him. I loved him, but—"

"But?"

"It was like watching an alcoholic drown in booze. I couldn't make myself step in and stop it. I kept hoping that he'd come to his senses. I did love him. Yet he'd changed so much . . ." Her voice trailed off.

Her hand, tight on mine, felt a little chilled. I hesitated before asking, "Would you have left him?"

"Not then. I might have, but he left us first, didn't he? Long before you told him to leave. I don't know what I would have done. If you get him back now, will he be the man I married, the man who was your father, or the man who couldn't stop gambling?"

"I think he deserves a chance."

"You would. Then give him that chance, if you can. But don't beat yourself up if you can't. I think it would be cruel to keep him trapped in limbo."

"Do you believe in hell?"

She took her hand away. "Not exactly. But if I did, I think that's where he's been for the last few years, don't you? Not able to return or move forward. I think he'd tell you to do what you have to do."

"If only I knew what that was."

She got up, put her tea in the microwave to heat it up again, and said, her back to me, "You'll figure it out."

The appliance dinged, masking my reply, which was probably

wise because she hated hearing me say things like, "Whatever the fuck that might be."

I was handling the laundry when Evie called. I'd been out for a long run, winter day or not, because when the semester started, I knew coach would be jogging our legs off, season or no season for field hockey. I pried my phone out of my pocket. Not a good sign, that. I might have to start running on a daily basis. My jeans shouldn't be quite that tight.

"Tessa, Tessa, Tessa!"

"Ohh-kay. That would be me."

"Did you get the invite?"

I glanced around the laundry room before answering, "What invite?"

"Party, this weekend, Hiram."

"Oooooh."

Evelyn pounced. "Good oh or bad oh?"

"Neutral. Meaning, at least I know why you're so excited and I may have to turn the volume down." I stopped sorting clothes for a minute and leaned one hip against the washing machine as it churned. "Is this the big everybody-meet-everybody luncheon?"

"It is!"

It looked to me like this was going to be my week for coming clean. I was going to have to pull her aside and tell her about the birds and the bees and fairies and magic. "Saturday?"

"Yes. Late lunch, around three PM. You're coming, right? And your mother?"

"Wouldn't miss it." Actually, I would if I could, but only because I'd met my quota of running into brick walls this month and it was still really early in January. "Don't embarrass me by asking him to marry you again."

Evelyn's voice dropped a tone. "I won't. That was really stupid of me, wasn't it?"

"Not stupid, just extremely premature. If he's the one, you've got time to get to know him first."

"With these butterflies?"

"I think those butterflies might be hormonal."

"Never!" But Evelyn laughed. It was good to hear that rather than a frantic explanation of why things had to be the way they were, from her point of view. Maybe there was hope for her yet.

The dryer buzzed. "Gotta go, I need to lay these clothes out so they don't wrinkle. I'll give you a call when I get my own invitation."

"Done deal!" She signed off, and I bent over to disperse the load. I wouldn't get the mail for a few hours yet, so I buried myself in chores.

As it turned out, it didn't come in the mail. Hiram delivered our invitation in person, our front porch groaning a bit as he ascended it and stood at our front door, very formal.

The dryer buzzed again from the laundry room in the back as I opened the house for him. "Is this about Saturday?"

"It is. And I hate to trouble you, but I need a word or so."

"Hiram! If you're trouble, I need more of it. We've biscuits and jam left over from breakfast—go help yourself while I move the clothes over?"

"I will, indeed. Peach jam?"

"Raspberry. Home put up."

He smiled broadly. "Don't mind if I do!"

When I showed up at the kitchen table, he had a spread of biscuits, two kinds of jam, one jar of honey, and a pot of wonderful-smelling coffee brewing.

He also had my mother's binder under his left hand, a third of it read. He closed it and put it aside when I sat down. His brows had settled deeply over his eyes.

I buttered a warm biscuit half, discovered he'd found peach jam in the pantry, and decorated my snack. "Everything all right?"

"So far."

He didn't look it, and I wasn't convinced, but Iron Dwarves weren't easy to pry words out of if they don't want to talk.

"Evelyn is excited."

"I know." His face twisted wryly for a few brief seconds. "Any chance you could calm her down?"

"I will do my best." I dusted crumbs off my fingers. "I'm glad you're doing this. It's really important to her."

"I am honored to be in her regard."

"Don't sound so stuffy. She's crazy about you, and I know you care for her."

"I do. I'm aware. I'm just not certain . . ." His gaze dropped.

I leaned forward and supplied an ending to his sentence. "That you have a future together?"

"Aye, that would be it."

"So, you should quit it if you haven't got the courage to stay in it."

"Well, now . . . I don't like hearing that. Broadstones are not quitters."

I decided to point out the obvious. "Nor are they mired in convention. Look at your own father. He fell in love with a harpy, no matter what the others said."

Hiram sat very silent for a long moment, an index finger ticking on the kitchen table. He cleared his throat. "He did, did he not?"

"He certainly did. And although they had their troubles, I venture to say they loved and respected each other in their own ways for decades. Goldie speaks very highly of him."

"I wouldn't want to live separately the way the two of them did."

"I shouldn't imagine Evie would either. It's a little early to be thinking about that now, though."

"I like to plan for contingencies." He devoured a raspberry jam biscuit in one bite.

"My advice would be to take it slowly and carefully, at least until after Statler's inauguration in two weeks. If you rock that boat, all your hopes will sink. Evelyn won't be able to save either of you."

"He's a strong man."

"And powerful. If you have to go up against him, it will be like those rams that butt heads against each other for days."

"Bighorn sheep."

"Those would be the ones."

Hiram laughed. "You've the right of that one. We would, indeed, butt heads until one of us fell over."

"Not good for anyone."

"No." Hiram's gaze drifted downward, glancing over my mother's dissertation, and I thought I saw a wince. He pushed away from the kitchen table. "I'll see the two of you?"

"Long as we have an address."

He dropped a gold-edged envelope on the table. "Now you do." He gave a bow. "Thank your mother for the biscuits. She has a delicate hand with them."

He left, the house softly creaking with each footstep as he did.

I picked up the invitation and slid it open to stare at the address, not at all surprised to find that he owned an estate house in a very good part of town, edged with woods and bordered by a small creek, and likely to have cost more than I could possibly imagine. I would definitely have to have a sit-down with Evelyn before the dinner.

I could hear Mom vacuuming somewhere in the living room and what passed for a parlor/dining room, heralded by Scout's somewhat panicky retreat to the upstairs. Brave as my dog could be, he'd never quite gotten used to the vacuum cleaner. I followed him up, determined to get that journal and more reading done.

Flopping down in my chair, feet up, dog at one knee, I pulled the journal into position . . . and then noticed a ragged edge of a page I hadn't ever seen before peeking out of the top. I leafed forward and back until I found the damage. Someone had ripped nearly an entire page out of the journal, something I had never noticed before. The spine held a ragged, jagged edge, of which only one word could be seen. Half a word, in truth. A name? A description? Nic—whatever. I stared at it and then read forward and afterward quickly to see if I could pick up the full name and context.

I finally dropped the journal on my lap. Someone had been into Mortimer's diary in the last few days. Someone didn't want me learning what the journal could teach me.

HARD AS IT was to skim through the entries, because Mortimer wrote in great blocks of exposition and description, I went through the next thirty pages as quickly as I could, hoping to pick up some sense of whatever it was that had been torn out.

He did mention a "great blight" upon the city and territory of Richmond, and he didn't refer to the Civil War, near as I could tell. He was writing about the last fifty years or so, although the root of the blight went back to the founding of the country itself. That sent a shiver down the back of my neck. I closed the journal around my finger to bookmark it and considered his writing. If he meant a person, it would have to be someone like himself, or Steptoe, or the professor. Someone or something with a lifespan covering centuries. Or a dynasty of power. Either way, it would be formidable. Someone or something that would think nothing of getting me out of its way. Or my father. Or anyone who was a mere mortal. The realization gave me a chill that sank into me and wouldn't let go.

Had that blight sent an agent into my house? Why not take the entire diary? Well, no. That would have immediately set off questions. But whoever had ripped out the page hadn't done it neatly, and I might never have noticed it otherwise because I usually skimmed Mortimer's words, looking for only the essential bits that might apply to my father. No one could know my method unless they'd been reading over my shoulder—at that thought, I did look over my shoulder in case something invisible resided in the corner of my room—sheer idiocy, but I felt spooked. My prowess with my stone shields and my field hockey stick only went so far in defensive work.

And, it seemed, I wouldn't be able to trust the Society either for lessons or schooling.

I got up. Scout followed me downstairs, watching quizzically as I stuffed the journal into a bag and then hid the bag inside a half-full cereal box in the pantry. Not terribly original, I admit, but what agent of a centuries-old blight would be that familiar with modern American cereals?

Then I trotted downstairs to look at the professor's stack of boxes. The sound of someone rattling around in the kitchen reached me. "Mom?"

"No, ducks, it's me," Steptoe called down. "Problem?"

"No." I thought about it. "Yes. Come down for a moment?"

He cleared his throat and came down the stairs slowly. "It's like being scalded," he told me.

"You didn't say anything earlier."

"Earlier we knew the house had been broken into." He chafed his arms a bit. "What is it?"

"I need the boxes the way they were."

"All scattered about? Are you bat-shit crazy?"

"Probably. I don't want them shoved about, but in the order . . . do you remember what we found where? Not the proper order but the mismatched order."

Steptoe humphed. "Since it's you, I could. And will." He bent over and unstacked the boxes. I helped getting them all on one level and then sorted again into the way we'd found them, although much neater. Scout whined once or twice from the stairs. I stood back and looked at them.

"Nope," I decided. "Back the way they were."

Steptoe rolled a dark eye at me. "Seriously?"

"Yes." I bent over and began to move and stack boxes myself. After making a disgruntled noise, he joined me.

He stood and clapped his hands on his trousered thighs when we'd finished. "Done?"

"I think so."

"And what was the point of all that?"

"Someone didn't want me getting into the professor's things."

"No? Then why did we just play *Jenga* with them?"

"They were mixed up, deliberately out of order. Whoever did it, hadn't planned that either you or I had a sharp enough memory to put them back in their proper place. At first, I thought the mess was deliberate, and it was, as messes go. But this order is deliberate, too. You and I both remembered it keenly. We put everything back in place expertly. Why?"

"I don't know about you," said Steptoe with a sulky curl to his bottom lip, "but I'd find it hard to forget now."

"Yes, but under normal circumstances, we'd have hardly paid attention to any of them, except for the leaker. Yet we did. Keen attention. As if they'd been bespelled." I put my hand out. "Got a pocket knife on you?"

He stared at me. "Why?"

"I'm going to cut that one open." I pointed at a box on the upper end.

He flexed his hand, and a nail lengthened into an impressive razor-sharp point. "That one?" he confirmed before stepping forward and slicing it free. He waved his hand, and the nail disappeared.

I took a minute to handle my shock and surprise before approaching it and unfolding its cardboard ears to see what lay inside. I have to admit, I forget from time to time what Steptoe is and what he might be capable of. I reminded myself that it would be careless to do so again. His menace didn't simmer just under the surface the way Malender's did, but he was, when all was said and done, a demon.

And right now, a slightly discomfited one.

The books inside still smelled a bit of smoke and water from the fire which had destroyed the professor's home. Their spines were mottled, titles and authors near impossible to read. I dipped a hand inside, still operating on what I could only call instinct. Something resided inside this box that I wasn't supposed to find.

"What are you looking for?"

I glanced quickly at Steptoe. "Harry Potter's Defense Against the Dark Arts textbook."

His jaw dropped for a moment as he stumbled for a word, and then he simply shut his mouth and said nothing at all. While he went silent, a book seemed to rise up out of its position and into the fingers of my hand. I pulled it the rest of the way out and examined its front cover.

"The Enemy and How to Defeat It," I read.

Steptoe visibly paled. He tried to reach around me. "I think that should go back in its carton."

I held it out of his reach. "Why?"

He mumbled something I couldn't understand.

"What?"

"Starting a war, are you? That's the only thing that book is good for."

I thought about Malender's chilling warning. Someone had marked us for harm. "I think this book might possibly be perfect. Let me tell you why . . ."

"Can you tell me upstairs? This is getting to me." He chafed his suit coat sleeves again, and he did look a bit frazzled, his normally wavy hair gaining strands that seemed to want to float off by themselves.

I locked the box flaps into place and waved him to lead the way. Halfway up, I turned about. "Don't worry, Dad. I have this handled."

I didn't, not yet, but I would.

Steptoe didn't like a word I said about the journal which had been altered. He sat and simmered, rather like a pot put on to boil, and I wondered if steam would come out of his ears as I finished.

"You didn't tell me most of that earlier."

"I told you about the Butchery, even when I thought I couldn't tell anyone."

A sound came from the kitchen doorway. My mother entered and sat down, her chair scraping across the floor as she did.

The two of them traded looks. "She's been holding out on us."

"That she has."

I thumped the book which now rested on the kitchen table. "Not anymore."

My mother took a deep breath. "What about the Butchery, again?"

"It's a bar. A popular night spot at the edge of Old Town, but I saw things there that nobody should ever see. People on hooks hanging from the ceiling, like meat carcasses, but they were . . . alive. Mostly. Ordinary people. I couldn't help them. I had to run or be caught up myself."

"Actual bodies?"

"More like souls, I think now." A shudder ran through me.

"Should you call the police?"

"I don't think so. It's more like it resides in two worlds at once. Ours and its. I doubt if anyone would find anything." I looked at my mother. "You already know magic has a dark side."

"Yes, but I didn't think I'd find you wandering about in it!"

"I'm not. But . . ." I flipped my left hand over, palm up. "This is power. People will cheat and kill for power. That's nothing new."

"What are you going to do about it?"

"I'm going to study this book and then, when we go out to dinner Saturday night, I'm going to make sure the Iron Dwarves promise to help."

Steptoe thought on that a bit. He nodded to my mother. "Might be a bright idea, that. They're judges but also a bit on the marshaling side of things."

"More than the Society?"

"Heaps more."

She rubbed the bridge of her nose as if a headache might be settling there. "All right then." She stood, pointing at me. "No more midnight rambles without telling me where and why you're going."

"Yes, ma'am."

"I mean it."

"And so do I." I nodded sharply. I noticed then she'd dressed for the office. "Where are you off to?"

"Campus. The university is starting a roster of on-line courses, and I've been asked to train for it."

"Wow. They're really moving into the twenty-first century."

She gave a half-laugh. "I'm not sure it's an honor. I think most of the teachers are too unfamiliar with the Internet to be useful."

"Well, that's not you."

"Not at the moment. We'll see how well I cope once the instruction gets going. We only have a few weeks before the spring semester starts. Today we show up, and tomorrow morning the IT team goes to work showing us what to do and how to work with their programs."

"You'll be great," I told her.

"Remote learning. It could just be a phase."

"At least, you're still teaching."

"For the moment." She waved and went out the kitchen door to the driveway, and we could hear her car leave. And I realized I'd missed yet another chance to ask her if she'd had company the other night. I huffed at myself for being careless.

Steptoe swung around in his chair. "You do know how much trouble you've been in?"

"Trust me, I know."

"We can't help if you don't spill the goods."

I moved around the kitchen, restoring lids to jam jars and putting them away, sweeping crumbs off the table, and generally just not looking him in the eyes.

"Tell Carter any of this?"

"I did, yes. Finally."

"Good. 'Cause I'd hate for him to blame me if something happened to you."

"He won't."

Steptoe's face sagged into unhappy lines. "Sooner or later, everyone always blames the demon." His tail wilted.

I took the dirty dishes from him, loaded the washer, and decided we had enough to run a cycle. "Where did you run off to?"

"When?"

"Earlier."

"You might say I had a bit of demon business to attend to." He rocked back in his chair.

"And did you?"

"Not exactly."

I saw a gleam in his eyes. "What, then?"

"You know that black sooty stuff that leaks from one of the professor's boxes?"

I nodded.

"I got a bit on my handkerchief, right, and took it to a friend to be analyzed," he said proudly.

"You did? And what did they say?"

Steptoe cleared his throat. "Vampiric dust."

"Vam what?"

"Vampiric dust."

I sat down quickly, asking, "What on earth is that?"

"In great quantities, it can be a shroud, like the one wot covered Malender." A bit of his cockney accent sneaked into his words.

"Imprisoned him," I corrected. "Well, he's shed of it now, one way or the other."

"True right. You have anything to do with that?"

"Salt."

His eyebrow waggled in surprise. "Salt? Must have been a ton of it, then."

"Close." I flexed my left hand about the maelstrom stone. "Why would the professor have anything like that in his goods?"

"Ever see Peter Pan?"

"A few times. Why . . . oh . . . the missing shadow."

"Something like that, I think." Steptoe's tail came up and wrapped partway about his waist.

"The professor had part of a . . . a shroud from somebody?"

"'e had my tail, didn't he?"

"He definitely did. Vampires are real?" Not that I hadn't believed Morty, but the fact was a difficult one to accept.

"We told you they were. Real, rare, and nasty. Not that I think the professor would be intemperate enough to try to bind a vampire to him, like he did me, but he had something to do with one, some time or other."

"But we boxed all that stuff up. I never saw anything like that."

"Nor I, ducks, but it was in there somewhere. Maybe in a hollowed-out book or some such. He was a good and devious wizard in his day." Steptoe stood up. "Cost me a pretty penny to get that analysis. I have to go pay up now."

"Doing what?"

He laid his index finger alongside his nose. "That's for me to know, and you to wonder. But it won't bring any harm home, I promise that."

"Better not," I said to his back as he left. I waited a few moments, listening to the house settle in the winter air, getting used to just me and the dog. When I was certain I was well and truly alone, I went to the pantry and got the journal out of the cereal box.

Scout and I took up a warm corner in the living room, me on the couch, and he stretched across my feet while I went in search of answers to questions that seemed ever more complicated.

The journal fell open in my lap, Mortimer's exquisite cursive easy to read, and yet difficult because it was so different looking from my friend, although I could hear his bass voice booming through the sentences themselves.

Then his words reached out and gripped me.

It is well known the power that resides in a name. But there are names which dare not be uttered even once, let alone thrice, for that being will hear and know and appear. The calling of a true name will breach even the long-standing protection of a threshold, and the intent of the visitor called in is never anything less than evil. Yet mortals seem slow to learn this truism and John Graham Andrews slower than most.

Finally, my dad, fully mentioned. My jaw dropped. Holy shit. Had my father summoned something?

CHAPTER TWENTY

WHO GOES THERE?

WHAT HAD HE done? What had I done? Had I put all this into motion?

I forgot to breathe for a long moment and then made a greedy gulp for air. This couldn't be. Not right under our noses, more or less. Steptoe would surely have noticed the remnants of such an action, and the professor, too, and I couldn't count Carter out. It might not have been recent, but it surely would have left a sign if a traumatic summoning had happened in this old house. Surely.

Wouldn't it have?

Would the summoned one have stayed here before making a break for the outside world? And if it had happened, they would have acted upon it. Perhaps even ending it, and I would never have spent those hellish last months in high school, and Mom . . .

No. I couldn't think that we would have been saved, because the past was past. No changing it. And we'd made it through, hadn't we? More or less intact? In some ways, better than we'd been before. My mother and I trusted each other truly and deeply, bonded by adversity and blood, and we were all right.

Only my father suffered unspeakably. I couldn't believe that he deserved it.

I bent over the journal again, reading as swiftly as I could, taking care not to skim if I could help it. I ran across Devian's name and stopped, reading the sentence several times to see if the silver-eyed, deadly elf was the name I sought.

No. Mortimer's entry dismissed him as little more than a devious, back-dealing personage to be watched carefully for the future. That future, I thought, had bothered me quite a bit, but it had taken Devian a few decades to get there.

And then, thirty pages and nearly two decades beyond the torn page, I came across a new personage.

Nicolo.

I leaned close to the pages.

Vampire. A master of centuries, hidden under our noses, and yet as woven into the fabric of Richmond and its Virginian environs as any being can be. We will have to root him out very cautiously. Nicolo is magic incarnate, wrapped in spells and wards that defy decryption. His instinct for survival and cruelty is vast. He protects and stokes the prejudices of old, to his advantage. There are few vampires and fewer alive who have studied them success-fully and can be consulted. All I can do is watch, wait, and learn . . . and pray no one breathes his name. Devian is said to be one of his puppets. And then along came John Graham Andrews, up to his neck in debt and desperation.

Cold fingers trailed down my back, leaving a chill dancing in their wake, despite the warm dog across my feet and ankles, and the furnace vent blowing softly from above in this corner of the room.

Nicolo would certainly match the scrap of a page which had defiantly remained in the journal. The notion of such a being would also certainly explain why no one spoke openly of him. Did Carter know of him? He had to, through the Society if no-where else, but perhaps even through his position with the po-lice. Vampires had to feed, didn't they?

I stood up, dumping Scout off my feet. He shook himself awake and trotted after me as I made my way to the cellar stairs and down to the limbo which imprisoned my father.

I centered myself in the middle of the room, where I could feel the chill despite the optimistically redecorated tile and walls and recessed lighting. Hiram and his crew had modernized the place far beyond its dirt floor, and plank shelves on stacked cement bricks, and rickety forgotten furniture. There hung little in the way of shadows, but an atmospheric depression filled the room. I'd gotten as used to that as my father's presence, never bothering to wonder if it could mean anything more. Now I did.

I held my hand up and the beady Eye of Nimora opened without reservation. My father's ghostly appearance looked like little more than a mirage, wavering transparent before me, but I could see an expression on his face, alert and listening.

"I came across a name in Morty's diary. Does Nicolo mean anything to you?" Scout leaned against my leg heavily with a little dog moan. The moment the words left my mouth, it felt as if something massive pressed on me, waiting, pushing, preparing to spring open. My throat closed a little bit in a spasm, and I coughed to clear it, not helping much. Upstairs, in the kitchen, keys and pots and pans clanged back and forth in a loud cacophony of sound and alarm.

"No," I told him. "I won't be saying it again. But is he the one?"

More rattles and clashes and then the sound of one of the pots falling off its hook, crashing onto a counter and then bouncing on the floor above.

"I'll take that as a yes, and a warning."

The noise ceased abruptly. Definitely a warning. "Is it about the stone?"

A single clang came from the upstairs kitchen. My hand shook slightly. "What does the stone have to do with it?"

My father's lips moved, but I couldn't hear him speak. Only a breathy sigh reached my ears.

"Had you found it? Were you negotiating with him over it? Gambling debts and everything? Or was this elf Devian the middle man?" Why I questioned him when he could not give an answer I could hear or know, I didn't understand, but I felt I had to. I had to know what had happened so I could unwind it.

The chill around me intensified as my father drew close. His mouth still moved, yet I could not gather his words.

Then his fingers brushed against my left hand, and in a movement too quick to deny him, he took the stone out of my palm.

I stared at it in astonishment as it floated in the air before my eyes. My hand felt empty. Abandoned. Icy cold. The stone rarely left me except when I willed it free, to save lives, and then it returned to me as quickly as it could. It chose its holder. It moved on when it was ready, unless the possessor had died and it had no choice. Yet he'd taken it without resistance.

"Wh-why did you do that?"

I caught the breathy whisper then. "It's what he desires and what will defeat him."

At least, that's what I thought my father said. Before I could blink, the stone pressed back into my palm again, warming, eyes still open. The cursed gold ring that had been the professor's and which the stone had eaten, fell chiming to the floor. Two things now it had given up: the null stone and then the ring.

"Okay. Was that supposed to happen, too?" I bent over and picked up the thick, 24 karat gold ring that would only have fit my thumb without falling off. "This belonged to Brandard. It was cursed."

"Not anymore . . ." and then my father retreated to the far side of the room. A cloud of cold went with him, all misty like, a fog moving across the tiled floor and gathering at his feet.

I looked at him. Possibilities swarmed through my mind. "If N—if the vampire is ended—are you freed?"

The apparition shrugged. My father did not know either.

I threw him a kiss and a promise. "I'll be careful." Scout and I clattered back upstairs where the dog threw himself against my ankles again and skimmed his lips back to show his teeth in a rumbling growl.

I unwrapped myself and tried to step around him, but Scout matched my every move, determined to stay between me and whatever it was he sensed. I had the journal tucked in my waistband and pulled it loose. Back into its bag and cereal box it went, although Scout's positioning impeded me, causing a handful of cereal to dance across the kitchen floor. He inhaled the bits and gave a choking growl as he retreated back into guard mode.

"Don't eat while you're snarling." I put my hand on his broad head. "What's going on?"

I'd only said the name aloud once. Just once. Like not thinking about the word hippopotamus, I couldn't get it out of my mind, but I wouldn't speak it. Broad daylight outside or not, I didn't dare. I had no ideas whether anything ever said about vampires in the movies or in books or folk tales were real. Was sunlight their bane? Garlic? Holy water? If I invited one in, was I as good as dead . . . or worse?

Correction. I did know something. Thresholds held a not understood but powerful gate against the uninvited, supernaturally speaking. Morty had spelled that out. I'd ferreted out a likely book from the professor's stash that might help as well. I'd have to prepare myself, without his phoenix wizardly help, and likely without the Society as well. If Carter found out I was up to anything, he'd probably put a very quick stop to it. The trick with him would be for me to get involved and then ask for help when I'd gone beyond the stopping point. I have friends I can call on, but first I need to find out what needs to be done, and how much help I'm going to need finishing it. I made this mess. I have to dig my way out of it.

I went upstairs toward the bedrooms, the path of least resistance to Scout's obstinate guard. From there, I stood in the hallway before looking to the tell-tales to see if they had reacted to whatever bothered my pup.

There are reactions and there are *reactions*. I don't think I've ever seen the tell-tales with their petals reaching to the sky, their tiny leafy arms standing up straight as well, their faces stark with floral alarm. I think each and every one of them had a panic attack.

Which meant I should, too.

Whatever signals they might be sending to Steptoe, he was undoubtedly too far away to intercept. He'd only know what had happened after the fact.

I spread my hands and concentrated on displaying my

shields. Then, having to nearly vault over Scout, I went into the professor's old room where the curtains still hung with just a slit open between them, to look out upon the front street. I wanted to brush the old lacy fabric aside to see better, but I didn't dare. Not with the hair rising on the back of my neck, my dog growling beside me, and the tell-tales frozen in silent screams in their hallway vase.

Peering out the window, I scanned the street. Broad daylight, more or less, with shadows lengthening for the shortness of the day. I stood back so that my breathing wouldn't condense on the window panes, giving me away. I needn't have—I couldn't breathe anyway. Something lurked on the sidewalk below.

It wasn't nighttime, so the eyes did not gleam as ferociously red-coal brilliant as they had during the dark. But they still glowered, amidst a shadow so black and shifting and sharp angled that it could not possibly be natural. As before, its form mutated as I watched, growing and shrinking, edges jabbing and then receding. It looked as if it wanted to devour whatever it could: sidewalk, lawn, house, and inhabitants. Then it would withdraw and curl up, before surging forth again. Their attention stayed rabidly on the front of the house, lower level, and I had no desire to direct the stare toward me. I felt melted and unnerved enough. To add to my fear was the realization that this was the third time I'd seen it, and in the magical world, three times is a summon.

Whatever it was, daylight didn't deter it. Nor the dog or the tell-tales or the fact that Steptoe lived here now. Or whatever protections the professor had laid when he was here.

I stepped back and away from the window slowly, so as not to stir the curtains at all. I did not want that thing, whatever it was, to know I watched. Had it been in our house? Had it had a presence that my mother accepted and invited in? No . . . if she had, it would have no compunction about coming in now. Once invited, the threshold seemed breached for that being. I wouldn't have to worry about calling its name if the doorway couldn't hold it back. So . . . no. That weakness, at least, shouldn't exist. I prayed it didn't.

I took another step backward and tripped over Scout. My

maelstrom-constructed shield bounced off his hard head without a sound from him, and I threw my arm about his neck. "Are you all right? Are you? I could have cut your head off!"

He snuffled into my hold but didn't seem to have tweaked a single hair in my accidental assault. I pondered the top of his golden skull. Was he immune to it? Or just so darn thick-headed he didn't notice it bouncing off? If he was immune, that could have consequences that I should note. My shield had worked in defense against Devian and his troops, but it might not in offense. All the more reason I should crack that book I found in the cellar and see what I could learn. My father was but a thin shadow of himself, and time seemed to be running out.

Already on the floor, it seemed logical to crawl into the hallway before standing. Scout threw his head back so that he could look up at me, worry in his doggy eyes. I rumpled an ear. "I know," I told him, although I really didn't and had no idea. We were alone in this, the two of us, for the moment.

And then I felt it. The gloom that had been ballooning inside the house seemed to implode suddenly, my ears popping and Scout giving out a yelp. A noise followed the extreme silence, and I realized we were no longer alone.

I lunged for my bedroom and grabbed up my field hockey stick, my backup, and spun out my shield a little larger. We could go down the front stairs, or we could try the back ones at the end of the bedroom hall—scarcely used and often overlooked. I didn't know the squeaky boards on that stair but knew they would bring both of us out into a part of the house which would be unexpected.

Unless our visitor had heat vision and hearing beyond reason. In any case, I didn't anticipate outrunning them. I was in it for the fight.

I stayed as close to the banister as I could and found that the boards there were as quiet as I could possibly hope for. I went down with Scout on my heels, nose to the backs of my knees.

CHAPTER TWENTY-ONE

SOS

HAD THAT ONE naming called a vampire into my house? Or had the specter outside decided to break in if it could, and do whatever damage it wished? Or was it some other dread being I couldn't readily identify? Halfway down the stairs, I paused and whispered as quietly as I could. "Carter, Carter, Carter."

He would come. I knew he would. But in time?

Horror movies never quite got it right. They have the creepy sounds, the erratic and unreliable lighting, the inadequate knowledge of the foe to be faced—but they never seem to mention the smell. A stalker has a body in the attic, his ode for the girl he covets, having taken out her mean girl rival. But does anyone smell the corpse? Ever?

Something crawls out of the sewer and into the bent old lady's backyard, sending her fuzzy little dog into fits . . . but does the overwhelming aroma of sewage ever warn anyone?

Zombies creep up behind the teens in the abandoned high school lab, and putrefied flesh is dripping off them, but no one ever says, "Ew! What is that stink?" and turns around in time to book it out of there.

Not this time. The coppery scent of blood seeped throughout the house, filling my senses, making me gag at the thought of it: wet, slippery, crimson. On its heels came another odor, a little harder to place, maybe that of a very enclosed and molding crypt, and finally a nose-searing layer of acute peppermint essence as though the owner tried to mask its actual aroma.

We made it all the way down the stairs into the back of the dining room and kitchen area before Scout let loose an ear-blasting sneeze. The peppermint, I guessed. Whatever advantage I had just vanished.

It spoke to me. "Show yourself."

I stood, back pressed to the wall, Scout half behind and beside me, and decided not to answer. The speaker did sound a little like Gollum, impressing me, and not in a good way.

I could feel the presence before the intruder turned the corner and entered the dining room.

Dark elf, I thought, looking at him. Not particularly tall—his brow probably wouldn't measure up to mine—but filled with wiry strength it seemed, encased in supple leather from neck to toes, black leather that looked as soft as butter. It had been torn in places, stitched up finely, leaving scars. Wounds where a knife had slit through the leather first? Or perhaps just a frugal being who didn't like changing outfits and repaired instead of replaced.

The smell of blood and decay rolled forward even stronger, and the peppermint followed when it said, "State your name."

"No."

"You know what I've come for. Give it over."

It smiled, a one-sided tilting of lips that were too thin and without real color, and where humor never reached the eyes at all. I couldn't even tell what color the eyes were from where we stood. They might have still been somewhat red. Whatever color, they were definitely glaring at me. This might have been the being who had chased me that night, but the minty odor told me it wasn't. It roiled with the same intense menace however that had frozen my reactions then but did not now. Because I was prepared? Because fool me once, you can't fool me twice? I didn't know but found myself grateful that my mind and body seemed in full function. One of us wasn't getting out of here alive.

I smacked the hockey stick against the floor. "Get out of my home. If you think you were invited or summoned, you are wrong. Your presence is revoked." It sounded formal, in case that might do the trick. It didn't because it just stood there. In fact, it might have inched a bit closer. I considered adding the only name I had, but I didn't think this was the big guy himself, more likely a second or third in charge. And I had no idea how it got in. I didn't want to open a door even wider.

Then it launched, faster than the blink of an eye, and if I hadn't thrown my shield up, it would have struck right at my throat. It slid off with a grunt, belying its need for air, while I slammed back against the wall, both shoulder blades stinging, and Scout barking sharply behind me as he found himself squeezed. He wanted out. He wanted in on the attack, but I dared not let him free. Could he even survive the vampire's touch, let alone its strength and ferocity? The pup was braver than he knew, and I was more afraid than I should be.

The hit proved to me how strong the damn thing was. I couldn't take too many of those and stay on my feet. It intimidated me and knew it.

I reacted to the lunge a bit slowly, considering. I skewed the shield about, presenting its edge and thrust at the slightly dazed vampire who hadn't anticipated a recoil—and scored. I followed up with a clout from my stick to the being's head, heard it crunch in satisfaction, and then heard the sounds of both the near-separated arm heal back with a sloppy slurp and the head bones crackle back into place.

Oh, lord. They did heal as quickly as rumored. Maybe even quicker.

I struck at it again, full face, shoving it back as hard as I could. Felt like running into a brick wall, but I managed to get enough room to slither sideways. I found myself at the corner of the dining room table where the crew and I had held many a strategy meeting as well as meals, and the large redwood chair which had been Morty's and now reigned as Hiram's stood between me and my foe. A terrible match to the maple set, it was the only furniture that could bear an Iron Dwarf's weight easily.

It hissed as the chair firmly blocked it from me. I thought of what the professor had told me so long ago when we'd first become friends. That redwood had a virtue not unlike rowan, a guardian wood, a barrier against malevolent magics. I couldn't haul the big framed piece of furniture about with me, but I could keep it between us for a bit. We dashed back and forth, slashing at each other until I was out of breath, but the vampire had no need for air. It curled its lips back over its gums and very, very sharp teeth. I chopped my shield at the vampire again and hit, solidly, but it also struck me, a back-handed swing that I couldn't scramble away from.

My arm instantly went numb and icy. I dropped my hockey stick, unable to grasp. Hot tears sprang to the corners of my eyes at the pain and shock. I thought my limb would drop off and almost hoped it would, taking the anguish with it. I stood unable to move at all while the vampire decided to flank me. I tried to swallow a whimper without much success. It threw a strangled sounding laugh at me.

I clenched my teeth and shuffled one foot, slowly trying to unfreeze. I couldn't just stand still, or it would charge again. Frustration bubbled out between my lips. I would die here, rooted in place like some idiot plant if I didn't shift my weight. Hold my own. Think of some cursed way to get back in the fight. My pup butted up against me, bumping one hand, and knew instantly from my reaction. I couldn't move, but Scout could.

He leaped out from behind me, teeth flashing, clawed paws scrabbling, and the vampire gave way, retreating hastily. Tingling started in my arm as it did. I managed to kick myself farther behind the redwood chair for safety and croaked a call for Scout.

My pup would have none of it. He'd tear this enemy to bits. He'd run him out of our home. He'd scare the being so badly the vampire would not dare to tread the earth again. With a roaring growl, Scout attacked. He leaped in a golden blur.

The vampire scooped him out of midair and held him up, teeth at his throat. I screamed as it did. Teeth flashed and sank in. Scout flailed, paws and tail thrashing to get loose. The creature flexed long, pale fingers to hold him tighter and dipped its head lower. I couldn't watch—flesh would rip and blood gush— but they did not. The vampire gave a long hiss and tossed him aside, his body slamming onto the floor. Scout went still, eyes rolled back, but only a few red drops bubbled out.

The blood must have tasted awful. The vampire kicked his limp form aside in disgust and jumped at me, landing on the seat of the redwood chair. It shuddered and danced but bore the insult of the redwood. It reached for me triumphantly. A jagged line of warmth lit me from my toes to the top of my head.

Scout had given me the time I needed to move again. I sliced crosswise at my attacker, and hot crimson splattered me and the chair, sizzling as it touched. I shrugged out of the spray as the vampire curled in upon itself. In a blink of my eyes, it healed. But its anger didn't dissipate. I bent and grabbed up my hockey stick, considering breaking it in two and shoving it into the vampire anywhere I could, staking it. With any luck that would at least slow it down.

Outmatched, I knew I couldn't stay out of its reach much longer. My right arm still ached beyond belief, and holding the stick seemed an impossible task to ask of it. My shield construct wavered ominously. The stone drew from me, my reserves faltering.

Where was Carter? Had he not heard my plea and summon?

Or anyone else? Anyone. Except my mother. I didn't want her here, to see me fall. Never.

From the kitchen, a terrible metallic ringing began, loud and clashing, angry and alarming. My father, doing what little he could. It was enough. The vampire straightened and looked askance to see who approached to help. I struck, cleaving its face in two. Undead flesh sloughed off bone even as bone itself parted and gave way. The odor pouring out of the wound near strangled me, and I recoiled.

Then it, too, healed before my very eyes, an impossible thing. I had no hope unless I could take its head off entirely. Only now, enraged and bold, it wasn't giving me a second chance. It bounded off the chair, recklessly throwing itself at the shield, uncaring at what damage it might feel, knowing it couldn't be stopped.

Not unless I was awfully lucky.

I hacked and slashed with my stick, stumbling away from the chairs and table, trying to give myself enough room to act and react. Leaving the redwood behind emboldened the vampire. It grinned, slashing at me with both hands swinging, fingernails elongated into hard as ivory talons. I ducked and twisted, hearing them swish closer and closer until the realization hit me that it toyed with me. Like a cat playing with a mouse.

My shield grew more and more compact until I had barely more than a Frisbee in size left in protection. My hand burned with the heat of the stone. Angry with me? Or desperately trying to conjure up more energy from somewhere, anywhere.

Behind the vampire, Scout heaved to his feet and shook his head. A few drops of blood ran down his throat ruff to his chest, but he didn't look that badly damaged. Dazed, though. He staggered a step toward me, and I was too busy watching him to duck.

I should have ducked.

Really.

Blinding pain exploded along my chest, neck, and the side of my head. I could feel myself tossed to the side as my feet went out from under me. My shield disappeared. My hockey stick dropped. And then, in a cloud of darkness, the rest of me followed to the floor.

Black, all black—and a stunning bolt of white light pierced my closed eyelids and took all my sight and senses from me.

CHAPTER TWENTY-TWO

SAY MY NAME (PART 2)

"HOW MANY FINGERS am I holding up?"

My head hurt. My whole body hurt. Someone had dropped a brick wall on me. Make that two or three brick walls. I couldn't even *see* any fingers. I thought vaguely that I might know the voice. I groaned, the action piercing my throat like a sharp knife. I must have been trying to lean up a little because I collapsed flat onto the floor again. Nice floor. Soft floor.

"Tessa. Open your eyes."

I couldn't. Why didn't they just go away and leave me alone? Broken yet comfortable. Did I still have two hands and two feet? I patted them on the surface under me. More of a convulsion, actually. A possible yes. The movement gave me a recoil of hurt, though.

"A world of hurt." I think I mumbled that. I know I sure as hell thought it.

"Who am I?"

I opened my mouth, only to be rewarded with a drink of cool, soothing water, much needed. Except that I had been trying to do something even more basic, like breathing. I coughed, choked, and hacked. Then I curled a finger or two, asking silently for water again. This time I got it down my throat successfully.

"Doesn't look good, guv."

Second speaker sounded familiar, too. I thought about it

for a very long while and realized I had lapsed back into unconsciousness where it felt much nicer to be. Not as painful or demanding.

A hand lifted my head up. The nice feeling fled abruptly. "Come on! What's my name?"

"Wanna sleep." Broken glass seemingly filled my throat and mouth as I tried to complain. I shut my mouth firmly, determined not to try that again.

"Hospital . . ."

"No. Not secure enough and we don't need questions asked. Tessa. Listen to me. Who am I?"

My lips felt crusty and dry. I licked them. Salty. Very, very salty. Had someone tried to make a pretzel out of me? I felt all twisted up and overbaked. I squirmed a bit. More crunching beneath me. Sand? What the heck . . .

"Carter," I got out. "What is this stuff?"

"Thank gods."

He had come. Strong arms lifted me and half-pulled me into a lap. "That, Tessa, is salt. You're drowning in it."

I wrenched my eyes open and saw his face, his blurred face, looking down at me. "Salt?"

"A shitload of it."

I turned my gaze, agony piercing my head and neck as I did, to see a bowler hat, snapping black eyes, apple cheeks, and a fashionably suited man also looking down at me. "Steptoe?"

"In the flesh! Now be quiet and have some more water before you dry up."

Carter put a bottle of water to my mouth, and I gulped happily. Well, not too happily; everything still ached beyond measure. I managed to wiggle a few fingers. "Pup?"

"Out back, growling at shadows, but he's fine. A slight limp. You got the brunt of it."

I locked my unreliable sight on Carter's face. "Tell me you got it. Tell me there's nothing left but a greasy smear." I knew now what that white flash had been . . . nothing less than Carter's arrival and fury. My sun lion.

"We got him."

"Good. Beyond good." I felt woozy again. "Did you know the floor is really, really comfortable?" I drifted off again.

By the time I woke, dusk had fallen, I'd been moved to the sofa, and my dog had draped himself over my legs and feet. Carter, my mother, and Steptoe ate delicious smelling shortbread cookies while debating my general health. Mental and otherwise. I could hear their suppositions as they drifted out to the living room. I don't know if I was insulted or just intrigued.

I pushed a hand out from one of Aunt April's antique but welcome afghan blankets. "Leave any for me?" They came over to answer.

"A whole platter," Simon said, looking a little peeved.

"I'll share."

"That's the sport!"

I rolled an eye at my mother. "Does Mom know?"

She sat up, straight and indignant. "Of course I know. I'm here, aren't I?"

"I mean . . . everything."

"I swept up a barrel of salt. I damn well know quite a bit."

"Okay." I didn't want to mention anything Carter didn't want her knowing. I settled for putting my left hand in front of my face, making sure my stone was still in place. I tapped it with my right pointer finger. "It came for this."

"How did it get in?"

"No idea. I felt it arrive . . . this incredible pressure and then my ears popped . . . and I knew something was in the house."

"But you didn't let it in."

"No way." Someone had put tea into a bottle container for me. I sipped at it, feeling the cool soothing nectar of tea and sugar make its way into me. "Good thing you thought of the salt, Carter."

"It was descending on you like a cloud when I got here. You conjured up that yourself."

"I did? Did it work?"

"Kept the vampire busy until I could dispatch it. We might remember that for the future."

"There had better not be a vampire in the future!" my mother snapped. Both men stepped back a little.

I cleared my throat hesitantly. It did not reward me with sharpness and agony as it had earlier. I might even be able to swallow a cookie. I had half of one nibbled down when something else occurred to me. I pointed at Scout. "It didn't like Scout's taste."

Carter looked at my pup in surprise. "Oh? That's . . . interesting."

"Worth remembering." Steptoe took a promised cookie from my platter and bit into it with a satisfied sigh. "Not just a dog, obviously."

My mother sounded a tad unhappy. "He's not?"

"Not entirely."

"I thought he was a Labrador retriever."

Carter smiled encouragingly. "Oh, he is. Also a bit of a mutt. We're not quite sure what the other bloodline is. Elven hound, most likely."

She set a cup and saucer down on the coffee table. "Good elf or bad elf?"

"Let's just say there are no bad dogs if they're raised right." And I think Carter had the nerve to wink at her.

Something else struck me. "Oh! How are the tell-tales?"

"They can only take so much shock. I've pulled them for now," Steptoe told me. "I'm going to swap them for a new, hardier bunch."

"What will happen to these?"

"They'll return to their beds. Grow a bit. Recover. They did the best they could."

"No one expects the Spanish Inquisition," I told him.

"Too right."

"If no one let the creature in, I think we have to consider the possibility that the threshold may have been breached before you even moved in here."

"Before—" I paused. "My father?"

"Seems likely. I don't know if a welcome wears off or resets, although frankly I would think the professor had circumvented that, but it seems he didn't."

I scrunched around on the sofa to have a better look at my

mother. She wore a silk shirt and jeans, her light blonde hair held back with a colorful headband, her eyes a bit shadowed. "Did you have a visitor the other night? Tomato soup and grilled cheese sandwich night?"

"I did, but—" she paled. "That couldn't have been that . . . that . . . thing."

"Not the vampire who came here today, but it could have been a Master."

She shook her head in denial. "We met at the university coffee bar. After the classes for online teaching, and he'd just come from the bookshop, putting in his semester order for textbooks. We've met up several times. He's new to the campus and Virginia. It seemed a neighborly thing to do. I didn't . . . you don't think . . ."

"We don't know what to think," offered Carter. "Any chance we could meet him? Name?"

She paused, looking thoughtful.

"Mom. We would like to know."

"I just hate to rope anyone in on this. It can be very complicated." She met my gaze steadily.

"Don't I know it. But Carter can probably check him out without his even suspecting." I snagged another cookie while deftly moving the plate out of Simon's reach. One of the cookies slid off and fell on Scout who, to his credit, took a thoughtful sniff before devouring it.

"He has his doctorate but doesn't go by it. Meyer Gregory."

"American?"

"Maybe. He has a very slight accent, maybe Germanic. Something. Definitely not a Southerner. Please be as discreet as you can. He seems well-spoken." She stood up. "And now I'm going to clean the kitchen up, and I suggest Tessa gets some more rest."

She hardly needed to suggest it. After my third cookie, my eyelids started sagging to the point where I either couldn't see straight or saw three of everyone. I yawned. Carter leaned down, gently peeling Scout off my legs, and sat me up.

"Can you walk?"

I was not too tired to blush. "Of course, I can walk." I stood up and proceeded to sashay toward the stairs in three different directions before I got my inner compass straightened out. Common sense prevailed, so I leaned on him heavily as we made our way up the front stairs. I pointed across the house. "I heard it in the kitchen area," I told him. "And came down the back stairs to surprise it. Would have made it, too, but Scout sneezed at the bottom."

"Sneezed?"

"The thing stank. Blood and mold and dusty—and Altoids. Really strong peppermint. Like all the Christmas candy in the world, laid end to end."

"Huh."

"Curled its lip and got to the dog. If it looked human enough to pass and was trying to hide its breath, I could see it, but it didn't, and it wasn't."

"Interesting." We'd reached my bedroom door, and he nudged it open with his shoe, guiding me inside.

"I had to call for you," I said.

"And it was a good thing you did. Salt slowed it down but wouldn't have stopped it. It had orders and a certain desperation about it."

"You did kill it."

Carter sat me down on the edge of my bed and carefully took my shoes off before fluffing my pillow. "I did."

"Damn thing healed every strike I got on it. Spooky."

"They can do that, I hear—but know this. It couldn't have taken much more. You damaged it almost to the point where it couldn't regenerate anymore. You almost drove it back into the ground."

"I did?"

"You did."

"It outlasted me."

"Yes. You might have tried a fireball or two."

I blinked. "I didn't think of it! I had trouble thinking at all."

"Part of a vampire's glamour. Steptoe had that vampiric dust analyzed, he told me. I got a touch of the remains. We'll see if it's the same creature."

I shook my head and immediately regretted it, as great, dizzying waves rose up to greet me. "I don't think so."

"It would explain how it breached your door. Part of it was already inside."

"Oooh. Maybe we should burn that box."

Carter squeezed my shoulder, his hand warm and strong. "We've already removed it and put a warding around it in the garage. I also put new runes on all the doorways and window frames. Even the chimneys and the plumbing vents."

"Boy, ain't nothing getting in here now."

He grinned. "Not unless you give it an invitation."

I made a cross over my heart. "Not this gal."

Leaning over, he kissed my forehead. I wrinkled my nose. "Call that a kiss?"

"For now, yes." Then he added in a whisper, "I'm very thankful you're okay."

"Tell me that when I'm able to walk straight again."

He laughed. "Deal."

And then he closed the door after him, leaving me alone with my throbbing head, lips that still tasted faintly of salted pretzels, and a body that hurt all over.

Scout snuffled from the hallway. I got out of bed to get him, settling for crawling along the floor. He crawled along after me as if I'd invented some new game, and we both got back in bed. The house felt a bit chilled, so his sprawled body warmed mine as I huddled under the comforter, thinking too many thoughts.

And no one but me seemed to have noticed the two fang marks on the inside of my left elbow while I wondered how much blood had been taken and if I might be poisoned. Was that even a thing? I should ask, but it would mean more questions back at me, and I really didn't feel up to it.

The last thing that drifted across my mind was the look on my mother's face when she talked about Dr. Meyer Gregory. Was he a deceiving Master or had she just been impressed by a nice guy? Had she betrayed us unwittingly—and if she had, and Carter or I found out, how do we stop her from doing it again? And how could she even think about moving on, with my father stuck in limbo? But if betraying ran in the family . . .

What if I had the stuff in my veins (or missing from my veins) to be the traitor myself?

CHAPTER TWENTY-THREE

INVITATIONS ONE AND ALL

I ROLLED OUT of bed cautiously the next morning and checked the weather on my phone. It promised to be a miserable day, the first of three miserable days in a row, but a glance out my window told me I might have time for a run before it started.

I didn't want to run. That brick wall which had fallen on me left bruised and cramped muscles that insisted on staying motionless, but I knew from experience that I needed to move. I also needed to run because field and track season awaited me. I dressed with a moan here and a smothered gasp there, grabbed a fleece hoodie, and went out. Rain and sleet hung in the dark clouds overhead, promising a deluge soon. I ducked my head down. Scout trotted beside me, not as unhappy as I was for the exercise, but not altogether go-lucky either. I had, after all, not fed him first.

We had a route, the two of us, which would measure at the minimum five miles and if I added a loop, would be closer to seven. Seven is a good measurement for me, distance as well as minutes count, and I did my loop at the beginning because if I waited twenty minutes, I'd chicken out. I knew my work ethic today absolutely sucked even though my body relaxed as I moved, and most of the sore spots lessened.

The wind rose, and clouds began to swirl even more ominously. I'd been jogging/running and moved up my pace, wanting to get home before the skies opened up. A warm shower sounded a lot more desirable than icy sleet. More posters fluttered about the circuit I took. Dogs and cats, gone missing, right out of their backyards. I didn't like what I was seeing. Was the neighborhood harboring a would-be junior serial killer? Or was there a creature feeding hereabouts? Had my recently deceased vampire been snacking? Or, more mundanely, Virginia had coyotes, though they were seldom seen, they were definitely about. They might be patrolling our part of Richmond. I tried to convince myself of that.

I might have been leery about going out on my own, but a smallish brown-and-gray–speckled owl came out of high branches, circled above us once, and got into position overhead. It soared along with us. I was at least being watched, at most escorted, and it felt friendly. Whether Carter had let Goldie know I needed some assistance or if the harpy left orders on her own, I had eyes in the sky. Worries that it just might be me and Scout against a coyote pack evaporated.

Scout moved with me effortlessly, tongue hanging out just a bit, soft ear flaps on alert, and tail wagging with his body movement and also because he just loved to run. He'd started off a little stiff as well, poor guy, but I knew I'd been right to bring him along.

By the time we got home, the blood sang in my ears, the hoodie felt almost too hot, and my feet let me know I should buy new running shoes because I could feel the pavement keenly through thinning soles.

Mom's car, in the driveway when I left, was now gone, so she was off to the campus again for her training classes. I showered and clattered downstairs in fresh clothes and better sneakers and fed Scout who had parked himself under the kitchen table and watched with soulful eyes until I filled his stainless-steel bowl.

"Simon! Need breakfast?" Paused by the counter, I waited for an answer but got none. It bothered me that Steptoe had a project or errands going that I knew nothing about. How much trouble could a lesser demon working on redemption get into? But the house lay absolutely empty. Run me up a tree and call me a possum, but they'd left me all alone again. I hadn't thought that possible after yesterday's battle. It wasn't until I sat down that I saw the professor's handbook sitting by my placemat, with a tiny Post-it Note on the front cover. I recognized Carter's scribble: Study.

I mock saluted as I dropped my plate filled with waffle and scrambled egg next to it. "Sir, yessir."

He'd even put a bookmark in the slim book for me. When I opened it, it fell out of the pages inked: Fire and Lightning Offense.

Or that's what I thought it said. Ink had faded, whoever had written it had terrible penmanship, and it looked like the language itself wasn't quite English. That, I'd become used to in some of the professor's other books. It seemed language evolved far faster than civilizations and humans. At Skyhawk, we'd listened in lit class to how Shakespearean plays actually sounded, and it was a revelation.

As helpful as the booklet tried to be, it had one caveat. To use a fireball or a lightning strike as a weapon, one first had to be able to produce basic flames or an electrical sprite. I could do one if not the other. A sprite was a fairly impressive lightning phenomenon rarely seen, and I certainly had no idea how to reproduce one albeit this one should be in miniature. I gnawed on the crisp corner of a waffle while Scout rattled his empty pan, hopeful for a refill. How does one produce an electrical spark? Static electricity perhaps? I leafed back and forth, finding no hint on producing the core of the spell. Either one could or couldn't, it seemed.

But I had fire. It seemed rather lame and mundane compared to the other, as if one was a scooter and the other a hot sports car. I pushed the book aside and finished my breakfast, rather than get syrup and jam drops where they didn't belong.

Scout put his head on my knee and whined. I looked down. He rolled his eyes up at me.

"Oh, all right."

He settled down to munching as I cleaned up the dishes and sat back down. Then, remembering something, I got back up and leaned into the dining room where the big table and chairs sat, and Hiram's redwood chair.

A black gash along the back marred the big thronelike chair, but otherwise it seemed to have weathered yesterday's assault in fairly good shape. Here and there I could see the random sparkle of a salt crystal winking up from the floor. I'd sweep and mop again. If I thought I'd just imagined the whole scene, I looked at proof I hadn't.

With a shudder, I sat back down to my study book.

Scout settled with one paw on my foot, and the rest of him splayed on the floor. I looked down for a moment, remembering when we'd gotten him that, although he'd been half-grown, he hadn't taken up half of the space he did now. He wasn't quite a pup anymore.

Rain started in a soft patter against the kitchen door. It sounded mild compared to what we expected around noon. I squinted at the spell book, conjured up a fist-sized fireball, and stepped outside to aim it at some overgrown bushes in the backyard.

It sat like a bowling ball over my palm, and I could feel my limb protesting at its density. I released a bit of it, lightening the weight so my arm wouldn't break off at the wrist. Took three breaths, eyed my potential target, and let go with an overhand baseball throw that tweaked my shoulder a bit.

Red and orange streaked across the yard and dove at the sedum border near the back wall, the flowering plant tucked in for the winter and frost; otherwise it would have taken up half the yard. The fireball exploded at the perimeter, sparks going up like a Fourth of July fountain, smoke hanging in the air, plants curling back into ash. The only thing missing was a whistling scream as it detonated.

I blinked.

Then the weather descended and whatever damage I had wrought quickly drowned and sluiced away, threatening to sweep me off my feet as well.

Lesson One: less is more, and definitely easier to handle. No, make that Lesson Two. Lesson One was that I was definitely capable of doing the spell.

I conjured up another fireball, the size of a tennis ball, and bounced it up and down a few times to see if there was any danger of it backfiring on me. Didn't seem to be. I took a step rather like a pitcher in motion off the mound and fired it toward a corner of rather pesky and thorny weeds that survived frost, drought, direct sun, Scout, and whatever else could be thrown at it. It almost survived my attack. There wasn't much left but a charred patch, but I bet myself that come spring, it would be green and growing again.

Maybe we should buy a goat.

I ducked my head and ran for the shelter of the house as the rain got colder and pea-sized hail began to bounce over the drive and lawn. By the time I got inside, my clothes were drenched and the noise of the hail could be heard drumming on the roof. It had stopped by the time I changed clothes, but the steady surge of heavy rain stayed. The house grew colder, so I bumped up the heat. The old furnace started up with a roar and sent out gusty clouds of air that grew hotter as it fell into its routine.

I pulled out an old notebook from one of my classes, copied the spell, and made appropriate notes. I would have to manifest and throw right-handed, tender though it seemed to be now. Less energy and possibly protection on my palm might help. No sense having two hands out of order.

Midafternoon, the mail came. I put up the hood on my second fleece covering of the day and made a mad dash in and out. Little of importance filled my hands, although my mother would argue with me about the letter from the university later, no doubt. Still too stodgy to rely on email, they send pompous missives from time to time. I'd never been impressed. I put her mail on her desk and then retreated to mine, of which there was a confirmation from Skyhawk Community about my spring registration (done online) and then a manila envelope without a return address. Curious, I opened it and dumped out a glossy, trifold brochure extolling the virtues of the Butchery as a meet and greet place for the hip.

I dropped it as soon as I saw it.

A taunt. A dare. Perhaps even an invitation. I swept the envelope and its contents off the table and got ready to dump it in the trash, but something halted me. Scout had been asleep on the floor and raised his head to eye me speculatively. I leaned over and waved the brochure to give him a sniff. "What do you think?"

He gave a mild sneeze before rearing back and out of reach.

"Yeah, that was my impression." I blew a short breath out, decisions colliding in my thought pattern. I'd show it to Carter when I next saw him, but no . . . I wasn't going on my own. Couldn't. Shouldn't. And definitely never alone. Seriously. But tempted. Someone knew I didn't like to back down. That the more in-my-face someone got, the more I stuck my chin out and went right back at 'em. Had they been talking to my coach?

I was not even much tempted. I'd come too close to losing my life and soul, and Scout as well. I knew I needed solid backup before I went after the vampire who might have caused all my father's misery. The minion had scared me. Terrified me. The Master would undoubtedly be worse.

That didn't mean, however, that I couldn't work on some planning and scheming.

I thumbed through the offensive magic manual, looking for some more handy spells to bulk up my attack because I intended to be right there, on the front line, when it got its reckoning. Because when I get intensely scared, I get angry. When I get angry, I get stone-cold determined. Might be a hot tear or two in the corner of my eyes, but they didn't fool those who knew me. This thing that sent me the brochure thought it knew me. Knew where I lived and that I was aware of where it operated. Knew my buttons. Decided to push them.

Boy, was it wrong. If anyone was going to push buttons, it would be me.

Smiling to myself, I began reading voraciously.

After two days of sleet, rain, and studying, I had an arsenal I could tuck into my hip pocket and feel I could do a fair amount of damage with. I also felt as though I'd put a dent in our good table.

Steptoe, in either the house or the garage, but definitely out of the weather, poked his head into the dining room.

"Still at it?"

"I think I've learned what I can."

"Excellent. How about a cuppa? I'll have it ready in a jiffy."

"Sounds great."

"Any cookies about?" he asked hopefully.

"Maybe. Check the tin."

We kept our extra cookies in an old fruitcake tin, but with Steptoe and Brian/the professor about, we rarely had extras. You'd've thought with one of our houseguests missing, that the odds of extra cookies would have increased, but it seemed that Steptoe was determined to fill the gap. I could hear him bustle about in the kitchen and give out a triumphant "Aha!" It looked like cookies did seem an option.

Moments and a teakettle whistle later, he brought in a tray of the spoils and set it down between us. He raised an eyebrow as I closed my book.

"Do you any good?"

"Yes and no." I sugared my tea (far less than he always did) and balanced the spoon on my saucer.

"Problem?"

"I don't have the basic foundation for some of the spells. Don't know how to skin shift, and I've never had much luck with sympathetic magic."

"Not making any voodoo dolls this week, eh?"

"Nope." I watched as he expertly doled out the cookies between us. "Don't think I'll need it with the three spells I can conjure. I could use a dozen flash-bangs, however."

"What? Oh."

He seemed disturbed enough at my request to not notice the cookie crumbs that escaped the corner of his mouth.

"Is there a problem with my asking?"

"No, no. Would half a dozen do?" He wouldn't quite meet my gaze.

"Of course!"

He beamed a smile then and told me he'd have them in a day or two. Still not looking me in the face, he finished his tea and cookies, waiting politely for me to finish mine, and then whisked everything back to the kitchen to be washed, leaving me wondering.

I felt fairly certain more chemistry than magic went into his little bombs, but I could be wrong. How vital could recharging be to a lesser demon? I'd never found an answer to my earlier ruminations. I still didn't know, and he didn't offer an explanation. But I had my fireball and something called icicle, the opposite, and I learned how to make salt clouds on purpose. Since we were fairly near a salt ocean, I had a source which wouldn't make that spell too awfully difficult or damaging to the environs. The spell book reminded me constantly of the imbalance that could happen if something were created out of nothing because nothing did not exist. Nothing in magic was a different locale being robbed of its asset to give me my something. Robbery could not be tolerated well at length. Magic and Albert Einstein coexisted rather well.

Had I just asked Steptoe to steal a substance he wasn't able to manage at the moment? I thought about it before shaking my head. He'd be all right. I could depend upon him as a friend, but he'd always had his own self-interest at heart, too.

I tucked that book away in a different cereal box. We'd have to buy more cereal if this kept up. My hip vibrated as I did. I fished out my phone and saw Evelyn's ID.

"It's almost Saturday!" she squealed in my ear.

"Indeed, it is." And I reminded myself I needed to have The Talk with her. "What's the weather like?"

"Better than yesterday. News channel says the storm is on the way out, so it should be cold but decent for our luncheon. Where have you been?"

"Studying. I need to get a head start."

"I hear you."

"Any chance you can drive over?"

Evelyn paused. "If I can't, Daddy will get me a driver."

"Any time," I told her and offered my excuse: "My closet's a mess."

"Seriously, Tessa? You never know what to wear!"

"Not unless it's a hockey game." I smiled.

"I'll be there in an hour or so!"

"See you then." I hung up and looked about, knowing I would

have to pick the house up a bit or my mother would frown at the thought of company walking in. It wasn't messy, but it wasn't exactly tidy, either. I yelled around the corner, "Evelyn's coming over!"

"Ah well. Shall I make myself scarce?"

"Nope. In fact, you can even let your tail hang out."

"I beg your pardon!" Steptoe peered out of the kitchen.

"Really," I told him. "It's time Evelyn saw a little of the truth."

He leaned a shoulder against the door jamb. "My. Think she can take it?"

"If she wants to date Hiram, she has to be able to."

His tail came around him, its spade end dancing a bit in the air. "Maybe Hiram should be the one to tell her."

"I don't think he has the guts."

Steptoe arched an eyebrow. "Now, ducks. He has laws he has to observe, and maybe you should, too."

"I think my friendship with Evie is more important than Hiram's shyness. Anyway, do what you want." I waved a hand at him. "Disappear if you feel better that way."

"I do hate being on display."

"Then go on." I returned to straightening up the dining room, and then drifted into the living room. "Whatever you think is best."

He didn't answer, and from the silence in the kitchen, I realized he'd left the house for his informal workshop in the garage. "Coward," I muttered to myself. I puttered around, continuing to talk to myself and Scout as I went room to room and finishing upstairs, where I hung the outfit I'd picked out earlier just in case I needed her critique.

She didn't bother to ring or knock, just charged in, promptly slipped and fell on her bottom in the foyer. She sat there blinking as I ran down the stairs at the noise.

"What happened?"

"I think the door hit me on the way in." She raised a hand to the back of her head and rubbed it. I thought of all the new wards we had on the house as I reached down to help her out.

If she hadn't been a friendly, would the magic have taken her head off? We'd have to be careful around here, making sure we escorted visitors over our thresholds.

Scout came clomping downstairs and danced around Evelyn, delighted to see one of his favorite people. She got over her slip and fall as she ran her hand up and down his back, fingers scratching as she went. She followed me upstairs, letting me know she'd driven herself but that there was a little ice on the road and she couldn't stay late because the freeze might get worse. Then Evie came to a halt in my bedroom. She swung about on me.

"That looks perfectly acceptable. Have you no taste?"

"It's complicated."

She bounced to a seat on the end of my bed. "No, it's not. There are primary colors and fabrics, and then complementary—"

"No. No. Don't. Stop," I said flatly and to my surprise she did, laughing softly.

"So are we making secret plans on how to get my parents to accept Hiram? Goody."

I sat down on the small chair that matched my flea sale desk/nightstand. "Sort of. I have something I should tell you, but it's difficult, and I'll warn you right now, you may not want to hear it. If you don't, tell me because I can't take it back later. Like our old history teacher used to say, you can't unring a bell."

Her expression closed a little, and a tiny frown marked her brow. "Are you going to tell me Hiram is dating someone else? Or married?"

"Not exactly. Actually, this is more about me than Hiram."

She put her hand on my knee. I could feel the tension even through the jeans. "Are you all right?"

"I am, but—I am also weird. Want to hear everything or not?"

"You're not dying of anything fatal, are you?"

"Not that I know of."

Evelyn took a deep breath, tucked her wheat blonde hair behind her ears, and looked solemn. "Okay, I do declare myself ready." She straightened up and put on her earnest face.

"You might have noticed things have been a bit . . . strange since last spring."

"Just a little. But like my mama always says, you don't know what goes on behind closed doors. You've had a rough time since your dad disappeared. I can't judge you." Now she says that. I had different memories from years ago, but she had evolved from frenemy to best friend.

I took a deep breath. "You might after this."

Evelyn frowned. "It is about Hiram, isn't it?"

"Not exactly."

"You're not trying to break us up!"

"No." Although, if she didn't take what I had to say—well, it could. I rubbed my nose which seemed to have developed a sudden itch. I was, in a word, frank. Often called tactless. Or blunt. I tried to think of how my mother would phrase the information. No one else in my circle could be a role model. Steptoe could be even harsher, the professor had never tolerated fools . . . although, to be certain, Evelyn was not a fool. Maybe a little stupid in love. I finally offered, "I don't want you to misunderstand me."

She rocked back. "You are trying to break us up! You've never approved of us. I knew it. I knew it all the time."

"That's not true. You know it's not."

She shook her head quickly, saying, "Sometimes I think I don't know who you are. You've changed so much."

"We've had a peculiar year, I admit, but I've gotten stronger because of all of you. My family. You make me better."

A strange expression passed over her lovely face. She cleared her throat. "What you say and what you do are reconciled, showing your nature to the world. Let that never change and your path will be true."

Great. Now she was reciting Shakespeare to me again. I fidgeted a bit on my chair, pushing her hand off my knee and said testily, "You're not hearing me."

Evelyn blinked rapidly several times. She put fingertips to one eyebrow. "Sorry, Tessa. I keep . . . my thoughts blank out now and then . . . maybe I'm the one with a fatal illness." She looked very pale.

"Don't say that!" I grabbed up a pillow. "Lie down. That was quite a slip you took in the foyer."

She fell over and stared up at my bedroom ceiling.

"Sometimes I hear myself and I think, who do I think I am, some bloody Juliet? And a little voice inside answers me, you say what you must. It doesn't even sound like me when I talk to myself. I don't get it."

"Do you remember it?"

Evelyn shook her head slowly, blonde hair cascading over the pillow. "Not most of the time. You want to talk about weird, this definitely is."

"I think you might be psychic."

"Hey! That's not nice."

"Not psychotic, doofus, psychic. Like, sometimes you know things before they happen."

"Oh. Really?"

I nodded. "Absolutely. You've told me things that were spot on."

"Hmmmm." She rotated onto one elbow. "Sixth sense." She pointed at me. "And I still think you're trying to come between me and Hiram."

I let out a long sigh and then I realized she'd already told me what she would listen to: me, showing myself and my true nature. I'd start with that.

"This is me." I held my left hand up. She'd never really had a good look at it because I usually wore wrestling gloves, cunningly made half-gloves that covered the palms, a little classier than most half-gloves. I know she'd thought it an eccentricity, fingerless coverings and all. The stone caught a stray bit of sunlight that had managed to break through the storm and shine through my bedroom window. It made the maelstrom stand out.

"Oh . . . my." Evie leaned so far forward to look, I thought she'd slide off the bed's corner. "That—that looks like a rock. It must hurt something awful. How did it happen and why hasn't it been removed?" She sat up to get a better look at it. I could tell she itched to touch it. I would have, too.

"It can't be." I stroked the swirled caramel-and-gold surface. "It's like marble, and I can hardly feel it anymore. As for how it got there—it's magic."

"Magic," she repeated flatly.

"It exists. Believe me. It's turned everything inside out for me, but it exists and the possibilities are . . . well, they're all knotted up and I'm still trying to untangle them."

She didn't blink. I waited a long moment and then decided maybe she had stopped breathing. "Did you hear what I said?"

"About what?"

"The . . . stone. Magic."

"You said you couldn't take it out. How awful. You've had that since last spring?" She skirted around my reveal a little, like sliding on an icy bit of road.

"Yup. It happened about the time the professor's house burned down, and his . . . nephew . . . came to live with us." I really had the feeling she was only hearing half of what I was saying as she ignored the obvious. Could the maelstrom stone be blocking me? She watched me with a look of utter calm and a lack of comprehension.

She reached out and took my left hand. "You said it can't come out? How can that be?" She stroked its glossy surface, and I felt it shiver through my entire body. I didn't want her touching it, not in any shape or form. The stone was mine.

Then her slender fingers tugged on it and the stone slipped right into her hand.

My jaw dropped. Thoughts stampeded through my head, the foremost of which told me she couldn't have it. Not yet. Maybe never. "Give it back!"

"Okay, okay. You're right, it's weird." She pushed it back into my palm and it sank like an anchor into my skin and senses.

I tried to wiggle it, but it seemed firmly in place again. Two slit eyes opened up to look back at me. Now seemed a poor time for the Eyes to wake up, but I had to roll with it, and I needed her to understand. "Okay." I reached for Evelyn. "This is going to be stranger."

"What?"

"I'm going to show you what the other world looks like."

"What other world?"

"The magical one. It exists. Think of it as an alternate band of existence with different rules of physics that overlaps ours, just like that sci-fi movie we really liked."

"The one where he gets killed over and over until he finally solves the problem."

"Maybe not that one. The one where the two lovers keep missing each other and then finally catch up and everything is happily ever after."

"Sure." She didn't look or sound convinced. Her hand felt a bit chilled in mine, but I attributed that to the stone whose warmth began to spread throughout my body. I stood up and drew her to her feet. "This way."

I took her to the new bouquet of tell-tales in the hallway niche.

"Oh, what cute roses. That's a new bouquet. You'll have to tell me where you bought them," she began, and then looked a little confused. "They're . . . looking at me."

"They're not exactly roses. They're a plant of some sort that is aware. Alive. They react. Each has their own psychic abilities and, well, they act like a home security service."

"What?"

"Look closely."

She did, and then she recoiled slightly, unnerved, I think, at what had to be flowers but weren't as the Eyes of the stone revealed a bit of the tell-tale's nature. "What . . . what do they do when something happens?"

I looked to the tell-tales who were slightly apathetic to me at the moment. "Show my friend how you sound the alarm."

A ripple went across the bouquet. Most of them had been looking at us. Petals opened slightly and elevated, not a full-flung "Help!" though Evie would get the idea. Her mouth hung ajar for a second.

"They look scared."

"Yup. They send off a high-pitched signal, too, if something is really happening. I'll spare you that one." I wasn't about to tell her they could stun an invader if it got close by. I didn't know how much Evelyn could take in.

Yawning, Scout trotted out of my bedroom and leaned against

my leg. I swept the Eye of Nimora over him. I rarely take a look at him under the influence, but I knew that Nimora could pinpoint some differences in him from the average dog, and I heard Evelyn breathe out, "Oh, my." She squinted slightly. "He's not just a purebred Lab, is he? Some kind of designer breed?"

"We don't quite know. Maybe elven hound in him."

"Elven?" She added, "Come on!"

I inclined my head. "Elven. Like *Lord of the Rings* and *The Hobbit*, elven."

"They don't exist."

"Somewhere they do." I pulled her back into my bedroom. "And so do wizards and dwarves."

"Tessa!"

I crossed my heart. "Please keep listening because I'm going to be talking about Hiram, and he'll tell you more, but sometimes you need to ask the right questions."

She dropped my hand suddenly. "I don't think I want to hear anymore."

"We're right at the most important part. Please."

She looked out my window, rather than at me, and faintly answered, "All right."

"I don't think there is much doubt that you love him and he loves you."

The line of tension in her shoulders relaxed slightly.

"But he is not what you think he is."

She got fierce then, swinging around to glare at me. "And there you go again! Putting him down. He's honest and intelligent and a gentleman!"

"He's a dwarf."

"A what—no, don't you go making fun of his height! He's tall enough for me."

"Not making fun of him, not at all. He is a very good person and one of my best friends. And he's years older than he looks and will live years longer than you or I. He's an Iron Dwarf, bound to elements of the earth; everyone in his clan is, and he is always very, very careful around you to protect you."

"Years longer . . ." Anger faded from her suddenly, and she

seemed to deflate. She gave a slight sniffle. "We shouldn't be together? You're not saying that, are you? For real?"

"No. I'm saying it could be difficult."

"He's never said anything."

"He can't. Magic is like that, Evie. That side can't admit it exists because this side knowing might tear their world apart. They've always been very careful and secretive."

Sulkily, she said, "You found out."

"I wasn't supposed to. You're right. And now I'm up to my neck in it. And you will be, too, so you need to know."

"But he has a home. And a business, a good one. You can't be right."

"I am."

"What about wizards? Like Gandalf or Dumbledore?"

"More like my old professor, but yeah."

She sucked in a breath and sat down again, suddenly. "This isn't happening."

"Tell me about it."

"Are you sane, Tessa?"

"I hope so. If I wasn't, I don't think I could show you the few things I have." I didn't want to tell her that was the tip of the iceberg because I wouldn't have believed me, and I'd been through all of it.

"So I need to ask Hiram if . . . if we have a future someday. And ask him about his clan. And maybe . . ." She glanced up at me. "Have you ever noticed how the house groans and creaks sometimes when he's walking about in it?"

"Trust me, I have. Iron Dwarves have a lot of weight to them."

She exhaled. "I thought it was just me."

"If only." I rubbed my hands together. "How about some tea?"

"And brandy. I could use a bracer."

"Just a shot, then. I don't want you driving with a buzz."

"Deal."

We both went downstairs to the kitchen. The last thing Evie said to me was, "Does your mother know?"

"Oh, yeah. And she's not extremely happy about most of it."

A pot and a lid rang together on their hooks as we entered.

She looked at them. "It's like this old place is haunted. I've always thought you had a poltergeist living here with you."

I thought about telling her about my father and decided against it. "And you wouldn't be far wrong, but that's a story for another day."

"Mercy," she answered and sat down for her tea with brandy.

CHAPTER TWENTY-FOUR

PARTY CRASHERS

STEPTOE SHOWED UP the morning of the big luncheon and dropped eight flash-bangs by my breakfast plate. I'd hoped for more but gave him a bright and thankful smile anyway. "Thanks!"

"Anything for you," he responded as he disappeared toward the mudroom and the back door. I heard the cot squeak as he dropped onto it, and a soft snore followed almost immediately. He must have been up all night making my ammo.

Mom smiled as she listened and then began to finish her breakfast.

"You're coming, too, right?"

"I wouldn't miss it. But I'm taking my own car."

I considered her. "Why?"

"Because I have a plus one."

My mind genuinely boggled. "Say what?"

Her smile tightened a bit into self-satisfaction. "I'm picking up someone."

"You don't have to drive your car to do that." My thoughts still scrambled around. She had a plus one? Why? And "Who?"

"You'll meet him when everyone else does."

Him? The very word made me narrow my gaze. It had to be that Gregory guy. I said carefully, "Is that wise? We don't want to violate anyone's threshold."

"We won't be. I don't think I need to remind you, but all of the people who've come into this house in the last year or so, have been friends or projects of yours. With this singular exception. Trust me, he is a perfectly normal person. Is that all right with you?"

"Not exactly. It sounds like you've given up on me and Dad."

"I haven't given up on your dad as your father, but I gave up on him as my husband months ago. He's betrayed everything we'd promised each other."

"I'm doing everything I can."

"And did that everything include putting yourself in the way of a vampire? I didn't even know they existed."

"I didn't either, not really, and I had no idea—"

Her eyes flashed. "That's the point. You have no idea of the consequences. You just charged ahead into this totally unknown territory."

"I should have let the professor burn to death?"

My mother stilled. Her jaw worked slightly before she answered. "Of course not. That is . . . he did, but you saved Brian."

"I saved them both."

"By keeping your own counsel, which isn't as wise as you think it is. I don't like being left out of your plans and escapades. I don't want to lose you, too."

I felt like hitting something, so I slammed the side of my hand on the table, jarring my teacup and saucer. "You're the one walking away from Dad. I told you I'd fix it—you just need to give me a little time. I will do it."

"I'm not blaming you for your father's mistakes and you shouldn't either. I know you're trying to find out what happened. But I have to have a future." She gave a half-smile. "You won't always be here."

"So now you're telling me this new guy is your future??? That happened fast."

"It hasn't happened at all! Honestly, are you learning dramatics from Evelyn?"

"Great. You don't approve of my regular friends, either."

"I didn't say that."

"It seems to me you kinda did."

"You're jumping to conclusions."

My face had warmed and even my ears felt hot. I tried to

rein in my anger though not too successfully. "I'm concluding that you don't trust me to put things right! I'm going to get Dad back."

My mother sighed. "And I'm trying to tell you that, here or not, I'm not certain your father has a life with me. Have you cured his need for a gambling high?"

"I should think being stuck in limbo for nearly three years would do that."

She said quietly, "You'd be surprised what the addictive personality will go through to avoid change. I don't want to argue with you. I know you're doing all you can. I'm just telling you that it may not be enough for me, that it won't restore things to the way they were."

"And you've got a new guy."

"Just a friend."

"I can hardly wait to see the proof of that!"

She wrinkled her nose. "Rude, as you would say." She put her fork down.

I looked at my plate where my sunny side egg had gotten mixed up with my potatoes as intended but all of a sudden looked very undesirable. I shifted. I didn't need our family dynamics screwed in addition to everything else. We'd always had each other's backs, and she was treating me as a partner—or trying to. "Sorry. We're both adults here. It's just . . . odd."

"I know it's difficult for you to hear."

"You've got that right."

Her expression softened a little. "You know we were married just out of college. He hadn't been hurt yet, and had gotten a job which was more of a sponsorship for his golfing. I started to earn my masters, taking advantage of a fairly good salary he'd begun to earn. We weren't rich by any means, but we did put a decent down payment on our little house. Then I found out I was pregnant with you."

I eyed her. "Didn't they have birth control then?"

"Of course, they did. But miscalculations do happen. You know who saved us?"

"I have no idea."

"Aunt April. She baby sat you for two years while I finished school, and then your Dad hurt his shoulder, and we had to start over. Luckily, my masters gave us some stability, and his sponsorship was with a local insurance company that took him on as an underwriter. She kept everything on an even keel. Sometimes she came to our home and sometimes I dropped you off at hers, the one with the greenhouse we both loved." The one she'd had to sell to pay off her own gambling debts. That vice ran deep in the Andrews bloodline.

"I don't remember her at all."

"No. Your father put some distance between us when he had to take a real job. I could never understand why. She came through when we needed her again, though."

That she did. Our creaky, quirky old house was one of the few investments she'd been able to hold onto, or we would have been truly homeless. I stabbed at my plate again and decided to change subjects. "We have enough serious worry with Evelyn swooning over Hiram."

"We certainly do."

We continued in silence while I wondered if I had a plus one. Carter, if available. I hadn't heard from him over the past few days, so I had no idea. Not that I needed company or an escort, but it would have been nice to have the moral support I suddenly felt that I desperately needed. I dropped a toast corner to Scout, knowing it would never hit the floor. My mother left me alone at the table.

I wouldn't tell my father. I don't know what the two of us would have to go through to get him out of limbo, but worrying about my mother wouldn't help either of us.

My phone sat on the kitchen table, showing me that the weather would be very chilly but no snow or ice, having thawed out the day before. I decided to take Scout along with me and texted Hiram to ask if it would be all right.

He answered immediately with permission, adding, "Bring Carter, too."

I returned, "Carter goes where Carter wants to go."

He sent me back a winking emoji, and I signed off at that.

That left me with a few hours to kill while waiting to go.

Evelyn texted twice so I talked with her, to calm her down.

Told her to lay off the caffeine, but I don't think she took my advice.

One of those invite notices appeared on the front porch from the Society reminding me that I had a schooling meeting the next day. I considered it for a long moment before ripping it into confetti, dumping the bits into the kitchen sink, and setting them on fire. I didn't want anyone to have any doubt about my reaction to the summons. If they couldn't protect students like Sophie, I no longer wanted anything to do with them. The Society faced corruption from the inside out, and I didn't want to be involved. The professor had been right in his summation about them. If I had to go through every miserable book stored in the boxes in the cellar, I'd school myself on what I needed to know. I had those three new spells under my belt, and there were more where those came from.

My room smelled like dog. Normally, not an unpleasant smell, but since he was going to a party that afternoon, I decided a bath would be in order. He still fit, more or less, in the humongous sink/tub in our laundry room, so we trotted in there and lathered up nicely. Luckily, Labs are water dogs, and he loves it, rain or shine, although he would much rather I turned on the sprinkler and let him romp through it. The wintry day, however, suggested that our sprinkler fountain might freeze in midair and be relatively useless.

Scout did not, in any way, shape, or form, like the hair dryer. I didn't scold him much, and even laughed when I got his lips splayed out, baring his teeth, as if he faced into the wind. He chuffed at me when I was finished and went to sleep under the kitchen table, head on paws and facing pointedly away from me.

Nobody liked me today, it seemed. "Fine," I told him. "Going upstairs to dress."

I chose leather pants to go with a nice silk blouse, and a weather-wise coat that had seen better days but would be warm and comfortable, and I'd shed it when I got in the house anyway. The flash-bangs went in an inner pocket meant for sunglasses. I could hear Mom fussing around a bit in her room and getting ready to leave.

She gave a faint goodbye, and then I heard her car start up. So she wasn't even letting the plus one come to the house first?

I frowned at myself in the bedroom mirror and arranged my hair about my face and shoulders. Brunette, as always, and the light dusting of freckles that sunnier months gave me had faded over the season. Maybe I should coax Evelyn into giving me highlights. That might be interesting. Blonde or purple? I'd distract her with that query if needed.

I'd just slipped my feet into some nice ankle boots which I rarely wore, and which I kept on the top shelf in my closet, away from enthusiastic puppy teeth, when my phone buzzed with a text. I smiled as I read it to myself. Carter, on the way over, asking if I thought he'd forgotten?

I might have, but I wouldn't admit it. I sent him a few hearts and a bunch of smiley faces.

It was nice, I told myself as I put my phone away that neither of us took the other for granted. Scout and I waited at the front windows for his car to pull up and then ran out before he could open his door, our breaths white and misty on the afternoon air. The sky glittered a brittle blue, not a cloud in sight besides the ones we were making.

Scout hopped into the back seat as I scooted in, the heater warmth hugging us close.

Carter grinned at me. "I should think you'd be a little more careful about what car you're getting into."

"Right, huh." I fussed for a moment because I hadn't discussed the taunting mail delivery from the Butchery.

Like the sun lion that seemed to be his magical alter ego, he sensed my nerves. "What is it?"

"Is it possible to let something in just by saying its name *once*?"

His amber gaze locked onto me. "It could be, if the being were powerful enough. I've only heard of it once or twice. For instance, if you were to think of our friend and sometimes nemesis, he could appear, but it would be extremely rare. I'd ask why you're asking, but I think I know. Who are we talking about?"

"I don't want to say."

He leaned out and fished a pocket notebook out of the car console. "Write it down." He pushed the notebook into my hands.

I frowned down at it. "In blood?"

"Great gods, no." Fumbling about, he found a stub of a pencil and gave that to me, watching as I started to write Nicolo.

He grabbed my hands before I got more than Nic down. "Stop."

I looked up. "Seriously?"

"Extremely seriously." He pulled the book and pencil away from me, muttered a few words and a golden blaze flared out. When it receded, he put everything back in the console. "And that was undoubtedly how the minion got into your house. Why were you even aware of his name?"

"Morty's journals. He speculated that my father had gotten involved."

Carter pointed through the car windshield. "When you have the Sight, drive down Monument Boulevard someday. You'll see shadows where there should be none, draped about most of the statues. Upon the flags that shouldn't be flying anymore because they represent a heritage that we need to leave behind. He uses our past, our guilt, and misguided pride against us. He's ensnared most of this state. We're fighting our way through, but it's like slogging through red clay. Nothing good comes from that Master."

"So I should stay away."

"You need to be told that?"

A bit of shame arched through me. "No. Not really. But what if he's the only way I can get my father freed?"

"He would never give you the information you need. The only thing we can do is destroy him and hope that unbinds all that he rules."

"Could that happen?"

"Maybe. It isn't certain . . . and it would take an army, Tessa, one I'm not sure I could raise. He's been entrenched in the South for, probably, centuries."

I thought of all the bodies/souls I'd seen twisting on meat

hooks in the Butchery when I had been trapped. "Bigger than the Mafia? Or a drug cartel?"

"Not necessarily bigger but more buried and infinitely more powerful. Let me think on this a bit, and don't you dare go acting on your own."

"I won't." But something twisted inside me, and I thought: unless I have to. Unless that's what it took to change what I had done to my father and save him.

To distract myself, I leaned over so we could kiss. I loved the way my mouth melted into his, and the sensations sang all the way to my toes and back, comforting and sizzling all at the same time. When he leaned away from me to put the car in gear and pull away from the curb, all I could think of was that we should kiss more often. The thought occupied me the whole way across town to Hiram's home.

Make that estate. We parked at one end of the circular drive, where there was just enough room, the rest of the area already occupied. I saw a lot of SUVs, tires and fenders spattered with dirty ice and dripping dry. We got out with Scout trotting at our heels, stopping once or twice to throw his head up and smell the air. Trees peppered the lots everywhere on the street, evergreens straight and limber, their branches clear, their bodies tall against the wind and weather. I could smell a bit of sap myself, against the crisp afternoon. I liked the neighborhood and wondered if any of the clan lived here besides Hiram.

Evelyn must have been stationed at a window, waiting for us, because she rushed out before we were more than a third of the way to the door. She looked gorgeous, fitted slacks, a fitted coat with a beautiful blouse underneath, her hair knotted in fashionable braids, and her eyes shining with excitement. She reminded me of Christmas mornings and Santa. I dropped a hand to Scout and softly told him "Off" so that he wouldn't bounce up in similar joy.

Evelyn got in between us and locked her arms in ours. "Isn't this place fantastic? It looks and feels like Hiram."

"It does." Carter shot me a look over her head, and I gave a little nod. Yes, Evelyn knew more than she did before I had talked with her, but I had no idea if she'd discussed it with the Iron Dwarf at all or not.

"You're the last to get here, and I think we're all ready," she bubbled and gave my arm a squeeze before breaking free and breezing toward the open door.

"I'm not sure if I'm ready for this," I said, but Carter laughed at me. I found it funny as well, and when we entered the doors, we were both grinning from ear to ear.

And then I saw my mother and her plus one across the foyer and vast living room of Hiram's home.

CHAPTER TWENTY-FIVE

WHO GOES THERE?

IT WAS THE fedora that struck me. I knew that hat, knew it from the Societas Obscura meeting, knew that the man wearing it had gotten close enough to influence me, to give me advice, to coax me into behaving. I didn't know who he was . . . a little taller than my mother, about the same mid-forties in age, well-dressed if a bit behind the current styles, with a nice mustache across pleasant features. They stood far enough away that I still couldn't get a clear look at his face, but he seemed nice-looking. Though if she thought he was just some scholarly civilian who'd happened into her sphere, she was terribly wrong. I needed to tell her that.

Our gazes met for the barest of moments, and then he turned his back to me, taking my mother by the hand and drawing her into the kitchen and great room where refreshment tables glistened with glasses and dishes, and they disappeared among the crowd. I saw a number of Dwarf clan members among the diners.

"What's wrong?"

I wondered if I should drag Carter into our family disagreement, before deciding on the negative. We'd sort this out together, if we still had a together. "Nothing. Everything is fine."

"Fine," he repeated. "That's one of those trigger words, isn't it?"

I punched him lightly in the bicep. "Stop it."

"Fine. But you will catch me up later." He took up Scout's

lead. "Looks like Hiram has a screened-in porch. Let's go mingle."

We found Hiram and Evelyn's parents (and Evelyn) there, as well as three other high-powered couples from the city council. Hiram was explaining how he'd inherited the lot and commissioned a builder, as though no one ever built custom homes anymore, but if anyone knew custom, this crowd did. Everything looked to be going well until Hiram flicked a look at me. His brows knotted, and I swear a storm cloud settled across his forehead. What was that for?

Oh, wait. My talk with Evie?

I mouthed, "I can explain" to him, but he turned a broad shoulder to me, ignoring me further. Wow. Maybe I should plan to leave the party before it got any harsher! Carter bumped shoulders with me as he reached for a drink and offered me one, hot cider from the luscious smell of it. I sipped at it cautiously as we approached everyone. Evelyn's mom swung about.

"Tessa! You're looking beautiful tonight."

She made it sound like such an exception, I wondered what I looked like other nights, but made a gracious sound anyway. Mr. Statler merely nodded a greeting but did not stop his conversation about property and conservation and ease ways, to which Hiram responded only, "Naturally." The other two couples looked as if they hung on every word until Scout decided to bump a leg, nosing out an hors d'oeuvres plate that was sagging too temptingly close to his level.

The whatever it was, I didn't get a good luck at it, disappeared with one slurp.

"Goodness," chirped the redhead with silvery highlights. "That was quick. I didn't even see your dog."

"I'm sorry, really. Can I get you another . . ."

"Pâté, but no thank you. He did me a favor, really. Luncheon will be served shortly, I understand, so I shouldn't be eating now anyway." The woman gave Scout a congratulatory pat and set her empty plate aside. Scout promptly sat and watched her closely for seconds. Her mouth curved. "No pressure, I see."

Mr. Statler looked to the redhead's husband. "A great sense of humor. No wonder you told me she was a keeper."

That drew a quiet chuckle all around, as I dropped a hand to Scout's collar. "Have some place I can put him for a nap?"

Hiram pointed a blunt finger to the screened-in area. "Also, there's a brook that runs along the edge of the property. He might enjoy a walk out there later." He barely finished the sentence before turning away from me again. I seemed to be making missteps in my relationships all over the place. Iron Dwarves didn't seethe, but they could certainly grow cold and judgmental.

Evelyn caught up with me as I put Scout into a comfortable corner. "He's a little uptight," she confessed to me.

"Tell me about it. Did he get angry with you?"

"No, not really. I did have the feeling that he might not have told me, and that bothers me. How long would he have waited? Would I have never known? Or was he thinking we'd just run our course and he wouldn't have to."

"I can't answer that for you."

"I know, and I don't want you to. I want *him* to, but this isn't the time or place, I guess." She brushed her hand against her forehead, putting some stray stands of hair back into position. "I just don't know if I can wait." I was glad to see she didn't have crazy eyes.

"Whatever his plans, we know that Hiram is one of the good guys. He'd never knowingly hurt you, even if his hesitation is driving you a bit crazy."

She rolled an eye before acknowledging, "Yeah, he's definitely a gentleman. He seems to be getting along really well with my dad."

"What about your mom?"

"She's always been the suspicious type. I had to do an end run around her just to stay friends with you."

That surprised me. Well, it did, and it didn't. I knew well the suspicion that had settled on our little household years ago, but not that her mother had bought into it. "Wow."

"That's why I got to drive you home from campus so many times. Her way of checking on you to make sure you were doing all right."

As if I might go bad like a carton of dairy shoved into the back corner of the refrigerator. I gave Scout the Stay signal and trailed Evelyn back into the main part of the house. "I had no idea."

"She can be subtle." Evelyn wrinkled her nose slightly. "Unlike my dad who is . . . how shall I say it . . . relentlessly forthright?"

"And you're a happy blend of both."

"Thanks! Did you get a look at the menu?"

"Not had a chance."

"Oh, let me show you." She dragged me right past our little group, leaving Carter behind, and into a living room/dining room area that was dominated by an L-shaped table, with porcelain and good crystal and sterling silver, along with place cards and small menus tent-folded and sitting on each plate. It looked like something out of movies and society scenes. In a way, it made me uneasy because this was not the Hiram I knew, the young man who enjoyed pizza or taco night. Not the builder who'd redesigned and constructed our new cellar. Nor the Iron Dwarf who lived in a fantasy old forest with his clan. Was this version of Hiram even real?

I looked at the card. We had soup and salad coming up . . . well, not soup. Bisque. And not an ordinary salad, but a salad du maison. And then a fowl dish and a beef dish. Then fruit and cheese. And a tartlet of some kind following. He'd obviously hired a catering company. I don't know what I'd expected. Ribs and potato salad, maybe.

"Looks good," I told her. Evelyn beamed as she put the card down.

"Fish if no one wishes beef."

"Oh, I'll take a filet mignon any day."

"I bet you would."

We sauntered down the length of one of the tables, eying the place cards. "Did you help pick the food out?"

"Nope. He did it all on his own, with suggestions from the caterers, of course. They're the same people that are going to do part of Dad's inauguration."

"Ah. Makes sense." We turned at a junction of the tables where I discovered my mother and her intended sitting about half a world away from mine. I stared down at the cards and wondered if I should swap them out, just to be ornery.

I didn't have time because Evelyn stopped all motion and stood stiff and quiet for a long moment. She half-turned then and looked at me with her eyes very wide. "Change is coming. An unimaginable disaster for the nation. We will not meet again for many months without risking our lives. This will be one of the hardest trials our country, our world, will ever face. Remember."

Then she closed her eyes for a long count before opening them and taking a deep breath.

"You've got to stop doing that," I told her. "It's getting scary."

"Oh, shoot. What did I say?"

"It doesn't matter. Doom and gloom. Real fun party stuff."

"Well, you're a big help."

I shrugged. "Call them as I see them." But I wouldn't forget what she said nor could I match it to anything I knew might be happening down the road. Her words had been too vague, except maybe the "disaster" one. "Don't think about it. It wasn't personal."

"It wasn't?"

"Nah. You just threw shade on the whole nation, that's all."

She pulled out a dining chair and sat down abruptly. "Oh, wow."

About then Scout let out a sharp bark. It violated his Stay command, so I went to see what the problem could be. He jumped up and danced around a bit, telling me that he needed a potty break. I hadn't taken his leash off, so I grabbed it up, found my coat in a pile on the sofa table in the foyer, and made my excuses for both of us.

Outside, sharp, cold air bit at my nose and cheeks and whistled about my ears, but Scout trudged into it briskly with his head up and his tail in a determined wave.

I talked to him as we slow-jogged toward the outer boundaries of the property. He had a fence, of sorts, out of trimmed hedges and trees, but nothing solid and impenetrable. Wildlife, deer and such, could wander in and out as wished. I could hear the brook, which sounded to me more like a river, and it hadn't frozen solid although when we came across it, the banks sparkled with a rim of ice. Scout bounded in for a drink and nearly as quickly bounded out. He found a tree to decorate with pee, and a fallen log to investigate for rabbit warrens underneath it. That brilliant blue sky overhead seemed to have dimmed a bit, muting to more of a stormy gray and blue canopy . . . or maybe I'd wandered into a different forest.

It felt different. The bird songs and animal chatter I'd only half-heard ceased altogether as the fringe of wilderness went ominously quiet. I told myself that, between Carter and Evelyn, I'd been spooked. The silence meant nothing. Scout dropped back to pace me, his wild enthusiasm now measured. His ears and nose went on high alert. What was he scenting or trailing? Whatever it was, he devoured it, yet he didn't gallop ahead to meet it. Something made him cautious or protective of me.

The icy cold of the day faded. A kind of humidity set in, and I could smell freshly turned and fallen leaves as though it were only an autumn day, a season long gone by. The brook sounded louder, its burbles uncongested by any ice at all. A soft breeze ruffled the trees. I looked up and saw not only the evergreens but huge chestnut trees here and there which no longer grew in Richmond or most of the east coast since the blight wiped most of them out. I stared at their mighty and widespread branches, alive with vibrant fall colors. How did Hiram manage to save these . . . or was this even modern-day Richmond? It felt different and smelled different, and eventually a few murmuring sounds crept back in that I did not recognize. That alone sent twinges of alarm down my back, and I knotted my hand more firmly about Scout's leash. My stone hadn't reacted, and I had my bracers on, and they stayed quiescent, too. That did not soothe me at all. Then I heard the distinctive crack of a branch breaking, and the noise of brush giving way. Something paced us on the other side of the hedges and branches, as footfalls reached me.

I searched the shadows which had become thicker, but I couldn't see through the foliage. Scout halted with me, his ears perked forward, his whole body straining to catch—what? My hand curled even tighter about his leash. I didn't want him bolting off. He wouldn't run, but he might attack, and that could be disastrous. Was this friend or foe?

Something quite possibly not human and definitely not four-footed. Or maybe it was. The forest closing in about us muffled the approaching sounds. Hooves? Boots? I couldn't distinguish it. Something that trod through an entirely different time of year, bringing a warning warmth with it, and a strangeness that made my throat tighten. The only thing I could feel happy about was that I did not smell that coppery tang of spilled blood or decaying flesh the vampire's minion had brought with him. Or peppermint strong enough to burn the fine hairs out of my nose! I knew it wasn't another minion, but I had no idea what a Master Vampire might smell like. Wrapped in magic and wards, Morty had written, and likely disguised beyond recognition. He could be pacing us now. I tried not to think of his name, but that didn't succeed. I wouldn't breathe it, though. I wouldn't!

Leaves crunched. The aroma of another season rose heavily into the air. Another bush noisily gave way as though our stalker no longer cared about stealth. I dug my phone out to call and found the screen black and unresponsive, dead as it could be. Replacing it in my pockets, I took a deep breath quietly. I'd have to name names three times to get anyone here—wherever it was—if they could get here.

Then I slipped my hand inside my coat and touched the lumpy bulk of Steptoe's flash-bangs. They might not stop whatever menaced us, but they would certainly cause a distraction while I got up the salt incantation. Then, depending on what I could discern, I would prepare one of the other offensive spells and hope I didn't set the forest on fire. Not that I thought I could, but the impossible autumn season might just be dry enough. Then Scout and I would have to run for our lives.

But I wasn't without options. Swallowing down the fear that tried to push up out of the pit of my stomach, through my chest and into my throat, I spread my feet a little to center myself. I prepped myself for some spell dropping.

And that's when the being strode out of winter, backdropped by the greenery and orange, yellow, and red color of leaves that had yet to fall in an autumn that couldn't be, and crossed the brook.

So tall that his head seemed wreathed in lower tree branches, he wore a fringed deerskin shirt and trousers, and moccasin boots that laced high on the ankle. I'd never seen anyone like him in person although he looked as though he could be a member of the Powhatan tribe, but Virginia has nearly a dozen indigenous tribes he could have hailed from. None of them dressed like this on a day-to-day basis, but he had. We traded looks, his fiercely brown eyes locked with mine, as I felt a shiver run through Scout. The quiver on the stalker's back looked well-stocked with arrows, and he carried his bow loosely in his left hand. I didn't know what I could say to him, and he didn't look like he wanted friendly conversation.

A squeak finally escaped my throat: "Who?"

He took another step forward without answering. Scout skinned his lips back. I froze for a moment as his body came free of the branches, and I saw that he carried a rack of antlers on his head and those mostly hadn't been branches at all. Not human, quite. More than. Someone on a level with Malender perhaps. A deity who looked distressed to find me in its territory. He nocked an arrow onto the bow as he raised it. The thought ran through me that it was longbows that ended the protection of medieval armor. That arrow looked like it could split me in two.

I got hold of a flash-bang and tossed it, to keep him at a distance, fearing those sharply pointed horns. It didn't go off as it should, but it made him drop his bow as it sizzled and smoked. He held his free hand up, and the explosion fizzled away with a tiny burp. I debated tossing another but figured it would be a dud as well. I hadn't wanted to pick a brawl at all and told myself he'd started it.

"That technology is useless in my realm," the being said. "But if it is a fight you want, I am willing to give it." He pointed at Scout. "Down."

My pup hit the ground belly first as if he'd been shoved into position. Although he shook all over, he didn't move. The command I'd taught him was Settle, but the intent in the being's words had been clear. Just as clearly came the notion that we were in trouble. "I didn't come to fight. I don't know how I got here. We'll just leave."

"Not before I judge you for your crimes."

Positive we were neck-deep in trouble, I tried to call for Carter, but the words died in my suddenly dry and choking throat.

"This is my world," the being said. "The day of my ultimate reign is nearing, and you trespass. How got you here, and what brought you?" His words tightened into menace and ended in a low growl.

I didn't know who he was, but my heart froze clear through my chest and the sinking, icy feeling plummeted to my feet.

Behind me, another voice spoke, and it wasn't Carter.

"Let them go."

I inched around enough to look behind me, and there stood my mother's Plus one. He'd been avoiding being clearly seen all afternoon, but now he stood. Fedora in place, and a grim expression riding his features, but it was the eyes, the eyes so close to me that I couldn't miss seeing them, recognizing the expression that I had once known so well. I got out one surprised exclamation.

"Professor!"

HE TILTED HIS head a bit and put one arm in front of me, herding me behind him, and didn't answer. I moved, but Scout did not. My rescuer repeated gently but firmly, "Let them be, Huntsman; your time, as you well noted, is not now."

Huntsman? The Great Hunt huntsman? The Wild Hunt? What had we just run into on the edge of Hiram Broadstone's estate? I knew the myth. I knew the terror and yet necessity of such a hunt . . . but I had no idea of its range. I hauled on Scout's leash, but my paralyzed dog could not stir.

The professor, not my crusty old professor of a few years ago—but then what phoenix wizard would want to be reincarnated as a doddering eighty-some-year-old?—nudged Scout with the toe of his shoe.

"Release the dog."

"I think not. He is one of mine, I believe, stolen when the year was young. I reclaim him."

"Stolen? Or misplaced because you have grown lax in your duties over the forests?"

They stared daggers at one another.

The professor waited a moment before continuing, "He has a new partner now. I propose this to you: let him live out his years with her and fulfill his bond, and when her life is done, take him to join you then. You are immortal and can afford a loss of a few years on that scale."

A few years? I was only gonna get a few years? Way to make

me feel better. I wanted to yelp in protest, but my lips and throat closed again. I couldn't tell who had really silenced me: the Huntsman or the wizard, but it seemed a moot point as neither of them would want to hear the blistering words I wanted to say.

The Huntsman lowered his head a bit as if he thought to charge us, wicked antlers and all, but it seemed he merely looked down upon my pup. When he looked back up, it was at me. "He seems well. Hearty and happy. He would have protected you against me. Your guardianship is adequate. If I release him to you, I expect that he will be kept as he deserves, and kept well." The being stepped back and flicked his hand. Scout immediately leaped to all fours and backed up to guard me from a better position. "A deal is struck. His life will be bonded to yours until the need is ended, and then he returns to my pack."

And suddenly, in the forest behind him, beings melted out of the woods in an eerie silence. I realized that he had only made noise in his earlier approach to alert or alarm me because this legion following him struck no earthly notes of their passage. And they possessed an absolutely ethereal quality. Horses too thin and elegant to be real. Riders upon their backs with horns or whips in their hands, hair and lips pale, elven or even more transcendent. Slender hounds loped about them, the Great Hunt rallying for its leader, and I couldn't look at them anymore. They were too terrible to watch, and I didn't want to be forced to join their ranks.

The phoenix wizard murmured, "That would be wise, Tessa," as he noted me inclining my face away from them. He dropped his arm which had been shielding me. "Another time," he said to the Huntsman.

"One day I will come for you."

"Well I know it. But that day is not today."

The Hunter only gave a frown for an answer.

A white-haired rider on the Hunter's flank raised a curved horn without valves that gleamed bronze, centuries old, and blew a charge on it. They all, Huntsman included, disappeared as if they had never been there. A cold wind keened through the woods. Autumn colors faded away again to bare branched trees and shivering evergreens.

We waited a long moment, and then the professor relaxed. He stood still as I swung about on him.

"Why didn't you tell me? What are you doing with my mother? Where have you been? What was that all about?!"

"I've been assessing the situation. I am not the old man you remember, nor the young surfer dude you used to refer to. But I am, indubitably, me. I have recovered most of my studied arts, my prime, and lately, a job. Not that I need one, I have caches of wealth scattered about, but I hate being idle, don't you?" He smiled faintly at me, a good-looking man in his forties, with a tinge of auburn in his slightly waved hair, and a bit more of the red in his mustache, and he looked good enough in his fedora to bring hat wearing back in style. He lived, and breathed, and carried an undeniable charisma. I almost understood why my mother considered him at all.

But he hadn't answered my questions. "What about my *mom*?"

"That is a bit more of a ticklish situation."

Winter rushed in about us and my teeth chattered once before I gritted them again.

"Shall we get back to civilization and discuss this?"

I realized then why Steptoe had been in and out of the house so much, to the point of exhaustion. He'd been seeking, his tail had told him the professor had to be near despite what he'd vowed to me, but his search had been in vain. "What have you done to Simon?"

"Led him on a merry chase, I'm afraid. The imp deserved it. I can't afford to be pinned down at the moment, and I'd ask you not to reveal my identity."

I waved a hand in the air. "How can anyone not see it? Not see *you*."

"Mary didn't. Or Carter. Even Scout here didn't sniff me out. Only you." He stopped and looked into my face deeply. "I'd like to know how you did."

"Your eyes. I couldn't miss it once I got close enough. Eyes are the windows to the soul and all that."

He gave a soft grunt before stepping back into motion. "Then I'll have to make sure that no one gets that near, I suppose."

"Your blasting rod was stolen."

"Retrieved, not stolen."

"You?"

"Of course, me." He reached over and took up my ring hand. "I'd like my ring back, too." His finger rubbed over the knob under my glove.

I peeled it off and then the ring, dropping it into his palm. "I think the stone ate the curse out of it."

"Let us hope so." He rubbed the thick gold jewelry a moment. "It seems probable. How did you get the stone to cough it up?"

"It just did. Maybe it knew you would be coming by to get it."

"Hmmm. We need a few ground rules. I've my doctorate, but you need to refer to me as Mr. Gregory. It took me a good bit of effort to replicate my degrees and credentials, and I don't want you to sink them in a moment of youthful exuberance. Still, you don't have to call me doctor."

I rolled my eyes. "You sound like an eighty-year-old. Do you talk like this to Mom?"

"Not if I can help it." A gleam lit his eyes for a moment.

I tapped the brim of his hat. "What were you doing buried in the Society crowd?"

"And it's a good thing I was because you have a temper for which you have no excuse. My excuse is spying on the enemy, as it were. But, no, I didn't realize you'd been asked to come in or that you would have agreed to it."

"You just walked in?"

"I have European membership that can be verified. I still have a touch of an accent, if you listen closely."

"Yeah." I thought about it. "Is that French or Irish or both?"

"Yes." He pointed ahead of us. "We shouldn't be seen walking in together." He nudged my shoulder to set me in the direction of the back doors, as he swung around to the front.

I stopped. "You didn't answer me. What about my mother?"

He disappeared around the brick corner of the estate, ignoring me. I took a few steps to go after him, but Scout wound about my ankles and tangled me up. I bent over. "Whose side are you on, anyway?"

Scout gave me a good slurp up the side of my nose and along my cheekbone as if to apologize. I looked after the wizard. Maybe the dog knew what he was doing.

As we drew near the back door, I could smell the luncheon with its heavenly aroma. Evelyn grabbed me up after I settled the dog and guided me to my seat which seemed to be insanely close to her parents, her, and Hiram, while my mother sat half a table away. I tried not to stare at them, finding that nearly impossible until Evelyn joggled my elbow.

"Isn't that true?" She smiled brightly.

I blinked. "What?"

"You knew Hiram's father." Evelyn gave me a look that chastised me for not listening.

"I did, and he was a good man. I've known Hiram longer, though, but I can see Morty's influence." I dipped my spoon back into the bisque, hoping I appeased Evelyn. "I've met Hiram's stepmother, too, an independent thinker and doer."

"Oh, a stepmother," cooed Mrs. Statler. I wasn't sure if that was a southern Bless Her Heart moment or not. As my Aunt April explained to me once, Bless Your Heart can be taken in two ways: one, genuine but most often, a rather judgmental observance. Aunt April only said it—rather blurted it out from time to time—in sincerity. But I hear the phrase dropped often enough to know mild condemnation when I hear it.

I smiled at Evelyn's mom. "You should meet her sometime. She's like you, unique and quite intelligent." A little flattery never hurt.

Mrs. Statler smiled. "My, my," and pushed her empty soup bowl a little away from her.

Under the table, Evelyn's knee nudged mine but in what context, I had no idea. I finished my soup as well and split a delicious, fresh-baked roll with Carter. I wanted to whisper my discovery in his ear and knew I couldn't. Someone might overhear, I couldn't predict his reaction, and the professor had asked me not to. At least one of those considerations kept my lips sealed.

Evelyn kept passing me the ball on extolling Hiram's virtues, along with his entire clan, and I responded without trying to sound as though she'd hired me to do a medicine show shill. I knew Mr. Statler would catch on fairly quickly and kept my participation down to as few murmurs as I could.

Every once in a while, I'd look down the table and see my mother laughing at something the professor must have said or sharing a small plate of food with him. She looked happy. Carefree. Adult in a way I hadn't seen her look in many years. Carter caught me watching them.

"Who is that fellow with Mary?"

"The one she told us about, the new doctorate at the university. Seems to be a nice guy."

"And you're okay with that?"

The fowl dish had been delivered. Duck, I think, from the looks of it, with the delicious scent of plum sauce. I stabbed it with my fork. "I was told it was none of my business."

"Oh." He watched me taste my tidbit. "Good?"

"Yes."

"I meant the duck."

"So did I." I met his slightly amused expression. "I don't want to talk about it."

"Fair enough."

I leaned a bit on him. "Is this the first time you've been to this home?"

"Yes. It's really something. I think I could fit my entire apartment into the living room."

"Actually, I'm more curious what you think about the grounds." I cut off another piece of the duck, enjoying it more than I meant to.

He took a moment to dab at the corner of his mouth with a napkin, a stalling move since he hadn't made a mess yet. "Any particular reason you're asking?"

"I was wondering how one could go for a walk along the tree line with one's dog, start out in winter, and end up in Halloween."

"Interesting. I take it this happened to you today."

"Only time I've ever been here." I enthusiastically scraped up the last of the plum sauce with the side of my fork. I licked it off and shook it at Carter. "This is seriously delicious."

"Want to finish mine?"

I eyed his plate. I did, but it wouldn't be fair, so I shook my head. "No, I'm good. I hear filets are on the way."

I watched as diners up and down the L shape finished their courses, got new refreshments, and sat back in contentment, not full but with their taste buds hopefully tantalized. Hiram caught my eye.

I ducked back in surprise. He had looked stormy still, and I couldn't understand what I might have done. Did he know about the Wild Hunt? Had a complaint been lodged? Or was it still about Evelyn? I couldn't tell if Evelyn had even remembered a word we'd exchanged, let alone taken it seriously.

Servers came in with trays, offering the filets at rare, medium rare, and medium well . . . I took mine at medium rare as did Carter. It was interesting seeing some of the choices. Then potato casseroles followed, au gratin or mashed, and a profound lapse in conversation followed that, punctuated only by the sound of sharp knives on porcelain, the scooping of serving spoons through the casseroles, and low sighs of appreciation. I didn't even need a knife for my tender filet, although I considered keeping one for self-defense later.

After dinner and various desserts—the catering company had gone all out and prepared trays of different goodies—people began saying goodbye and drifting off. The Statlers left but not without a hug to Hiram (from Mrs. Statler) and a hearty handshake (from Mr. Statler), and a long kiss (from Evelyn, naturally) so it looked like that had gone well.

Hiram dipped by our chairs long enough to say, "Stay behind. I need to talk with you."

My mouth dropped a bit in surprise because talking looked like the last thing on his mind, and hanging lips seemed unseemly, so I promptly filled it with chocolate éclair. Carter said to me, "Wonder why?"

I shook my head before licking a bit of whipped cream off my lips. "No idea."

Desserts and coffee finished, everyone took a look outside,

declared that night would be dropping soon, and off they went. Soon, it was only me, my mother, the professor, and Carter . . . and an uncanny number of clan Dwarves who descended from the upstairs as if they had just materialized there. The house bore their weight admirably, just an occasional groan of its massive timbers and stonework here and there, as it filled with them.

I recognized most of them from the primeval forest they rightly called home, but they weren't there; they were here. We gathered in the great room, and as big as it was, I felt stifled and closed in, a feeling I didn't care for, and which Hiram had never given me before. It didn't help when I saw the diadem of the Eye of Nimora appear and work its way forward to Hiram who put it on solemnly. My mother retreated to my elbow to ask, "What's going on?"

"I have no idea. Perhaps the . . . doctor . . . knows."

She frowned slightly at me. I gave a diffident shrug back. I caught a side-eye from the professor, but he said nothing. I could see him move a little protectively toward both of us. Carter put his hands on my shoulders and moved up close behind me. I could feel his warm breath on the side of my neck as he leaned forward to whisper.

"That gentleman seems familiar."

I closed my eyes, willing my body not to react in any way at all. Carter added, "Never mind. It's just me. I wonder what's going on."

Hiram raised his deep bass voice just a bit. "Quiet, everyone. It's time."

Time for what, I had no idea, but the feeling lanced through me that I wouldn't like it. I didn't act on my impulse although the professor did. The man I'd been told to call Dr. Meyer Gregory answered back, "Not here and not now."

"You have no say here. This is a trial and the court is convened."

"A trial?" My mother caught up my hand then. "What does he mean?"

"He's wearing the Eye of Nimora. I know you remember that jewel . . . and the crown is said to see the Truth. He's prepared to judge." Her skin felt slightly chilled as she gripped me in answer, and I could feel the fear in her. I rubbed my eyes with my free hand, as shadows surged in and out of the crowd and I tried to clear my vision. What did I really see mingling among the gathering? I couldn't tell, but I didn't like it. I thought of what Carter had told me of the corruption braided into the very fabric of our proud town, going back decades and even centuries. I hadn't raised my hand, hadn't called upon my stone to see with its shard of Nimora, but it seemed the Sight descended on me after all.

Carter called out. "Just who is on trial here?"

I recognized the blue plaid colors of the Waterman clan as one of its elders stepped forward. "We are here to accuse Mary Andrews and Tessa Andrews of breaching the veil of magic and threatening our very existence. If this duly convened court finds a verdict of guilty, the punishment is death."

It would be correct to say that I had had quite enough of people wanting me deceased.

CHAPTER TWENTY-SEVEN

WAIT JUST A DAMN MINUTE

"DON'T TELL ME this is just another ploy to get the stone." I brought up a handful of fire, but Carter reached out and absorbed it before I could even feel the heat.

Ignoring what I'd just stated, Carter said smoothly, "I was not aware that sentencing came before the trial, but I am aware that it should be commensurate with the crime. You're not in any way advocating for a fair judgment."

The Waterman opened and closed his mouth indignantly several times but didn't get a word out as he was jostled back in the crowd. Hiram put a hand up. "He speaks truth. We are ahead of ourselves. I do, however, have evidence." He reached back to a drawer in the sofa table that adorned the foyer, nestled in a little alcove leading to the stairs. He pulled a binder out of that drawer, and I recognized it as matching the binders of my mother's dissertation. Banded to it were several disks. It looked as though Faith Hawkins had not carried out her secretarial duties.

My mother made a low sound deep in her throat. "He's stolen my materials."

The professor said nothing, but a tinge of heat rose up the back of his neck from his collar. I hid my smile, recognizing the signs of his irritation. Between Carter and our phoenix wizard, I felt safer than I had in weeks. Carter turned his head to one side, assessing Gregory closely, and then his mouth fell open.

The wizard looked back at him, to give a slow smile. My

mother, however, hadn't noticed a bit of the exchange, nor Carter's startled response. She squared her shoulders. She glanced at all three of us, took a stance, and said to us, "I've been silent long enough. I've got this."

She looked at Hiram and the crowd of Iron Dwarves ringing him. "Do you all believe that I have exposed your secrets to the modern world?"

Dark shapes rose and danced among the agitated crowd and fell back where they could barely be seen. Like the watchers on our street below our windows, they had sharp-angled and angry shapes. I shook myself a little, trying unsuccessfully to rid myself of the phenomena. I scanned Gregory's and Carter's faces to see if they noticed anything, but they showed no awareness. Was my Sight just particularly sensitive for this?

Hiram shook the binder. A female voice called from the rear of the crowd, "That speaks for itself."

Mom gave a little nod to Hiram. "It does speak. Have you read it all the way through?"

He did not answer immediately before saying reluctantly, "Not entirely."

"Then your evidence is incomplete. You should be ashamed of presenting that."

Hiram's cheeks reflected his heat. "I read enough!"

"Then tell me how you reached your conclusion." My mother refused to back down.

"You list evidence of another world in proximity to your own. You cite examples in literature and song . . ."

"Poetry and plays, stories old and new, imaginings drawn from every culture. Imagination is the keyword here. Did I give nonfiction citations? Actual verifiable incidents?"

Again, Hiram hesitated. "I haven't run across any. Yet."

"Because there are none in my paper. And, Hiram Broadstone, if you had read my dissertation to its inevitable conclusion, you would know that I posited not that there was a real magical world, but that because of humanity's dreams, fears, and hopes we created a world of magic to meet our needs. It weaves throughout our music, our tales, our paintings, our ingenuity, our writings . . . but we cannot prove it exists. We only want it to, sometimes in the small measures of magical realism and sometimes in great doses of popular fiction. *Fiction*. But my work is not presented as actuality. None of my footnotes and citations refer to concrete examples or witnesses of real magic. I could, if I wanted, gather a few." She looked around the room and spread her hands. "I've been aiding and comforting and being friends with many of you this last year. Have I ever asked any of you to give me proof of who you are or what you can do? No, I haven't."

Without waiting for an answer, she took a deep breath. "In short, just wait a damn minute before you accuse me of betraying you. I'm well aware that you knew of my husband's heritage long before any of this. Did any of you take Potion Polly into your confidence and help her stand against those who accused that healer of witchcraft? Did you take her aside and tell her: we understand what you are, and what you're doing, and you're a member of our family, too? No, you let her drift without rules and aid. April Andrews rode a good luck streak that made her, for a short while, a wealthy woman of property. Did any of you stand at her elbow and tell her that a price would be paid, ultimately, for that luck, and it could be dire? Did you tell my husband, John Graham Andrews, the same? No. You kept yourselves apart and secret, kept the rules obscure and unavailable, and now—only now—do you reveal them, and expect us to understand what we've violated and that you anticipate punishing us. That is reality."

A Timber Dwarf woman at Hiram's elbow, her face twisted unhappily, spoke up. "It matters little whether fact or fiction if it is believed. It has the potential to destroy us. I believe we should treat this as we have always treated such threats. Extermination."

"She's right. It matters not her intentions but her deeds. That book will be the death of our peace, and probably of us as well."

I searched for the speaker but could not quite locate her amidst the Iron Dwarves shifting back and forth in their anger and concern.

Darkness hopped in and out of them. It choked me a little as it approached, as if it had substance more than shadows. I didn't want whatever it was touching us. I looked to Gregory and Carter to see if they noticed yet, but they did not seem to. What is it that they missed and I found?

"I understand your need for secrecy. Your worry and anxiety. But your response will only make things worse, if the worst happens. If you choose to run, you will be chased." My mother crossed her arms over her chest. "Outdated thinking, if not downright murderous. That won't stop publication. I've paid for it, and it's been scheduled. There are two things that can happen: it can be published and virtually ignored by academia, which is more likely than you think, or I can withdraw it from publication, pleading mental illness or some such, and beg for an extension to rewrite and present another dissertation. I'd rather not do the latter, because there is good reason to believe I'd be fired and possibly have great difficulty ever being hired anywhere else, and I would like to have a future. But if you have us killed, the paper will still be published. I have duplicates of what you've been handed. There's no stopping it at this point that way. I have you at a standoff, and I do trust that most of you have sense and fairness built into every bone of your bodies."

I doubted it, based on what I'd been viewing. Not among the Broadstones, for which I thanked mercy, but many of the others. Someone had breached this branch of magic long ago, become entrenched, and now exerted whatever influences it could, and called for my death.

It might be because we'd broken unspoken rules, but it was just as likely that the maelstrom stone was coveted, and a reward had been set for its recovery—over my dead body. If it had to be that way, so be it, but there was no way I was going to let my mother die as well. I reached inside to center myself for an offensive spell, on edge for when I would have to detonate it.

"Lies and more lies. The paper is already being talked about at the university. There are plans to take it wider as a textbook. We'll be revealed across the nation!" Then I spotted the speaker, none other than Faith Hawkins herself. A double threat, that woman . . . no, triple. Buried in the Society and University academia, and here in the dwarf clan.

"Totally untrue!" My mother raised her voice as I'd seldom

heard her. The crimson beam of the Eye cut across the room in answer, but it had become impossible to know what it responded to. Who lied? It did not point to anyone but everyone.

The crowd began talking among themselves, only Hiram silent, his gaze fixed on the two of us, his mouth a grim line. The foyer filled with the altos and basses of their tones, and the floor shifted as they moved restlessly. The entire house sounded with their weight and unease. They conferred and argued, grumbled and declaimed, and I could not read their expressions well enough to know if anything my mother said could make a difference. They judged her with every exchange.

I had the distinct feeling that, although he'd read part of the manuscript that day he'd sat at our kitchen table and after it had been delivered to him, the trial had not been his idea. We did have a friendship, and it was that strong. I watched the crowd around him, looking for someone insistent, someone traitorous. Someone had been the instigator, the perpetrator of ill-action, someone who had to be wreathed in darkness wrought by Nicolo or worse. Goldie had warned me days ago, and I'd nearly forgotten. I saw one face that stared at me belligerently. It shocked me to see a transparent, oily black shroud like the one I'd banished from Malender wrapped about the squared form, but when I returned that stare, they shuffled back into the crowd, unwilling to be seen. A vampiric shroud, Malender had told me. Steptoe had confirmed it. A coffin that ate its wearer from the inside out, renewing itself constantly as the being inside shrank and shrank . . . Malender had only survived because he seemed to be a demigod, and I'd showered him with salt. It seemed not quite visible to the dwarves, for no one reacted to it, but I knew what I'd seen: a horrible imprisonment that drew upon the life and soul of the prisoner to keep itself strong and functioning. I knew I had the instigator. Now to call her out and see if I could force her true colors to show. She'd kept herself hidden for months, perhaps even years. Time to reveal her for what she was. Before I could do that, however, trouble bubbled over.

Someone called out, "Lies, all lies. Humans lie, we know that."

My mother drew herself up straighter. "Did the Eye of Nimora judge me? Did it?" I couldn't see her face, but I knew her piercing blue gaze swept the crowd. "I'm sorry that you can't value my friendship as I have valued yours. But I won't stand silently while you threaten my daughter and me." She turned on one heel. "Nor, I believe will Carter Phillips or the man you know as Meyer Gregory but who was once known to me as Brandard. I will not threaten you with the powers of a phoenix wizard or a sun lion as you've threatened me, but I do have friends and allies. If you unjustly find us guilty, you won't be able to impose your sentence."

Havoc broke out. Gregory reached for my mother's elbow and turned her aside slightly and she managed a small smile at him. "Did you think I wouldn't know?"

"Madam," he said solemnly, "you and yours have always happily surprised me."

I took advantage of the pause to point out the woman who, unsuccessfully, tried even more forcefully to move toward the rear of the pack. "There are not many Fire Dwarves, I believe, but I name that one as traitor." Her determined shoving to get out of sight gave her away, or perhaps it was that cloud over her. No matter. I saw her, and she couldn't hide from me. "She's the one who helped the Eye of Nimora be stolen by elves and tried to frame Goldie Germanigold. She misdirected Mortimer Broadstone to his untimely death. She's lied to all of you. And, unless I'm greatly wrong, she is servant to a dark master."

She flared up as I thought she would, but I had been prepping my ice spell quietly while my mother spoke, and I let loose even as she did. Dwarves scattered. Hiram did not hit the floor, but he did duck as he swung about. Hail peppered the hallway as she burst into fire. The blaze died away with a hiss, wreathing her in smoke. She bared her teeth and tried to push her way free of the gathering.

"Jocosta Flintridge. Stand your ground."

The young woman did not, shoving her way out of the press, and took to her heels to the back of the house. I let Scout off his lead, saying only, "Trail."

He took off, and I ran after.

Hiram did as well and caught me for a step or two. "Don't," he warned. "Justice waits for whoever goes out that door!"

He fell behind, unable to match my speed, and I had no idea what he meant until I burst out onto the driveway and saw Jocosta halted, her arms up to protect her face, Scout afraid to come closer, as Malender stood and uncoiled his great whip of razors and flame.

CHAPTER TWENTY-EIGHT

NOBODY EXPECTS THE SPANISH INQUISITION

"STAND," COMMANDED MALENDER, "for you are filled with crimes unbowed to justice. That is my job, and I will have it." His declaration sounded overly formal, but then Hiram must have called him in to deal with a guilty verdict. The scourge coiled about his booted feet, its orange glow reflected like small suns on his black leather pants, his shirt opened at his throat, and his wavy hair seemed slightly blown back from his face from a wind that did not touch me. His presence filled me with fear that I had not felt around him for seasons. He did not look at me, however, his bright green gaze fixed on poor Jocosta who looked as though she might melt into ashes right there on the drive. "You have been judged."

"No! Not me. Her," and Jocosta flung her hand to point in my direction.

His body did not move, but his glance did, taking me in, and returning immediately to her. "They called me here, but I have no need to rely on the judgment of Iron Dwarves. I know sin when I see it. Punishment is mine to give out."

I thought I knew what he had planned, and although I had run after to catch Jocosta, I didn't want to see her flayed alive with the scourge. And I certainly didn't want that deed to be on Malender. As terrible a being as he could be, I'd never sensed evil in him. "Let her go, Malender."

"She deals with untruths that bring death. She deserves the justice that I am intended to deliver."

I could see the shroud about her. Could smell its rank and oily odor. Could almost feel it as if I touched it, greasy and slimy beyond measure. Surely Mal could as well. If he did, he would know instinctively what it was that drove Jocosta to her crimes because a similar shroud had enveloped him for decades.

The deity looked at me again. "You have brought me back to my true self. Do you regret that?"

"Regret freeing you? Never. But can't you see that she's as possessed as you were? That Nicolo has his hooks in her?" The air shuddered about me at the sound of the vampire's name. I shouldn't have said it; I knew that too late now, but how else to tell Malender without saying it? My throat suddenly went dry, and I lost what other words I would have added. So I brought up my salt spell, and—with a few passes of my hands and a choked word or two that might not be enough—I dropped the cloud over Jocosta Flintridge.

He stepped back hastily, having been deluged before and not enjoying the sting. His whip hissed and spat as the flames ate bits of excess crystal bouncing about the driveway.

As for Jocosta—it buried her up to her neck, after having appeared over her and cascading down and around her, and she began to weep. Whether in pain or fear, I couldn't tell, but I felt sorry for her. Her wails filled the air. I knew the caustic effect the salt had on her shroud and how she must be blistering as it ate away her binding. Did she miss it as well? Would being expunged that way destroy her as it had almost destroyed Malender once?

I put a hand out toward Mal. "Help her!"

"She would have seen you dead."

"She couldn't help it; she was too far gone. Can't you do something?"

"I am Justice."

"Justice is not worth it without mercy," I told him. "Maybe your world is filled with absolutes, but mine is pretty . . . wibbly-wobbly."

His brows rose in his elegant face. "Wibbly-wobbly?"

"Yes!"

"And what might you mean by that?"

"Nothing is all black or all white. There are shades of gray everywhere."

"This is where many humans go wrong. They misjudge their errors. This is why a being like myself must exist."

"Everyone needs mercy as you needed it once. I believed in you. You scared me to hell and back, but I believed in you."

"I owe you a life-debt. Very well." He stepped close to Jocosta, his boots crunching on the salt, and his gaze locked onto her pale, tear-soaked face. "Your life has been begged of me. Do you understand?"

I backed up a step. "I didn't ask that of you," but Jocosta's response overrode mine.

She whispered, "I can see again."

Had the vampire blinded her to everything but his will? Perhaps. I didn't know what she meant, but I could hear the change in her voice.

"I asked if you understood what Tessa Andrews wants of me."

"M-mercy."

"I am not inclined to offer it." Malender bowed his head a moment, a stray lock of hair falling onto his forehead. He seemed to be contemplating.

I became aware that Carter stood at my left elbow and the professor at my right. "Be careful," Gregory warned. "He is borne into his full powers now and not amenable to mortal persuasion."

Carter disagreed. "He has always listened to Tessa. Or at least had a dialogue with her."

Malender lifted his head and looked toward us. He gave a nod of acknowledgment and recognition before adding, "You would both be wise not to interfere with me."

Did I want to see the deity of Justice brawling with my sun lion and phoenix wizard? No, I most certainly did not. It could very well turn into a scorched earth battlefield, and I don't think Mal had any idea that the Wild Hunt ranged not far from Hiram's backyard and might be pulled in as well. It would be a war of supernatural powers such as the modern-day world has never seen. No, I didn't intend for this to be any sort of a last stand for any of us. I ventured, "That life-debt."

"Yes." His brilliantly green eyes rested on my face with their stern gaze, but I could see a little gleam in them as well. I amused him, for reasons I had never understood. He tolerated me as I gathered he tolerated few people. He seemed to be waiting for something.

Carter put his hand on my wrist. Warm, comforting, and his touch requested my attention. "Do not," he said, "ask for her life in exchange for your life-debt. It is worth more than you know. We will find a way to save her."

Advice on making deals with deities, huh. I should respect his words; he knew what he was talking about. If I had any doubt, the professor said on my other side, "Listen to Carter. It could be vital."

I could only think of one battle where it might mean everything to have Malender on our side, and that thought gave me pause. I spread my hands. "I didn't ask for it to be canceled by saving Jocosta, only that you find within yourself some small pity and understanding. I'm not giving her mercy, you would be."

"Yet knowing what I am, and what I must do having been restored to myself, you should realize the difficulty of what you propose."

I exhaled forcefully, a little afraid of the word games he seemed to want to play. I decided to call Malender's bluff. "All right, then. Do what you have to," and began pivoting on my heel. I caught sight of Carter's amazed expression, and hidden humor on the professor's face, shadowed by that fedora. "I'll be greatly disappointed in you if you can't find that in yourself, but it's your choice, so I guess I'll have to accept it."

My words hung palpably in the air between us. Malender stood as a powerful, charismatic being. I'd always been in awe of him and that would never stop, but, yes, I'd be really disappointed if he couldn't look at Jocosta and see that Nicolo had enslaved her will and controlled her. Who could have stood up to that? He hadn't, once upon a time. I don't know how long Nicolo's vampiric shroud had surrounded and cut off Malender, but it might even have stretched into centuries. Could he not look at a Fire Dwarf now and understand the surrender?

"You did not dare to remind me of myself." He echoed my thoughts as if having read the last of them.

"I didn't think I had to."

Malender tilted his head ever so slightly. "No. No, you do not." He chopped his hand in the air and rain began to fall, heavily, from skies that had been cold weather clear a second ago. The drops drenched Jocosta who eventually stood, freed, in an ankle-deep puddle while the professor had opened an umbrella ridiculously big enough to cover all three of us. Not a drop of rain, naturally, touched Malender. His whip stayed, lethally sharp and flamboyantly aflame, pooled in loops about his booted feet.

"Your people," he said to her, "will undoubtedly have other punishments. You can treat them as an interruption of your life or an enrichment of the purpose of it." He gave a slight bow in my direction. "Tessa of the Salt." Malender snapped the whip up, so that it revolved about his torso, and disappeared in a haze of smoke that smelled of cedar and a touch of sulfur.

Jocosta collapsed to her knees, put her hands to her face, and began to cry again, a quiet, heart-wrenching act of sorrow.

The professor had evidently been holding his breath, for he gave a low growl and muttered, "That was close."

Carter caught me by the chin and turned my face toward his. "You take the oddest chances with magic."

"Do you think he heard?"

He didn't ask who. He knew. Carter shrugged slightly. "Likely. If we're lucky, it will have been just enough to pique his interest, not enough to come investigate. He knows where we are, currently, and Hiram's clans generally have good defenses against him."

"Jocosta didn't."

"No, but I imagine the clan elders will be discussing that deep into the next few nights. How did you know?"

I shook my head slightly. "I *saw* it. I couldn't understand how none of you seemed to see it, too. I knew, after what Malender had been through, how it must have been agony. Carter, I've seen those souls on their hooks at the Butchery."

"You seem certain."

"I couldn't mistake it."

The professor had unwound himself and began walking back to the main house. We trailed after, Scout trotting quietly by my side.

"I've been working on the task force trying to pin down his bases of operation."

"That's what you've been doing."

"It is. He's mostly underground, with tentacles everywhere, and his forces are as deeply interwoven into his doings as they can be. We can't really shake anyone loose to give evidence against him, and we've never been able to get anyone under-cover with him. His control is legendary. That's when I realized what he was, and why we couldn't get to his operations. But imagine my telling the DEA or FBI that we're hunting a vampire."

"No one would believe you."

"Exactly."

Hiram and others buffeted past us, going to Jocosta and raising her to her feet, some gentle and some shouting at her. I looked back over my shoulder. "I feel sorry for her."

"That says more about you than her." Carter put his arm about my waist, drawing me close, so that we walked in tandem, keeping each other warm, Scout trailing.

"What do you think is going to happen to her?"

"No idea. However," and he looked at the bank of windows by the door in use, "I'd say everything we did was closely observed."

"But my mother . . ."

"You have to be on guard."

"I'll turn them in if I have to. Anyone who threatens us." I put my head on his shoulder. "It would be nice to have it in writing, though."

"Oh, they won't do that," said Gregory. "That would put them in a very precarious position having asked for the death penalty in the first place. No, it's likely that they'll bluster a bit, step back, and put it on hold. It is, also, still possible for Mary to put in a rewrite of sorts that might soften her view."

The Mary in question joined us on the steps and heard the last few remarks. "No," my mom said. "I don't think I'll be doing any rewriting. The kernel of my paper is, after all, the veil that hides magic."

"Please understand, Mary, that there is an enemy which will use that paper as justification for its actions. The matter won't stop here."

She and Gregory traded a long look. "Are you certain?"

"Nothing is certain about that enemy except that he has many strategies. His roots go back centuries. I am shocked that he found a way into the clans, a near impossible group to infiltrate. But Tessa has something he covets, and he'll do what he must to attain it, in addition to his many other misdeeds."

"Is there a way to stop him? What if she gives him the stone?"

"And add to his powers? No way, Mom. I'd have to be crazy to do something like that." Or desperate. I might become desperate at some point, but I wasn't yet.

"In the meantime," Carter added, "We have already stopped several attempts, so we're ahead of the game. He knows he has an opponent with allies and powers. He'll be cautious."

"How about we convince him to quit?"

Carter shook me lightly. "Don't even think it."

"We have to do something."

"We," he said firmly, "will think of something."

Hiram joined us as we walked into his house, the warm air inviting and still smelling of the afternoon feast. He cleared his throat. "I owe you an apology."

"Maybe."

He twitched a bit at my answer. "You have to understand my concerns."

"You might have discussed them with us first, you know."

He gave a little salute to me. "Well I know it. Circumstances, however, seemed far different at the time. The dissertation shocked me. I'll admit I feared to read it completely."

"At least you found your traitor."

"That we know of. It is like that old saying, one bad apple spoils the barrel. Have we more? I'll be busy determining that. I'd like to know how you saw it in her."

I could see the weariness and worry in his eyes. "It was the Sight. You have it, don't you?"

"We do, and yet we didn't see her in a true light. How did she appear to you?"

"A vampiric shroud wrapped about her. It might have been difficult to see apart from her normal shadow, but I could tell."

Hiram muttered a curse to himself before noting, "We shall have to sharpen our skills. As much as we avoid the modern world, we seem to have lost our ability to cope with it. The traps are many."

"I'll help when I can, if you need it. What are friends for, anyway?"

A troubled look ran across his face so quickly I wasn't quite sure I'd seen what I'd seen. He put a thumb into a suspender strap, looking away from us, and mumbled, "Our friendship is, at best, strained and must stay that way for the moment. The clans are not as forgiving, and it will take months, perhaps even years, to clear their minds on this. Tessa, I need the journal back as soon as possible. It wasn't mine alone to surrender, and it belongs with the clans. I'm sorry to have to tell you this and I hope you understand."

My mom stepped forward and gave him a slight hug. "We do. Now you have to understand that a dissertation isn't a best-selling novel and not likely to have many readers. It'll stay mired in academia."

"You need to give yourself more credit. What I read was quite enjoyable and gave credence to my fears."

"Well, thank you, Hiram. We look forward to the day when you step into our house again."

He did not respond to that, but lines etched a sad look into his face.

I thought a minute. "I'll forgive you for a box of chocolate éclairs, if you have any left over."

His eyes narrowed a bit as he thought and nodded. "We very well might. I know I ordered extra."

Sure enough, the catering company coughed up a pink doughnut box filled with éclairs and a waxed paper bag full of bones and scraps for Scout. I accepted them with open arms as the pup danced about my feet, and we took our leave. It wasn't the apology I needed, but for the moment, I'd take what we could: our lives and éclairs.

The weather held as we drove home, Mom's car following ours, and Scout making impatient noises in the backseat, eager to get at his doggie bag, but I could see clouds boiling on the horizon. Winter seemed far from being at bay, and if not tonight, then tomorrow would be bitter and slushy. Carter and I didn't say much, both of us somber because of losing Hiram. It might be temporary, it might not.

Entering our neighborhood, a dog's body lay splayed across the road. Bloodied and limp, obviously dead, but not obvious if it had been hit by a car or what. Carter came to a stop.

"Stay here."

I had no intention of arguing with him. He got out and bent down just long enough to get a close look before straightening and returning.

As he put the car back into gear, he said, "Nasty bit of work. Has this been happening around here?"

"Unfortunately, yes."

"Do you still do your training in the area? I know you run. Don't. Something is at work here, something vicious."

"Got it. Not even with Scout?"

"He'd give his life for you, but if you don't get in that situation, it would be even better."

"Okay." Scout's head hung over the console between us, his eyes wary as he looked from one to another. I pushed on his muzzle, forcing him back. "Not now," I told him and after another worried eye roll, he retreated.

"What do you think it is?"

"Other than something that enjoys killing? No idea. I'm worried about Steptoe, though."

"Simon? Why?"

Carter wouldn't take his eyes off the road to look at me.

"Not Simon!"

"He is a demon, even if a lesser one."

"He's come over to the light side!"

"He's trying, but he has basic impulses he might not be able to deny. I don't know enough about them to tell you how his metabolism even functions."

"On hot tea and cookies, if I had to make a guess." I stared out the side window. An intense sadness settled about me. I hadn't freed my father, I'd lost Hiram, my mother's career could be in jeopardy, the professor was back but wasn't, and the rest of my world seemed to be in upheaval as well. Our death sentences hung suffocatingly close. There were times when I couldn't see the victories for the losses.

We both lapsed into silence until Carter pulled in the driveway. He turned about. "Don't do anything foolish."

"What, me? Foolish?"

"And stubborn." He leaned forward to kiss the tip of my nose. "I'll call in a bit."

"My cell phone is portable. I could be answering it from anywhere."

"I expect you to be at home."

"Yeah, yeah, yeah." I swung my legs out and instantly felt a cold that wanted to settle into my bones, brittle and deep. My nose went icy, along with my ears. I balanced the box and bag while I stood. "Coming in?"

"No, work to do. I took the afternoon off to be with you."

"Awww. That's so sweet."

"Isn't it? Save me an éclair."

I looked at the box. Hefted it to make sure it weighed sufficiently enough that there would be leftovers. "You've got a chance. No guarantee, though."

"Don't make me put a spell on you."

"You can do that?"

"Well," Carter answered. "It depends on how I rank with you compared to how chocolate éclairs rank with you."

I raised an eyebrow. "It's going to be very, very close."

Laughing, he reached over to pull the door closed after me, and as the car pulled away, I could still hear his cheer. It sounded nice.

Scout danced around my feet as we went inside. I'd left the furnace on at a reasonable level, so it wasn't cozy warm but neither did the house hold a chill. I dropped the box and bag on the kitchen counter, calling for Steptoe as I went to the thermostat and boosted the heat setting.

"Simon! I've got pastries from the luncheon!"

My voice echoed through the empty house. Mom hadn't come home yet with the professor, and who knows what they were up to. I didn't want to think about it. I peeked in the mudroom to see if I'd caught him napping on his cot there, but it stood empty, with a few rumpled blankets to show he'd been there once upon a time, just not now. I had no idea where he could have gone or what he might be attempting to do, only that it was unlike him not to be about. Was he still out chasing the elusive professor's trail? I'd missed him before. Now I was just plain worried about him.

In the kitchen, I had to give Scout some of the scraps promised to him before he had a conniption fit and to reward him for his good behavior under stressful circumstances. I decided to reward myself, too. I snagged an éclair and went upstairs for a nap. Being unconscious for a while appealed as a really sound solution to the day. I put my pods in, tuned in the music, and closed my eyes.

Evelyn's call woke me, but only because the phone vibrated somewhere under my chin and shoulder. I answered with a yawn.

"It went great, didn't it? Don't you think?"

"It seemed to." I tried to stifle another yawn. "Did you get any feedback from your parents?"

"Dad liked him. Mom seemed cautious."

"You didn't hit them with anything like 'this is the guy I want to spend the rest of my life with,' did you?"

"Not exactly."

I rubbed a bit of sleep from my right eye. "What do you mean by that?" Silence from her end. "Evie."

"I told them that I hoped they liked him because I could see myself in a relationship with him. My father said 'Fine, I don't like you flitting about,' and my mom said, 'It's a little early, but he seems nice.' Honestly, do they even see me as an adult?"

"They do, and that's okay, then. Would you rather they'd gone all Romeo and Juliet on you and forbidden you to see him?"

"I guess."

I sat up and stretched before putting the phone to my ear again. "What did you expect?" She was twenty-one, I was twenty, I doubted if any of our parents looked to marry us off yet.

"More enthusiasm?"

"Maybe," I suggested, "if you waited until after the inauguration and your dad settled into office, they might not have their minds full of other business. They're busy right now."

"True! I need to remember that. The caterers were great, weren't they? I think our reception will go well. I'll have to re-mind Dad to switch the menu up a bit."

"But keep the desserts!"

"Definitely. It should go fine."

"If we're not in a snowstorm, agreed."

"I looked the weather up," Evelyn said seriously. "Cold with overnight freezes, but no rain or snow. Tuesday night should be fine."

"I don't know who decided to invent swearing-in ceremonies in the middle of January, anyway."

"I think it's supposed to be a comment on the survival of the fittest."

I laughed at Evelyn. "You could be right."

Now it was her turn to yawn. Before she could sign off, I stopped her. "Wait. You haven't had anything strange happening around your neighborhood, have you?"

"It's gated. Not much of anything happens here. Why?"

"Oh, pets missing, that kind of thing."

"How awful! It's not . . . not supernatural, is it?"

"I don't know. If you hear anything, you'll tell me?"

Evelyn took a breath. "Of course! Now I'd better go to sleep before Mother comes in and tries to take my phone away."

"Good luck with that!"

And then she was gone, and the silence seemed immense.

I slouched back down into bed. Scout gave a little whine at being disturbed and rolled over on his back. We slept until the sound of Mom doing early morning laundry woke us.

She was all dressed and ready to leave, one hip up against the dryer and her phone in her hands when I leaned around the corner.

"It's Sunday," I informed her.

"It is. And I have a date for brunch."

That thought lurched around in my skull a bit. "Really? Seriously? Who with?"

"You wouldn't know her. She's also on the department secretarial staff—Becky Sawsmith."

I wondered if she was lying to me because I really hadn't ever heard the name before. "Ummm. Okay."

"It doesn't hurt to be nice to all the secretaries once in a while. They do a lot of the work behind the scenes. It's the secretaries that have always pitched me as a professor. I need her balance against Faith Hawkins if I intend to put my paper into publication. I've got recommends from most of the committee. One way or another, I intend to end this."

"Ah. So you fill up your schedule as you fill up their stomachs?"

"Believe it or not, yes, if it's the only way to get classes assigned and get the presses rolling." She slipped her phone into the outside pocket of her purse. "What's your day going to be like?"

I looked at the baskets on the floor. "Finishing the laundry, for one. And then I have to go online and do some work on my spring semester. They're nagging me for a major. I have my schedule, but they're not happy."

"Still?"

I shrugged. "Haven't told them."

"You don't look like you've any idea, either."

I sat down on a rickety old three-legged stool that we'd inherited with the house. It was at least as old, if not older than Aunt April, and we had put it in the laundry room to keep it clear of Iron Dwarves who could reduce it to kindling and splinters. "Once upon a time, I wanted to be an architect. Gave up that idea. Too expensive and a wee bit too much math for me."

"I had no idea. Architecture?"

"Buildings fascinated me. It's different now. Maybe I've

grown or changed, but it's not the buildings anymore, even though they're magnificent. It's the people who need them, want them, live in them."

"But you want to do something . . . ?"

"I still want to build bridges, but maybe . . ." I paused, suddenly unable to say what I wanted.

She waited, a slight smile on her lips, for me to find the words. I managed. "Between people."

"Like a psychologist?"

"Not really. Maybe a mediator." One of her eyebrows arched up. I waved a hand. "I know, I know, I've a temper, and it sounds stupid. I know. But if there were a way to get people to sit down and listen to one another, it might help, right? Everyone deserves a voice. I read today that people listen so that they can respond, but they should listen so they can understand."

"I think this is personal for you."

I nodded slowly. "Yeah, I guess it is. Losing Hiram and all . . . he should have come to us and talked it over, first."

"I agree. Now all you have to do is find a job that fits that description."

"I'm not sure there is one."

"Diplomat, although you're talking about a smaller scale."

"Maybe."

"I don't see you in poli sci. I think you should look into culture and ethnic studies."

I didn't have any of those classes in my background. "Why?"

"You need to know and understand the peoples of the world, first, before you get into the peoples of the unknown world. Their likes and dislikes. Their ways. Their taboos. The commonalities as well as the differences. You need to have a very thorough knowledge of what you'll face when you sit down to work with them, don't you think? Anthropology and cultural studies will give that to you. Some of it is guesswork, admittedly, but many cultures have survived to modern times. I think you'd be good at it."

She made sense. I put a finger up. "But I have no background in it yet. I would have to add a year, maybe even two in order to graduate Skyhawk and more years at university beyond that."

"If you do, you do. Anything worth having is worth working for, right? Whether you study here, or if we have to move, you'll be able to find the classes you need. We'll get through it. And just think, with your background—and mine—you will be an expert in fields that haven't even been invented yet." She straightened. "I hate to leave now, but I have to. Talk more when we get home?"

"All right, but I still have that paperwork to get in."

She smoothed my cheek as she passed by. "Don't fret over it. They'll change it for you if they have to. College counselors have learned to be flexible, if nothing else."

CHAPTER TWENTY-NINE

SWEARING IN AND JUST PLAIN CUSSING

THE CROWD CAME winter-prepared, with stylish puffy coats, faux fur, and even a few well-lined leather dusters as they pressed close to the platform to see and hear their mayor's swearing-in. A few carried protest signs because that's what we do if we don't like the results. The outgoing mayor, a popular African-American, smiled as the Statlers assembled on the platform. The former mayor, far from being old in years, was headed to a higher elected office, so good humor reigned all around. Three years' term length made it difficult to be un-happy with the office for too long, so there was that. I followed at Evelyn's heels, having been designated her moral support, and I had no idea what had happened to Hiram. She hadn't sobbed on my shoulder, so I figured nothing dramatic. Perhaps he'd had to work, or maybe the Statlers hadn't wanted to unveil him as her companion just yet. I spotted Carter, working the crowd as security, but he looked up at me only once, his atten-tion intent on his job. He and his workmates stood out, not in heavy, heavy coats but scaled down for easy access to weapons and movement. They wore vests and such under their shirts, I could tell. I would worry about him in the biting cold, but he carried a fire within him that would keep him warm. The other security wouldn't be so lucky.

Mom and the professor had paper cups of steaming hot cider in their hands, near the front row, and saluted me as I sat down next to Evelyn. Evie stared at them a moment.

"He looks familiar," she whispered to me. She'd left Hiram's party before the big reveal. I hadn't told her and debated a moment or two whether I should. I realized that her high-pitched squeal of amazement might jar the proceedings and decided later would be better.

Gregory gave both of us a look as if he could read minds before ducking his chin down a bit to listen to something my mother had evidently been saying. They shared a soft laugh. My stomach did a little flip. Was he courting her? How could he? And how could she dare allow it? My father was still around, if imprisoned, and I was this close to getting him sprung. I could feel it. Why could she not wait a few more weeks and then make up her mind?

Although, from the way we had talked, she'd already waited years. I hadn't seen it, hadn't noticed, couldn't know what they'd been going through before. I only knew the tragic end result. It made my insides want to curl up and ache. I could feel the tension all the way up my throat and into my jaws. I stared out across the gathering celebrants until Evie nudged my knee with hers.

"You look angry."

"I'm not." I was, but she was right. This was her father's ceremony, and the people in front of me were looking forward to the swearing-in and then the lawn supper promised. Behind us, I could hear the caterers working efficiently. There wouldn't be any chairs, but the tall tables waited to hold plates and platters of great food. Overhead, the sky stayed a brazen blue, with fingerlings of clouds that skirted through quickly and without threat. Perfect weather for a winter's day.

I could see the security moving about, nothing too drastic, just staying with the ebb and flow of the attendees. But one woman drew my interest. Not terribly tall, but with incredibly good posture and high-heeled boots to die for—and a long, black coat that must have been mink or sable, a bold statement. Real fur had almost dropped out of garments entirely, but this . . . well, I don't know fur, but looking at it, all I could think of was a panther. Sleek. Primal. Lethal.

That last surprised me as I thought it. What if Morty had been wrong and Nicolo was not male but female? What if? And yet I couldn't convince myself that a Master Vampire would be working the spectators out in the open and as effectively as she was. But as I lost her and found her again, I thought my assessment correct. She looked positively predatory. I shrugged that off to a bit of paranoia, but she definitely worked the crowd, going from a set of attendees here to another set there. She generally got welcomed, but there were a few who turned their backs on her. As I watched, I couldn't help the feeling that I knew her, that I'd seen her before, but I couldn't place her, and—of course—she didn't get near to the platform for me to see her face.

Evelyn must have caught me staring, for she leaned over a bit. She murmured, "Nice coat, but I'm glad PETA isn't here."

"Real fur, you think."

"I do. I don't approve of it, but it's well tailored."

"Who is she?"

I felt Evie shrug slightly. "Don't know her. She came to my dad's transition office a couple of times—the place has been full of dealmakers since the election—and I know he doesn't particularly like her."

"But you didn't catch a name?"

"No. She has this slight accent, though. I want to say it's French, and she looks like a European with money."

An ice-cold feeling lanced through me. "French?" It couldn't be . . . she had died . . . an enigmatic sorceress who, once upon a time, had been a love of the old professor, and who played fast and loose with the sides of light and dark. But Remy was gone, wasn't she? She wasn't a phoenix wizard like the professor. She couldn't just reappear out of the flames, reborn. No. It couldn't be. I had both liked and hated her. She'd helped me once or twice, then turned about and nearly killed me herself. I couldn't trust her as far as I could throw her.

But she had been undeniably sleek and fashionable, beautiful and definitely French.

Remy? Alive? Or Undead?

I put a hand to my throat to call up that warmth of Carter's love, that spark that lay buried within to kindle the reassurance I needed. I leaned so far forward out of my chair, I almost slid off the edge of it, straining to see the woman's face. Would I recognize it if it was her? I told myself it would not matter. I had the Sight now, without depending on the tiny Eyes in the stone very often. If she turned and faced me, from anywhere in the first eight or nine rows of viewers, I would see her face well enough to recognize her. Or would I just deceive myself into believing I saw someone I could not possibly see?

My mother frowned slightly and pulled on Gregory's arm. The two pushed as close to the platform as they dared. Carter had to stop them, but we all knew he wasn't going to throw them on the ground and cuff them.

The newly reconstituted professor peered up at me. "What is it?"

"I saw somebody."

"There are literally hundreds of somebodies standing out here. Anything more specific?"

"It can't be, and I can't verify it, but . . . there's a woman working the crowd. Hand shaking and so forth. Making contacts. Offers. I'm not sure what she's doing, but I'd say she was working, somehow. It could be Remy."

"Re—" he blinked. "Can't be."

"Tell me that! But she's rumored to be European, most likely French, and she has the style."

Evelyn pulled me back on my chair and shushed me. I could see the officials on the platform getting into their positions and the affair getting ready to start.

The professor put an arm about my mother's waist, and the two of them carefully melted back and disappeared among the viewers. Unseen, I rolled my glove off my hand, and rubbed the stone, willing it to awaken. It did. I wanted clarity.

I raised my hand to fix a bit of hair back into place, giving the Eyes a chance to swing over the area as I turned my palm outward. What did they see? What did I See?

Whether Remy or not, she sensed the interest and left, for the only thing I could spot definitely was the woman striding to the back of the crowd, across the field to the parking lot, and away. A lost opportunity, of sorts.

But I'd been right about one thing. The person held power. My stone and its eyes recognized that much and telegraphed it to me. So much power that I felt grateful it hadn't been unleashed on the unwary and innocent. I could see the aura rippling, not only about her as she strode away, but in her wake. Those touched seemed to know it in some small way, a shiver and a fidget, a fuss with their coat or sleeve or, like myself, with a strand of hair that wouldn't lay quite flat. They couldn't have told me what they felt, but I could see their reaction and I knew. A ribbon of oily smut marked her path. Some of those she'd approached shrugged it off; others seem to be tangled hopelessly in it, faint as it was.

I didn't like what I saw at all.

What had she intended to do if she had not been noticed and her own senses made her wary? An assassination? Or just bribery and politics? Or was she tagging souls that were vulnerable to being ensnared and taken?

I shrugged my hand back into my glove and tried to look alert as the ceremony began.

Since I was only an observer and not a participant, other than in the prayer and a few other rituals, I pondered over the sights that worried me. Thoughts blew through my mind like storm clouds on a wild and blustery day, seething and then thinning to nothing, boiling and churning, only to disappear. I had no proof of my suspicions other than that a personage with a lot of sorcery had walked through, working their will here and there, and left.

What did we intend to do about it?

Hiram joined us after the ceremony, among the cheering. He wore a classic Armani suit and looked quite at ease in it, leaving me a bit surprised at his style. Perhaps Evelyn had coaxed him into it. He ducked his chin at me.

"Tessa."

I tried to smile back, but his frown discouraged that. He stood back a little, unwilling to even get within a certain distance of me, as though I could contaminate him. Then I saw the handprint on his right shoulder, sooty looking with a faint sour smell to it. He'd been marked.

Something had to be done. I couldn't leave Hiram under any influence that woman, whoever she was, might have left on him. I put a hand behind my back, centered myself, and brought up a pinch of my salt incantation. Weight filled my palm. With a slight smile, I murmured that I needed to find my mother, stepping past them and into Hiram's personal space, patting him on the shoulder as I passed. The handmark hissed as it faded away under the crystal assault.

Salt went every which way, but he didn't seem to notice. Evie said, "Oh, my goodness," and reached out to brush the shoulder of his suit off. She raised an eyebrow at me, but I just shook my head and kept walking. No explanations, not today. Hiram, still unaware, took up her hand and spirited Evelyn away to enjoy the catered lunch.

My plans to find my mother and Gregory went awry. I couldn't spot them at the buffet tables or eating areas. Left without a partner as Carter continued to work security, I stood at a table with a small plate of goodies and picked at them. I wouldn't have eaten at all if I thought the other sorcerer had gotten near the caterers, but I hadn't detected any interference. The stone's power leeched off mine, so food seemed to be in order. Evelyn swung by my table long enough to leave another pink box of éclairs with me, laughing at my surprise as Hiram then steered her away again.

At this rate, I might even get tired of having them for dessert. When I got in the car, I kicked my heels off and wiggled my toes. Turned the heat up to full blast and the radio followed after.

I drove up to hear Scout barking hysterically and wildly in alarm. I could clearly hear the dog's distress and threw myself out of the car. The entire house lay in late afternoon dimness, not quite nighttime yet but definitely gloom-ridden. Shadows arched everything. The fact that Scout barked loudly and vehemently somewhere near the side door sent me scurrying, wondering what could be happening. I yelled at myself for not coming home sooner.

The porch light, on a motion activated switch, blazed golden into the dusk. I couldn't see much except that I was too late.

Simon lay sprawled on the drive, limp and unresponsive, blood pooling underneath him with his suit coat torn to shreds as was his bowler hat. My heart froze.

I RAN TO him and fell on one knee, not even feeling the pain or
the numbness of my bare feet in the coming evening freeze. All
I could think of was that I had to stop the bleeding, but there
was so much and from everywhere, I had no idea where to
start. And his jacket, his magnificent jacket that carried invisibility within it, flapped in shreds amid a rising breeze that carried a spiteful chill on it. The coat was and wasn't an intimate
part of him. It might even have been a second skin, even though
he'd lent it to me once. I didn't know. I'd never asked . . . and
he'd never told me. Scout hunkered down a few feet away from
us, whining. He wouldn't come closer. I didn't yell at him for his
cowardice. He was still just a pup, if a nearly grown one, and I
knew he was sensitive to the magic side of things, both light
and dark.

Little sparks of fire burned here and there among the slashed
skin and clothing and, heaven help me, all I could think of was
Malender when I saw that. He'd come for Steptoe, and I hadn't
been here—none of us had been—to protect him. When had
Justice been here? Before or after the ceremony? After, it must
have been because the pool of blood was still warm and spreading. Then again, I had no idea what a lesser demon's normal
temperature might be. I wondered what might have pulled Malender here? The animal deaths? Did he think Steptoe had gone
rogue? Then I saw the faint debris of flash-bangs among the
flickering flames. Simon might have set the flash-bangs off too

close to himself. Out of desperation, a last stand defense? I peeled my gloves off, cold or not.

I tried to pull the biggest gashes closed, willing the stone to go red-hot and cauterize them, but it was too late to stop the overall damage. I had to do something, had to restore my friend to what he had been once. Flesh closed in ugly purple welts, and yet he still bled as I leaned over him. Simon's eyelids fluttered, and I stopped, paralyzed. He lived? I hadn't quite dared to believe he could.

His hand closed on mine, his eyes fully opening. "I been tailin' it, you see? Keeping you lot safe. But it caught up with me first. No help for it. Too fast for me. Moves like a whirlwind of knives."

He looked it, caught in a tornado of slashes. "Just stay with me."

"No worries, ducks. Too late for me."

"Never! I'm here. I . . . I've got you."

He coughed, a wet, choking sound. Blood trickled out of his lips as he did. I couldn't bear it.

"Don't you dare die on me."

"It's been a good gig. Time to bow out."

"No!" I passed my left hand over him again, flesh sizzling as the maelstrom stone did the work I willed it to. It hurt him, I knew. The heat sizzled my flesh as well. He jerked and groaned with every wound shut, and yet the bloodstain beneath him continued to grow and spread. How much blood could one body hold? "I'll bloody kill Malender," I said grimly as I sealed another huge slash.

"Too wrong. Wasn't him."

"Had to have been. I've seen that whip of his!"

Steptoe tried to bring his head up, his skin as pale as I'd ever seen it, the English rose blush of his cheeks gone. "Look in th' yard. 'Tweren't him. I did . . . what I c-could."

"Don't you leave me. I'll be right back." I stumbled to my feet, angled across the driveway and then saw the ungodly mess scattered over the backyard. Something had killed a large gray-and-white owl there, feathers everywhere, the bird's body twisted and ripped, in a heap.

But it was Goldie herself that tore through my sight, and the havoc she'd wrought, that filled the backyard. Her beautiful armor, ripped apart, her bow broken, her sword shattered into needle-like shards, her bloodied and contorted body surrounded by no less than four vampires, only one of which stayed in one piece.

The other three had been mangled, limb from limb by Goldie. She might have prevailed but for that last bloodsucker. I could see her throat torn open, his arm still over her torso where it had fallen, talons out, a piece of her bow buried in his chest as they'd both fallen. They'd taken each other down in one last, mighty struggle. Death throes wet the browning grass with blood and more feathers, and rags of the black shrouds the vamps had worn . . . I stood and stared, voiceless, in grief. Shock filled me, and I staggered back, my fist to my mouth.

What had happened here, at my home, while we were gone?

I made my way back to Steptoe and squatted down. I took the cuff of my sleeve and wiped his mouth dry.

"Goldie?"

"They got her, but it took all of them."

He gave the slightest of nods. "She watched th' house. Got caught up in it. No match for her either. Was the last watcher that got us."

My stomach clenched in reaction. Dying, dead, gone, and lost forever. My eyes stung as hot tears spilled down. "Did you fight for her?"

"Best I could. It got both of us, th' bastard."

I couldn't call Carter, still embroiled in the event cleanup and debriefing. I'd seen enough of the Master's minions, all spiky and jagged, nothing human, but I wasn't about to let him walk away this time. I should never have let that woman go at the swearing-in ceremony, nor the creature that I'd spotted outside the house. Had to have been one of Nicolo's. This was my home and my family, and I'd failed to defend it. Never again. I could and did cry out the only other name that came to mind. "Meyer Gregory!" Three times only, and then, my face smeared with tears and blood, I kept trying to keep the life in Steptoe.

"Don't be crying for me."

"Then you stop dying on me. You're my friend. You're like my favorite uncle. You're part of my family! Fight for us, Simon."

"Can't be helped, luv. Can't be helped at all. We gave those suckers a good battle and lost." His words wheezed. I barely understood him, but I did.

A steely resolve filled me. I knew where to find the bastard. Where to free other victims. Alone or accompanied, I knew where I had to go because Nicolo had been *here*. I brushed my sleeve over my eyes to see better.

The professor did not materialize out of thin air as summoned. Instead, a screech of car tires stopped at the front of the driveway, doors opened and slammed, footfalls ran toward me, and then warm bodies surrounded me as I shivered.

"I can't—I can't stop it. He just keeps bleeding." I took a sobbing inhale. "And Goldie's dead, in the yard."

"Good gods," the professor said as he bent over and ran the tips of his fingers over Steptoe's forehead. "Who did this?"

"Can't say his name, but I'm going there. We've waited too long. I'm going to put an end to him." I flung my arm out and pointed to the backyard. "Out there."

"Mmmm." The professor left to see the carnage out back, and my mother slipped close to my side, putting an arm around me, warming and steadying me.

"It looks bad," she murmured.

"I don't see how he's held on this long." I passed my palm over an upper arm wound, but nothing happened. Futile, it had given him all it could. Weakness ran through me, we were both tapped out, me and the stone. The professor returned and got down on one knee, too. He took up Steptoe's hand.

"There's not much I can say."

"I'm going," Simon answered, weak voice barely above a whisper.

"Then there's this I will do—for Tessa as much as for you. You've earned it." Gregory took a small pen knife out of his pocket and made a cut against one fingertip and held it, dripping blood, over the pool under Simon. Crimson streams mingled with a faint humming sound. He said a few words that might have been Latin or maybe Celtic or maybe even Sanskrit.

How would I know? His blood continued mixing with that spilled out of Simon as he finished in English. "You are hereby released from any bond I have placed on you, free, old friend, your redemption finished and successful."

"Free?"

"Always and forever."

A long breath quavered out of Steptoe, but he hadn't quite let go. He looked for me, and found me, eyes bleary. "Watch your backs, mates. Th' bastard is offering immortality for the stone."

"We'll keep her safe," Gregory told him.

"Do that, guv. I may be back, if I can." His eyelids fluttered again. His chest heaved up and down with a guttural sound and, at that, I heard his death rattle. I began to cry again before he ceased breathing.

My mother held me close, and I realized she cried as well. She drew me up onto my feet. Leaning together, we supported each other.

Steptoe's body turned to ash, blood and all, crumbling away, every scrap of flesh, cloth, and hat felt, until nothing at all remained of him, not even his precious tail. Scout got to his feet, tiptoeing close to join us and cautiously sniffed the now empty driveway. I forced myself to inhale. "Just like that?"

"Another plane, another form of existence. He doesn't have a soul quite like yours, but he does have an essential existence. He's not gone, in the way you might fear. But you're not likely to see him again in your lifetime or even mine." Gregory looked thoughtful for a long moment.

"What of Goldie?"

"Yes." Gregory turned on heel. "That might be a tad difficult. Her nest will not be happy, but they should be notified. They will want her remains. I'll take care of the vampire carcasses."

I swallowed, not anxious to be confronted with harpies who were likely to be extremely unhappy. "Okay. I'll be here for them."

"You," my mother said firmly, "will put on shoes and have a heavy coat ready. They'll let you know when they're here. In the meantime, we'll be waiting inside." She took my elbow to guide me away while I heard the professor chanting something to the wind. Even upstairs in my room, while I changed and dropped my dress in a bloodstained heap in the corner, I could hear his voice carrying.

By the time I was done, all sunlight had left the sky, and a sliver of moon fought with cloud cover to be seen, its silvery light dappling in and out. Mom stood in the kitchen. We waited.

We could hear the beat of wings, even against the growing storm wind. My pulse quickened in anticipation. Would we have a fight on our hands, or would they take their leader and sister and leave quietly? I ought to say something to them, but I had no idea what. I'd never had a sister.

But I knew what it had been to lose a father and a best friend. Loss is loss. I'd put my slippers on and hung my jacket over a kitchen chair, so I picked it up now and went to join the professor as we answered the summons at our door. He said softly to me as we crossed the threshold, "Best not to invite them in."

"Really?"

"Goldie had steady moods compared to most harpies I've treated with. They can be a nasty-tempered race."

"Understood. What should I say to them?"

"No names. None at all. Do you understand? We cannot risk drawing his attention. He's already been awakened. We don't want to draw him here. It's best you say nothing at all. Let me handle the details, mmm?"

"Yes, sir." I fell in a step behind him, willing to let the professor take the brunt of the encounter. Following behind him, I marveled yet again that the stoop-shouldered old man I knew so well was gone, morphed into this man in his prime with a stride I had trouble matching. Broad-shouldered and slim-waisted, he looked as if he could hold his own in a tussle, even against Carter. I did prep my ice spell as I hurried after, taking advantage of the lowering clouds and nightfall.

Up and down the block of our street, and even the block behind our house, the lights suddenly dimmed into twilight. I couldn't tell if that happened through harpy magic or if it was the professor's doing, but the flight came in, virtually unseen by any but us, winged women in armor as they ringed my back-yard. The only thing not the least bit menacing was that they hadn't pulled their weapons. Not yet. Wings spread and beating gently, they lowered until their booted feet almost, but not quite, touched the browned grass. A ginger-haired woman led the formation.

Gregory reached inside his overcoat and withdrew the crystal-headed cane I knew well, shrunk down in size to fit his inner jacket. It lengthened from baton size to full-fledged cudgel as he did. The diamond-like knob drew on whatever illumination the failing streetlights could muster and burned in reflection like a silvery moon. Without his saying a word, the cane identified him to the incoming flight. They touched ground as if reassured.

The head of the formation rested her gaze on him. "Finally returned, wizard?"

"Not quite in the nick of time, it seems. I mourn with you all the loss of Goldie Germanigold." He spread his hands over the strewn remains. "She fought a bitter battle against a Master which should not be named, and we lost one of our own as well who came to her aid." He paused, before thumping the end of the cane upon the ground. "We will avenge them both."

The redhead, her glorious hair cascading down over her shoulders, her armor dyed in stripes of black and amber, considered him before answering, "We wish you success. We accept your account now as it is, but if we find out later than you have not told us the entire truth, we will return for you."

"I would expect nothing less."

I stirred behind him, feeling insulted, and he waved a hand back at me to still my restless movement.

Two other harpies took a canvas sheet from a backpack one of them wore and dropped it on the ground. In minutes, they had gathered up what remained of Goldie and wrapped it tightly in their tarp.

"What . . . what will you do for her?" I blurted out, unable to stay quiet any longer.

The professor winced.

"She died in combat. She fought well and hard and nearly won against impossible odds."

The redhead assessed me before answering, "She is a sister and a war-leader and one of the best of us. She will be honored highly and remembered."

"And her eggs?" I pressed, knowing she had never incubated any of them to life but that she always intended to, someday. We had talked about her progeny months ago, while on another quest of sorts.

"They will be raised, and her young will be taught of their heritage." The redhead eyed me sternly. "And what will you do for her memory?"

"I intend to cut out the heart of the son of a bitch that killed her."

The harpy gave a grim and lopsided smile, capped with a brusque nod. "So be it. Good hunting."

She signaled the wing and they rose in their pattern, one of them carrying the tarp bundle close to her chest. Wings surged and they disappeared into the gray-and-black clouds lowered in the sky.

Gregory let out a heavy sigh. He turned to face me. "I should have expected it, but when I say keep silent, it would be best if you listened."

"Obedience has never been my strong suit."

"As well I know. I don't believe you did much damage, but you need to understand your promise of vengeance will be remembered."

Fury rose inside of me. "I won't be hunted anymore! It's my turn now. I've had enough—and I intend to put a stop to it. I'm going after him."

He waved us inside. "Now to consider plans. From the way you talk, I gather you know where the Master may be most vulnerable."

"I have a pretty good idea," I admitted.

"Carter will have my hide if I let you go haring off to avenge our friends. We must plan—and plan well."

We retreated and prepared to start a war council. It would

be awfully short of our usual number, which hit me with a sharp pang somewhere close to my heart.

I should have expected that the wizard wouldn't take being disobeyed lightly because he put something in our second cup of tea that put us out cold, me and my mother, and we barely made it to the living room sofa and armchair before passing out.

CHAPTER THIRTY-ONE

SERVED COLD

IF MY TONGUE and mouth hadn't been all swollen and yet dried out, I would have given Gregory an old-fashioned talking-to. But whatever he'd used gave me a persistent hangover and required two or three glasses of water to drown. Instead of yelling, I sat and gave him the stink eye as he bustled about the kitchen making scrambled eggs and toast for my mom.

He paused by my plate, spatula in hand. "Want any?"

"Dough." I sounded like I had the worse nasal cold.

"Hmmm. All right then." Gregory nodded at me and passed me by while I glared daggers at his back. I thought I heard a muffled snicker.

Jabbing my hand at my drink glass, I slogged down more until I felt like I could talk somewhat reasonably. "When id Carter coming?" Still a trifle nasally.

"Soon. He has to do a bit of research, and the police computers seemed to be the best option." Gregory checked out the expensive, antique watch on his wrist. "It's three AM. Time and tide will wait for us."

Mom discreetly shoveled half her magnanimous portion of eggs onto my plate and pointed at it. I didn't want to eat, but it seemed mandatory, so I did.

Huh. Truffle salt and chives, along with a bit of American cheese improved the standard fare. Not that I would compliment him. No need to add to his ego. I did wonder where he got the seasonings, though, because I knew what we had in our cupboard and it didn't include what I tasted. Had the old—hmmm, middle-aged—guy developed some sleight of hand in the months he'd been gone? Or had my mother just been holding out on me? I stabbed my fork full and enjoyed another mouthful. Really good. I evidently made enough noise chewing and swallowing that Gregory turned around and saw me.

He didn't say anything, but I saw the faint smirk on his face as he put the cooking pan aside and refilled his coffee cup. It might have made me smile, once upon a time, but not this day. Not with losing Hiram, and then Steptoe, and Goldie. It made me realize how much darker the world could get . . . and had already gotten.

"It's just us," I stated the obvious.

"So it appears, but we are not woefully insufficient. Your abilities have grown, and your discipline. We have no need to worry about Carter, even though it is close to the dead of winter. I myself am robustly skilled once again. We should have enough in our armory to do what's needed." He paused. "Any flash-bangs left?"

"About eight, I think."

"Excellent. I hoped he'd been up to leaving you with ammo."

"He struggled with it."

"Did he?" The professor looked thoughtful again. "Not on my account, I believe. Demons need their own renewal now and then, and he must have been fighting that off. It explains, to me anyway, how he lost his final battle. Normally, Steptoe would have inflicted a great deal of damage himself."

"Renewal?"

"Yes." The professor topped his coffee cup with a bit of cream and sugar to it. "Don't ask me about the process, I'm not privy to his ritual. Most of them are a bit unsavory, but I do believe he would have amended it to fit his new path of redemption."

I fussed. "There have been missing and slaughtered animals all over the neighborhood."

"Not Steptoe's doing! No, more likely that of the minions sent to keep watch on you."

I felt a little better. "You're certain?"

"Fairly certain."

I settled back in my chair, aware that he wouldn't say anything more on that subject and found myself glad he didn't.

My mother let out a long, drawn-out sigh.

"Problem, Mary?"

"I'm sorry that Hiram and the others have withdrawn their support. I wish he would have finished the dissertation and understood it better. He's still distant."

"But you're letting it stand?"

"I am, Meyer. I worked hard on it and think it's of benefit. Perhaps one day we'll have a chance to meet the other side face-to-face and value each other. Who knows? It might even come about with Tessa's help."

"Oh?" The professor gave me his attention.

"I put in for my major, cultural and ethnic studies. I want to help the peoples of the world accept one another. Diplomatically, if no other way."

"Commendable. And your abilities may be very helpful in that. Or not. You might be considered part of the enemy."

"I'll face that if it comes to it," I told him.

"Your obstinacy can be an asset as well." He rested both elbows on the tabletop and leaned forward. "Do you think you can definitely verify it was Remy you saw?"

I'd almost forgotten her. I shook my head. "Couldn't see her face well enough. She ladled out bits of vampiric shroud here and there, tagging different people, without any real goal that I could see. She even hit Hiram, but I cleaned him up. He had a marking, here," and I indicated my shoulder.

"How?"

"Same thing I used on Malender. Salt."

"Basic. Cheap. Not often a method that would come to mind."

"Better than garlic and holy water?"

"Measurably better. The other two don't have many results that I've seen. Rowan wood crossbow bolts are remarkably effective, however."

"And who has one of those?!"

Gregory waggled an eyebrow at me.

"Of course, you would," I conceded.

As I spoke, the side door to the kitchen opened with a swoop of frigid air, and Carter stomped inside. "Would what?" He'd evidently caught what I'd said.

"Have a crossbow," the professor answered him. "Come in, come in. You've a choice of hot tea and brandy or some fresh brewed coffee."

"Yes." Carter flashed a grin as he sat.

My mother quickly fixed him a mug of one and teacup of the other. He shot the coffee mug in two gulps, black, and then wrapped his hand about the tea and inhaled the smell of Earl Grey plus some decent brandy wafting off it.

"Cold out?"

"Of course. Too cold to snow, they tell me."

"We've weather moving in. That'll change in a day or two."

Carter looked dubiously at the professor but did not dispute him. My mother slid a warm biscuit with butter nearby and he gave her a grateful look. Half a biscuit in, he noticed the silence the rest of us sat in. "It's too quiet. What's happening?"

"We had an attack here at the house. We lost Steptoe and Goldie as they tried to defend the home."

He dropped his cup, caught and juggled it in time, and set it down in its saucer with a rattle. "Dead?"

"And gone. We can only be happy that they kept the place from being infiltrated. The house harbors nothing. It is safe."

"That must have been some battle."

"Brutal but quick," I said, my voice thickening as tears brimmed in my eyes again. "Over in minutes. Vicious. Nothing left but shreds."

Carter reached out, pulled me in, and held me close without saying a word. He knew, just knew, how I must be feeling. The tears fell, but I did not sob because he steadied me. I listened to his heartbeat and felt that warm glow he'd left inside me heat up just a touch, so that I would know. After long moments, the shoulder of his shirt damp, he pulled back.

"So . . . what are we going to do about it?"

"The Butchery," I told him. "I think his power center is at the Butchery, but not the bar. He . . . he transcends time, somehow."

"And you've been there. We've discussed that. In the time-displaced building."

"Very eerie and yes. I've been in and out twice now. Once in a dream and once being pursued. I think he opened the door to me." Carter knew, of course, but my mother and Gregory needed to be filled in. I uncurled my hand on the table and rubbed my stone. "He'll do it again. Third times pays for all, right?"

"Carter seems to be familiar with this, but I am not."

"I can't comprehend that," my mother piped in. "Karaoke nights and all? I know it's popular with the university students."

"It's popular with everybody. But it has two faces, and the second one is grim. I had a nightmare about it, went in search of . . . I don't remember what now . . ." I did remember, too clearly, but I wasn't about to tell her what I'd encountered. "I walked in and it had reverted to its original purpose, a meat and carcass butcher's shop, from old days. But people hung on its hooks, people in terrible pain, and I couldn't help them. I almost lost myself in there." I paused. "Evelyn called me to an exit I hadn't been able to find, and I fled. It was a dream, so her presence seemed logical at the time. I think I saw souls, but I can't be sure. Then, the other week, when a car came to get me for the Societas Obscura meeting, I got into it. It was the wrong car, but I had no idea. I didn't realize it until we neared Old Town, and I was locked in. I busted out and ran through the back alleys. Something stalked me, and it took everything I had to evade it as it tried to herd me toward the Butchery."

"You didn't call for help?"

I hated to see the fear and concern on my mother's face. "I couldn't. The whole area seemed to be a dead zone. My phone went dead. The stone leeched away at me until I nearly dropped, and then suddenly, everything came back to normal. I don't want to go back, but it seems clear that it's the center of strong magic. I've been taunted to return. When I go, I intend to take some serious firepower with me."

"Some would say," Meyer suggested, "that we give him the stone and walk away."

I narrowed my eyes as I looked over at him. "Give a powerful being even more power? No one in the state . . . maybe even the coast . . . would be safe."

"I'm glad you realize that." The professor gave me a nod. "I wanted to be sure we had a fighter."

"Fighter, hell. I said I'd cut his heart out, and I will!"

My mother stirred. "I'd rather you didn't get that close."

"This is one enemy we can't fight at a distance. And it looks as though we won't have aid. The Society won't. Hiram's clans are out. Only Goldie would have answered our call, and she's gone. Simon, too. That pretty much leaves the three of us." I wiped my face dry before adding, "And Malender."

"Mal?"

I tapped my index finger on the table in front of the professor. "He owes me a life-debt."

Carter asked sharply, "You didn't redeem that for Jocosta."

"Tried not to."

"You're sure."

"Pretty sure." He was there, but evidently the words exchanged by me and Malender had been private. Still, I thought I could count on Mal.

"Well then. He'll be formidable as well, and we know he has a score to settle against the Master. Added incentive."

Carter finished his drink. "Intend to include him in our planning?"

"No. Best not. I think Tessa should summon him when we need him. Otherwise, he might find a way to back out, saying that he needs to be neutral as Justice. We call him in when we need him, Tessa tells him she's redeeming the life-debt, and he can't forbid her."

"We want to be very careful where Malender is concerned."

"I saw the scourge. He has become the powerful deity of old, but I'm just as willing to believe he would rather not be the person he has been created to be. We can't, however, promise him change. He is as he must be."

Wow. That sounded like the handsome being was just as imprisoned as he had always been, although by a different master.

The professor patted my wrist. "You're not condemning him. Malender will fight for you if given half a chance, and I think he will find it fulfilling."

"Really?"

"It's hard to tell with demigods, especially one that's been as hidden away as he has for eons, but he knows the world has changed while he has not."

"Demigods fade because no one believes in them anymore?"

"Sometimes." He pushed his chair back. "Now, given what we saw at the swearing-in, we may have Remy to contend with as well as the Master."

"Remy?" repeated Carter, stunned.

I nudged him. "Surely you saw her working the crowd?"

"No. One of the other guards did mention a pushy woman, but I didn't think anything of it. A lot of the onlookers seemed a bit discontented. We did a lot of calming down and soothing. If you saw and recognized her, we'll have to assume it's because she wanted it. Decoy, maybe."

"Precisely. Remy stirred the pot. Or someone very like her."

"But she's dead."

"Undead," I corrected him. "Probably."

"I can handle her," Gregory stated.

"Like you did last time? I don't think so." They had been lovers once, I knew, from when the country and both of them had been relatively young. Magic ages mortals differently. The last time I'd seen Remy alive, she'd been vibrant and beautiful in her way, and younger even than my mother, and the professor had been a crusty and irritable eighty-something. I'd found out a little bit about their history the hard way. She'd nearly killed me more than once. Saved me at least once on another occasion and warned me about shifting alliances. Experience told me she should know, if anyone, about changing sides.

Gregory's face blushed a little, and he turned a bit so my mother couldn't stare him full in the face. "Another lifetime ago."

She leaned toward him, their shoulders brushing. "I understand that." She cleared her throat. "If we're picking this battle, and the Butchery has to be approached through its veil, it seems that we have to have bait. I'd rather it not be Tessa."

"I agree, but we may have no other way to force his hand." Carter's expression hardened.

I drew a circle on the table in front of me. "I don't think we're going to need to do that."

"What do you have in mind?" Carter's tone went even, but underneath the tabletop, our knees touched, letting me feel the tension running through him.

"Evelyn opened the door out for me last time. I think she can open the door in."

"Statler? Why on earth her? And how?"

"Because, professor, she's a seer, and a rather good one. She doesn't channel it often—it seizes her—but she can see into times and places others can't. Forward and backward. That sounds like an ability we can use to access the Butchery. She can see when that door opens and get us through it. She's been incredibly accurate."

"And if you have Evelyn," Carter added, "you'll get Hiram."

"That, too. A very upset Hiram."

"Seers don't work like that."

"She has done it before. I think she can do it again. How else can she see into the future? And Hiram won't let her come along by herself."

"It could be a great deal riskier than any of you think. None of you have seen an Iron Dwarf go berserk. I have. He could be a devastating ally . . . or he could aim all that destruction at us. You'd have to convince Evelyn it's necessary, and I'm not at all sure you're up to that." Gregory reached for his coffee mug, noticed it was empty and set it back down with a clatter.

"She's new to the idea of magic, but she gets it. A lot happened while you were gone."

"So it seems." He checked his wristwatch. This time I got a good look at it and found myself impressed at what might be a vintage Rolex. He must have some impressive hoards of goods hidden about the states that he'd put away through the ages. "It might be worth the peril. Understand, if anything happened to Evelyn, you'd have the clans down on our necks. If there's anything left of us."

I considered it before shaking my head. "You're right. Too much to ask of her. I don't want to be foolish or stupid."

"It's late. I suggest everyone retire and get whatever sleep they can. More plans and action to come tomorrow." The professor stood briskly, the movements of a young man, and once again I found myself a little surprised by the new person he'd become.

My mother walked him to the front door while Carter stayed behind with me. He traced the outline of my face gently, brushing away a stray bit of hair, and smiled at me.

"You're not talking me out of this."

He made a sound that was not quite a chuckle or a grunt. "I didn't think I could. This is for your father as well as Steptoe and Goldie."

"Damn right. I don't know how my father got mixed up in this, but he did, and if there's any chance I can free him by bringing down N—the old Master, I will."

"There's a reason he hasn't been removed. I can almost certainly tell you that, every decade or so, there've been a number of attempts, and all have failed. I've been on assignment, trying to detail his various workings. He's devious, calculating, and has no conscience whatsoever. He'll be difficult to stop."

"We haven't tried yet." We leaned together, foreheads touching. "The stone will get us where we need to be."

"He'll see through any illusion." His warm breath feathered across my face.

"It can be removed—if it wants to be. We know he covets it." I kissed him, ever so slightly. "I'm betting that if the stone thinks it has an opportunity, any prospect at all, of inhaling some of that vampire magic, it will."

"He'll snatch it out of your fingers before you could blink."

"Not if I'm Seeing. I won't let him."

He kissed me back. "Tessa. I think the professor's right. We should go in without warning, and that means soon. We need some sleep and fresh ideas."

"I have ideas."

He did laugh then, backing away and standing up. "So do I, but not now, not tonight."

"Chicken."

"Bock, bock," he said softly and made his way to the front of the house where my mother had evidently just said good night and stood framed in the porch light as Gregory drove away.

They gave each other a half hug, and I watched from the warm foyer as the winter evening tried its best to freeze our doorway. She closed the door firmly and locked it.

Mom faced me. "Ready for bed?"

"Yes, but I'm going downstairs first."

She nodded. Hesitated half a beat before saying, "Don't tell him. I'll do that."

"About what—oh. All right. That seems fair."

"Thank you."

She went upstairs, Scout following at her heels, evidently quite happy that somebody in the building had the good sense to head to bed.

I had business elsewhere. The cellar door creaked a bit as I opened it, and the light flickered twice before it steadied and shone truly. Both surprised me as did the feeling of spidery webs as I descended the steps. What the hell? I brushed away at my face, disliking the feeling, and then I realized I had blundered into a few of the milder wards protecting the basement room. Annoyed, I complained, "It's me!"

Arms flailing a bit, I reached the stairs' bottom and vigorously dusted myself off even though I knew the webs had to exist only in my imagination. I grumbled for a minute before raising my hand to search for my father, the Eyes open and looking.

I found no sign of him. My heart did a skip-beat of anxiety. "Dad?" I turned on my heel, scanning every inch, even the shadowy corners, of the room. Finally, I spotted what I both feared and hoped would be him: little more than a wavering mirage in the farthest corner away from me. Even my Sight showed little more in the way of detail. I wouldn't have known what it was I saw except that I knew what I'd expected to find.

"That's got to be you, Dad. Somehow. You're scaring me, you know."

The mirage strengthened a bit, coming nearer, and I felt a bit of the coldness that ghosts are supposed to bring with them. "You can't give up like that. We're very close to doing what we need to get you back."

The faint chill danced across my face, brushing the hair off my forehead as if a hand reached out. The faintest whisper reached me. "I know . . ."

"You have to hang on."

"The stone."

Was he arguing with me? I could no longer hear him well enough to make out his tone. I could not see his transparent face with any expression. The agonizing thought that I was too late hit me. "Don't give up! Don't you dare quit on me." I'd implored Steptoe with the same words. It hadn't helped then. I feared it wouldn't now.

"The stone."

I cupped my hand to the empty air, stone flashing a bit in the artificial light, its marble depths showing creamy brown and obsidian and gold highlights against the parchment background. I'd often thought it would make a beautiful pendant, carved down, without its magical tendencies. The edges of the stone cooled, telling me my father touched it.

"Let me in."

The voice, stronger, even if the image wasn't. I was startled by his demand. "What? No. It will gobble you up, Dad, and it won't spit you back out. You'll disappear." I curled my hand up tightly, shutting it away. "I don't know why you'd want that. We've got a team. We're going after that son of a bitch and taking him down. Not just for you. He's woven evil throughout the fabric of the whole city. We're taking that out."

My fingers went icy. I could feel other fingers clawing at my own. "Let me in."

Fear, absolute terror, at losing what I'd already actually lost, and never really recovered, no matter what I tried. The feeling went to my core. "I can't do that. You don't know what the stone will do. I have some idea."

My father pried my hand open with cold and brittle fingers. Again, his thin and whispery voice. "Let me in."

"No way."

A sudden blast of energy knocked me off my feet. I hit the floor, rump first, elbows and feet thudding down next in absolute surprise as I gasped. My hands went up in the air. And then my stone inhaled what was left of my father.

CHAPTER THIRTY-TWO

INTO THE ABYSS

"OH, MY GAWD." Numbness claimed my entire arm. I sat and watched my limb shake. Energy thrilled throughout it, pushing pins and needles every which way until, finally, I could slightly feel again. Not pleasantly. I flexed my digits. They moved stiffly, with an ache and a buzz, as though I had suddenly become partially paralyzed. I rolled my arm about, the strange feeling of its not being quite mine flowing all the way up to the shoulder. What energy he'd had left, he'd expended to get the stone to take him, and it had.

The knowledge that I'd lost him, truly lost him, flooded me. Hot tears began sliding down my cheek. "What did you do? Why?" I shook all over, my arm tingling as circulation fought to return. "We had the key, finally. Why did you quit on me?" Then I gathered myself, not to stand but to try to hold myself together, crouched there on the cellar floor. "We're so close! I needed you to hold on. To give me a chance. To believe in me. And you have to go and quit on me."

I tried to scrub my cheeks dry. Words kept tumbling out, even though I knew I talked to someone who was no longer there, not in any way. "What am I going to tell Mom? How am I going to tell her I failed?"

I didn't know if I had the sheer guts needed to go after Nicolo now without freeing my father as a motivation. I had no idea if I could do it, even with my friends helping. How could I ask them to sacrifice everything when our goal had vanished? I cradled my face a moment.

"The professor came back. We had the odds, a genuine hope, to get you out of this. Why didn't you believe me?" I had to wipe my nose on my sleeve. Let out a string of cuss words that would have curled both my parents' hair if they'd heard me. What you can learn on a field hockey team, right?

Not that it helped any except to get my breathing down to normal again. I heaved one last sigh. Gone. I'd lost him. My nose stung and my eyes burned and I knew I'd cried ugly and would again when I tried to tell Mom what had happened.

"What am I going to do?" Things had gone incredibly dark. I wiped at my eyes again.

"Tessa. Listen to me."

Words flooded my mind, and it was *him*, strong and bold and doing the fatherly bit. Tears welled up once more.

I swiveled my head about. Maybe there was hope after all. "It didn't work? It didn't take you? Where are you? I can't See you!"

"In the stone."

He wasn't gone, but he wasn't free, either. "How do I . . . what can I do about that? Damn stone does what it wants to. I don't know if I can make it release you."

"I'm where I need to be and you can listen."

I stood up, went over to the bottom step, and sat back down. "All right." I hiccoughed faintly. "Because if you did this on purpose, you'd better have some idea of how all this is going to turn out!"

"Something of an idea."

"It had better be a blockbuster."

And my father began to tell me the tale of how he got himself into this fix.

I listened, tamping down my reactions, aware outside myself that it was like listening to an AA meeting. This was how I got trapped. This was how I fell . . . and fell . . . and finally reached bottom. It hurt to hear him tell me things I had never known for certain but that my mother and I had guessed as we lost our credit cards, our home, our bank accounts.

Flexing my left hand in and out, trying to force away the feeling that it wasn't entirely in my control, I sat as quietly as I could manage. The professor would have been impressed. I chewed on a corner of my lower lip to keep myself still. Certainly, my father had to feel my thoughts tumbling about him, angry and definitely conflicted, but I didn't speak them aloud. I listened as we went down the rabbit hole, literally, to the bet that would settle all other bets . . . if he won.

I straightened at that. We'd finally hit pay dirt in his confession, and he stopped talking.

"Take note," he said.

"Oh, I am. This is the Master who made the offer, right."

"None other."

"So Mortimer guessed correctly about your downfall."

"Somewhat. I was hooked, no doubt about that, and I won enough to make my heart race, and to pay off Aunt April's debts and everything seemed exhilarating. I couldn't lose! Then everything went cold. If it weren't for bad luck, I had none at all. I tapped out, bankrupted every source I could touch. Nothing worked. Then I was offered a deal. Poker game, high stakes, and if I won and delivered, everything would be wiped out and I'd be funded again." My father's voice lowered. "My opponent had an idea he had something valuable, a relic, but had no real idea what it was. He had just enough talent to perceive a bit of its power. He played for money, and I cleaned him out until he finally put that stone up in the last stake."

I blinked. "The maelstrom stone?"

"Yes. The Master wanted it although he had no idea of its worth either, but he needed to study it. I would retrieve it and turn it over to him."

"So you won it."

"I did."

"Did it embed in you?"

"No. But I felt it keenly. For the first time in years, I knew clearly what was right and what was wrong, and that I shouldn't keep my end of the bargain. Knew it better than I knew my own name. It became clear to me that the fellow who'd lost to me would come after me as well as the Master. I'd frittered away the two of you and my home, but I remembered this old place of Aunt April's, empty and unused. I came and went through the cellar window. It was a nice hidey hole while it lasted."

"It didn't last, though, did it?"

"Not quite."

"Who was the loser?"

"At the poker game? Fellow by the name of Parker. A Judge Parker."

"Oh, shit, Dad. He's a real piece of work."

Well, that explained what happened to Goldie and his animosity toward me. I knew he'd abducted and held her at one time before I decided her missing along with the Eye of Nimora was more than coincidence. He'd hated me at first sight when I crossed him. Parker had to have had Nicolo all over him for not giving up the stone when asked and then losing it—not to mention stealing the Eye without knowing its true function and trying to auction it off elsewhere. Parker would have been desperate to make amends. "I know him," I said. "The Society has him under wraps, for now."

"He is, unless I miss my guess, dead and gone. The Master has little patience."

"Couldn't happen to a nicer guy. I can cross him off the list of uglies we might meet, then."

"Most likely. I doubt the Master would have lifted a finger to keep him around."

"So what happened? I found the stone in the old cabinet down here, wedged into a locked drawer. Shed some blood on it by accident and BOOM—it buried itself in my palm and that was that."

"It chose you, for whatever reasons it had. It is, in its way, sentient. Magical, in any way you might want to describe it. Parker had to have been lacking in talent to not be able to recognize its potential. I saw it the moment he put it out on the poker table. It burned right through me. A blood bond . . . well, in your way, you invited it, and it answered. It won't leave you easily."

"Tell me about it. I've had people try to kill me for it."

"And that's what we face now. It took a while for the Master to learn I had no intentions of relinquishing the stone. He came here looking for it. I did the only thing I could do. I hid."

I thought of the way I had hidden that night not that long ago, when I felt thinned out and all but invisible, the maelstrom stone pulling me into transparency. "You stretched out."

"I did. And kept doing it, praying he wouldn't be able to sense me or grab a hold of me. I'd already hidden the stone, but even though it hadn't claimed me, we had a connection. It pulled and pulled on me until I had almost nothing left."

I knew the feeling, terrifying and yet the only thing that could have saved me at the time. I remembered thinking then how, in some ways, it paralleled my father's existence. "I know," I told him.

"Show me."

I didn't want to but reeled out my memories of that horrible night and the thing that had pursued me, and how close I came to losing myself altogether. A long silence followed. I don't know if my father could tire in his current realm of existence or what had happened.

Finally he sighed. "I would have warned you if I could have."

"About using the stone? Or the Butchery?"

"All of it. You have this life outside the house, and I had only this life within it. I couldn't begin to guess what you were up against."

"And if you had known, did you have the training or ability to teach me?"

Another pause. Then, reluctantly, "Probably not. We had some minor talent. Hedge witches, they would have called Polly and Aunt April. Myself? A minor magician, at the most. I had some telekinesis, that's why I excelled at golf, though I didn't know why then. And luck. I had good fortune until it turned on me. I knew games of chance, and the odds, and how to push the odds in my favor, but the adrenaline betrayed me. The Master amplified my telekinesis for that last gambling bout. He made a sort of mage out of me."

"And the price."

"Price?"

"For every action, there is a price. Magic demands its price. You knew that, right?"

"Not precisely."

"Well, trust me, I do. The stone feeds on my essence and if I overuse it, I drop. There are other spells that take their toll as well. The professor has shown me that it is a law of the universe, and we have to be very careful what we do."

"Are you?"

"I try."

"So now we go to face the Master."

I stood up on the cellar stairs, my ass beginning to feel the chill and unrelenting hardness of the step. "I go, but not alone."

"It's my fight, too."

"You're the reason I'm going!"

"Not entirely," my father said. "You have that streak of responsibility I never had. You want to see the Butchery dismantled and those souls freed."

He was right. I'm no hero, but I'm not going to turn my back on a soul in pain if I can help. And, I intended to leave the Master without the ability to hunt anyone ever again. "You've got me there."

"And you've got me here. You need to get me as close to the Master as you dare."

A lump filled my throat and made it difficult to swallow for a moment. "I have to?"

"You do. The maelstrom stone carries me, and you carry the stone."

"He's a vampire."

"I know. But none of you can wound him if you can't break the cocoon of wards and spells he has wrapped about himself, going back forever. It's armor for him and it's been very effective."

"And you think you can?"

My father answered, "You'd better hope I can if the rest of you want any chance at all of surviving the encounter."

"You think your hedge witchiness is a match?"

"I think that if anyone can put a crack into his wall, I can. I intend to be a crowbar. Once there's a crack, he's vulnerable. It'll be up to the rest of you to pry it wide open."

I wanted to believe he could do it. I needed to. But I couldn't, not quite. There was no way I couldn't take him; the stone had him, and where I went, the stone went. No possibility of leaving him behind.

But I couldn't depend on him.

Not from years ago . . . and not now. I said nothing. I don't know if he could read my thoughts.

I hoped not.

CHAPTER THIRTY-THREE

A DOOR OPENS

I GUESS I slept. I got in bed and then got out of bed when Scout roused me in the early morning, but if I dreamed or worried or schemed, it stayed a blank in my mind. I took the quickest of showers, before the little wall heater in the bathroom could even get the room warmed up, and the sting of the water's cold edge warned me that the day would be even colder. That would be good. Not many people out and about, and hopefully the rocking place that the Butchery claimed to be after four PM would stay quiet until then.

I called Evelyn to see if she might come and help us. No answer. I stared at my phone for a few minutes, debating whether to call Hiram. Deciding on no, I laid my clothes out and got dressed for a cold and rugged day. I don't know if the others planned to hit today, but it seemed our best bet. Our walls might have ears . . . it had been breached once or twice and who knew what might have been left behind. Can spiders hear? Lizards? Maybe there was a bat up in our attic, unseen but watching. We told ourselves it hadn't been infiltrated, but I didn't feel certain. The tell-tales in the hallway had given up, wilted over the lip of their vase. I didn't know if it was because Steptoe was gone or because they'd just been shocked beyond their capacity. Nothing held certainty anymore.

Scout put his wet nose on my ankle as I searched for a pair of pants that would be warm and also protective. I threw my leather ones up on the bed and then began scrounging around looking for a two-shirt combination. A nice silk shirt I rarely wear would go under one of my tough flannel shirts, and I have my jacket with the inside pockets still lumpy with a few flash-bangs to go over that. Why silk? I remember reading they could slow down, even stop arrowheads. The Mongols wore silk-reinforced body armor. This baby wasn't made as armor but did call itself dragon silk, and I liked it, so I'd bought it. Any advantage at all would help.

I also have a silver choker necklace that I'd bought with scraped-together money right after my father left, in my Goth period which had lasted all of two months. It encircled my throat nicely, about two inches tall, and I clipped it on. The metal warmed slowly against my skin. If we didn't go to war today, I'd wear it again tomorrow . . . and the day after that and the day after that until we did.

As I prepared to actually get dressed, something fell and hit the floor with a clunk. I bent over to see what it was and decide if I wanted to retrieve it or not. Whatever it was, disappeared somewhere in rug wrinkles. I had to get down on one knee and finally pulled it out from under my bed and looked at it in mild surprise, an object I had totally forgotten I had. It might be useful. I stuffed it in my pants pocket and finished getting dressed.

The rest of the trip downstairs, I pondered what to do with my mother and my dog. Scout wouldn't want to be left behind, but my mom—well, she was a fighter. I knew that. But I also knew she didn't have the offensive or defensive skills to be any help against the magic we likely faced. Would she be content to stay behind and wait for news of the outcome?

No, she would not.

I thought of draping her with a garlic bulb necklace, but the professor had already said they were relatively useless. I doubt if he'd give an amateur his crossbow. If Steptoe had survived, I'd pair him with her as guardian, fighter, with that invisibility suit coat of his as a final line of protection—but he hadn't. I would give her flash-bangs. That might be enough to give her the option to turn and run.

Then I realized if we called in Evelyn, we had pretty much

the same problem. Two innocents, unprepared to protect themselves. I mean, I know my mother could swing a mean bat or hockey stick if she had to, but Evie?

Then again, Evie would likely have Hiram. I couldn't be sure what Hiram would bring to the fray, but I figured it would be impressive. I walked into the kitchen determined to call him anyway and see if I could emotionally blackmail him into shielding her and helping us.

I stopped dead at the sight of a full table: Gregory, Carter, Hiram and Evelyn, all passing about a huge vat of coffee while my mother took a pan of biscuits hot from the oven. She said she'd always been considered a Yankee, but she still made the finest deep South biscuits I'd ever eaten. Scout immediately loped over to Evelyn and put his head on her knee, rolling his brown eyes up at her in his best begging expression.

I stated the obvious. "I'm late to the party."

Evelyn pulled out the last available chair next to her. "I had a feeling I should be here." She looked back over her shoulder at Hiram. They traded a fond look. "He convinced me I shouldn't ignore those feelings any longer."

"Really?"

Hiram didn't really answer, just made a short bass rumble as he reached his massive hand for a mug of coffee. He wore a shirt of chain mail that looked as if it had been around, but repaired and nicely kept.

"You look prepared."

"I've my ax and shield in the car."

He was.

That left my mom. As I sized her up, Gregory said, "She's taken care of."

"How?"

Mom rebuked me. "Don't be a doubter, Tessa."

I curled my fingers around an unclaimed mug and pulled it toward me to add cream and sugar. "Curious."

"She's bespelled."

"Until you drop?" I raised an eyebrow at our wizard. I took a cautious sip. The coffee was gloriously hot and wonderfully flavored. Someone had ground some good beans and brought them to our kitchen.

"I won't drop." Gregory gave me a hard look. "None of us will."

"Today is the day?"

Carter nodded. Jam dotted the corner of his mouth. I so wanted to kiss it away yet knew I couldn't, not in front of everyone. Scout left Evelyn and came to me, leaning heavily on my legs, and rolled his eyes up at me. I gave him a flaky corner off the first biscuit that came my way. I opened my mouth to tell everyone about my father and the stone, but my father's voice flooded my mind.

"Don't."

So I didn't, instead stuffing another bite in before swallowing the last completely and dabbing the melted butter off my chin.

"Manners," my mother chided.

"Sorry." A few crumbs flew out, and I ducked my head. I could understand why Dad didn't want them alerted since his plan stipulated that I get overwhelmingly close to a set of very sharp fangs. Carter wouldn't allow it if I telegraphed it early, for which I felt grateful and annoyed. If I had to do what I had to do, it would be nice to have backup.

Evelyn asked, "Why do you need me?"

"You open doors."

She tilted her head. Someone had braided her pale blonde hair tightly and wrapped it closely about, so that it couldn't be grabbed. I imagined it was Hiram, who had obviously been in a pitched battle once or twice, and had had Mortimer as one of his instructors. I ought to have my brunette hair fixed as well and cleared my throat to ask if she or Carter could do it, but my father's ghostly voice stopped me again. Seriously? He wanted the vampire to grab me by my pony tail and reel me in?

Yes, he did.

"Doors?"

"You can see into the future enough to wedge our way into a protected building, we are betting."

Evelyn frowned slightly. "I dreamed of that last night, I think. Two paths, one victorious and one disastrous. I don't remember much more than being terrified. But the door, yes. A thick wooden door, chestnut wood, with a great carven B on it, and slightly scarred from many passages over the years. Worn and antiqued."

She nailed the description. I hunched down on my chair and decided to rub Scout's soft ears and neck wrinkles to hide my upset. I told him what a good dog he was. I really had no idea of my father's exact plan, but my feelings about it grew worse and worse. If Carter or any of the others heard a word of my intention, I'd be hog-tied and left by the side of the road.

I had a couple of aces in my pocket that I dared not think or talk about because it seemed very probable that I would be argued out of them. Beyond that, I had my three offensive spells, my bracers, and whatever shields the maelstrom stone could produce before my father took it over for his offensive. I had my own trusty hockey stick as well.

Gregory put his hand on my shoulder, startling me a bit before I shrugged him off. "No spells for me. Mom needs all the power you can spare."

He patted me instead. "You've a point. And, I trust, Carter will be looking out for you."

Carter assessed me before smiling a bit, that little offset dimple in his chin deepening. "She'll be fine." He dusted his hands off on his napkin. "When do we want to bring in Malender?"

"Not until we're deep enough into the Butchery to see our target."

"You're going to ask him to help?"

I nodded at my mother. "He owes me, and he has a score to settle with the Master, as well. We can't be sure he'll help, but I think he might." I paused for a minute. "That's right. You've never seen him in action."

"No."

"He looks like a troubadour. But he's got abilities and power."

"If he'll use them on your behalf."

"He owes me a life-debt. He damn well better help."

Something flashed deep in her eyes, and I don't think it was aimed at me. "He'll get a swift talking-to from me if he tries to back down."

Gregory chuckled softly at that. "The being is a demigod, Mary."

"I assume he's met a mama bear or two and knows what to expect."

Carter bumped a shoulder against mine, muffling his laughter, as my mother sat up straighter in her chair. He said, "I wouldn't bet against her."

"So it seems." Gregory pushed his mug and plate to the center of the table. "Are we satisfied with our planning? Prepared to go? Have advice from our seer?" He fastened his attention on Evelyn.

"May the odds be in your favor," she quoted back at him. "Actually, high noon seems to be a good time, from what I've sensed and felt."

"Excellent for me." Carter took her advice well. He needed the sunlight, whatever he could absorb of it, although his powers also had a stored battery component to them, which made him doubly dangerous. He didn't need daylight to flex his abilities though it helped now and then. If Nicolo had been an old-time, myth-ridden vampire, the daylight Carter could shine on him alone would have made the being dry up and float away. Unfortunately, he wasn't. Everyone about the table took out their phones and put them on silent.

Gregory joined in. "I've reinforced the wards as I can. Tessa, your father will be alone here, in the cellar, but I trust he will not be disturbed."

"Hopefully not." I bent out of my chair and hugged my pup, then massaged him lightly up and down his flank. "I'm sending Scout with Mom, a little extra protection."

"Oh?" Gregory eyed the two of us thoughtfully before adding, "Good idea."

Did he have some idea of what I planned? Possibly. But if today wasn't a day to pull out all the stops, I didn't know when one would come. I thought of something else that might be important. "Oh! And a word . . . well, it sounds silly but if you smell strong peppermint, duck. The Master's minions seem to soak in it. I didn't get close enough to Remy to know if she did as well, but it seems to be a fetish with the old vampire. He doesn't like the smell of the Undead."

We took three cars: Hiram's SUV with Evelyn, the professor's somewhat sedate sedan with Mom and Scout, and I accompanied Carter in his SUV. Few people were out on the road, it being a work day, and true to the weather forecast, one of bitter cold and low humidity, too chilled to even snow. We didn't get many days like this in Richmond. This front had edged its way down from Canada and would be gone in a day or two, most of its nasty effects across the Great Lakes and into the Midwest before turning our way. We just caught an edge of it, and I could only be happy that was all.

Old Town seemed very quiet, streets near empty, the carousing waiting for Happy Hour and evening. Classes hadn't started up yet, so the students and the Gen Z and Gen Xers weren't about, likely at work, before showing up to drink and circulate. Carter gave an approving murmur. The less crowd/witnesses we had to deal with, the better.

We parked a bit up the street. When the professor and Mom drove up, I settled Scout in the front seat and gave her the leash. Gregory went to mull over some last details with Carter, and I said to her, "When the time comes, let him off the lead, and let him go."

"Time? What time? What are you talking about?"

"You'll know. Trust me, you'll know." I hugged Scout again. "You're the best boy, you know that? I love you. You stay my good boy."

Scout wiggled a bit and gave me a sloppy kiss, before sitting back on the car seat and giving me a worried look. It matched the one my mother wore. I shoveled out four flash-bangs and pressed them into her hand. "If they come out of the building and after you, throw one or two at their feet. Make sure you throw them hard enough to crack like an egg, all right? It's called a flash-bang and you'll see why. It'll slow them down enough for you to run or drive away. Save two for the worst."

"What are you up to?"

"I can't say, not just yet. But you've got to know, we're going to need everything we've got to put this guy down."

"Please come back to me."

"I will definitely do everything I can to do that." I hugged her, too. I whispered in her ear, "I never told Dad, but I think he knows about Gregory. He's okay with it."

She hid a sniffle as I moved away. I turned my back on them and willed my feet to walk me away or I never would have left.

Evelyn and Hiram stood, arms hooked together, on the sidewalk just out of range of the Butchery's front windows. He had a wicked looking double-headed ax in his right hand, and since I'd seen him work on a demolition and construction crew, I knew he had the muscle to wield it. A slightly dented shield leaned against his leg. His chain mail looked like pewter in the light. He held a vest hooked on his thumb and threw it toward me. "Not much, but it will help."

I caught it. Heavier than it looked, but when I shrugged into it, the weight distributed nicely about me. It looked as if it could be made of the same stuff as my bracers. I rolled one cuff up to compare. It did match the bronzed metal of my armament. "Nice. Thank you."

"Not as good as my mail, but it'll do you. Better than nothing."

Evelyn stirred. "Are we all ready?"

I fetched two flash-bangs out of my inner jacket pocket, a little tough to do under the vest, but I fumbled them out. Two more rested inside, but I wouldn't use them until the last minute—whenever that was. Like I told my mother, it was one of those things you'd know when you saw it.

"Ready," Carter agreed.

"One moment." The professor lifted both his hands and chanted a few words that sounded harsh and booming against my ears. When he finished, the whole world seemed muffled. I think my head had been stuffed with fog and cotton. Gregory gave himself a pleased nod. "Muted. We shouldn't draw too much attention."

Evelyn pulled away from Hiram. "Are you all certain you want me to do this?"

"This is our only way to catch the Master at a disadvantage, and believe me, he must be caught and dealt with. His shadow is knotted through the countryside, drawing it down into a mire from which it might never return if we don't act." Gregory met her question squarely if somewhat dramatically, but it was her kind of language.

She inhaled. Said, "I know Tessa believes in you."

As if my judgment could be depended upon. I almost spoke up to argue with her. She trembled, her slender body caught in a whirlwind, and put one hand up to shade her eyes. "Open, oh doors of breath and morrow, let fate come in." Somewhat Shakespearean; I wondered if it would work.

The immense brick building that had warehoused a near three-hundred-year–old butcher and slaughter shop and now a modern-day bar and restaurant/dance hall shuddered at her words. I could see the shimmer of time move swiftly across its feature as if years ran across it.

And then, with a moan and a creak, the massive wooden door swung open.

I wondered no more.

CHAPTER THIRTY-FOUR

FATED

THEY RUSHED US. I don't think any of us expected that, but a wave of peppermint essence hit us suddenly, and I had just enough time to yell, "Incoming!" before the threshold filled with snapping fangs and supernaturally quick bodies. I spun Evelyn out of my way, put a bracered arm up and caught a mouthful on it. With a certain satisfaction, I felt them crack and splinter as the vampire fell back. Like a serpent, he recoiled, smacked his lips, brought new fangs down, and struck at me again.

He might have gotten closer if not for meeting with Hiram's ax and losing his head over it. As it fell to the sidewalk, body tumbling after, I recognized the too pale but still insufferably arrogant face of Judge Parker. I kicked his remains to the side and ducked as Hiram yelled at me to, and his ax swung over me again, effectively cleaving another minion in two from head to toe. I didn't recognize her.

Gregory brought one down, tangled in webbing as Carter torched first his opponent and then Gregory's victim.

Just like that, the doorway cleared.

It looked incredibly dark inside. Musty and filled with the dust of years. The sting of candy cane aroma faded. The coppery tang of blood and . . . spilled beer? . . . flooded us in its wake. I didn't know if they'd been waiting for us or if the four vampires were always at the door. They hadn't been when I'd entered those earlier times, but those realities had been even more twisted. Parker, though, had to have been a "new hire" since I'd last seen him at the Society meeting. He wasn't what I would have called Bouncer material. I hoped Sophie had evaded his grasp.

Thinking of her, I conjured up that small bowl of light Sophie had taught me to conquer and stepped inside, my throat dry and my ears stinging. In the somewhat dulled atmosphere, footsteps shuffled beside me, but I couldn't quite pinpoint their position with respect to mine. I knew my friends were with me. I guess that's all that counted. Air pressure imploded slightly nearby, making me jump, but I didn't know what caused it.

Carter muttered a word or two in the shadows and grabbed for my hand. He caught me up after first fumbling and twisted my hockey stick out of my fingers, pressing a hilt of cold metal in its place. I lifted it up and stared at it.

It was a wicked, wicked blade. Not a straight-edged sword but more like a blazingly sharp sickle had met a sword and conquered it. The point end of it bent cleverly. I flicked a look at Carter, my sun lion. "Egyptian?"

"It's a khopesh. You can hook shields and other weapons with the end, but the sickle blade is extremely sharp. Use it well."

"Why didn't you give it to me outside?"

He smiled, his teeth dazzlingly white, as if the sun itself shined there, and answered, "I didn't have it then."

He could do that, I knew, transport to the sands of his eternal magic and back in a wink if he had to. He'd taken a calculated risk, based on the need he saw, and whatever energy he'd expended, he'd pay for later. Beyond the journey itself, the destination carried severe consequences of its own. Creatures prowled there that would pounce and slay if they had the chance. But he'd done it and come back safely. He'd also told me, in his way, that he had an escape route planned for me. I knew I'd have to stay away from him if the mission went sour. I had a fate I intended to carry out.

I saw he carried a similar weapon, although his was longer and straighter, as if a Japanese katana had influenced ancient

Egypt as well. He carried the smell of hot wind and burning sands with him, and a wedge of white-gold light spilled across the Butchery floor in front of him as if the world had cracked open. It revealed the blood-and-guts–stained sawdust, splintered bones, and joints with sinew and tatters of meat still hanging from them among the blocky tables and accoutrements of slaughter. Beyond, I could see the dark shapes of bodies dangling from meat hooks hanging from racks in the overhead beams.

I took my hockey stick back from him and shoved it under my mail vest, in the back between my shoulder blades.

We halted and fanned out a bit. Evelyn had stayed at Hiram's flank. I frowned her way. "You should get out of here. Safer outside."

"Then how would you all get out? I stay." Her body chimed slightly as she moved a bit closer. I could see then that he'd equipped her with a long duster coat of mail, dainty and silvery and, I swear to the good Lord, it must have come from lore straight out of Tolkien. I'd never seen anything like it. Unless someone hit the floor, did a slide and attacked her ankles, she looked protected from head to calf. I would never have believed it if I hadn't seen it. She must have been wearing it all along, but only the ancient magic interred in this lair revealed it. I would have whistled low in admiration, but my throat and mouth had gone dry.

"Let your light go," Gregory told me. He pulled out his cane and the diamond end did a much better job of illuminating the room, so I snuffed out my bit of light. With the crescent that beamed from the cane and from Carter, we had no need of my small contribution.

Chains unwound. Bolts and screws squealed, metal twisting inside metal. The entire warehouse stretched before us answered to our appearance. A low moan began to run about the room, undeterred by the professor's previous spell. Wood creaked and sounded as the building felt the weight and anger of Hiram's Iron Dwarf heft. The floor echoed with a low moan of its own. I had never heard metal groan before, though, and the noise of it raised every hair on my body. It also screeched, so high a note I could barely hear it, nails on a chalkboard sound. A steady clink, clink, clink punctuated it. The professor's mute spell had no purchase here at all. I wanted to shutter my ears against the noise. Unnatural. Threatening. The smell of rust filled the air.

A voice split the noise. "Showtime, my loveys." A beautiful voice, strong and elegant, compelling. The building was cavernous enough that it should have echoed, but it did not—it shot into us, a sharp arrow of command. I gulped as it reached me, for I knew who must have spoken. Felt glad I'd never heard him speak before because, if I had, I wouldn't have thought he could ever be defeated. He compelled me, and I tried not to think of what his command to me might be. Now I was in the fight, with no way to back out.

A turning of the screw whine answered. Every occupied meat hook swung about to face us, its unfortunate occupant stirring. I didn't know what armor Nicolo carried, but these poor souls hung as his shield. My left arm pulsed. For a moment, I thought it was my father, flexing his strength. But no. It was the barely healed bite mark, stinging and pulling at me. I fought the urge to answer whatever command Nicolo had just given his nest.

Carter acted, swinging about at the chain, with a flash of sunlight up his arm and sword as he struck. Metal exploded as they met, the hook, the blade, and the light. Bits of shrapnel spit past my head, and I ducked out of the way. Out of the corner of my eye, I expected to see the body spill onto the flooring. Instead, it sparked and disappeared.

Was that the way a soul flew home? Or had it died? Had we set it free or destroyed it?

No time to wonder or mourn. Gregory moved from body to body to body; his voice chanted, unafraid, touching bare hands to captive bare hands as he ran through. With each he touched, a small sun answered and the captive left. Carter took the other side, tamped down his sunlight bursts, preserving what energy he could.

Not all left in brilliance. A staggering amount dissolving into a sooty, oily cloud, melting onto the floor and billowing up in my direction. The stink they carried threatened to suffocate me as I swept my khopesh. They reached out with grasping hands and kicked with sharp-toed shoes. Failing that, they simply tried to use the brunt of their bodies as battering rams. As one clutched at me, I spun about to strike, expecting to hit a fragile body. Instead, the sickle sword and my arm felt the brunt of hitting a wall. I almost dropped my weapon. I jumped aside instead, and raised my left hand, calling forth my salt spell, as little as I dared and hoping it was as much as I needed. My attacker dissolved into a puff of obsidian smoke. Lesson learned.

Spinning about, I came face-to-face with a captive. In the sepia hues of the Butchery, I almost didn't recognize her, but I did. Her golden complexion faded, her youth and perkiness drained away, Sophie swayed on the hook in front of me with closed eyes.

No. Not my Miss S'mores.

What would happen if I attacked her chain? Fear galloped through me. I couldn't bear the thought that she might not survive. Her eyes came open, and then awareness flooded her face.

I had to do something. I swung the khopesh at the overhead stud holding her. Metal clashed against metal. I felt the blow all the way to my toes, and my ears rang with the noise.

Then a white flash nearly blinded me as Sophie disappeared. A dazzling white spark flew up to the ceiling and away. Free. I had no way of knowing if I would be so lucky next time. I prayed that she'd been so newly caught, he hadn't corrupted her.

I tossed handfuls of salt ahead of each sword sweep. Toss. Hack. Jump away. Repeat. My actions took a lot more effort than Gregory or Carter expended, physically, but when I could glance at either one of them, their expressions were strained, their foreheads dotted with sweat. We worked steadily to clear a pathway into the Butchery, a slog at best, a retreat here and there when necessary.

And we hardly made a dent.

I thought we could advance, but squeaky rollers overhead brought forth row after row of bodies. Gods above, he must have hundreds entangled in his net. What false promises he must have caught them with, as he had my father, decades of mortals too desperate and too eager to avoid his traps. I began to notice the clothing they wore and realized the styles stretched across generations. We were, after all, in a niche of time that was of Nicolo's own making. By what magic, I didn't know. His ripples stretched across ages, and once his captives got dragged into here, it seemed a kind of stasis existed.

I brushed my own forehead dry on my sleeve. Behind me, somewhere, Evelyn screamed. Her terror undulated, loud and all too real. I jumped back but could not see her or what frightened her. Hiram gave a battle cry, his bass tones shattering the noise of the Butchery's wood and metal, and I hoped she would be all right. That he would be all right.

That sidestep, that moment, nearly undid me. Hands ripped at my left arm. Salt danced and fell uselessly to the floor. Nails like talons ripped at my palm. Teeth snapped in my face as I punched away my attacker. I looked square into the face of my high school history teacher, one of my favorites, a master of the pun and one of the good guys, I had thought. His expression twisted grotesquely. Darkness billowed out of his mouth as he strained to get me. I kicked out, and the meat-hooked body spun out, arms flailing, as the being, no longer human in any way, wailed. The crude rolling system overhead dragged it away as my teacher hissed in frustration.

It had almost had me. I could feel blood dripping from my hand and wiped it off on my leg.

"Easy, Tessa," my father said.

He could, no doubt, feel the energy level of the stone keenly, and warned me not to leave him little or nothing to draw upon.

I didn't care for a few seconds. The professor and Carter switched sides, as their attacks became less effective. Or perhaps the captives became stronger the deeper we got into the old Master's stockpile. No time to wonder why.

Darkness roiled up, solid and threatening, eating not only

all the light we'd brought in, but the energy as well. I could feel my throat tightening. My eyes stinging. My palms, both of them, aching. The khopesh acted as if it wanted to twist in my hold and turn on me. Could it? Or did I stand in the way of a magical wave that permeated every fiber of the Butchery? People caved in here. Gave up. Wasted away. Died, hopeless. I could *feel* it.

"Now," commanded Nicolo, still unseen.

From behind the dread and swaying bodies of mortals, vampires came gliding.

Did I expect wings? A few had them. Some approached with duster coats spread wide, to inflate their size and confuse the target of their forms. Canines flashed, and the whites of their eyes, and the pale moons of their faces where undeath had leeched all natural color from their skin, no matter what they'd been born as. Did they smell of peppermint?

No. They stank of carrion. Befouled blood. Decaying flesh. They might have been promised immortality, but no one promised them health. The wave that flung themselves on us might have been zombies except they were not falling apart. Magic and hatred strung them together. The stone spun out a shield for me, a small and easily maneuvered one.

A woman descended on me. I saw her eyes flash. She didn't breathe except to express sound, drew in breath and released it, hissing, as she closed on me. The khopesh caught and hooked her by the wrist as she reached for me. I shook her off it and aimed the sickle at her neck.

It worked remarkably well. Her head tumbled off and her cloaked body sank into cloth and ashes. I only had to do that about a thousand more times.

They learned quickly. Instead of coming at each of us one at a time, they came in coordinated swarms. Backing up, I prepped my fireball and tossed it into the depths of the dark wing throwing themselves at me.

Gregory shouted, "Don't use ice, whatever you do. We need our footing." A wave of vampires came at him, threatening to pull him under. He went to his knees anyway, hands beckoning and calling forth his spells. Lightning ripped about him.

I heard him. Understood, although barely, and instead reached in my pocket for a flash-bang. A vamp came at me, choking me with its smell as I dodged to the side and lobbed my grenade in the professor's defense. It scattered the vampires who didn't burst into flames and let him make it back to his feet. No time for gratitude, as one of them bulled its way into my shoulder, knocking me off balance. I twirled about and Hiram caught me. His ax swept about us like a great pendulum, aimed from side to side, and the obsidian wave parted. He set me back steady, nodded, and moved back to wherever he'd come from.

Back to Evelyn, I could almost be certain. A ray of light illuminated him for a moment, a sign that she held the door open behind him. We had a way back but not for retreat. No. We had to finish what we started or Nicolo's revenge would spill out into the city. He didn't have to threaten us. I knew it in my bones that our attack would unleash whatever restraint he might have.

"You've got to get to him," my father whispered to me.

"I know." I just didn't know how. My arms ached. Blood and weariness sang through my body. How many swings did I have left? Not enough.

Not nearly enough to cut through this swath and make a difference. How could he have held this many Undead under his sway, without leaving traces?

And then they dropped from above. Fast and deadly, with moves that I could hardly parry, my position getting driven back and suddenly I found myself back-to-back with the professor.

He breathed hard. A welcome and reassuring sound.

"Now," he muttered, "would be a good time to summon our friend."

I looked and saw the three of us boxed into a corner, of sorts. Carter spewed light and fire again, restrained, and I couldn't tell if he had begun to run low or if he was still rationing his ability.

No idea where Nicolo sat in power.

We wouldn't make it, wherever it was. Not without help.

"Malender," I called. Two opponents dove at me. I ducked under the arm of one and spun off the cane of another with a crack against my elbow that rang through my bones. "Malender, Malender, Malender!"

My movement exposed Gregory, but Carter stepped into the gap. I danced around to flank them and would have brought up my salt, but my body refused to do it. Just a glitch, a blip, as I could feel spell weariness drift through me. I couldn't be burned out. Couldn't quit. I'd come to fight. Fight I would until they dropped me. But they weren't going to find it easy!

A new opponent stepped into the gap. Confident. Grinning. Bleached-out face and talons came at me. He looked as if he could have walked the streets of my town any time. He didn't smell like spoiled meat or candy canes. I could have passed him at my college campus or the local diner and never noticed. Dressed like the others, all in black, not so much because he would have worn that normally, but because it gave him camouflage at the Butchery, I supposed. He moved on me so quickly that my bracers took the brunt of two sweeps meant to open my wrists like fire hydrants. His eyebrows raised.

"Niiiice." His hiss flowed over me like ice water. "I will take those for myself."

I countered with the khopesh, but he ducked away from the sickle blade and grabbed at it, tearing it out of my hands.

Fingers empty, slightly amazed, I just stood flat-footed. A deadly position. The vampire laughed, a hollow sound, and came at me swinging my own sword.

And then there was Malender, between me and the vampire, his whip cocked. Without a wasted movement, he swung the whip, slicing the being up, setting its clothes on fire. My sword clattered to the planked flooring. I swooped down to retrieve it.

"My life—"

"I get it. Your debt is being redeemed. And what have we here? Ah. Nicolo's lair." Only Malender didn't pronounce it as I'd been thinking of it. He gave it a definite Italian accent and twist. Knee-co-low. Malender bared his teeth in delight. He strode forward, lashing his scourge from side to side, catching vampires and hooked bodies alike, clearing a path that we eagerly followed. Finally, I could see the racks clearing, empty hooks rattling past us.

Far from easy, we slogged forward a step at a time. The meat hooks kept rolling in, but the influx of vampires slowed. We caught a breather, fighting one at a time, until I could see the back of the building and the magnificent being that wrought all this death and fury. He sat on a block table, waiting, well-dressed in a modern-day smoking jacket and slacks, eyes glowing a bit in the dim light, hair down to his shoulders and curled at the ends. I dared not look longer than that as I could feel the magic seething out of and around him. It plucked at that bite, too, as if I were an instrument he could hope to play.

Blood slicked the floor under my steps; from what, I had no idea. One of us? Maybe. From slaughters earlier? Possibly. From those hanging on the meat hooks? Maybe. Some of them appeared to be physical as opposed to spiritual, but I couldn't tell the difference easily. Did Nicolo treat this place as a pantry, with prime meats to be aged before being devoured? Legend said that vampires only drank blood, but from what I'd seen, that might not be the truth. Legend also talked about ghouls. Where did the dividing line fall?

I did not have time to parse good from evil. That seemed self-evident. Malender's whip either freed captives or sent them cascading into flame and ash. There was no in-between. Justice dealt with them one way or another. He showed no signs of slowing down, stringing us behind him in his wake. My steps faltered now and then as I fought to keep my swings strong and straight. Vampires fell back, retreating to a more advantageous spot instead of rushing us head on. Rather than overwhelm us with sheer numbers, now they began to resort to strategy. It told me one thing: Nicolo didn't have unlimited resources. He had a bottom he didn't want to reach. The only question now was whether we could hang on long enough to reach that.

Every fiber of my body ached. I felt as though I'd just played a doubleheader of field hockey and both shoulders had gone out. My knees throbbed. Even my toes protested with every step. Weary. I was so tired. I could just lie down on the floor and—

"Tessa!" My father's voice, sharp and loud. "Pay attention!"

I stumbled. Felt as if someone had thrown a bucket of cold water into my face. My eyes went wide. I'd been falling asleep on my feet?

The old Master had been glamouring us. I joggled Gregory's elbow and then Carter. "Look alive," I warned them.

As I glared ahead of me, I could see Nicolo, in person, now on his feet. I could see his eyes, dark and vibrant, his persona as striking as Malender was handsome. He looked pleased. He reached behind him and drew a long, wicked-looking blade off the block table. I knew its like or thought I did. I'd faced samurai sorcerers once with swords like that. Maybe they'd been in concert with him, maybe not. They were dead and gone.

I survived. Thrived, even. Loved. Learned. Breathed.

I smiled. And that, more than anything we were doing as we battled to draw near him, disconcerted him. His own expression faded. I think he'd just begun to realize that, although our advance slowed a bit, it continued. His minions hadn't turned us back, not yet. Had not even injured us grievously, although we had Malender's help for that turn of fortune. Behind us, Hiram and Evelyn kept a path of retreat open, just in case. If anyone in this battle was cornered, it was him.

And he didn't like it.

"Now we take him," my father urged.

"Now?" I couldn't see a way to get closer, without ending up stuck on a spit.

"You have a way." He sounded confident and a bit scornful. The shield on my left forearm disappeared abruptly.

I hadn't done that, he had. I frowned and repositioned my stance, my left side now very vulnerable.

I found myself to the fore of our little phalanx. Shaking my head, I attempted to fall back. A tall shape glided in next to me, hard fingers wrapping about my bicep and tugging me out of position. My pony tail suddenly yanked my head about. Captured, I looked up into Remy's Undead face.

She still looked human. French, with a nose just slightly too long, high cheekbones, hair smartly brought back into an upsweep, her eyes now of indifferent color but highlighted with an ironic glimmer.

"You still look elegant," I said, words tumbling out before I could catch them.

"And you are still intolerably naïve."

My scalp stung. Caught in her grasp, I could scarcely move, but I wiggled my hand, palm up. "He wants this. Take me to him. We can settle this right here, right now."

Remy considered me. I had no idea if her orders had been to kill or capture, and for a long moment, I wasn't certain she remembered either. She jerked on my hair again, and I bit back a scream. I dropped my khopesh to enforce my surrender. That stirred the vampire into motion. She dragged me across the floor, sawdust puffing up about my boots, the smell of old blood wafting up, as Nicolo watched us intently.

Malender held his scourge quiet, also staring, even as Carter moved to his elbow and must have said something, for Malender nodded sharply, dark curls on his head bouncing a bit. Flames licked the whip from handle to end and settled, like a fire that had been banked.

I passed Gregory and threw him a look. A plea, I supposed, in case what my father and I hoped to do might turn ill. I didn't want to end up on a meat hook, even if I had to burn alive from toe to head to avoid it. He couldn't do that, I supposed, and ever face my mother again, but I hoped he might have something up his sleeve.

Remy yanked on my arm to hurry me up. I wouldn't have time to say goodbyes. I did look back over my shoulder to Carter. I mouthed "I love you" to him. Did he catch it? I didn't have time to know as Remy swung me about and I hit my knees in front of Nicolo. She finally let loose of my hair. Her steely hand moved from my elbow to my shoulder, and dug in. I wasn't about to move if she could prevent it.

He had a classic Roman nose which I could see when he looked down at me. Italian complexion. Undeniably attractive, if short in stature. Brunette hair as straight as a stick until its slight curl at the collar, a modern, razor cut. Not a hint of peppermint about him, oddly enough. Perhaps he just soaked his vampire ghouls in it to keep them sufferable. His clothes looked fairly new and pricey, but his arrogance seemed priceless. And why not? He'd lived ages longer than anyone else in the building, except perhaps for Malender—and Malender had been his prisoner once for an unimaginably long time. Long enough that the modern magical world had forgotten Mal and what he represented, and he had even forgotten himself.

If Nicolo had been clever enough to entrap Malender, I held out little hope for myself.

"We have the stone," my father whispered encouragingly.

I kept my gaze on Nicolo's chin, unwilling to look him in the eyes. "The stone," I said, and my first words failed me, sticking in my throat and inaudible. I cleared my throat. "The stone," I began again. "Ransom for Richmond." I trembled. The old scars of that vampire bite on the crook of my left arm pulled on me. Made me want to be obedient. Coaxed me into submitting. Laughed at me for trying to stay untouched. It battered at every defense I had built up over the years. Being alone. Being scorned. Being abandoned.

I fought back. I wasn't alone, loved ones and friends surrounded me. My moments of ridicule lay years behind me—and what teenager hadn't felt some despair? Only one person, my father, had left me willingly. I straightened my spine and stared back at the beautiful creature in front of me. His eyes held depths of vast experience, but I saw no love, no mercy in them. No humanity. I turned aside his compulsion and waited for him to answer. If he thought I would throw myself at him, bitten or not, he was greatly mistaken.

Nicolo's lip curled a bit. "Indeed. Why not call out parlay like one of your myths and see if we can negotiate?"

"I am serious. I won't give up the maelstrom without compensation."

"I won't entertain your offer. I can kill you on the spot—or have you killed—and the stone will be mine."

"No, it won't. It will go to where it wills. I can hand it to you, and you can hope you can keep ahold of it, or you will lose it if you slaughter me." I willed conviction into every word.

Nicolo's mouth twitched. He took a step to one side and looked at me from a slightly different angle. "Bold if foolish."

"I have what you want. The advantage is mine."

"Careful," my father cautioned.

From what had happened to him, and to me, it seemed the stone had a mind of its own and would be possessed by the person it chose, not the other way around. But then, that was just two examples. I could be wrong. I desperately hoped I wasn't.

I waved my hand slightly, palm outward, flashing the stone at Nicolo. His desire for it gleamed deep in his eyes. I had him. We had him. But did we have a deal of any kind?

He straightened. "Your life and the lives of your friends here, for the stone. That is the best I intend to offer."

"Malender is among my friends."

A twitch of one cheek. "Very well."

I heard the whip snap behind me, a minor undulation, expressing Malender's distaste for the proceedings.

Nicolo bowed slightly at the waist, bending toward me. "I will warn you. If anything happens to me, the will that holds all these beings in check, disappears. Chaos will descend upon you. They will go into a blood frenzy if I do not hold them back."

Oh, that didn't sound good at all. I had been afraid since I entered the Butchery and found, to my surprise, that I could be terrified still further. My bones ached with it.

"He's bluffing," my father responded.

But was he?

I dipped my right hand into my jacket inner pocket and shoved myself to my feet. Remy swung about on me, mouth open, canines glittering, jaws snapping. I pushed a flash-bang into her teeth as she came at my throat, teeth clicking together. Her savage attempt to bite me shattered the weapon. I ducked away just as it exploded. Remy's loveliness detonated all over me and Nicolo, a gory, slimy, crimson mess. The rest of her body fell with a resounding thud. I drew the back of my wrist over my eyes to clear them.

"I won't be messed with."

Nicolo didn't move for a moment. Then he reached into his pocket and withdrew a large, white silken handkerchief and cleaned his face off before dropping the sodden fabric to the sawdust and floor. Then he smiled. "You will take her place if our deal falters."

He thought he had me. Perhaps he did. I could feel the wrappings of magic, old and new, extremely powerful as it clung to him, armor that I did not think the four of us could penetrate even if we all hit him at once.

My father told me, "I've got this."

It was a gamble. We both knew it. And the high of the prospect of winning or losing gripped him tightly. It always had and always would, even now. I could feel the hum of tension in the two of us.

"Pluck it out."

I picked at the maelstrom stone, and it gave. Not easily. I felt a wrenching that went deep, deep inside me as if I tried to turn myself inside out, like nothing I had ever felt before from it, as though I betrayed it. It hurt worse than anything I'd ever endured, physically and emotionally. It questioned why I wanted it gone, the bond we had, all of it, all the partnership of magic that we had ever worked together and I simply told it that it was time. In turn, it gave way, accepting that I knew it had to go. Spasms ran the length of my body and then, suddenly, stopped. It agreed to leave me, this time. Why, I could not know, not for sure. I remembered a dream from not all that long ago, but long enough that my magical experiences had exploded exponentially since. In that dream world, Malender had stood next to me in a meadow, taking the stone from me, saying, "This is the way the world ends."

A prophetic warning. I took a deep breath, praying he would be wrong, and freed the stone entirely. I held it up to give Nicolo.

He reached for it, lightning-quick vampire reflexes that I anticipated. Our hands coupled, the stone between them, neither one of us owning it, the two of us sharing it.

That's when my father struck.

It felt like a bomb going off.

I went blind.

CHAPTER THIRTY-FIVE

MISCALCULATIONS

NICOLO LET OUT a roar. It shattered through my skull, a pounding sound of triumph. Then he closed in on us, my Sight flashed back, the Master Vampire nose to nose with us. He screamed inside my skull. "No, my puppet, you haven't got me! I made you a mage, and you wasted it. Lost your way. Lost our destiny. Could have been more if you wished, in my dominion, but no. You gambled it away with every decision you made, and now you are mine, and the stone is mine!"

He heard my father through the stone. Our advantage of surprise, spent. Our attack, thwarted. He had magic, yes, but he had a force of will he'd built up over years and years of rule, and one, no two, mortals could not hope to penetrate that.

My pulse roared in my ears, and I dropped to my knees again, still holding onto Nicolo's ice-cold hand and my maelstrom stone. I saw nothing different in the wrappings of magic crowded about him. Did it work? Could it work?

My father cried inside my head. I thought it might be for me and realized that it wasn't as he crooned in despair, "Not enough, not enough!"

I wouldn't let it end this way. I couldn't. My father, my friends, all ringing me, all in death's way. The stone still drew from me. This was the moment in which I had to double down or lose everything as my father had. I wouldn't do that. I couldn't. I reached inside and found that golden spark buried deep inside me, the love and care that had been gifted, Carter's sunlight, and I brought it up. Lit myself from inside out, built a roaring fire out of it, let it sear me until I wanted to scream from its perfect agony—and I released it.

The stone vibrated in my hand. Grew warm and then hot as my energy poured into it. Nicolo tried to turn it aside, that beam of hope and light. I could hear his skin sizzle as he refused to drop the stone. And I still had one hand free.

I fetched out the nullifier, that near forgotten relic, from my pants' pocket and jammed it against Nicolo's trousered leg. If there had ever been a more appropriate time to use it, it came now. It sparked and bucked in my fragile hold. He shouted as it fastened onto him, and levin fire danced around my fingers. I didn't know how long I could hold it or how much it would take. This was all I had. I'd put all my cards on the table. It would either be enough, or we would die trying.

"Now!" I cried.

Soot rained from Nicolo's form, spilling out onto the Butchery floor as his protection split. He let out a bellow and kicked me and the nullifier away, but I heard, I swear I heard his armor crack as it splintered. Shards spilled out among the soot, hard, crystalline daggers of broken spells. We danced around them, for they looked as lethal as any blade. Around me, Gregory leaped to my side and Malender joined him, spells and whip deafening me as they attacked. Carter circled around behind the Master.

Nicolo fought back. Faster than I can track, he struck and lashed out, and Gregory and Malender answered his blows. Two against one, and yet not enough. They were busy defending us and themselves from the others who had gone wild. Malender reared back on one heel and brought his whip up, and Gregory joined him, his cane blazing with blue-white fire. Side by side, demigod and phoenix wizard, they laid into Nicolo with everything they had.

About me, vampires screeched in high-pitched anger, and I could hear them take to the rafters and tables to leap at us. Whatever happened between Nicolo and the stone, he had lost control of his mob as threatened. We might fell him and yet be engulfed by the ravening creatures he'd created.

Someone—it had to be Carter—pushed my khopesh back into my hand. I almost dropped it, shaking as I did, as it filled my left hand. I wasn't ambidextrous, but I blinked hot tears back, and closed my grip tightly, prepared to swing away. I'd let go of the stone, yet it stayed in my mind, in my possession as if it hated to let me go. Some chance would be better than none. My sun lion brought up his power, energy crashing into the ravening wave of vampire servants.

Nicolo let out a groan as we both pulled to possess the maelstrom. Flooded with golden light straight out of an eternal desert, I fought to get on my feet and take the stone away from him. My tears matched his as crimson drops flooding down his vampire face. I only noticed mine as they pattered down upon my hands, red as they could be.

I could feel my father fading. Wayward mage that he had proven to be, yet he'd taken this last true pathway, and now found himself defeated. His desperation flooded me. He said, "Forgive me for not loving you both as much as I should." It sounded final.

Our only chance to win sank into failure. I turned a bit to scream, "Get him!"

I'd emptied all I had. Reserves gone, I swayed and staggered as I readied to fight.

Carter and I moved back-to-back again, and I let go of both of the relics, turning my thoughts to survival, abandoning my father once again. The nullifier disintegrated; I swapped my khopesh to my dominant hand. We hammered the vampires who dared to close in. Unceasing numbers. Too strong, too hungry, and far, far too many. We might lose, but we would take as many with us as we could.

My father's voice went silent. In the corner of my eye, I could see Nicolo fighting off the whip, his sword blade silvery as a kind of darkness began to fall about him.

Talons slashed across the side of my head. It stung like a bitch, but at least I still had my head on my neck. I swung back with the sickle blade, connecting with a dark shape I could only sense. I didn't hear a thud. Damage done but not enough. Wetness dripped off me. My blood? Remy's? The attackers?

A beam from an open door fell over us. Nicolo frowned at the brightness, retreating a step or two. I heard Evelyn call out, "I'm losing the door. Retreat! Come back!"

No roar from Hiram. He must have his hands full protecting her, and we could no more retreat than we could have grown wings. My arms grew heavy and my legs leaden. I no longer saw individual targets but a wave of figures in dark clothing descending upon us, over and over and over.

Then Gregory let out a triumphant grunt. I turned my attention a fraction to see him and Malender bearing down on Nicolo—and the Master giving way to them. He roared, and the scourge lashed over his throat, slicing it through, his cry truncated sharply. A bolt of lightning fire from the professor took Nicolo's head off completely.

The stone thunked to the floor. The samurai sword followed.

Nicolo's body did not disintegrate until Carter loosed his sun lion and then, eerily, the body went to particles, his clothing falling limp as it did.

The vampires screamed.

Not a one of them dropped, to follow their Master. We were up to our necks in a swamp of vamps, with little hope of getting out.

I thought of one last desperate outreach. I maybe had one chance left. I pulled out my last ace, the forbidden one hidden up my sleeve. I cleared my throat to summon.

"Herne, Herne, Herne. Bring your Wild Hunt, and I return the pup that is yours." He hadn't given me his name, but hey—wasn't that what the Internet was for? You'd best believe I'd looked it up.

Outside, somewhere, my mother waited with Scout. I'd told her she would know when to let him go. I prayed she did.

A bugle call blasted the air. The entire front of the Butchery blew away, and the forest came tumbling in. Branches pushed through. Fresh air and pine and the sound of clean water rushing through river banks still hidden shoved inward along with hoof beats and the triumphant call of a master Huntsman rallying his pack. They stampeded in, and Nicolo's children fell before them, as did the bodies still writhing on their hooks.

Some survived. Most did not. None of the vampire ghouls made it out.

The four of us gathered together, wearily, chests heaving as if we'd run a marathon, our weapons pointed to the floor, and watched in muted awe.

The Wild Hunt swept the Butchery clean of all its inequities, galloping round as they did, until finally the great Huntsman himself reined to a stop in front of us, and slid off his silvery white horse. Scout trotted up to join him, his sides splashed with blood and gore, his ears perked, his attention rapt upon the pack master.

Herne lowered his antlered head, his face somewhat amused as he took in Malender. "Justice," he greeted.

"Justice," Malender returned. "Although I am but one and you are a multitude."

"Join us and you need never be alone again." He put a broad hand forward.

I think Malender hesitated. Perhaps not, because they clasped in a handshake, and Mal's scourge dropped uselessly to the floor, disappearing. A steed of pale gold, its saddle empty, trotted up, and Malender mounted up with a single, graceful jump to take up its reins. He looked toward me and gave me a little salute.

"Farewell, Tessa of the Salt. I shall remember your lessons of mercy." He reined his steed in behind the Huntsman.

I faced Herne. "I am grateful you answered."

The primal being considered me. I thought I'd said it carefully enough, but my heart thudded in apprehension once or twice. When I'd looked up the Huntsman's name, I'd also found useful information that one should never thank a fairy directly lest trouble ensue.

He pronounced, "A debt is canceled. A future is given. It's as it should be."

The Huntsman whistled. The Hunt behind him began to ride away, toward the open forest which ought to have been a city street but hadn't always been and quite possibly wouldn't be in some far-flung future. Soon, only the antlered immortal and my dog remained.

He dropped his hand down to Scout's head. I couldn't say goodbye to my pup. It sounds silly to say, but I'd already lost so much. I didn't think I could bear losing him, too, but a promise is a promise. The words stuck in my throat. I settled for merely nodding at Herne.

"He has proven his loyalty and his place. I return him to your charge . . ." and the Huntsman paused before saying ironically, "Tessa of the Salt. For as long as you shall live, which hopefully will be long, indeed."

Scout didn't hesitate. He jumped into my arms, a big enough and heavy enough burden to knock me on my tush. I hugged him close, too tired to cry for happiness.

I didn't see the Huntsman leave.

The Butchery repaired itself behind him, I guess, because suddenly it became a popular bar and restaurant and karaoke inn again. Evelyn and Hiram joined us, Hiram dirtied and bloodied like the rest of us, except for Evie. Her armor served her well, for she had not a hair out of place or a single drop of bloodied sawdust on her. She bent over as she kicked something on the flooring.

"Don't—" I started but not in time, as the maelstrom stone promptly buried itself in her left hand.

"My, my." She tapped it. "Wasn't this yours? But it's hardly there at all. It doesn't look the same."

I leaned in to look at it. It wasn't, diminished to barely the size of a quarter. "May I?" I stroked a fingertip over it.

My father no longer inhabited the stone. I had no idea where he'd gone. Heaven, I suppose, if such a place exists. I hoped it did. He'd given all he could. What further amends could anyone make?

Hiram shoved the door open, and we shuffled out after the two of them. My mother stood nervously on the sidewalk, leash and harness dangling from her hands.

"Thank god," she said.

"Gods," Carter corrected, and, "Yes."

She and Gregory hugged, and walked away, Gregory's head bent down to her as he filled her in with such details as he wanted her to know.

Scout stayed tight at my calf as we walked down the street. Something tickled in my left palm; I sneaked a peak when Carter couldn't see.

A thin and wavy black line lay across the lines of my hand. Not a scar. Not the normal lines every palm developed over the years. Something that looked as if a fine-point marker had traced its ebony path across my skin.

Somehow, I knew that if I pulled at it, I'd bring a long, black whip curling out of my hand, a whip with razor-sharp thorns and flickering flames. I closed my eyes briefly. I might have to call Malender back and return his parting gift. If he'd answer. If he'd accept it back. If he even truly existed in my world anymore.

It's good when Councils of War turn into Councils of Peace. Or, supper, as we call it at my house. Gregory entered the house last, finding Carter and me, Hiram, Evelyn, and my mother all sitting about the table enjoying a hearty bowl of soup with fresh-baked rolls. I'd come in late as well, determined to make up for it, so I barely slowed in eating. He motioned for my mom to stay seated, went to the tureen, and served himself, snagging a second basket of rolls as he did.

"It looks," he announced, "as if we are all here." Then, with a flourish, as if he'd had a third arm and hand (I hadn't noticed he did, but he produced an object out of nowhere), he sat a black bowler hat on the table between us all.

I gave a gasp and half-choked on my soup spoon. "Is that—?"

"It certainly appears to be," Gregory answered smoothly.

My mother stared at it for a long moment. "Then where is the rest of Steptoe? I've never known him to miss a meal if he could help it."

"Likely not completely about. I suggest we put the hat on the back step, with a small bowl of cream, and see what happens." The professor picked up a roll and thoroughly buttered it.

"Treat him like a brownie?" Carter peered at Gregory over the rim of his coffee mug.

"Precisely."

"But he'll be back?"

Gregory tilted an eyebrow at me. "I really can't say."

"Can't or won't?"

"Both." He devoured half his bread in one bite, chewed, and swallowed deliberately before continuing. "This is beyond my experience. If he's in the process of restoration, this is decades before I would have anticipated it. That could be a very good . . . or very bad . . . thing."

"Not bad. Couldn't be," I remarked. "He is just leaving us word that he's coming back home." I have even less experience than the phoenix wizard, but I have tons of faith in Simon Steptoe.

"That's the idea! Be optimistic." Gregory paused. "Any more tea in the pot?"

"Always." Mom got up and whisked herself off to the stove to brew more. She looked over one shoulder. "I can tell you have more news. Out with it."

It startled me a bit that my mom and Gregory had begun to know each other so well. In the weeks since the Butchery debacle and my classes started, I must have missed some of the subterfuge. But then, with the change in my schedule plus track and field demands, I've been busy.

Gregory put both hands on the table. "The news is that the death sentence for Tessa has been lifted. She no longer possesses the maelstrom stone, and no one is seeking it. The small marble that Evelyn holds is far from the magical relic that it was perceived to be—"

Evelyn opened her mouth to argue with that, but he put up an index finger and stopped her. Looking at her, he finished, "I think it's fair to say we should let that perception rest. If it decides to change opinions, it will do so in its own time, but you, Evelyn, are far safer if it appears to have no value."

"Amen to that," Hiram said. He had been sitting back in his chair, hands folded over his stomach, with a plate full of roll crusts in front of him. I could tell that he'd been through at least one pan just by himself. No wonder he looked contented.

Gregory paused as the kettle began to whistle on the stove, and the pot got refilled and steeped, and his cup once more brimmed with freshly brewed tea. "Now, as to the sentence pronounced on Mary . . ."

"Still?" She paled a bit.

He nodded. "However, I got that dispensed with this afternoon."

Mom sank down into her chair. "Thank heavens."

"Oh, you needn't have worried, I have you protected, but now it's official."

"Whatever did you do?"

"First, we changed your dissertation. From the title 'Through a Broken Mirror, How the Modern World Overlooks Magic' (I believe that was it, wasn't it, Mary? Or something like that.) to 'How Mankind Constructs Imagination and Needful Magic through Creativity and Folklore.'"

"Humankind," my mother said, with a frown.

"Ah, yes. I'll have them edit that to humankind. Is the rest acceptable?"

"It's changed but not. I suppose it will do. But why does that make a difference?"

"Instead of proposing that Magic exists and our ignorance of it is because we simply can't see it properly, the new title suggests that we invented it because we are a creative people and inspired to experience what doesn't exist to fulfill ourselves."

My mother unfolded and folded her napkin a few times, aware that we all looked at her and Gregory waited for an answer. Finally, she remarked, "But it does exist."

"It most certainly does, in the Arts. Which is what your dissertation delineates, and quite well, too. We aren't ready for anything closer to the truth yet." He reached for more bread and soaked it in his soup. "By the time Tessa here graduates with her advanced degree, we may be ready to start exploring further options."

"I hope so."

Carter slid his hand over to cover mine. "We have time."

With my other hand, I dropped a sizable chunk of my supper to Scout's eagerly waiting jaws. It never would have hit the floor, that I knew. For years and years ahead of us, I hoped.

Evelyn smiled. "So all's well that ends well?"

"Except for that prophecy of yours." I frowned in spite of my relief.

"The one about hard and challenging times ahead?" She shrugged. "Doesn't every unknown day fit that?"

"Sometimes." I looked about the table.

The wintry day had turned to sunset, and its color streamed in through the kitchen window. Fabulous red-and-pink hues lined the western sky and promised that tomorrow would be a glorious day. Spring would come someday, and all the days of the year as it should following. My heart lifted as Carter closed his arm about my waist and held me close.

I leaned on Carter. "I think I just learned a universal truth."

"Mmmm. And what would that be?"

"Life is meant to be good."